To my father, Zibeon Kikuyu,
for preparing the soil of my soul for The Word,
and my mother, Rose Kikuyu, for giving me a
strong perspective on African
traditions and beliefs.

I also thank my lovely wife,
Talu, for her support and my wonderful
daughters, SimSim and Nissa for their
encouragement.

Special thanks to my father-in-law,
Eliakim Masale and Mama
Joyce Wakesho.

Acknowledgments

My deepest thanks go to John Croft who took this project and ran with it. I also thank Beth Woodard, Ajema Kikuyu-Ngumba, and Carol Shumway for their support, suggestions, and corrections.

I also extend deep appreciation to the following who, directly or indirectly, made this project a reality:

Chris and Linda Davenport, my brother-in-law, Duncan Mwakio and sister-in-law, Corrine; Pastor and Mrs. Ronnie Rodgers; Dr. Anne Parker; Patrick and Sandra Muasya; Joseph and Mercy Kamau; Lee Kirkham; Dr. Roger Bohanan; Tony and Edie Tolar; Pastors Robert and David Doleshal, the deacons, and members of Desertview Baptist Church - Gilbert, AZ; the pastors and members of other churches we attended, namely, Parklands Baptist Church - Nairobi; First Baptist Church of Euless, TX; Lighthouse Baptist Church - Azle, TX; Retta Baptist Church - Burleson, TX; PrimeTime Valet, TX.

I thank the following who read a chapter of the book and made suggestions and corrections:

Pat Evans, Patricia Escarcega, Diane Dorman, Douglas Gaer, Ray Sheppard, Dr. Rose Nyunja, Ellen (Mama!) Kersey, Jim Jacob, Lisa Brown, Dave Shue, and John Chawanga.

I also deeply appreciate my brothers, sisters, friends, and relatives who have played a part in shaping me for the better.

In memory of Egadwa Kikuyu,
Nyawira Ngumba, and Aggrey Muserah.

ISBN: 1453838813
EAN-13: 9781453838815.

This is a work of fiction. Names, characters, places, and incidents are either the product of the author's imagination or used fictitiously. Any resemblance to actual persons, living or dead, events, or places is entirely coincidental.

Website: sonoftheoracle.com
Email: tsihugwa@sonoftheoracle.com

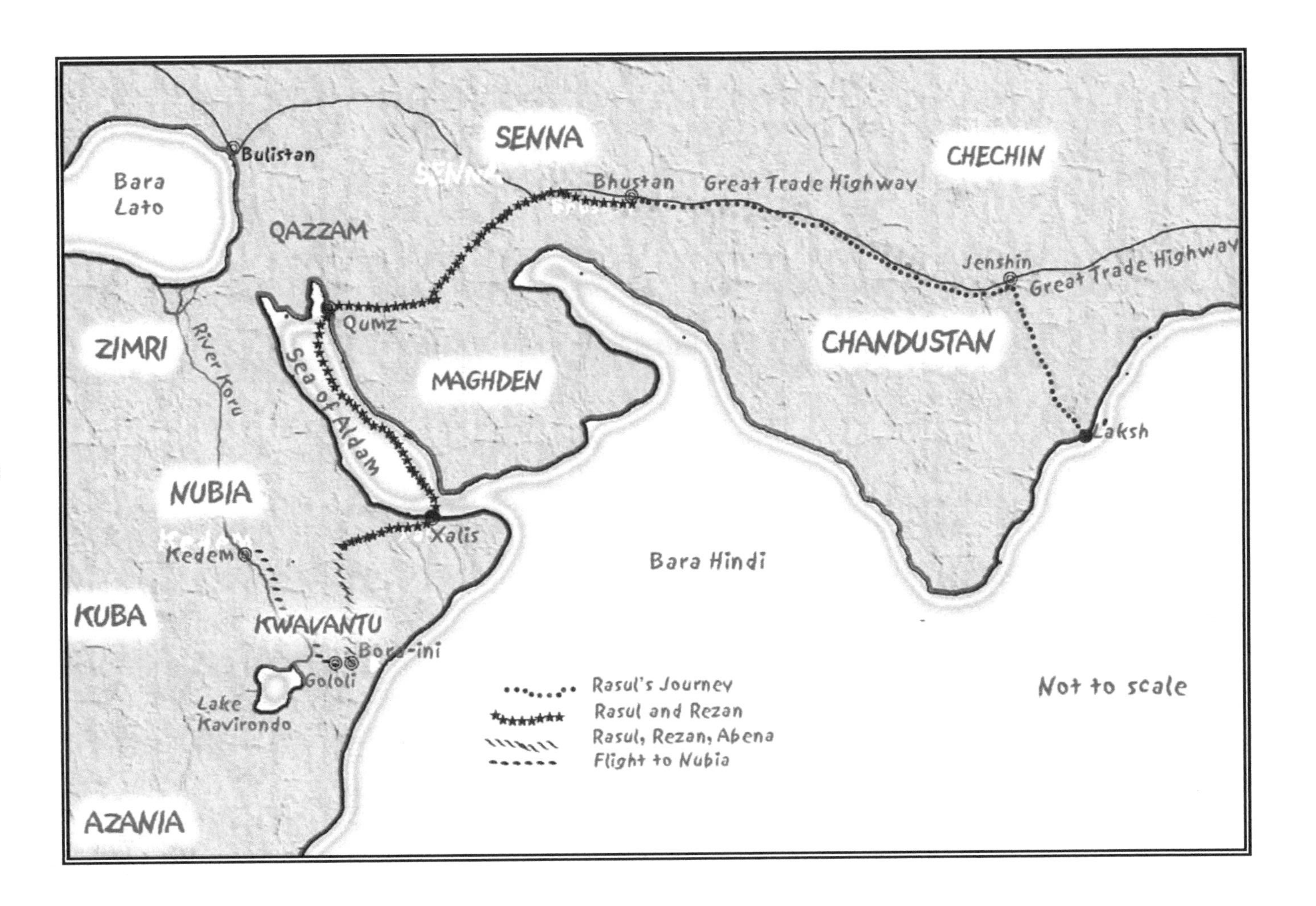
Bara
Lato
Bulistan
SENNA
CHECHIN
Bhustan
Great Trade Highway
QAZZAM
Jenshin
Great Trade Highway
Qumz
ZIMRI
River Koru
CHANDUSTAN
Sea of Aldam
MAGHDEN
Laksh
NUBIA
Xalis
Kedem
Bara Hindi
KUBA
KWAVANTU
Gololi
Lake
Kavirondo
Rasul's Journey
Rasul and Rezan
Rasul, Rezan, Abena
Flight to Nubia
Not to scale
AZANIA

CONTENTS

Son of the Oracle

Part One

prologue

The Plains of Sacrifice and the Shrine of the Oracle were sacred to the Bagololi. Good spirits and the ancestors had breathed their blessing upon this land. The calm winds that blew across the plains, the mild climate, and natural beauty attested to the goodness of this place. In the distance lay rolling blue hills with Lake Ementi in the foreground reflecting the hills and the sky. The River Dzodzo snaked across the plains like a long umbilical appendage to the lake. Dotted across the landscape were huge rocks nature had shaped to resemble animate objects. They had names like "The Skull," "The Sleeper," and "The Lion."

Strangely, the Bangoma, arguably the most licentious clan in Gololi, were the honorary custodians of the sacred land. The other clans regarded them as a cursed community with little respect for tradition. They had the highest number of children born out of wedlock. Incest, which was taboo, occurred with alarming frequency with little consequence to the perpetrators. No other clan had as many murders and assaults as Ngoma. Over time, the large number of men married to strong wine had led to the decay of morals. Many had not seen a day of sobriety in a long time.

The women, not to be outdone, also boasted a share of heavy drinkers. They had earned the right to drink in the company of men who had long accepted them as equals. When they trudged home, women spewed profanities as hard as men did. Vicious fights broke out everyday and someone was bound to walk home a bloody mess for the most trivial of reasons.

However, a few individuals in Ngoma somewhat redeemed the name of the clan. One was the elder, Lemba, along with his wife, Sabet. They were childless and Lemba confounded everyone by refusing to take another wife with whom he could raise progeny. He knew people laughed behind his back saying he was not a man because he "shot blunt arrows." Were it not so, they argued, he would have taken another wife to prove himself. Lemba saw no point in giving them the satisfaction. He was content with his wife though disappointed that she had not born him children.

Sabet had her own share of problems. In the eyes of some women, she was a broken pot that could hold no water and they considered her incomplete as a woman because she was barren. She was unhappy and it strained the marriage. They visited the *mganga* frequently. He administered potions and performed rituals to ward off the spirits of infertility. Season after season they went to see him, but after many moons and a trail of sacrifices it was clear his powers would not work. Sabet was undeterred. She insisted that they should visit the priests of the Oracle on the Plains of Sacrifice. Though he was skeptical, Lemba agreed to go for her sake. His friends, Vodoti and Sakwa, and their wives, Imu and Ajema, accompanied them on the trip. For the sacrifice, they took a pure white goat, a white chicken, and a basket of millet. They walked in solemn silence.

At the shrine, other people were already waiting. Everyone sat in an open area facing the raised altar where the priests received offerings during the Festival of Sacrifice - an event that took place every fifth harvest. The priests conducted the sessions behind the altar, out of sight. Two warrior guards noted the order in which parties arrived and summoned them accordingly. Those who had seen the priests took a different exit.

Though others had arrived before them, a different warrior emerged from behind the rocks and gestured toward Lemba and his company. The two warriors did not attempt to correct him. Lemba and his group looked at one another in confusion. The warrior signaled again.

"I think he's calling for us," Lemba said.

When they all started toward the altar, the warrior stayed them with a gesture and pointed directly at Lemba. Again, Lemba looked around and back at the warrior who waved him over before he disappeared behind a big rock. Lemba climbed up to the altar area and went round the rock. He came to a shaded area where a huge slab of stone lay over others like a roof. He was wondering where the warrior had gone when a voice spoke.

"Lemba."

He was startled and looked around to see who spoke. A man stood in a recess where two large boulders met. Lemba could not tell whether he was a warrior-guard, a priest, or a spirit-being.

"Do not be afraid. The Oracle has heard your cry and that of your wife, Sabet. She will bear a son, and you shall call his name Jani. The spirit of the Oracle will be upon him and he will be a joy to you and turn the hearts of your wretched people from their wicked ways."

When the fear subsided, Lemba reflected on what the man had just said. He thought of the unfruitful visits to the medicine man and almost smiled.

"How can I be sure of it? After all, my arrows are blunt and my wife is not entirely a young thing."

The man was silent for a while and Lemba knew he had erred.

"The King among kings sends me to give you this good news and you talk to me about dull arrows! Because of this, you will not utter another word until the words I have spoken come to pass. You may go."

The man turned and vanished in the dark recess. Lemba stood watching before he made his way back past the altar.

Sabet and her companions wondered what had happened to Lemba. They still found it strange that the guard had singled him out to go up to the altar. They also felt there was something odd about the guard who had called him. He was not dressed in warrior garb like the one who had called other groups, and he did not bear a spear or shield. Instead, he wore a gleaming sword at his waist.

"I'm a little worried," Sabet said. "How is it that the man called only Lemba? What are they doing to him back there?"

"We can't just go and check on him. We might upset the spirits," Vodoti pointed out.

"What shall we do?" Imu asked.

"We'll have to wait and trust he's fine," Sakwa said.

Just then, Lemba emerged. He had the appearance of one who had seen an apparition.

"Lemba!" Sabet exclaimed when she saw her husband. Breaking with protocol, they ran to meet him at the bottom of the steps.

"What happened back there?" Vodoti asked. "We were worried about you."

"Lemba, my lord," Sabet said. "What's wrong? Talk to me."

He shook his head and made a croaking sound. He could not speak. He motioned them to head back home. No one uttered another word all the way home.

When they got to the village, fellow villagers watched them keenly, but nobody dared ask what had happened. It would have been improper to do so. They all went to Lemba's house. They mostly sat in silence, only speaking in whispers when necessary. After observing a respectful interval, neighbors stopped by to find out what had happened. Vodoti related what had transpired. Sakwa and the women interjected periodically. They did not have the full story because Lemba could not explain what happened behind the altar. The visitors expressed their sympathy to the downcast Lemba. As dusk fell, the visitors took their leave.

Alone with his wife, Lemba motioned for Sabet's attention. When she looked at him, he gestured to her that she was pregnant. Initially, she was baffled and incredulous. Lemba repeated the gestures with equal seriousness and she began to believe him. She wanted to. Finally, she broke into loud chants of thanksgiving and praise.

"O Great Spirit, I thank you for hearing this old woman's cry and giving her a child. Long has she cried before you. Long has she endured the scorn of other women. No longer am I a broken pot. My womb shall be filled and bear fruit. Oh, how I thank you Mighty One! How I praise you for taking away my reproach."

She was not content to shout her praises within the confines of the hut. She went outside and paced the compound, speaking aloud for all to hear. A crowd gathered again on hearing the news. When they asked Lemba whether what Sabet chanted was true, he nodded in the affirmative. The villagers who were sober enough to care about anything were sad that Lemba was unable to speak, but delighted to hear that Sabet was pregnant. Men and women congratulated the couple on the good news, though some were too embarrassed to face them after what they had said about Lemba's impotence and Sabet's barrenness. Some were still skeptical, but in the days that followed, all signs confirmed the pregnancy. There was not a more joyous woman in the village than Sabet.

Chapter 1

the chosen bride

On a cloudless day, almost six moons later, Zai lay on the embankment in a state of semi-slumber induced by the meal he had consumed. The gentle evening breeze played on his skin like a soft, warm bedroll on a cold night. His cousins, endowed with more energy, were engrossed in a noisy game below. As usual, the animals needed little supervision as they grazed on the lush grass, which they would bring up to chew on the cud after dusk. Other than the sky falling, there was nothing of great concern, and he drifted in and out of sleep on a bed of bliss.

On the outbound leg of one of his brief visits to wakefulness, Zai noticed an odd cloud, shaped like a fist, cutting slowly across the sky. *Where did that thing come from?* His mind halted its somnolent meandering and engaged the cloud for a few moments, but soon released it. He was just slipping back into slumber when the unthinkable happened. With a sharp movement, the cloud spat out a bolt of pure light that hit the ground with a resounding "*boom!*" It was the loudest sound Zai had ever heard and the shock lifted him off the ground. Now fully awake, he saw his cousins scrambling up the embankment toward him, wide-eyed with fear. The animals had also scattered in all directions with the same panicked look in their eyes.

"What was that?" Boza, the younger of the brothers asked in a tremulous voice when he got to where Zai stood.

"I don't know," Zai said, looking into the distance at a spot where the bolt seemed to have hit. "I thought I saw the cloud throw a ball of light to the ground. It landed over there," he pointed. Everything seemed to have a residual aura at the point of impact.

Amit confirmed his impression. "Oh, I see it. The place is glowing!"

"I hope nobody's hurt. That was a huge bolt. The sound lifted me right off the ground," Zai said, breathing heavily.

"*Wah!*" Amit exclaimed. "It knocked me off my feet, too!"

"And it tossed me a distance from where I was sitting!" Boza chimed in.

"Come. Let's go and see what happened in the village," Zai urged.

They tumbled down the slope and ran all the way to the village without a thought to the animals.

In the village of Kilima, Ma'alia was grinding maize for the evening meal. She struggled to keep her mind on a task she had performed since she was a child. Worse still, she could not put a finger on what was bothering her. Certainly, her betrothal to Yossou was constantly on her mind, but it did not explain the sense of unease she was experiencing.

"Something's in the air. I can feel it," her mother would have said.

The thought of her mother brought on a fresh rush of emotion that further unsettled her. A lump suddenly formed in her throat and she could neither swallow nor breathe. Suddenly, the kitchen felt like an alien entity closing in on her. The rough mud walls took the form of a horde of hostile warriors. Churning emotions whipped themselves into thunderous sounds in her head. *She had to get out!* In a panic, she slammed the small grindstone on the larger one breaking it to pieces. At that precise moment, she heard the loud "*boom!*" of a thunderclap that shook the ground and sent a searing pain through her lower abdomen. Doubled over, she stumbled out the door into the evening breeze.

It was unusually bright outside and the light hurt her eyes. Everything – the trees, bushes, huts, even the ground, had a strange aura she had never seen before. She gulped, taking in a lungful of air, and leaned against the wall. She breathed heavily as if someone had held her head under water to the point of drowning. Each breath sent a fresh stab of pain to her lower belly. She shut her eyes tight against the oddly iridescent twilight.

After a while, she started to breathe normally and opened her eyes, but could not see clearly for the pain and tears. She blinked several times in rapid succession then wiped each eye with the back of her hand.

"Peace, my child."

The salutation startled Ma'alia. She looked around for the source, but could not immediately locate it. She shook her head to clear it, blinked again, and squinted. Then she saw him - a strange man at the edge of the banana grove. It was an odd place for a visitor to stand since most came by the path in front of the compound. She knew he was not from the area, but because of her limited exposure to other communities, she could not tell whence he came. She wanted to call for help, but the lump she had briefly forgotten reasserted itself, preventing her from making a sound.

Sensing her consternation, the man raised his right hand in a gesture of peace then lowered it as if invoking a blessing upon her. For a moment, the hint of a smile played on his lips. He dropped his hand and started to walk toward her with measured steps. Ma'alia's fear subsided when she realized that he was not intent on hurting her.

"Peace," he said again, stopping a few paces from her. "Daughter of Avantu, the Oracle smiles upon you."

"Wh… who are you?" Ma'alia stammered.

"Do not fear, child. I speak as the voice of The One who has chosen you for a great purpose. He has appointed you to bear a son. He will be known as King of the Avantu for seasons past and seasons to come. I speak the words of the Oracle."

"But… I… I have never been with a man. I'm only recently betrothed to Yossou, the craftsman, and as The Ancients are my witnesses, we haven't…"

"Your honor is not in question. It is the very thing the Great Spirit seeks - a vessel without blemish. The Spirit Father will come upon you, and you will bear a son. You shall call him Yssa. He will be great and will sit upon the throne of his ancestor, the great King Adu."

"What can I say?" Ma'alia bowed her head. "Let it be to me as the Oracle has ordained."

She closed her eyes to wipe her tears. When she opened them, the man was gone. She looked around, drained, confused, yet curiously elated.

"Ma'alia, are you alright?" She started at the sound of her name. It was her aunt, *Senge* Rodina. She held a clay shard with which to carry an ember. "What's wrong? To whom were you talking? *Ai!* Have you just seen a spirit?"

"I don't know. Maybe."

Rodina frowned at the strange answer. Ma'alia was not given to sarcasm.

"What's troubling you, child?" she asked. "You are acting like a pregnant woman."

"I don't know. Maybe I am," Ma'alia muttered softly, more to herself than to her aunt.

"What?" Rodina asked sharply.

She regarded her niece in bewilderment. Ma'alia made the statement while staring toward the banana grove. Rodina followed her gaze and saw nothing. Once again, she peered into Ma'alia's face, trying to make sense of her strange manner. What she beheld did not enlighten her. Rodina shook her head and stepped into the kitchen.

"*Vaya!* What's going on in here? Ma'alia! With whom were you fighting? Why did you smash the grindstone to pieces? Do you know how long it has been in this family?"

Senge Rodina's voice sounded like a distant echo. Even when she came out and spoke to her, Ma'alia only raised her head to give her a blank look.

"I might as well be talking to that rock over there." Rodina mumbled, indicating a big rock embedded in the ground a few strides away. She hissed in frustration and reentered Ma'alia's kitchen. She came out with an ember and strode toward her own kitchen where she set about preparing the entire meal. Her grindstone rasped impatiently to the accompaniment of her mutterings. Every now and then, she clicked her tongue to complete the vexed cadence of the grinding. Her children, Kalhi and Chanzu had learned to divine their mother's mood from the rasping tempo and would give her a wide berth tonight.

Outside, the import of the strange man's words gradually started to sink in. Ma'alia felt as if she carried the weight of the world on her shoulders, but was not sure she could handle it. She was barely a woman. She suddenly felt dizzy and her stomach heaved. She pitched forward, fell on all fours, and retched on the grass.

Ma'alia did not know how long she sat beside her stomach contents, but it was dark by the time she picked herself up, stumbled into her hut, and crawled onto her bedroll. She thought about the stranger's words and knew in her spirit that she believed him. She would become a mother without having planned on it. She also believed his words about the child's destiny and was willing to be the vessel for such noble use. *But will people believe me? Will they understand? They won't. I'll bear this burden alone.*

Her spirit began to spiral into a dark, cold pit of despondency. A storm whirled around in her head like imbuya - the fabled inner turmoil that could drive a man to jump off the edge of a cliff.

"Fear not, child. You are not alone," a gentle voice cut through her tumultuous descent.

Briefly, she saw a vision of the strange man smiling at her. A ray of light cut through the dark thoughts that had engulfed her. An invisible hand reached down, plucked her from the dark depths, and lifted her into a warm light. A serene spirit came over her and she fell asleep with a smile on her face.

Egadwa balled the last piece of *chima* and used it to chase the remaining stew around the bowl. He deftly tossed it into his mouth, chewed, and swallowed noisily. He drank water from the gourd and belched loudly, wiping his mouth with the back of his hand.

"She broke the grindstone, eh? Well, well! Maybe she's grieving her mother again. You know how close they were even when she was as a little girl."

"I know, Egadwa, but this is different," Rodina said picking up the gourds. "Honestly, I am worried. This evening, I went to get an ember from her fire. As I approached, I heard her talking to someone. She was outside her kitchen looking confused. When I asked her if she had seen a spirit, she gave me an answer that neither confirmed nor denied it. Now, here's the worst part. Without thinking, I told her she was behaving like a pregnant woman. You know what she said. 'I don't know. Maybe I am.' If she's pregnant, what will people say? What shall we tell Yossou? A young bride getting pregnant out of wedlock? That's sacrilege!"

"*Akh!* You're jumping to conclusions. She's just not feeling well. In any case, who would the father be? Ma'alia is not one to fool around. There's got to be something else going on."

"By the Oracle! I hope so. I guess there's nothing to do but wait until morning."

"Yes. Don't make more of it than there is."

"I won't," Rodina said, but her heart was still restive.

Almost a full moon later, Yossou was surprised to hear his mother calling him from outside his hut. Ever since he built his first *disi*, a bachelor's hut, she rarely set foot in his chambers. The only time she had come in and lingered, he was ill and she nursed him back to health. Another surprise was she had brought his breakfast. That was the preserve of his younger daughter, Temin, who would not let anyone else bring him food. He knew this had to be serious. He told her that he was decent and she could enter.

She set the food before him and sat down to make small talk while he ate. Yossou sensed she had something on her mind, but since she had brought him breakfast, he went along.

"What is it M'ma? What's wrong?" he asked when he finished.

Simi sighed heavily. "Son, I have grave news for you." She looked at him sadly. "You've been through a lot and I don't know how you'll take it."

"I've lost a wife and children. What more can life do to me?"

Simi took a deep breath.

"Ma'alia's relatives paid your uncle a visit yesterday. They did not want to spend the night because of the message they bore." She paused again. "They say Ma'alia is with child. They're sure you are not the father, but they don't know who committed the transgression. Ma'alia only gave strange responses when they asked her about it. As her relatives, they felt duty-bound to inform us of this development so as to give you time to decide how you want to proceed."

Yossou was stunned. He did not believe what he heard. His initial reaction was anger, frustration, and a sense of betrayal. He was glad they did not suspect him because the distance from Ronge to Kilima and their infrequent, chaperoned meetings gave them no window for a tryst. A relative always hovered in the background observing them when they met.

"By the Oracle! What's wrong with me? Why does something have to happen to every woman who comes my way? M'ma, how did Ma'alia turn to *this?*"

"Some things are hard to understand, son. I know the news is hard for you, but before we draw conclusions, we need to know the truth. We haven't heard Ma'alia's side of the story. If she behaved improperly, she's bound to tell someone. I understand she's not quite herself. Something's bothering her and sooner or later she'll talk to someone."

"This is a case for the elders. Let's stop all negotiations for now."

"That sounds like the best thing to do under the circumstances. I'll talk with your uncle Minadi and let him know how you feel. For now, we want as few people involved as possible. Word gets around fast."

"Do what you have to, M'ma. Yanze has been with the ancestors several moons now. I can wait a little longer. I was getting used to being alone, though it has not been easy because she was such a wonderful woman. You have been there for Simi and Temin, and I thank you for that."

"Oh, I love my grandchildren. After raising you and your brothers, taking care of them is nothing."

"Was I that bad?"

"Oh, as a child you were trouble. Something went right after you were circumcised."

"I became a man."

"*Ao!* I guess so." She got up. "We'll work this out, son. Take care of your heart." She laid a hand on his shoulder before she took the gourds and made for the kitchen.

Yossou sat alone in the semi-darkness contemplating the shimmering shafts of light that sliced the darkness from the holes in the roof. Thousands of tiny dust particles chased one another in and out of the darkness on the blades of light. They had fascinated him even as a baby strapped to his mother's back while she cooked. He would watch the beams open-mouthed, with a string of saliva dribbling onto her back. He repeatedly tried to grab the beams and seemed baffled when he came away empty-handed. Watching him was a source of great amusement for his siblings and cousins. They laughed until tears came to their eyes.

This morning however, there was little amusement or fascination in the beams. They were like blades that pierced him through and made his head hurt. Suddenly, he felt he had to get out for some air. With sharp, deliberate movements, he gathered his tools, strode out of the hut, and headed for the riverbank where he harvested grass. A light mist hung over the river. *This is going to be one of those days*, he thought.

By the river, Yossou picked up his sickle and began to swing at the grass. His mind went back to the conversation with his mother. The question kept coming to him. *Why? Why, Ma'alia, why?* He thought back to the times they had been together. He found her a little conservative, but warm and intelligent. He perceived she was a young woman who not only knew her role, but could also exercise independent thinking. Once, in their conversations, he had intimated women should be subservient to men. She was quick to reprimand him, stating clearly what she would and would not do. She still managed to convey it in a manner that was neither disrespectful nor combative. Yossou learned to stay clear of topics that would elicit such a reaction.

Now she was pregnant by another! It stung deeply that someone else would pluck the fruit for which he had waited so long and borne so much. *No*. He would not go through with the wedding. He would tell his mother and *Koza* Minadi to cancel the negotiations and arrangements. He did not want complications. He just wanted the thing to go away quietly so he could move on. Perhaps he would remain a widower the rest of his life. *Oh! If only Yanze were still alive! She was such a beautiful person!* It was hard for him to accept she was gone and that he had to start over. In Ma'alia, he thought he had found something akin to what he had with Yanze. She had just as strong a personality, was equally independent, and seemed loving and loyal. That is what had drawn him to her when he accepted his mother's invitation to look into the possibility of taking her as his bride. *Now this!*

He did not realize that his strokes had quickened and he was not cutting the grass with his customary precision. He was breathing heavily as he firmed the decision to break off the engagement. The reality of it dawned on him painfully along with something else. He realized he loved her. *He really loved her!* The proof of it was in the pain he was experiencing.

Why, Ma'alia, why? With every stroke, Yossou grew more agitated until he was hacking at the grass like a man gone berserk. Hot tears streamed down his face and sweat run down his forehead, stinging his eyes and blurring his vision.

"Whyyyyy…?" he cried, lifting both arms over his head.

He was about to bring the sickle down for a final stroke when a powerful hand grabbed his wrist. The grip was stronger than that of a champion wrestler and whoever held him knew precisely how to cause maximum discomfort. The pressure caused Yossou to drop the sickle. He saw a face whose age he could not tell easily. It was that of an elder yet with the freshness of youth. The man let go of his wrist.

"What has the grass done that you abuse it so? Are you not man enough to face your feelings without venting like a madman?"

"Who are you? What do you want with me?" Yossou demanded. He rubbed his wrist and felt it throb as the blood flowed again. Though the sickle lay by his side, he thought against snatching it for a quick strike. Besides, he knew it was no ordinary man who stood over him and such an attempt might turn out to be a very bad idea. The glint of a sharp sword tucked in the man's waistband further persuaded him of the wisdom of staying his hand. It had a handle carved in the form of a lion's head.

"Yossou, get your foolish pride out of the way. You make yourself judge over things of which you haven't the slightest idea. Are you so pure that you would put Ma'alia away without understanding the purposes of the Oracle?"

Yossou was surprised the man knew his name.

"What have I done?" he asked defensively.

"It's your rage. You want to break off the engagement. Indeed Ma'alia is with child by the Spirit Father. Yossou, though you have not known her, you will marry her and be a father to the child. You shall call him *Yssa*. He will be the Son of the Avantu, born to fulfill the purposes of the Oracle in the realm of men."

Then the stranger bent and put a gentle hand on his shoulder. Yossou could not hold his gaze and lowered his eyes.

"Be a man. Do the right thing."

He stood up straight and regarded Yossou with a kind look before gliding off. A mist had enveloped them during the encounter. Even through the sweat and tears, Yossou could have sworn the man simply faded into it. Moments later, he heard footsteps approaching rapidly behind him.

"Yossou, what's the matter?" Sande, his young apprentice materialized out of the fog. "I was making my way here when I heard you scream. I thought you were in some kind of trouble. By the ancients! You look terrible. Have you beheld a spirit or something?"

"I don't know what I saw, Sande. Take the day off. I don't feel well. I need to rest."

"But we have so much to do. I thought today we were…"

"We'll do it tomorrow. Let's go."

"Fine if that's what you want." Sande was baffled, but did not venture another suggestion. They went back to the village.

"What's going on with these two?" Minadi asked. "I've heard that Ma'alia is going about her duties as usual, but she still seems preoccupied. Now, Simi, what's this I'm hearing about Yossou?"

"Well, you know Sande - Yossou's apprentice. He and my son came back right after he had set off to work this morning, which is unusual. Sande called me aside and told me to keep an eye on Yossou because he was acting strange. He says that as he neared the river, he heard my son scream. When he got there, Yossou was on the ground in a daze. He also said Yossou thought he might have seen a spirit. I'm not clear about that part."

"*Woi! Woi! Woi!* Where is he now?"

"In his hut. He says he's not feeling well."

"What do we do?"

"I don't know. Let's leave him alone for now. We'll talk to him later."

"M'ma, *Koza*, let's proceed with the wedding. I'll marry Ma'alia as promised. I'll be a father to the child, as any honorable man should. It does not matter who the real father is. The child needs a father. I will be that father."

"Son, do you realize what you're saying? You'll be admitting that you impregnated Ma'alia before wedlock. You'll be stigmatized for life."

Yossou raised himself off the bedroll and leaned on one arm. He looked at his uncle who sat on a stool next to his mother.

"Let's continue with the arrangements. I will marry Ma'alia one moon before the rains. That way we, as the child's parents, will be married and there will be no room for speculation."

Minadi turned to his sister for reaction. She clapped her hands lightly, looked aside at the ground, and wrapped her arms around herself like a hen out in the cold.

"As you wish my son," she said. After some time she rose and left. Minadi sat a while longer and neither spoke. Yossou laid his head back down and stared at the roof.

Finally, Minadi spoke. "So be it."

He went to join his sister in her hut.

Chapter 2

the wedding

For a short period after her encounter with the stranger, Ma'alia was brooding and distant, but she eventually returned to her easygoing self. At a meeting after the experience, Yossou had told her he understood the pregnancy was beyond the natural and he would not hinder what the Oracle ordained. He would therefore proceed with marriage arrangements. From what little she knew, an encounter much like hers had brought about this change of heart. It was a great relief for Ma'alia.

A few days before the ceremony, the village women kept Ma'alia in seclusion, pampering her for the last time. They catered to her every whim in order to present her to her husband looking her best. The more ample the bride, the more beautiful and fertile the community deemed her. A scrawny bride was hideous - a shame to her family and bad luck to her husband. Fortunately, Ma'alia had gained weight and this would therefore not be a problem.

Preparations began in earnest seven days before the wedding. There was a steady stream of visitors in and out of the homestead. Simi and Senge Rodina were in charge of the arrangements, paying special attention to the food. They made sure there was plenty of millet flour for *chima* ahead of time. For this, they recruited several girls and young women to do the grinding. Minadi secured two cows for meat and checked with Malua, the famed brewer, to ensure there will be enough wine. A ceremony where the wine ran out was an embarrassment to the bride and groom, the family, and the community. It would be fodder for bards who immortalized both the famous and infamous in song and lore.

Chizi had worked her singers and dancers hard in the days before the wedding. Ziki, her husband, who was also the village crooner, coordinated the music and dance and worked out a loose program for the event. All ceremonies were largely extemporaneous, though built around key rituals. Chizi and Ziki usually composed new songs and dances or modified old ones to fit the occasion.

The morning of the wedding, the senior women of the village roused Ma'alia early for the bridal bath. They marched slowly while humming somber tunes. At the stream, three women washed Ma'alia, scrubbing her all over with *zola* leaves from the depths of the forest. They secreted a substance that foamed when rubbed in the presence of water. According to tradition, the bath purified and cleansed not only the skin, but also the spirit. People also believed the leaves had the power to prevent infertility.

When Ma'alia emerged from the water, the women dried her off and rubbed her down with special scented oils said to possess power to ward off evil spirits and protect her at the start of a new life. All through the bathing and oiling process, the three women intoned prayers for her health, wealth, and fertility. The rest stood on the banks, punctuating the prayers with choruses of agreement. When it was over, Ma'alia donned a simple garment and they commenced the slow march to the village.

Back in the bridal chamber, another group of women fussed over Ma'alia. They painted her face, adorned her with ornaments, and gave her final words of advice. They held nothing back when it came to intimacy and sometimes it was overwhelming. Ma'alia did not realize the women she had respected all her life had such a coarse sense of humor.

At the ceremonial square, people had started to gather. Most had done their chores early so they could spend the rest of the day at the wedding. By the afternoon, the crowd had grown considerably and there was a constant buzz of conversation. Children chased one another, screaming at the top of their voices. Occasionally, an adult would shoo them away or shout at them to be quiet. The children scampered off only to return as the excitement of their game picked up again.

Men and women sat separately. No one knew exactly how this came about, but legend had it that in the past, men and women sat together. On one occasion, a man thought his neighbor touched his wife inappropriately. According to the story, the aggrieved man promptly rose and brained the offender. Ever since, the sexes have sat apart. Conversation was largely within the respective groups, but it often flowed across the gender gap.

At one point, the men were discussing loudly who would win the upcoming wrestling match between Sela of Vogol and the champion, M'mata of Ronge. M'mata had felled his last seven opponents, but had struggled in the last match. Only his experience had given him the edge when he exploited a mistake his over-eager younger opponent made.

"I tell you, M'mata will not make it this time. Since Sela took up wrestling, he has floored five of eight opponents instantly. You see, being short and stocky, he gets beneath his man and throws him off balance before the opponent can react. It works all the time," Mena said.

"From what hole did you crawl you silly worm?" Orina demanded. "Have you not seen how intently M'mata watches his opponents when they fight other people? He studies them so by the time of the fight, he knows all their strengths and weaknesses. Sela will be on his back before your spit hits the ground."

"Honestly, this time, I'll put my shells on Sela." Jaran interjected. "He may be the newest and youngest fighter in Gololi, but he has that aggressive streak. Look in his eyes and you'll see he neither fears man nor pain. It might not be easy, but I think he'll take M'mata down."

Several voices tried to speak at the same time, arguing their case for either fighter. The argument heated up as supporters on one side tried to outdo the other in stating the case. Two men were already on their feet staring each other down. The shouting switched to egging the two to go at it.

Then they heard it - the distant singing of the bridal procession. The heckling and banter subsided to a low murmur. The two men who would have fought sunk into the crowd, which now focused on the reason for which they had gathered. As the singing got closer, heads kept turning in the direction of the sound. They had witnessed many weddings, but there was always something new and exciting about each one.

They could now see the bridal party through the trees as it approached, singing the praises of the daughter of Kilima. Each verse praised her beauty, kindness, gentleness, patience, prudence, and sense of duty. No one could see Ma'alia since she was one of five veiled girls among the women. When the procession was a stone's throw away from the square, a group of women broke from the crowd and ran to meet them. They were relatives of the groom. They did not join in the singing, but ululated periodically. The procession made its way to sit at an assigned section. The crowd now joined in the singing and ululating. All eyes were on the girls who were covered from head to toe with sheets woven from *junzi* fiber. A group of strong women in the party shot dark glances at the crowd, ostensibly to discourage speculation on the identity of the bride. It was all part of the show.

A powerful rhythm split the air, jolting the crowd from their deliberations. Bodies painted in bright colors exploded into the square at a dizzying pace. The dancers chased one another and gyrated to the delight of the crowd. Occasionally, one would break ranks to stand before a section of the crowd for a solo performance in which he or she would display his or her particular style. The audience responded with loud cheering and clapping. The dancer would then rejoin the troupe.

After some time, the dancers receded to the sidelines and a group of women took the stage. To the accompaniment of the musicians, their leader raised her voice and began to revile the groom while praising the bride. The other women responded on the chorus. They exaggerated his features, singing that Yossou had a big nose, but Ma'alia's was like a sparrow's egg. Yossou had a big belly while Ma'alia's was as flat as grindstone. Yossou ate like a pig, but Ma'alia worked as hard as an ox. On and on they sang to the delight of Ma'alia's kin while Yossou's people heckled them. Suddenly, a group of young men brandishing spears and shields entered the stage from all directions. They chased the women who ran away screaming in mock terror. The crowd loved it. The band of warriors came together and took up their own song about Yossou and his exploits.

He is as fearless as a lion
Yes, our Yossou is as fearless as a lion
He is stronger than the ox
Yes, our Yossou is stronger than the ox

They sang about his cunning, his skill, and his wisdom. They did not disparage Ma'alia at all.

The pace of the music picked up as the warriors dissolved back into the crowd and Chizi's dancers took center stage again. They performed a series of intricate dances that left the crowd roaring with delight. For the most exciting part, a dancer would break from the troupe to prance before a member of the crowd. The glaring and dancing feet were a challenge to a duel of dance. If the individual did not take the challenge, members of the crowd would click their tongues in disappointment and shout, "*Ao!*" or, "*Eesh!*" The timid person would slink to the back of the crowd in shame. The brazen would lock eyes with the challengers and rise as their feet picked up the rhythm of the music. They would glide to the center where they flew into a dusty blur of arms, garments, and stomping feet. The crowd showed approval with cries of "*Yee!*" or "*Eh-hee!*" When they felt a dancer had risen to the challenge, they would rush in, pick the individual, and carry him or her shoulder-high around the arena for a victory lap. Likewise, when a dancer did not match the challenge, members of the crowd would click their tongues in disapproval and shout, "*Eesh!*" or "*Ao!*" If the dancer did not take the hint, spectators would rush in and chase him or her away.

After a series of challenges, the troupe took the stage for a final performance. By now, the crowd was fully engaged, having participated and accepted challenges. It would be no surprise if some of them were included in Chizi's troupe at the next event. The music and dance reached a climax and a shout from Ziki brought it to an abrupt end. It was the signal for the *Sakul* or elder from the village of Ronge to speak.

Sakul Wiki-Zugu rose slowly and deliberately. He hawked and spit out a bolus of phlegm. It raised a tiny puff of dust when it landed and rolled, wrapping itself in a thin film of dust. Wiki-Zugu contemplated his missile for a moment then mentally dismissed it. He raised his hand for silence. The crowd quieted. With equal drama, he raised his head heavenward and intoned a prayer.

"Peace to all!"

"*Peace!*" the crowd responded.

"Peace, again I say!"

"*Peace!*"

"May the Oracle bless the events of this day and the ceremony we are about to witness."

"*Bless it!*"

"And bless those who have caused us to gather here."

"Bless them!"

"And let there be peace among the Avantu."

"*Let there be peace indeed!*" the crowd concluded.

Wiki-Zugu gave the crowd a moment to settle down then continued.

"The Great Spirit smiles upon a man who works hard and lives above reproach. Yossou is such a man." A murmur of agreement rippled through the crowd. "But death knows no such thing. It knows neither hard work nor laziness, neither youth nor age. It cuts down man and woman, the strong and the weak."

"*Oh, yes it does,*" several voices agreed.

"Thankfully, the Oracle smiles upon men and blesses them with the promise of new life." Wiki-Zugu turned to Yossou and smiled. "The hand of fate plucked a young, loving mother and wife from our midst." Turning to the group of veiled women he added, "But the Oracle knew and appointed another beautiful person in the bride who sits before us this day." He turned back to Yossou. "Yesterday, your sorrow was our sorrow. Today, your joy is ours. Peace be upon you all your days."

"*May it be so,*" the crowd responded.

Yossou nodded and murmured his thanks for the blessing. Wiki-Zugu sat down.

Next, the strong women stood and faced Yossou. Mideva, the short, stout one was their spokesperson.

"Stand up Yossou," she commanded.

He did.

"You say you want to get married. How many women do you want to marry?"

There was some chortling at this question. The strong women threw dark glances in the direction from which it came. The guilty lowered their eyes.

"There's only one I love and she's the one I want to marry today," Yossou answered.

Mideva half turned to the group behind her.

"Get up, girls!" she said sharply.

They also obeyed and lined up behind her.

To Yossou, Mideva said, "There are five young women standing before you. Do you know which one is your bride or should we pick one for you?"

Several people in the crowd raised their voices. Yossou only smiled and shifted his weight from one leg to another. He had been through this before.

"Remember…" Mideva continued, raising her voice above the crowd. "Remember if we pick a girl for you, she's the one you will marry. There'll be no turning back. Likewise, the girl you pick is the one you will marry. And you know if you refuse to proceed with either choice there's a heavy penalty for gathering people from all the villages here for nothing."

A rumble rose in the audience.

"I believe I can identify my bride," Yossou said patiently.

Mideva addressed the crowd. "You heard him. He's bragging that he knows his bride. What if he picks the wrong girl?"

Everyone in the crowd talked at the same time. The consensus was that he should marry his pick. Yossou stood silently, his hands behind his back, still smiling.

"You've heard what the people say," Mideva told him. "Now you must choose." She moved to the first girl in line. All of them, even under their covering, appeared about the same height and build. Mideva pointed to the first girl.

"Is this your bride?" She asked him the question, but looked at the crowd to draw them into the drama.

"She's not the one," many shouted, though a few voices called out to the contrary.

"No. That is not the girl I want to marry," Yossou answered firmly.

"Are you sure?"

"Yes, I'm sure."

"What about this one?" Mideva moved to the second girl.

"No. She's not the one for me."

"Do you really know what you want? You pick the wrong girl, you have her for life."

A lone female voice urged him to take the girl, to which a man charged the speaker to find another suitor for her daughter.

"She's not the one," Yossou said.

"Fine. And this one?"

"Not that one."

Mideva looked him up and down for a moment.

"I hope you won't regret this. You've turned down three girls already. One of them may have been your intended and you can't go back on it because you rejected them in the presence of this congregation."

"If I made the wrong decision, I'll live with it and honor the woman I pick. But I doubt it will come to that."

The crowd applauded his forthrightness.

"All right. Before you, stands a maiden as beautiful as any a man would desire. Is she your bride?"

"Again, *Senge* Mideva, beautiful as she is, she's not the one I want. I have yet to see my bride."

"Oh, now you've become like the spirits, eh? You're able to see beyond the nakedness of your eyes!" She turned to the crowd. "Who sees like he does? Is she the one?"

Members of the crowd raised their voices to express their opinions. Some even stood and gestured at Yossou, trying to shout sense into him. By the sound of it, they were evenly divided among those who thought she was the one and those who disagreed. Mideva let it run for some time then raised her hand to restore order.

"You have not helped this poor man come to a decision. I'll leave it up to him. Is that your final decision, Yossou?"

"Yes. She's not the one."

"You've rejected all but one." Mideva pointed to the fifth girl. "She's the one who will go with you to the ceremonial chamber - the one with whom you'll share life from this day on. I hope you won't regret having rejected the other four."

Yossou paused before answering.

"I believe she is my bride."

Once again, chaos reigned in the audience. Mideva let it run longer this time, alternately looking at Yossou and the crowd. He looked at her and crossed his arms. In response, she put her hands on her hip and planted her feet firmly on the ground.

"And you are absolutely sure?"

"Yes, I am." The crowd was now calling on Mideva to unveil the maiden. She turned toward them and raised her arms.

"He has spoken. Why wait any longer? Young woman, show yourself!"

The girl's hands came up slowly and took hold of the edge of the veil. Slowly, ever so slowly she raised it. The crowd egged her on.

"Hurry up. I don't have all day! I have cows to water and chickens to feed!" a man shouted.

"I'll be long dead by the time that face appears," an elderly man moaned.

When the veil had come up to her chin, the girl threw it back and the crowd gave a collective gasp. Ma'alia stood before them, positively glowing. She had never looked so beautiful. Yossou was in awe at her appearance. He did not hear Emesi ask the people to sit down or even notice when they did. He gawked at Ma'alia open-mouthed until a subtle clearing of the throat broke the spell. Everyone burst into laughter when he stuttered, trying to find his tongue. He flushed deeply and rubbed his nose in embarrassment.

"*Weeeh iyah!* It's over for him," a man said. "If a woman can have such an effect on him, she will sit on his head for the rest of his life."

"Oh, he'll be alright. Ma'alia is a good girl," a woman pointed out.

"I hope so… for his sake."

"Now then, let's continue," Emesi said when the laughter had died down. "Hopefully the man standing before us has recovered enough to know what's going on. Now, does this woman have family?"

"Yes she does," Egadwa said standing up. "Rodina and I have looked after Ma'alia as our own daughter. We stand here as her parents. And these," he said turning to a group seated around him, "are members of her family."

"Peace to you all," Emesi greeted them.

"*Peace!*" they responded.

"And does this man have people from whom he hails?"

"We are here to stand with Yossou." Minadi answered, also standing. "His mother is here together with his uncles, aunts, brothers, and children."

"Peace to you all."

"*Peace!*"

"Good. After what we've just seen, he'll surely need his family's support. Thank you, Minadi. You may be seated." Turning to Yossou he said, "I believe you are already aware of what is expected of you as a husband. You've earned great respect, not just in your village, but also in all Gololi. Therefore, I will not dwell long on that subject."

Emesi briefly outlined the duties of a husband as tradition dictated. When he finished, *Senge* Efi, one of the strong women came forward to charge Ma'alia with her responsibilities as a wife and mother. She prayed that Ma'alia would have many children and bring Yossou and his family much happiness. Efi then took Ma'alia by the hand and led her to her Yossou.

"We entrust our beloved daughter to you. Take good care of her and she will take good care of you."

"I will."

The crowd cheered. Efi stepped back to resume her crowd-control duties. Emesi took over again.

"Yossou, in the presence of this congregation, by the ancients, and by the Great Spirit, behold your wife!"

Yossou stepped forward and embraced Ma'alia with customary etiquette then sat on the stool while she sat on a mat by his side. Women ululated and the crowd raised a prolonged cheer. Emesi lifted his hands and shouted.

"Let's celebrate!"

On cue, Ziki and Chizi broke into a lively song as several maidens appeared from the cooking area. The first group passed out gourds to the special guests. Others followed with baskets of beef, chicken, and vegetables that the guests picked to fill their gourds. Another group of maidens handed the guests drinking horns, which their peers filled with banana wine. Having served the special guests, the maidens went on to attend the crowd. They dished out portions on banana leaves neatly folded to accommodate the food. There was plenty to eat and drink.

By evening, the celebrations were in full progress with much eating, drinking, singing, and heckling. On occasion, a song would require either one or both bride and groom to dance. They joined in and enjoyed themselves thoroughly. Yossou was not given to drink, but he had allowed himself a horn or two and it showed in his animated conversation and heightened sense of humor.

As night fell, groups of men still sat in the shadows, talking in low tones with their *sekes* or drinking straws stuck in pots of wine. The women whisked Ma'alia away for the last time while Minadi grafted Yossou into his group. The topic of discussion alternated between recent events in Gololi and words of advice. Since he had been married before, the men spared Yossou details they would otherwise have given a first-timer. The moon was out and most people had left for nearby villages. Those who came from further away simply walked up to their relatives, friends, or even strangers' compounds and made themselves at home. Among the Avantu, one was always at home in another's hut.

Ma'alia and Yossou had agreed that until the child was born, they would not be intimate with each other. However, not everybody knew the special circumstances surrounding this union and none of the people involved sought to divulge any information. According to tradition, the morning after the wedding, women from the groom's village would take the bedroll on which the couple had slept, and drape it over a low shrub outside the hut. If she were married pure, virginal blood would stain it. If not, the poor girl would have some explaining to do. She would suffer shame for having shared her fruit before it was ripe. There would be snickering behind her every time she passed a group of people. It was enough to deter a girl from succumbing to the advances of an eager male. Oddly, though, the community did not apply the same standards to males.

The problem had nagged Rodina all day. Though she was confident of her niece's purity, she would not be able to explain the lack of bloodstains. She pondered it while absentmindedly collecting the gourds brought out for the wedding. They had a tendency to disappear if not collected immediately. So preoccupied, she picked up more gourds than she could hold. A chipped gourd cut her as it slipped from her grasp.

"*Eesh!*" she cursed, looking at the bleeding finger. In the weak moonlight, the blood was an eerie black liquid that dripped onto the ground leaving dark spots. It gave her an idea. She would have to get to Kavessa, the milk cow discreetly, and then find Simi immediately.

"What brings you here at this late?" Simi asked, surprised to see Rodina. Emesi's homestead, where Simi would spend the night, was still bustling with activity.

"*Sshh!* Softly! Come. I need to ask you something." They moved to the edge of the compound away from the huts where there was constant movement of people, mostly women and children, between the huts.

"I'm sure you have the same concern I have about tonight. Ma'alia is like my daughter and I know she's a good girl. I also believe she did have an encounter with a spirit-being. You understand because Yossou experienced the same thing."

"Yes. It's strange indeed. And you're right. I've been wondering about tonight and tomorrow morning. Mideva and her women have inspected the couple's bedroll. They will bring it out tomorrow morning and there's no stopping them. Why? What are you thinking?"

"I know it's against tradition for the mother to get involved, but this is for my niece's sake. I'd hate to see her name tarnished for something she didn't do."

"Mideva's a tough one. She's posted lookouts around the chamber. She takes her role very seriously."

"There's got to be a way. Look. This is what I was thinking. I have…" Just then, a woman emerging from one of the huts noticed them. She walked over to identify them.

"*Chi!* Rodina! Simi! What are you conspiring?"

Rodina swore under her breath and hid the horn she carried in her hand.

"Oh, we're just talking about how the day went. I also wanted to talk with Simi a little about her new daughter so they can start off well."

Rodina hoped the explanation would satisfy the woman and send her off. Instead, it was an opening for conversation. The woman talked about how hard it had initially been with her own mother-in-law and how they eventually worked it out. She talked loudly, drawing attention. Two other women joined them and completely took over the conversation. Rodina barely heard what they said. She had almost resigned to the possibility she might not be able to help Ma'alia. However, she would not give up without trying one last time. It would have to be soon.

"Rodina, you're not listening. I asked you a question." It was the first woman who had interrupted them. Rodina cleared her head and apologized.

"Oh, I'm, sorry. I have a lot on my mind. I have to get back to my husband. Simi, I'll see you in the morning."

Beyond a certain time in the evening, it was strange for someone, especially a woman, to be out wandering. Rodina knew she was cutting it close. The night belonged to foul spirits, the occasional leopard, and night-runners. The latter, for whatever reason, were driven to be a nuisance after dark. They rustled the thatch on roofs, threw pebbles into huts, and broke wind so loud and so foul as to elevate it to an art form. If someone called from his compound challenging a person wandering in the dark and that person did not identify himself or his business properly, the challenger could raise a cry that would bring the villagers out with machetes, spears, bows, and arrows.

Rodina planted the horn at a specific spot then hurried to find Sabet, Ma'alia's cousin. In all likelihood, she would be at the bridal chambers. Sure enough as Rodina approached, she heard the high-pitched laughter and fast-talking that could only be Sabet. She was in a group of women putting final touches on the bridal chambers. Rodina realized this was her last chance.

"Rodina, you're still up?" one of the women said.

"Peace, friends. I had to discuss a few things with Simi, now that she's taking my daughter."

"Ah! Time to let go, mother. Time to let go," another woman said.

"Yes. Sabet, I forgot to give Simi a little potion for Ma'alia. You know how things will be tonight."

Sabet giggled and approached. It was common for a mother to give her newly wed daughter potions and ointments to make things go smoothly on her wedding night. Rodina tried to talk softly without drawing too much attention.

"I have no time to explain. They will not know each other tonight," she said bluntly. "But the bedroll must be stained. When you need to go to the bush before you retire, go behind the big tree over my shoulder. Between the roots, you'll find something you must either give Ma'alia secretly or do it yourself. Just find a way to save your cousin from ridicule."

"Rodina, that's impossible. All these women…"

"Sabet, find a way. Please try!"

Sabet saw Rodina's desperation and love for Ma'alia in her willingness to go to such lengths.

"I'll do my best," she said.

Sabet could feel the tension drain from Rodina even in the darkness.

"Thank you," Rodina said and strode into the shadows.

"Have you recently become a night runner?" Egadwa asked when Rodina removed the hide and stepped into the dark hut.

Before she could reply, Rodina stopped and registered the deep breathing of two individuals asleep in a corner.

"It's the children." Egadwa answered her silence. "They are here because the Sidzas are using Ma'alia's hut."

Rodina covered the entrance with the hide. "I was at the square to see Simi and Sabet and to give them a few suggestions. You know Ma'alia's in a delicate situation and we need to handle it carefully."

"Rodina, she's married and is now her husband's responsibility. It's time to step out of her life." The slightly slurred speech indicated Egadwa was a little inebriated.

"Yes, but like I said, I had to take care of a few things." She lay down beside him.

"Right. Oh, by the way, I don't know what happened to Kavessa. She seems to have hurt herself on a sharp branch or something. She has a small but deep cut on the inside right leg. I wouldn't have noticed it if she hadn't kept fidgeting."

Rodina cleared her throat. "Hmm. I wonder what happened. Chanzu didn't take her to the fields today."

"*Akh!* It's nothing. I rubbed some ash over the wound. She'll be fine in the morning."

"I hope so." Rodina wished it for a different "she" - one for whom Kavessa had given some of her blood. Rodina prayed that Sabet would find the horn and carry out the plan. Egadwa did not answer. He was already snoring.

After they had fussed over Ma'alia and ensured that the bridal chambers were in order, the women were ready to bring in the couple. Mideva dispatched one of her lieutenants to the men in whose company Yossou sat.

"Yossou," the woman said, "your bride awaits you."

"Thank you my daughter," Minadi replied.

The men detained Yossou a while longer. It would have been improper and disrespectful for the groom to rise immediately and follow her. A man should never seem too eager to go into his wife. After a suitable interval, Minadi announced he was tired and ready for bed. That was the signal to release the groom.

"Yes, it's late," Sakul Bonaya agreed. "And this man needs to attend to his bride."

"Be gentle, with her," Vakhum added.

"*Eh heh!* And don't forget what we discussed. Though you've been married before, remember that no two women are alike. *Eesh!* In fact no woman is like herself, so forget what you think you know about women and start afresh with this one."

"Thank you, *Koza*. I'll remember that."

They rose and escorted Yossou to the bridal chamber where the women waited. Mideva took Ma'alia by the hand and brought her forward. Sakul Bonaya nudged Yossou who turned and looked at him quizzically. Bonaya frowned and tipped his head imperceptibly in Ma'alia's direction. Yossou understood and stepped forward to join his bride.

"O, Great Spirit." Sakul Wiki-Zugu intoned. "We stand here this night to present to you this newlywed couple. Bless their lives together."

"*Bless them!*" The rest answered.

"Bless the seed of this man."

"*Bless it!*"

"Bless the seed of this woman."

"*Bless it!*"

"May they have many children."

"*Yes!*"

"May they find happiness together."

"*Yes!*"

"Bless this man and this woman."

"*Bless them!*"

"Bless them ever more."

"*Yes, bless them!*"

Having concluded the invocation, Wiki-Zugu looked skyward with arms raised for several moments before turning to Yossou.

"Take your bride. Love and take care of her."

Yossou took Ma'alia's hand and led her into the bridal chamber. A woman choked. All turned toward the sound. Sabet looked down so no one would see the tears. She thought back to what she had just experienced.

After relieving herself by the tree Rodina had indicated, Sabet found what she was looking for between two sturdy roots. A section of banana leaf covered the top of the horn and a thin strand of fiber tied it firmly in place. She was about to head back when she caught a whiff from it. She inspected the horn in the moonlight and found the leaf unbroken. Her curiosity piqued, she untied the chord and lifted the leaf. Nothing could have prepared her for what she saw. Slimy white maggots wiggled in a dark, evil-smelling, gelatinous liquid that flowed onto her hand. With a sharp cry, she dropped the horn and jumped back, staring at it in horror.

"What is it?" a woman called out.

"Something scared me. That's all."

"Useless coward!" the woman mumbled audibly.

Sabet paid no attention to the remark and shook her hand vigorously to rid it of the foul substance. She looked around for a kisasu plant, found one, and plucked several leaves with which she wiped her hand furiously. She rejoined the others, trying to remain composed. She ran into Mideva.

"You look upset. What is it?"

"Oh, nothing," Sabet lied and moved away.

"Why would Rodina do a thing like that? What purpose will it serve? Was it witchcraft?" she asked herself. She was even more confused when she recalled Rodina's apparent concern for Ma'alia. She will never forgive her for the shame Ma'alia would suffer in the morning.

"What do we do now?" Yossou asked. He felt surprisingly calm, having resolved to defend Ma'alia against any accusation of impropriety.

"What can we do?" she replied, carefully taking off the ceremonial gown. "I swore in my heart to the Oracle not to…"

"So did I!" Yossou cut her off a little more sharply than he intended. "I also honor the Oracle and stand in the faith of our ancestors. Since there's nothing we can do about it, let's talk about something else."

"I know. Whatever happens in the morning will happen. I'm just happy to be with you." She paused. "I love you, Yossou."

He gulped. She had never mentioned her feelings toward him until now. Sometimes he wondered if she was just going along because their families had brought them together. He had loved Yanze deeply and missed her, but he was sure of what he felt for Ma'alia as an individual and not as a replacement for his late wife.

"I never thought I'd hear those words from you. I was never sure. You always seemed to hold back."

"And I was not sure if you wanted to marry me because you needed a wife and a mother for your children or because you truly loved me. With time, I have grown confident of your love. The fact that you were willing to marry me in spite of my state reassured me."

Dealing with these subjects allowed the conversation to flow freely. They talked and laughed most of the night until they agreed they had to get some sleep.

"Sleep well, my love," Yossou said.

"You too."

He draped an arm around her belly and drew her to himself. She snuggled up against him, buried her head in his shoulder, and sighed contentedly. Soon they were fast asleep.

Yossou and Ma'alia were early risers, but they heard neither the rooster crow nor the birds chirping just before daybreak. Mideva's stern voice woke them.

"Are those who slept in this hut still alive?" she demanded. Yossou woke up with a start, his mind at first not registering the change in circumstances. He could see that it was already light outside. Ma'alia took longer waking up and looked at him dreamily. Suddenly, she stiffened and sat up with a look of horror on her face.

"What?" Yossou asked with concern.

"The day is well gone, Ma'alia," Mideva called out again before Ma'alia could explain. "We need to clean you up."

"I'm coming, Mideva. Give me a moment," Ma'alia shouted back. To Yossou she whispered, "I wetted the bedroll. Even as a child I never did that." She bowed her head despondently. Yossou did not know what to say.

"Did an ogre eat your legs or what?" Mideva asked again."

"*Vaya!* Give us a little time!" Yossou was starting to get irritated. He turned to Ma'alia. "Are you sure about this? Let's see. Turn over a little." He touched the spot under her thighs and felt wetness. When he looked at his fingertips, they were dark.

"You are bleeding!"

"What?" Ma'alia rolled on her hip to look. There was a dark stain the size of a man's palm on the bedroll.

"Do you feel any pain?"

"No, but I feel sticky between my thighs."

"Just what's going on in there?" Mideva seemed to get impatient herself.

Yossou got off the bedroll and sat on the floor arms locked together holding his knees at the elbows.

"Take to that woman what she wants," he said.

In a daze, Ma'alia got up, folded the bedroll, and carried it to the outer chamber. She took the ceremonial gown with her.

"I thought you'd never come out," Mideva chided. "I'll take that," She snatched the bedroll from Ma'alia. "Wait here," She commanded and went out into the sunshine. Moments later, Efi, one of the strong women brought a large gourd of water.

"Come, let's clean you up. Sit down."

Ma'alia accepted the cleansing ritual though she felt somewhat violated. Outside, she heard exclamations of joy and approval.

"Of course, she would not let us down," someone said.

Ma'alia suspected the stain on the bedroll must have elicited the comments. She did not know what to feel. When Efi finished, she asked Ma'alia to don the ceremonial gown then led her out to the courtyard.

"One of the men will come to get you, Yossou," Efi threw her voice into the inner chamber as they left.

Not long after, Sakul Bonaya came in.

"I trust everything went well, Yossou."

"As well as you'd expect." Yossou was non-committal.

"Good. The elders have prepared water for your cleansing. Let's go."

The sun hurt Yossou's eyes and he squinted before he got accustomed to the light. Bonaya led him to a booth behind the hut where Yossou found some warm water in a huge calabash. He shed his garment and squatted. He smiled to himself as he thought of the purpose for this early bath. He was as "clean" as he had been since Yanze's passing. He splashed water over himself to take his mind off the thoughts that threatened to breach his emotional defenses. This was not the time. He finished then waited a while to get reasonably dry. He then dressed and went to join Ma'alia and a group of others for breakfast.

The meal consisted of porridge, chicken, chunks of roast meat, roast potato, and cassava. This was Kilima's farewell to their daughter. It was a rather subdued event because there would be more festivities in Ronge. Afterwards, some young people from both villages put the couple's belongings and presents together. At midmorning, the party then started for Yossou's home. They would be there by nightfall.

Chapter 3

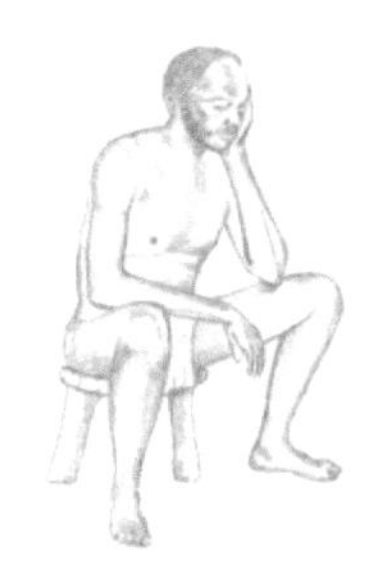

apart for a season

Marriage was a big change for Ma'alia. Sharing a bedroll with another adult - a man for that matter, was a new experience. Working closely with her mother-in-law, fitting in with the Baronge, and most of all, suddenly finding herself the mother of two young girls, all required major adjustments. Soon she realized the memory of their mother was still fresh in their minds and that she could never replace her. Ma'alia understood how they felt because she still grieved her own mother after all the seasons that had passed. Everyone had only good things to say about Yanze, and it was not just a case of the living talking well of the departed for fear she might haunt them. They all meant what they said. Besides, she had been the adopted daughter of Sakul Wiki-Zugu, the most respected elder in the village.

Yanze had also set a standard so high that anyone who succeeded her would have to be exceptional to live up to it. The elder Simi had raised eight of her own children, and after Yanze's demise, she had mothered Yossou and her two granddaughters. Ma'alia sensed a perverse pleasure in her mother-in-law for looking after Yossou again. Simi respected him as an adult, but to the mother in her, he was still her little boy. This inevitably led to tension between the two women.

Simi clearly resented the prospect of giving up the care of her son and grandchildren to another woman. This sentiment found expression in little statements of correction, ceaseless suggestions, or subtle gestures of exasperation with Ma'alia and the way she carried out her tasks. Like many mothers-in-law, she considered it her duty to teach the young bride to manage the household and look after her son.

Initially, Ma'alia could deal with both subtle and overt comparisons to Yanze, but after some time, it started to bother her. Knowing she had walked into the situation at a distinct disadvantage, she pointed out as tactfully as she could that she was not Yanze and she did not intend to become like her. She became increasingly frustrated, but found it difficult to open up to her husband about it. Her mother-in-law, though meaning well, stifled her with her controlling attitude. She decided what they would eat and when, assigned and supervised chores, and undermined Ma'alia's attempts to discipline the girls. Ma'alia could not help feeling Simi treated her just as she treated them. Her desire was to cook for her husband and feel like a woman in her own home. That was not the case and she was miserable. At the same time, she could not go back to aunt Rodina. If her parents had been alive, it might have been more palatable to say she was going back to her father and mother. But she was an orphan.

In spite of the inner turmoil, Ma'alia always put on a brave face. Sometimes when she was truly downcast, Yossou sensed it and asked what was bothering her. She could not bring herself to say his mother was the problem. She only said she was not feeling like herself, perhaps because of the burden she carried. She hoped he would dig deeper, but he did not reward her with any research. If anything, he found ways to avoid her until the spells passed. This only aggravated her further.

When Ma'alia was a little girl, her mother had taught her about the Great Spirit who knew everything. She said he lived beyond the skies, but could see into the realm of men. He knew when children were doing right or wrong, so Ma'alia always tried to do what was right. Her mother also told her the Great Spirit could do anything and she could ask him for help whenever she had a problem. She taught Ma'alia a short prayer.

"Great Spirit," she would say. "I need your help. Father of all ancestors, hear the prayer of your little girl."

Ma'alia had said that prayer in earnest when her mother died leaving her orphaned. Now, she was no longer a child and felt anguished in her marriage. She remembered her mother's advice and mouthed the prayer several times during the day. Unfortunately, the Spirit did not seem to hear. Little changed in her new home and she grew desperate. Her mother-in-law sensed her mood and asked what troubled her. Ma'alia could not bring herself to tell Simi exactly what she felt either. She was very much alone.

The opportunity to share her feelings presented itself one afternoon as they were crushing millet in a mortar. Women modified their conversation to the beat of the pestles, using the down stroke for emphasis. This particular afternoon, Ma'alia brought the pestle down with unusual force. Each landing accented the sharp release of her breath. She did not talk much. Simi stopped pounding, but Ma'alia continued a while longer until she realized Simi had stopped and was regarding her questioningly. Ma'alia also stopped. Deliberately, Simi sifted through the crushed millet.

"Are you not happy here?"

Ma'alia did not answer right away. She struggled to find the right words.

"Oh, I just have a few things on my mind. I have not been a mother before and I'm still getting used to it."

"There's nothing to it my child. Just take each day as it comes. The Oracle will take care of you and the child. Leave the future in the hands of The Mighty One."

Ma'alia found little solace in this advice and the patronizing tone in which her mother-in-law delivered it. But, she was completely unprepared for the question Simi asked next.

"Have you been preparing porridge for your husband?"

"What?"

"Is your husband having his daily porridge? I know you are with child, but you should still be able to feed my son."

Feed her son - a grown man? Ma'alia was puzzled. A moment later, what the older woman alluded to hit her, and she was disgusted and angry. She trembled and her lower lip quivered. In order not to say the wrong thing, she stepped away.

"Forgive me M'ma. I will go fetch some water."

Simi was about to speak, but Ma'alia had already tossed the pestle to the ground and walked away. She passed her hut and went down to the orchard where her Simi grew various fruits. People would not see her in the thick foliage unless they came looking for her. Out of sight, she put her hands on her head and muttered to herself like a deranged woman. The pain in her heart was unbearable. She paced aimlessly, crunching leaves underfoot. She frequently let out a strained moan as if doing so would squeeze out some of the agony.

When she could not take it anymore, she sat down on the thick carpet of leaves and undergrowth, propping herself up with her right arm. She, who was otherwise scared of anything that crawled or was slimy, paid no heed to the slithery vegetation under her hand. She wanted to cry aloud, but only continued to moan. She wanted to die. She wished she could join her parents beyond the skies where she would be free from worry and the grind of life.

She thought of her husband. She loved him dearly, but she had to compete with her mother-in-law for his love. The more she thought about it the less confident she felt that if he had to choose, he would stand with her over his mother. Gloomy thoughts assailed her, casting a shadow over her spirit. The constant buzzing of *onjiri* bored into her head, amplifying her forlorn mood and pushing her to the edge of sanity. An owl hooted intermittently in the distance - a haunting requiem to happier days past. Her fingers found strands of banana fiber, which she twiddled randomly in the manner of her thoughts. They took on a life of their own and her hands worked themselves to a frenetic rhythm. As they climaxed, she frantically reached for fibers around her and wove them into a three-strand cord with dexterity born of years of practice plaiting hair. Soon, she was on her hands and knees, looking for anything she could add to her lengthening cord.

Ma'alia gave no thought to what she was doing. She did not want to. She knew where she was heading, but did not want to stop. Another childhood skill kicked in. Girls were not encouraged to climb trees, but Ma'alia had never resisted a ripe mango or guava. She did not settle for the overripe fruit that fell to the ground, half-eaten by birds and insects. When boys were unwilling to share or get her a fruit, she would wait until they were gone then quickly scale the tree and have her pick of fruit. For a long time she thought no one knew of her exploits until Senge Rodina mentioned in passing that it was unbecoming for girls to climb trees. Ma'alia did not feel disinclined to go after her favorite fruits. She was just more discreet.

Now she threw all discretion aside and made for the guava tree in the middle of the orchard. With resolve in her heart and the cord over her shoulder, she laid her hands on the trunk and looked up to start climbing. Just then, she saw directly above her, a gray and white dove unlike any she had ever seen. It neither stirred nor fled, but fixed her a soft, penetrating gaze. It looked at her a moment longer then fluttered its wings and flew away through an opening in the porous canopy of branches and leaves. Ma'alia watched it fly. Her resolve crumpled and she sank to her knees. It was the briefest of encounters, but it touched her momentously. She shuddered at the thought of what she might have done. She trembled with relief that the dove had somehow averted the tragedy she would have brought on herself and her family. The compound in which a person took his or her own life was under a curse and it behooved the villagers to raze it to the ground.

When she at last regained her composure, it was as if a great load had fallen from her shoulders. The tears she shed washed her spirit clean of the morbid thoughts that had recently flooded her being. She felt clean and rejuvenated, holding no bitterness in her heart. She looked around. Everything seemed magically brighter and her mood reflected her spirit. Once again, Ma'alia picked herself from the ground, but this time her disposition was a complete antithesis of what she had experienced earlier.

It came to her as a deep conviction – a still inner voice whose message was unmistakable. *She had to go to her cousin, Sabet.* She could not explain it except it felt like the right thing to do. She went into her hut, packed a few items in her pouch before she went to join Simi in the kitchen.

Simi thought she was the best mother-in-law a girl could have so she wondered why Ma'alia did not get along with her as easily as Yanze had. She looked up as Ma'alia entered the kitchen.

"I thought you'd never come back"

"You are right. I might not have, but The Mighty One has different plans for me." She sat down.

"He has plans for everyone, Ma'alia. It just depends on what you desire and how hard you work for it."

"Yes. Speaking of plans, I'm going to cousin Sabet's tomorrow. I'll stay there until this child is born. Besides, she's many moons pregnant and could use some help."

Simi gave her daughter-in-law a long sideways glance.

"Just like that, you are going away from home?"

"It's best that way M'ma. I love Yossou and I don't want to trouble him and displease you at the same time. I'll return when my baby is born."

"Are you running away from your responsibilities? What manner of wife marries one day and runs off the next?"

"I'm not running away. I'll return when the child is born. For now, honestly M'ma, we both cannot live in the same compound. You are not leaving, so I will."

Simi was mortified. Ma'alia sat silently looking at the floor a while then stood up.

"I'll go to the river."

"I thought you went already. Isn't that what you said when you showed me your back earlier? I don't understand you."

Ma'alia did not answer. She picked an *ingata*, placed it on her head, and deftly hefted a pot onto it. She ducked at the door as she left the kitchen. Seeing her, the younger Simi fetched a smaller pot and ran after Ma'alia. The elder Simi watched them go, noting as if for the first time how gracefully Ma'alia walked. Balancing the pot on her head added flair to the smooth swinging of her arms and hips. *She walks like a queen mother. She's a remarkable girl.* Simi wondered if she had driven Ma'alia too hard in trying to make her the perfect wife for her son. She pushed the thought aside, unwilling to admit it to herself. Instead, she gritted her teeth and turned her attention to the cooking. *Going away? What's this world coming to?* The more she thought about it, the angrier she became and, in a perverse way, the better she felt about herself. Still, she was not happy with the situation. It was a paradox.

For Yossou, the cruel irony was that after several moons without a wife, he could not consummate his union with the one he had found. He loved Ma'alia dearly, but unfulfilled desire, the resulting tension, and Ma'alia's changing physical and emotional state began to strain their relationship. He also noticed the strained relationship between his mother and his new bride. It baffled him because his mother had adored Ma'alia before he married her and had recommended her strongly. She had also had excellent rapport with Yanze, so he could not understand why she could not get along with Ma'alia.

He sat outside by the door of his hut, watching a tiny black ant moving with great deliberation, looking for a morsel of food. It would latch onto something, only to let go and continue its search. Yossou felt like the ant. He was always searching, finding, and letting go. He had lost children and a wife. Now he was about to lose another. He lifted his head to look at Ma'alia who stood beside him. She leaned with one hand against the wall. With the other, she absently pulled at the straw on the roof.

"So you leave tomorrow, eh? Since when did women decide when they stayed and went?"

"Would you rather I told you, or simply ran away?"

"At the last moment? What will people think when suddenly you are gone? And we got married just the other day!" Yossou clicked his tongue in frustration.

"Yossou, I'm unhappy here. I can't do anything right in your mother's eyes. I'm no better than Simi or Temin. She's always telling me what to do and correcting me. This is supposed to be my home. I'm supposed to cook for you and your children. I'm supposed to help you raise them, but no! I don't have a voice. I'm just like a slave! I don't want to live like this. Since I found your mother here, I'll leave. Of course, it's not for good. I just want to go away until this child is born. By then, I hope things will have changed. For now, I can't deal with all this."

"You're not the only woman to have problems with a mother-in-law. Many women have been through worse. They didn't run at the first sign of trouble and things worked out in the end."

"Yossou, I'm telling you how I feel. Those women had their situations and handled them as they saw fit. Me, I need to get away. Can you understand that? Maybe not. You men never have to move away. You never leave your family. Your mother's here, your children are here, this is your home. How could you understand how I feel?"

"Come now. Let's be sensible about this. I'm just trying to see how moving away is going to solve anything. You say you'll come back after the baby's born. How sure are you that you'll have changed by then? How can you be certain my mother will change? I'm sure she's the one you would like to change the most. You'll only come back to the same situation and have to start over."

"I made a vow before the Oracle and the people that I'll be yours forever. I intend to keep that vow. I also vowed to The Mighty One I would be a worthy vessel for his son. That's another vow I intend to keep. This is what I must do in order to keep my vows. I don't want to go through suffering and heartache and do something to hurt this child. You've got to understand that."

Yossou caught the veiled threat and furrowed his brow, trying to decipher its implications. He had forgotten that Ma'alia's pregnancy had aspects of mystery to it. He also remembered that morning by the river when he hacked away at grass in a rage. He could still feel the strength of the hand that had gripped his wrist. He shuddered. He did not want to incur the wrath of the Oracle and spirit-beings sent to deliver His message in the realm of men. He regretted his impudence and listened to his wife with a different attitude. Eventually, he agreed they would stay apart until the child was born.

In the morning, Yossou assembled a small party to accompany them on the half-day trip to Ngoma. Though she was leaving for legitimate reasons, Ma'alia still felt like an outcast. She was leaving her husband and home to live in another village. Further still, she could not push aside the thought that the baby she carried was not her husband's. *Isn't this what they do to girls and women who conceive out of wedlock or are caught in adultery - send them away from the village?* She became even more depressed as they descended onto the Plains of Sacrifice and she looked to the surrounding hills. In the distance, the hill country seemed to mock her. Now she felt even worse about leaving.

The hill country was *Bagondi* territory. The rugged terrain was home to mountain goats, hyrax, serpents, and other reptiles. Little could grow on the wind swept crags that saw little rain and only nature's hardiest survived the hostile environment. To this land, society drove her rejects - murderers, adulterers, rapists, lepers, and the unclean.

Those who survived the first few days of expulsion were likely to make it because in that time they learned vital survival skills. The frail, weak, and dispirited rolled over and died. Few members of normal society ever ventured into the hills. The unintended consequence of ostracizing members of society was that they inevitably grew in number, learned to survive in difficult circumstances, and eventually formed their own communities. Because they held grudges against those who expelled them, the outcasts often descended on the villages in vengeful raids.

Another reason for the frequent raids was the scarcity of women in the bandit colony. In most, if not all communities, men often were the offenders and therefore more likely to suffer banishment. Since men outnumbered women, tension persisted with brutal competition for the women. The raids therefore served to replenish their coffers, release pent-up tension through skirmishes, and gratify their desires through the rape and capture of women. Many captive women took their own lives when they could not take the abuse any longer. Others became empty shells - caring neither what the men did to them, nor whether they lived or died. They were long dead from the rape, beatings, and abuse. Sujia was little more than a girl when the Bagondi raided her village.

She woke up to screaming and wailing.

"The Bagondi are upon us!"

Her mother burst into the chamber where she slept with her older sister and two half-sisters, dragging her younger siblings along. The older boys slept apart in their disi.

"Get up!" her mother said. "Quick! To the banana grove!" The girls were up and outside in a flash. Their mother waited by the door. When Sujia stepped outside, she saw her father attempting to fend off one of the raiders.

"Baba!" she cried.

"Sujia! Let's go!" her mother pleaded, as she dragged the children away.

"Go! Run!" her father ordered. Those words were his last. The momentary distraction was all the assailant needed to deliver the fatal blow. Sujia heard the sickening, cracking sound and a grunt. Her father fell with a thud. Sujia froze where she stood. The huge attacker stepped on her father's twitching body and came toward her. He had painted his face in war patterns and his eyes glinted wickedly. The machete in his hand dripped with her father's blood. When he reached her, he pushed her back into the hut without a word. He threw her roughly to the ground, forced her legs apart, and thrust himself viciously into her. He was not a man inclined to caring for his person. His odor and breath overwhelmed her. His body was as rough as his assault upon her honor. She had never felt such exquisite pain.

"Woi, M'ma! M'ma goi!" Sujia screamed, but it did not elicit any mercy. If anything, he got more excited and thrust harder and faster. Conflicting senses and emotions carried her to another world where there was only pain.

When he finished, the man stood and pulled her up by the wrist. He did not release her after he had yanked her back outside. He dragged her into her father's chamber and pushed her to the ground with a warning not to move. He started rummaging around looking for something. Sujia had never set foot in her parents' bedchamber, so she did not know what he sought. Apparently, he knew what he wanted and where to find it. He pushed the bedroll aside and found a spot on the ground. With a few thrusts of the machete, he unearthed some cowry shells, beads, precious stones, and other treasures wrapped in soft hide. He threw them in a pouch slung over his shoulder. He pulled Sujia back to her feet and went outside. He cackled what must have been a signal because there were answering calls from other parts of the village. The man then raced through the bushes heading out of the village, dragging the girl along. Three equally fierce looking men joined him as they ran. More catcalls later and other Bagondi, all breathing heavily from excitement, joined them. Some dragged women who were either crying, or like Sujia, were shocked beyond feeling. The raiders spoke various dialects of the Avantu. She could make out a few words from their whispered conversations, which they kept to a minimum. Her captor, she figured, was the leader of this raid. That would certainly make it more difficult to escape. When they had regrouped, the big man gave the order, and they began to walk quickly.

The raiders traveled most of the night along paths Sujia had never taken. For the latter part of the trek, the terrain became rougher and more punishing. The brutality of the raid and the rigors of the hike took its toll on some of the captive women and they were unable to continue. Whenever a woman became burdensome, men took turns raping her then put her out of her misery with a swift blow to the head. Observing this, Sujia vowed not to break down no matter what they did. Her nether regions were on fire and the blood still trickled down her thighs but she pressed on purely as a matter of will.

In the days that followed, Sujia learned, contrary to some accounts that filtered into the villages, that the life of a *M'gondi,* or bandit, was not at all glamorous. When they were not out on a raid, the men spent the time lying around, sleeping, playing games, or fighting at the slightest provocation, often with deadly consequence. They encouraged fights because they provided entertainment for a people with no purpose. They had no gardens to till, no wives or children to boast of, and no social structure with which they could identify with pride.

Sujia understood what it meant to be an outcast. A person was as good as dead. The only thing that these men and women had in common was the fact that either their communities had driven them out, or other outcasts had taken them forcibly from their villages. Other than that, no one cared for anyone else. There was little order in their rocky commune and even less attention to hygiene. When nature called, most went right where they stood, resulting in a perpetual stench in the air.

Asai, her captor, was not a good man. He had no patience, did not take kindly to criticism, and could not stand any of his minions overstepping their bounds. In the first few days of captivity, she saw him slay two men. One had taken liberties with a woman he considered exclusively his own. The other had merely spoken out of turn. Either way, Asai could not stand anyone challenging his authority.

Apparently, he had grafted Sujia into his pool of women because he kept her close day and night. It was not out of affection because he gratified himself whenever he wanted with whoever he chose. Every time he came to her, Sujia remembered the night the *Bagondi* had raided her village and taken her from the life she knew and loved. She remembered too, that he was the man who took her father's life and brought her into this bizarre universe. At such times, she still saw the light from the flames of burning huts playing on his painted face as he assaulted her. She still saw the glint in his eye. *She had to be strong.*

But she was not always strong. Sometimes when she was alone, emotions would burst to the surface and she would cry silently, but intensely. She yearned to see her mother, her brothers, and sisters. She even missed her stepmother in whose eyes she never could do right. Not knowing if they had survived tormented her. Worst of all, she remembered her father's last moments as if it happened just yesterday. She remembered calling out to him as he fought the big man. Had she not distracted him, he might have held his own, but because of her, he was dead. She could still hear the sickening sound of the blow and see his head crack open like a pumpkin. She hated herself for causing the death of the man she loved the most and was often tempted to take her own life. But that would be too easy. The most appropriate punishment was to live with the guilt, which was far greater than the abuse at the hand of her captor. It was a matter of time and she would find a way to make him pay for her father's death.

The answer came in the form of the thighbone of a mountain goat. One evening, some men shot the animal and had it for dinner. As with a pride of lions, Asai, who did not participate in the hunt, took the choice portion of the meat first. His deputies divided the rest among themselves. The women who roasted the goat could not partake of it. Out of necessity, they had refined the skill of sneaking pieces of meat into their mouths and chewing on the sly.

When he had cleaned the bones of meat, Asai belched loud and long then lay down to let the food settle. Sitting nearby, Sujia noticed a bone that he had crushed in order to get to the marrow. It tapered to a fine sharp point while the opposite end lent itself to the form of a handle at the joint. It was a ready dagger and she did not have to do anything else to it. With a little discomfort and improvisation, she could hide it in her modesty patch the next time he demanded her body.

Though girls were not supposed to handle weapons, her half-brother, Kanu, had secretly taught her to shoot with bow and arrow. She had become adept at it, even surpassing him in marksmanship. He was very proud of her and urged her to show her skills to their father, but she felt she was not ready. She continued to hone her skills with the bow Kanu had made for her, but had never killed anything. In captivity, she had been unable to lay her hands on a weapon - until now. She took the bone and hid it behind Asai's hut. Over the next two days, she formed a plan, mulled over it, and steeled herself to follow through. Her first kill would be a deserving animal.

On the evening of the third day after the hunt, Sujia made herself very appealing to Asai with subtle hints. She would let him catch her stealing glances at him then look away as if she were embarrassed he had caught her. At one point when she was close to him, she briefly brushed her breasts against him. He turned to look at her, but she acted as if it was purely unintentional. She augmented the impression she sought to make by touching his arm lightly when she asked him a question later. By the end of the evening, his eyes followed her around as she busied herself with the banal chores of the shambolic commune. She was not surprised when he hollered for her from his hut after dark. The plan had worked so far. She went to the back of the hut, retrieved her weapon, and tucked it under her patch to the small of her back before she went in.

Asai was all over her as soon she entered his odorous hut. He was like a beast that smelled a female in heat and could not wait to mount her. In a bold move that surprised even her, Sujia stayed his calloused, groping hands.

"Slowly, Asai. I'm your woman and I'm going nowhere." She affected a seductive rasping voice. "Slow down and enjoy these moments. You are always rushing things."

He slowed down grudgingly and let her take the lead. Guided by primal instinct and knowledge of men she had quickly acquired in a few moons, she began to stimulate him slowly. Soon he was moaning and groaning softly. She guided his hands and allowed him to explore her person in a measured way. She had to push them back every so often to stop him from getting out of control. Above all, she ensured his hands did not drift to her lower back. She continued to work his senses until he was gasping and breathing heavily. She rolled over on top of him and faced him in the faint light.

"You like what I'm doing?"

"Yes! Oh yes!" he gasped.

"You want more?"

"Yes! Don't stop!"

She smiled sweetly and slid down his torso. He closed his eyes and savored the millions of sensations that rippled through him as she played him with her hands and mouth. Sujia worked her way back up to his face, locked lips with him. The smell reminded her of the night when he had first assaulted her, and she recoiled in disgust. She managed to control her feelings and continue. She lifted her face and smiled at him again. He opened his eyes and ran a rough hand across her bare back.

"I have a gift for you," she said.

He laughed softly. "What gift?"

"A parting gift," she said, discreetly reaching for the bone at her lower back.

"A parting gift?" he chuckled. "Where are you going? Where can you go? I own you." The self-assured domineering tone crept back into his voice.

In the semi-darkness, Sujia's eyes turned into hard black pebbles. The smile was gone and she pulled her lips back in a tight line. Asai raised his head, trying to figure out what was happening.

"Remember my father? His blood calls. Goodbye."

He realized too late. In his arousal, he was slow to react. Sujia drove the bone deep in his throat and put all her weight on it. He still managed to toss her aside and pull the bone out. She scrambled to her feet and stood against the wall. Asai rolled onto his stomach, gurgling and rasping as blood spewed out of his neck and mouth. He shuddered then went limp. When he was still, Sujia went up to the body, snatched the weapon, and stepped back. After she was sure he would not move again, she kicked him and went to sit outside for the rest of the night.

In the morning, early risers woke to the sight of their leader's favorite girl seated by the hut, looking disheveled and glassy-eyed. In her hands, she held a bloodstained bone. No one asked her what she was doing because she was, after all, the leader's girl. Word must have gone around fast because more people came to stare at her. No one spoke.

The sun was well clear of the hills when Sujia finally stood up and stretched nonchalantly. The bloody bone in her outstretched right hand made for a particularly poignant pose. Her casual demeanor did not fool those who gathered, waiting for the rest of the drama to unfold. She turned round and walked into the hut. The watchers were appalled at what she was doing. When she finished, she attempted, with some success, to drag out the limp form of their leader by his right arm. After a brief struggle, she managed to get the top half of his body through the door. The head was missing. She trod on his body and went back into the hut emerging moments later, holding Asai's head upside down by the beard in one hand. In the other, she carried the dead man's bow. She had a quiver full of arrows over her shoulders. With equal drama, she walked right through the confounded watchers and placed the head on a boulder at a distance from the hut. The eyes were still open. Sujia walked back to the entrance of the hut, turned around, and notched an arrow. Realizing what she intended, the watchers hurriedly cleared the arrow's flight path, giving it a generous margin of error. Sujia pulled the string slowly, held for effect, and let fly. The arrow went clean through the left eye, knocking Asai's head over. Sujia looked around at everyone to see if she had made her point. No eyes challenged her. Satisfied, she made her way out of the colony and down the hill to the low-lying areas. After a long descent, she came to a creek at the edge of the plains. Hidden in the shrubbery, she bathed, ate some wild fruits, then slept hard.

The sun was already dipping when voices woke her. A man and a woman were talking a short distance away. Sujia carefully crept toward the voices. Through the foliage, she saw a beautiful young woman who could not have been much older than she was. Her companion, an older man, stood watching as she knelt to fill her water skin. She brought it to her lips and drank, letting out a sound of satisfaction at the end. But she did not look happy. She offered the skin to the man and he drank, handing it back to her when he finished. She refilled it and tied it shut. The man squatted beside the woman.

"I wish you didn't feel you had to do this. We can work it out."

"You still don't understand, do you? It's not only about what your mother said. Honestly, I don't know how I'm feeling. I'm carrying a baby that I have been told is of the Spirit Father yet I have not known a man. I pledged not to do so until I deliver this child, yet your mother asks me if I'm attending to your needs. Do you see how uncomfortable it is to be in my position? Besides, I wonder how many people are whispering behind my back that the child I carry is not my husband's."

"But I married you in spite of it. Yes, it took a little urging, but I did."

"We have come too far. I can't turn back now. I'll be gone a few moons then I'll return. That's all I ask."

The man lifted his eyes and appeared to look straight at Sujia. She held still, wondering if he had seen her. She silently notched an arrow, but he turned away.

"If that's how you feel, so be it. Come. The others are waiting."

He made his way back along the creek. The woman rose and followed. Sujia saw she was in the early stages of pregnancy. She watched them disappear and heard other voices in the distance. It sounded as though the couple had stolen away to try to resolve a disagreement. However, it was what they talked about that bothered Sujia. She could not grasp the idea of a Spirit Father coming upon a woman to give her a baby. She remembered her first experience with Asai and the rage within her started to boil over. She was angry that the Spirit would take over a woman body without her consent. She was angry with the man that he did not understand how the young woman felt. She was angry with his mother for whatever she had said to the girl. She got up and started the climb back to the colony furiously.

When she got back, it was already getting dark. She noticed the men and women treated her with deference. Someone had cleared Asai's hut of the body. They rightly assumed she would make it her home. One of the men brought her a bone leftover from the previous day's hunt and a large roast yam. She thanked him and ate absently. Later, she fell into troubled sleep and dreamt of a woman with a spirit-being hovering above her. The words about the Spirit Father choosing the woman at the creek to bear his child repeated themselves in her mind. It was the first of many nights they would haunt her.

Sabet was six moons pregnant and the baby had been increasingly active as the pregnancy progressed. One day, however, he suddenly stopped moving and Sabet was worried. When she expressed her fears, Ajema, her friend, told her this sometimes happened and the child would start moving soon. If there were no activity for more than three days, they would massage her belly with special herbs. If that did not help, she would have to see the medicine man again. Sabet groaned at the thought of those long and costly sessions with the *mganga.* She prayed her baby would move before she had to resort to that.

By the third day, the child had not moved. Even on the fourth, there was still no movement. Sabet started to despair. It seemed cruel that after The Mighty One had blest her, the child should die in her womb before she looked into his tiny eyes. The little fingers would not clasp hers as so many other babies had done. Even the ritual of counting to make sure he had ten fingers and ten toes would be meaningless. She began to mourn her child. When Lemba tried to comfort her, he only croaked, adding to her frustration.

"Come now, Sabet. Where's the hope?" Jani's wife, Imu, chided. "We are not sure he's dead. You can't lose hope now. You have a miracle child. The One who gave him to you will not deal you such a cruel blow." But she did not seem convinced of what she said herself.

In the afternoon of the fifth day, they were at the *mganga's* secluded abode at the edge of the forest with a white chicken for the sacrifice and anxious hearts. Even when the medicine man broke the chicken's neck and let the blood run over her distended belly, Sabet was still uncertain. On the way home, she sang funeral dirges, drawing people out of their huts to watch the sad company

"*Modi, vitu. Modi,*" they commiserated with her. Ajema and Imu did not sing, but they walked on either side of her with their arms around her. They knew how she must feel to have prayed and waited so long only to end up losing the child. To compound her pain further, she would have to carry the dead child until her body rejected it. Neither woman envied her.

They were almost home when they saw a party approaching.

"The village has visitors," Jani said.

"I wonder whose they are and why they are here," Imu added.

Even Sabet stopped mourning to look. When the visitors came within a stone's throw, she suddenly pulled away from her friends.

"Ma'alia!" she cried, running awkwardly toward the visitors.

"Sabet!" Ma'alia said, also starting toward her. Sabet faltered.

"*Aaoooo!*" she exclaimed stopping to clutch her stomach. In a moment, all the women were at her side.

"Are you alright?" they asked at the same time.

"The baby kicked me hard." Then the significance of what she just said sank in. "He kicked!" she exclaimed, looking around, eyes wide open, and a huge smile on her face. "My baby's alive! He's alive!"

"*Chi!* That's unbelievable!" Ajema exclaimed. All the women joined her in a group hug, jumping up and down.

Lemba croaked what would be praise and thanks upon hearing the news.

"You are a blessing, Ma'alia," Sabet said when the excitement had passed. "At the sound of your voice, the baby in my womb, who has not moved in five days, jumped for joy. The child you carry is even more blessed. My spirit tells me he will be greatly used by The Mighty One."

"I am nothing but a slave of the Oracle. He does as he pleases. He brings one down and raises another up. He gives children to the barren and the untouched. He has remembered you and me in wondrous ways. I am indeed happy for you, my sister."

They embraced once more before they shook hands all around. They made their way to Lemba's compound. This was indeed a day of celebration.

Ma'alia's first days with Sabet were most refreshing. They caught up on what was going on in their villages, lives, and pregnancies. Sabet loved having another woman with whom she could talk. Lemba's inability to speak had frustrated both her and Lemba and Ma'alia's presence was a mitigating influence.

However, Ma'alia soon realized the exact nature of people among whom she had come to live.

"Why is this woman here without her husband?" she heard people ask several times as she passed by. They did not care whether she heard them or not. It even appeared they wanted her to hear it.

"Don't you know her? She's the wife of the Oracle," a woman once answered. She lowered her voice to a conspiratorial whisper. "She's carrying his son." They burst into laughter. Ma'alia bit her lip and kept walking.

A few days later, she had an encounter that would change everything. On the way to the river in the morning, a young sot broke away from his friends and weaved toward Ma'alia. He walked inappropriately close.

"I'm divine," he declared. "I can also give you a child." Ma'alia stopped. The smell of stale beer on the young man's breath almost made her gag. He continued unabashed. "He will be great and will turn water into wine so I will never have to drink Bosela's poison again!"

He shrieked with mirth at his own joke, but his eyes did not laugh. They were lifeless, reflecting something that had long died on the inside. Ma'alia felt sorry for the poor creature as he danced around her, wiggling his pelvis obscenely.

"Come on. Surely, you want me. I can make you happy."

"Leave her alone, Edoni. Let's go," his friends urged.

"Oh please, I was just getting through to her," he said taking Ma'alia's arm.

She pulled it away. The sudden movement caused the pot balancing on her head to fall, breaking into several pieces. Edoni burst into uncontrolled laughter. He looked at his friends and pointed at Ma'alia.

"Did you see that? I made her jump," he uttered, still laughing. "Think what I would do if…" He coughed and laughed. "If she let me…" He coughed again this time with less laughter. He bent over and rested his hands on his knees like a spent athlete at the end of a race. Ma'alia walked away.

"*Weh!* Where are you going?"

She neither answered nor looked back.

"Edoni, that's enough," a young women in the group said. "We're leaving." Edoni's coughing grew worse and his breathing became labored. He fell to his knees. His friends helped him up and dragged him away as he coughed and cursed Ma'alia.

The encounter with the young drunk bothered Ma'alia deeply as she made her way back home. She did not know Edoni, but the eyes… something in the eyes troubled her. In them, she saw another person - a frightened child hiding behind the boastful bully.

"What happened?" Sabet asked when she came back without her pot.

"I met some of the nice young people of your village. They seem to hang around doing nothing."

"They don't want to do anything. Was one of them called Edoni?"

"Yes indeed. He's the one who made me drop the pot when he tried to grab me."

"Ah. That's a rough bunch. Their business is to drink cheap wine and harass people. Their parents and the *basakul* have given up on them. Even M'losi and his medicine could not turn them around. And where are you going again?" Sabet asked as Ma'alia hefted another pot onto her head.

"To the river. I was going to fetch water, remember?"

"Please be careful. I'm not sure those young people will let you off so easily especially since you're an outsider."

"An outsider? I thought no Avantu are strangers to one another. Yours is truly a strange village."

"I felt the same until I married into it. Now I'm used to it. This village has a different view on many things."

"Don't let it change you Sabet. You're the only sister I have. I'll be back."

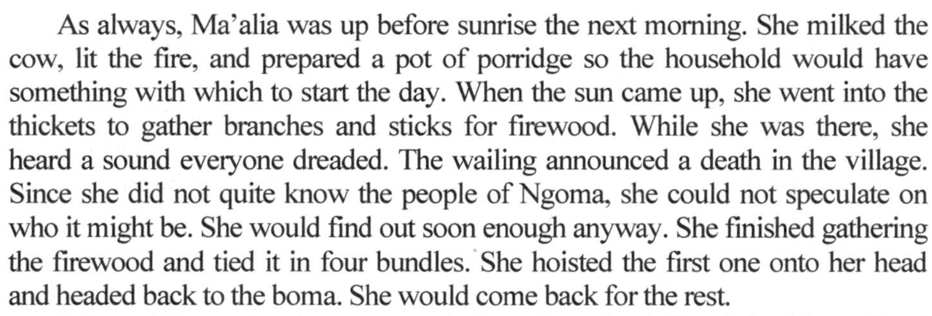

As always, Ma'alia was up before sunrise the next morning. She milked the cow, lit the fire, and prepared a pot of porridge so the household would have something with which to start the day. When the sun came up, she went into the thickets to gather branches and sticks for firewood. While she was there, she heard a sound everyone dreaded. The wailing announced a death in the village. Since she did not quite know the people of Ngoma, she could not speculate on who it might be. She would find out soon enough anyway. She finished gathering the firewood and tied it in four bundles. She hoisted the first one onto her head and headed back to the boma. She would come back for the rest.

Sabet was sweeping the compound when she arrived. She righted herself and placed a hand on her back when she saw Ma'alia. Her stomach had grown significantly in the time Ma'alia had been with them and she was due any time.

"It's Edoni." There was an ominous ring in the way Sabet said it. "His mother found him this morning. He had coughed up blood while he slept and drowned in it."

"Oh, poor boy!" Ma'alia was quite saddened by the death of her would be assailant. She wished it had not turned out this way.

"I'll stop by his place later this morning."

"I'll go with you," Ma'alia said. Sabet frowned. Apparently, she did not think it was a good idea but did not say so.

The wailing rose to a new pitch, indicating the arrival of a fresh group of mourners. Word of Edoni's passing was spreading fast. Villagers shouted it from one boma to another. When two individuals stopped along the path for a brief exchange, they mentioned it. Herdsmen passed it on as they made their way to the pastures and the river. By nightfall, all the villages will have heard the news. Relatives and friends would come to view the body before the *hayatma* carried the remains to the burial fields.

No one pointed out that Edoni might have accelerated his own demise with his poor diet and fondness for the cheap wine that practically cooked the user's innards. A few of his cohorts whispered he might have pushed his luck too far when he harassed Sabet's cousin, but they kept their suspicions to themselves. Whatever the case, he died young. However, one did not have to look far to see why Edoni came to grief so soon. His father's sunken eyes, protruding cheekbones, and red lips bespoke a hard drinker. The fruit did not land far from the tree.

Edoni's mother sat under the large tree in the middle of the boma, wrapped in a mourning shawl. Her family and friends sat with her. Edoni's rigid body lay on the ground by her side, wrapped in the skin used to cover the dead. Only his head showed. Whenever a close relative arrived, the mother would rise and join in the wailing. Mourners arrived at regular intervals, wailing and loudly proclaiming their sadness at the death of one whom they loved so dearly. Some ran up to the corpse, falling before it and demanding why he had left them. After the overt display of grief, women sat to console the mother while men comforted the father.

This was the scene when Sabet and Ma'alia approached the compound. They could have started wailing when they got within earshot of the boma, but they felt constrained not to raise their voices. Several mourners noticed them from afar. The message must have reached the grieving mother fast because she started shouting at Ma'alia from a distance.

"Get away from here you witch! Get away! How dare you show yourself on my land when you killed my son? Away!"

Sabet tried to explain that they only wanted to offer their condolences. It only made matters worse. Some women restrained the mother when she tried to rush Ma'alia. Two young men told them they were not welcome and must leave immediately. Ma'alia ignored them and continued to look at the disheveled wild-eyed woman who hurled obscenities at them. Something moved Ma'alia deeply. In the woman's eyes, she saw the same emptiness she had seen in Edoni's the previous day.

"I'm sorry for your son's passing, M'ma," Ma'alia said. She turned around and walked back home sadly.

For a moment, Edoni's mother did not know what to say or do. She struggled against the arms that held her then resigned, staring open-mouthed at Ma'alia. Paradoxically, those were the most comforting words she had heard so far. They also brought home the loss she felt, forcing her to face her grief in earnest. She let out a cry and collapsed, sobbing in her sisters' arms. Sabet who was puzzled at this exchange turned to follow Ma'alia. A new wail arose from all the mourners. Everyone cried, not just for Edoni, but also for the death of innocence in Ngoma that his passing symbolized.

In the days immediately following Edoni's death, Ma'alia went about her chores with a heavy heart because she felt responsible for it in someway. She threw herself into work to get her mind off the episode. She was so preoccupied with her thoughts that she did not at first notice the way the villagers reacted to her. She would come upon a group of people talking and leave silence in her wake. Those she encountered either lowered their eyes or glared at her. Tongues would click after she passed. People working in the fields or in their compounds straightened and regarded her with open hostility. No one spoke directly to her, but she soon got the message. She was no longer welcome in Ngoma.

Yossou could not shake off the sense of disquiet that lingered all afternoon. He was building a new barn for Lesiba, the elderly widow of the late Sakul Vudza. She had no family to help her with building or repairs. Yossou had taken it upon himself to make sure she did not suffer for lack of repairs on her structures or building new ones when the need arose.

This afternoon Yossou had asked Sande to help him since the young man knew how he worked and they would finish quicker. As the afternoon progressed, Yossou grew sluggish and distracted. Only because he had done the same thing so often was he was able to function. Well before sundown, he told Sande they would break to continue the following day.

Yossou made his way home, tactfully avoiding extended conversation with villagers he met along the way. Simi and Temin saw him from a distance and ran to him. He gave each of them a banana - gifts from Lesiba. The girls ran back to their grandmother's kitchen to enjoy the treat. Yossou put his tools away, found some water, and washed his face and arms. He did not sit outside because he was in no mood to chat. Only when darkness fell did he venture to sit by the door, hearing, but not paying attention to the chatter of his children as they bombarded their grandmother with questions. He knew his ugly mood was in large part due to Ma'alia's absence. He missed her more than he cared to admit. Tonight he felt it even more intensely.

"N'ne, when is M'ma coming back?"

Yossou shot upright. He had not expected that question from his children. He was amazed at how they quickly they adapted after having lost their mother only a few moons ago. They had taken it hard, but handled it better than he expected. When he married Ma'alia, he had anticipated some resentment toward her, and their attitude did not surprise him. His mother's handling of things did not help either. Asking for her was a new development. Before he could check it, a wave of emotion washed over him. He missed Yanze. Remembering he had remarried, he felt a little guilty, but he missed her because they had been through a lot together. She had given him nine children in the ten and one seasons they were married. All but two of their children had died before they had seen seven harvests. Yanze's reaction to the passing of their eighth child, Lukalo, especially affected Yossou. He thought back to that fateful day.

About mid-morning, Yanze was spreading a fresh coat of cow dung on the floor of their hut. Lukalo had just seen his third harvest and was playing with Simi, his cousins, and friends. Yanze could hear their shouting and laughter and paid them scant attention. Her youngest child Temin, born a few moons earlier, sat just outside the door with a chicken bone in her hand, alternately sucking on it and hitting it on the ground. With the child so pacified, Yanze worked entirely by rote, gathering the green, creamy dung in a cupped hand, and spreading it in smooth arcs.

Outside, play became animated, with the children squealing and chasing each other round trees and huts. Then Lukalo began to cry, saying he felt pain in his leg. Some of the children laughed, accusing him of feigning pain because he could not keep up. They laughed even more, saying his face looked funny and he dribbled like a baby.

Yanze sensed the shift in play. Instinct told her something was not right. She rinsed her hands with clean water and stepped past the baby into the sunshine. One look at Lukalo and she knew it was happening again.

"Why, Mighty One? Why? What did I do to deserve this? What did this innocent child do to you? What did all my children do to you?" she muttered bitterly. The questions, though lasting but a moment, encapsulated years of pain. Six of her children had died after showing similar signs. Now her eighth was going the way of his siblings. She walked up to her droopy-faced child. The other children fell silent and kept a respectable distance when they noticed her grave expression. Yanze lifted Lukalo gently and held him to her bosom.

"Go call your mother," she ordered one of the girls. "And you," she turned to the oldest boy, "go fetch Lukalo's dad. He's at N'ne Lesiba's. Run!"

The children sped away to carry out their assignments. She rose, took the sick child to the kitchen, and laid him on the floor. She fetched the baby and placed her on the floor as well. She started massaging Lukalo's face and left side of his body. She prayed constantly as she did so.

"M'ma," he whimpered, "thorns are pricking me here." With a weak right hand, he touched his left arm, leg, and torso. Yanze noticed this was the droopy side.

"You'll be fine, my son," she said without conviction. She drew a horn of water from a pot, gently raised his head, and held it to his lips. He swallowed some, but most of it dribbled down the left side of his mouth onto his neck and chest. She set his head down, put the horn away, and continued to massage him.

"What is happening to me?" he asked.

"Oh, nothing. You were running around a little too much. After you rest, you'll feel better." She wished she could believe herself.

A shadow briefly covered the doorway. Llesi, Yanze's neighbor entered the kitchen, breathing heavily from exertion.

One glance at the child on the floor was all she needed.

"Woi! M'ma goi! Not again, Yanze!" She stomped her feet and clapped her hands in frustration as she uttered these words. She fell to her knees beside the child. When she picked up his left hand, the lack of responsiveness confirmed her suspicions. She shook her head.

"I've got to get him to M'losi," Yanze said. "Carry the baby for me."

Llesi picked up the baby and Yanze hefted the frail child by placing her right arm behind both his knees and the left arm around his shoulders. By now, the neighbors had an inkling what was going on and lined the path.

"Modi. Take heart." They voiced prayers for the child and his family.

Yanze and Llesi hurried to the medicine man's abode at the edge of the village in a secluded heavily wooded area. Only those in need of treatment or divination veered off the path onto the trail leading up to his quarters. It burst into an opening facing a small rundown hut. Yanze, who had been here several times before, knew she had to wait a few steps into the clearing until M'losi asked her to approach. The wait could be as long as half a day. It all depended on where he was in his communion with the spirits.

Yanze did not sit as expected. She stood and fidgeted impatiently, taking her eyes off the dark entrance of the hut only to look at her son. Llesi sat down with the baby. When it started to fuss, she stuffed one of her breasts into its mouth. Temin squeezed the proffered breast and suckled noisily. Soon she was waving her arm and legs, crossing and uncrossing each big toe with its neighbor in contentment. The bliss on her face was in stark contrast to the strained expressions of the adults. Their heads jerked simultaneously whenever they heard a sound coming from the hut. Still M'losi did not summon them.

Suddenly, Lukalo's breathing came in labored gasps. He strained with every breath and exhaled in sharp puffs. His bony ribs rose and fell with each effort. Saliva hung from his lower lip and his eyes rolled, showing only the whites.

"No, my child! We are here! M'losi will help you!" Yanze sat down and cradled her son. He continued to breathe with difficulty and she massaged him in an attempt to relieve his discomfort. Llesi also reached out and gently stroked his head. Even little Temin tore her head away from the breast with a smacking sound. She looked at her mother first then Llesi. Since nothing registered, she lost interest and scanned with her open mouth for the nipple. She found it on the third pass.

After a while, Lukalo's breathing evened and he calmed down, though his eyes remained closed. It was an amazing transformation. He stopped dribbling and his face straightened. They heard heavy footsteps approaching rapidly. Yossou tore into the area and took a knee beside his wife.

"Oh, my child! My child!" he cried.

"You came at a good time. He seems better all of a sudden," Yanze informed him.

"Yes. You should have seen him moments ago. His face drooped and he dribbled like a baby," Llesi added.

"We might not need to see the medicine man after all."

As if to prove his mother right, Lukalo's eyes popped open, bright and clear.

"M'ma, you are beautiful," he said looking up at her.

The intense light in his eyes surprised Yanze. His voice, though faint, was steady. His forthrightness baffled them. A shadow fell over them. It was M'losi. A moment later, Lukalo, still facing his mother, seemed to adjust his focus to a point beyond her - beyond the present. A smile played on his face.

"I see beautiful people. There's so much light, M'ma - bright light. Aahh! I see the light!" His voice faded with each statement." They could barely make out his last sentence. "I go to the Light!"

He sighed deeply. The light went in his eyes, but the smile remained. He had breathed his last. Yossou looked at Yanze when she turned a pained face toward him. She did not have to say it. He knew she was apologizing for giving him children doomed to die in infancy. He touched her cheek gently.

"It's all right. It's all right," he said.

Her eyes watered and she squeezed his hand between her cheek and shoulder. They stayed that way for several moments. Once more, Temin ripped her head from the breast to stare at each adult before returning to it. Yossou, with one arm over Yanze's shoulders, could not bear to look at his wife or his child. He looked at the ground without seeing the two dark spots where his tears fell. Yanze's tears landed on her son's torso and rolled down his side. It was always hard to lose a child. Each loss tore open the wound that had not healed from the previous one. She cried for her son. She cried for each child she had lost. Llesi, at loss for something to say, hugged Temin closer and rocked her gently. M'losi bent and closed the child's eyes.

"Go bury your son. He's in a better place and shall suffer no more."

He turned and walked wearily back to his hut.

The strength of emotion he still felt when remembering his late wife and child surprised Yossou. Yanze never recovered from Lukalo's death. She lost the desire to live and succumbed to a series of illnesses that took her life prematurely. Yossou wiped away the tears and composed himself just as his daughters brought his dinner. Simi knelt before him and proffered a gourd with some water to wash his hands. He washed them then took the two bowls that Temin held before him. She also knelt at his feet. He thanked his daughters and they left. He began to eat without tasting the food. He did not finish it and called the girls to take the gourds away.

"Fetch my chewing stick," he told Simi.

"I'll get it." Temin said. She was off before her sister could move. Simi shook her head and headed to the kitchen with the partly eaten food. Temin came back with the stick. Yossou stuck it in his mouth and began to clean his teeth. Temin planted herself on his lap and draped an arm around his neck. She looked at him quizzically.

"Baba, you are sad," she said. "Is it because our mother died or because our new mother is not here?"

Yossou thought for a moment.

"It's a little of both, my child. I loved your mother a lot. She was good to you and your brothers and sisters. And you know what? She was also my friend."

"I know. N'ne told us M'ma was like her own daughter and she loved her as much as she loves all of us."

"Is that so?"

"Yes. And she says she loves our new mother just as much."

"You have a good grandmother, my child. She loves people and that's why everybody loves her."

"*Uh huh.* She tells us all kinds of stories about great people who lived a long, long time ago, and about the clever little squirrel who tricked Gunani the ogre."

"Oh, she also told you that story? I loved hearing that story when I was a child."

"Will you tell it to me please?"

"But you know it already. I've told it to you before."

"I know, but I want to hear it again."

"All right, then."

Once upon a time, there was a little squirrel called Kamuna who lived in a tree with his mother. On a huge tree nearby, an ogre named Gunani also lived with his mother. Kamuna and Gunani were friends. They played together and shared everything. One season, the rains did not come and everything in the land dried up. There was no food for the animals and they began to die. Kamuna and Gunani searched all over, but could not find anything to eat. Everything was dead, dry, or decayed. Then Kamuna came up with a plan.

"Look," he said to Gunani. "We'll die if we don't find food. Since our mothers are old and don't have long to live, let's kill and eat them that we may survive."

"That sounds like a good idea," Gunani agreed. "There's no need for all of us to die. Whose mother shall we eat first?" he asked.

"Let's eat your mother since she's bigger and will provide food for a long time."

"That's right," Gunani agreed.

He then went home and killed his mother. All three lived on the meat for several days. By this time, the clouds were starting to gather though the rains still did not come. Soon, the meat ran out and again there was nothing to eat.

"There's no more meat," Gunani said. "We'll have to eat your mother now."

But clever Kamuna had warned his mother and hidden her with enough meat to last a long time.

"All right. I'll go kill her so we can have something to eat." Kamuna pretended to look for his mother, shouting and hollering for her. He came back to Gunani and said, "I've looked everywhere, and I can't find her. She must have suspected what we planned to do and hidden herself."

"Aakh!" Gunani was enraged. "How could she have known what we were planning? Did you warn her?"

"I swear I didn't. She must have figured it out herself."

"I'm tired and hungry. I'm going to sleep. We'll find her when I wake up."

As soon as Gunani fell asleep, Kamuna went to his mother's hiding place and they ate of the meat from Gunani's mother. For several days, Kamuna pretended to be hungry and to look for his mother. Gunani, however, became suspicious because Kamuna disappeared at the same time every day for a long spell. When he came back, he did not seem hungry. One day, Gunani followed Kamuna as he made his usual disappearance and discovered where Kamuna hid his mother. He was very, very mad.

"You liar!" he shouted. "You hid your mother all this time with some of the meat from my mother leaving me to starve. Now I'll kill both of you and eat you."

Because he was weak from hunger, Gunani could not catch either Kamuna or his mother. They hopped from side to side and the clumsy Gunani could not decide whom to chase. Because he was hungry, he tired quickly. He went back and ate some of the meat Kamuna had hidden. He lived on it until the rains came days later, bringing life back to the land. Kamuna and Gunani became enemies and never played together again.

A noisy intake of breath told Yossou that Temin had fallen asleep in the middle of the story. He had become so engrossed in narrating it he did not notice. He smiled to himself and raised her to his bosom. He got up and took her to his mother's hut.

"M'ma, your grandchild is asleep."

"We're still in the kitchen," his mother answered. "Bring her here. She can lie here a while. I'll take her into the chamber later."

He entered the kitchen where Simi, his mother, and Simi, his daughter named after her, sat by the fire. Over the dying embers was a shard of clay on which they were roasting *zinuni* for a late night snack. The elder Simi unrolled a reed mat on the floor.

"Place her here."

The younger Simi looked up at her father and smiled.

"It must have been the Kamuna story."

"It was."

"She always asks for it and then falls asleep before it's finished. The funny thing is she knows the whole story herself. She tells it to me."

"Yet she still asks for it. I'm also going to bed. Sleep well." He ruffled Simi's hair and took a handful of the nuts on his way out.

"Sleep well," his mother and daughter replied in unison.

Yossou went into his hut and lay down, savoring the *zinuni*. He finished and fell asleep.

He had a panoramic view of the Plains of Sacrifice. He could also see The Skull, The Sleeper, and The Lion clearly outlined against the horizon. Something else caught his attention. Several dark specks circled over a particular spot. On magical wings, he zoomed in closer and saw a flock of vultures circling a woman. He could not tell who she was, but he knew intuitively she was with child. Then he saw what the birds were doing. They picked huge boulders from the ground with their strong talons then soared high to dump the salvo on the woman. She ran erratically with hands on her head as if that would protect her from the huge stones. So far, they had all missed. Yossou felt pained and helpless. He desperately wanted to go and rescue her, but his legs had turned to stone. He tried to shout, but his voice stuck in his throat. His heart was ready to explode. The woman ducked under the rock called The Sleeper where the birds could not get to her.

In a sudden strange twist, one of the vultures grew several times larger than the rest and went berserk. One by one, it attacked the smaller birds and ripped them apart until none remained. Their feathers darkened the sky as they spiraled earthward in a slow dance of death. When the last feather had fallen, the bird began to circle the woman with great deliberation. Finally, it swooped to the earth with a loud whoosh, picked up a boulder as big as a hut, and rose high in the sky. The woman, hearing the turbulence, looked up. Her eyes widened with horror as the bird began a rapid descent toward her with the massive boulder in its huge talons. Clearly, it planned to crush The Sleeper and the woman along with it. There was unspeakable hatred in its angry, yellow eyes as it plunged earthward ready to release the mighty missile. The woman covered her eyes with one hand and raised the other over her head in a futile defensive posture. Yossou was horrified to see that it was...

Chapter 4

saving ma'alia

Ma'alia collapsed on her bedroll the same night, exhausted from mental strain rather than physical exertion. After tossing and turning for what seemed an eternity, her thoughts merged seamlessly with troubling dreams.

Heavy dark forms morphed incessantly and weighed her spirit down. She tried to walk away, but they swirled around her, binding her in thick black vapors. She tried to yell at them to let her go, but the words would not come out. She could only manage a hoarse whisper with each attempt. As her desperation, increased, huge chunks formed out of the dark and hurtled toward her. The first few whizzed past. One finally struck her. It did not hurt her physically, but emotionally it was highly upsetting. Others soon followed and each strike added to her distress. She strained against the darkness and broke free just as another chunk whistled through the air and...

Thunk!

"Ma'alia!"

She woke up when Sabet called out to her. Next, she heard the distinct thud of a missile hitting the wall of the hut... then another... and another. Sabet was screaming, asking what they had done. Lemba croaked. Ma'alia realized that they were under attack. Justified or not, she felt responsible for their predicament, which probably had to do with Edoni's passing. Villagers blamed her for his death and as tradition went, they would level this compound. Those within would go down with it if they did not escape. She knew what she must do. She stood up quickly, removed the hide from the doorway, and stepped into the chilly night, fully aware she stood no chance in a hail of missiles.

"I'm the one you seek to punish," she called out to the unseen assailants. "Leave Sabet and Lemba alone. Take my life if you must hold someone responsible for Edoni." She took a few more steps into the open and stood still. She felt no fear. She faced the darkness and waited for the rocks to rain on her. Nothing happened. Then she heard rustling and multiple footsteps receding rapidly. For some reason, the attackers had fled suddenly. She remained at the spot several moments before walking back into the hut on wobbly legs. She replaced the hide in the doorway and buckled to the floor. She trembled with relief as the tension uncoiled from her like a remorseful python. She missed Yossou sorely. She wished he were with her so she could bury her head in his shoulder and cry. She would have loved him to stroke her hair tenderly and say everything would be fine. Her longing for him felt like a tight painful knot in her belly.

As she reflected on what had happened, she wondered why she was not buried under a pile of rocks. She also wondered if it was her imagination or it was a person she saw in the darkness when she turned to enter the hut. If so, he would have been standing by the hut behind her when she challenged her attackers. She also thought she saw the glint of a sword around the figure. She ascribed it to her highly impressionable imagination under the circumstances. She tried to sleep in vain.

Impressionable or not, there was no mistaking the sudden urge to leave. It came upon her well before cockcrow while it was still dark. She did not have much to take with her. The change of garments, a few shells, and trinkets fit in her pouch easily. She slung it over her shoulder, folded her bedroll, and placed it in against the wall. She pushed the hide aside and stepped outside. She started to replace it when she sensed a presence close by. She froze, not knowing what to expect.

"You are leaving?" It was a statement, not a question. Ma'alia breathed a sigh of relief.

"I have to, Sabet. I don't know what will happen if I stay here. I've already brought too much trouble upon you. I'm going back home. It's better that way."

"Many dangers await the lone traveler in the night, my sister."

"Greater danger will befall us all if I stay. I must leave now."

"I understand. Also, remember you probably saved my child's life. Perhaps it's the reason for which The Mighty One sent you here. I sensed in my spirit you were leaving, so I came to see you." She paused. "Go in peace. Perhaps we'll meet next market day after our children are born."

"Yes, we will. Stay well."

They embraced as close as their bellies would allow. Ma'alia broke the embrace and walked out of the *boma* onto the path.

"Ma'alia!" Yossou shouted and woke up.

He realized he had been dreaming. He was at once relieved and upset. He was relieved because the pain he had felt in the dream was palpable, but it was only a dream. Its vividness distressed him. This was the third time he had had the same dream. He knew Ma'alia was in some danger this very moment and the dream warned him of it. He had to find her.

Having come to this conclusion, Yossou did not want to think about it again lest he relent. Traveling alone at night was dangerous and downright foolish unless one had a compelling reason to do so. He felt he had one. He wondered who might be foolish enough to go with him. He thought of Sande. The young man was strong, hard working, and loyal. The lad was also good with bow and arrow. However, Yossou dismissed the idea of waking him in the middle of the night on a mere hunch. Wind maybe…? This was his problem and he would take care of it himself. He felt for his weapons in the darkness. He slung the quiver over his shoulder, picked up the bow and machete, and made for the door. He removed the hide, stepped into the crisp night, and covered the entrance again. There was no moon, but the stars gave sufficient light.

He heard a soft cough. Someone wanted Yossou to be aware of his presence and good intent. Yossou stood still and looked in the direction of the sound. He tightened his grip on the machete.

"Ready?"

That voice! It was Wind. There were stories that he could smell, stalk, and kill an animal without its ever being aware of his presence. He was the natural leader of hunting parties. Bards had already composed several songs in his honor as a living legend.

"I… I didn't…" Yossou, stammered at loss for words.

"Don't apologize. The lad said you needed help. So here we are."

"*Eh heh*," a second voice agreed.

"Sande?"

"Yes. You sent for me too, remember?"

"Uh… honestly I…"

"Didn't expect I would come?" Sande finished. "You are like a father to me. I would give my life for you if I had to."

"It had to be important for you to rouse us this late in the night. I imagine we are heading to Ngoma."

"Yes, Wind." Yossou was still confused. He had wished it, but he had not sent for them. Whoever had summoned them must possess great power of persuasion. He had no time to figure it out.

"You have your weapons and Sande has his too. Let's go."

Wind took charge and was off at a trot expecting the other two to keep up. The usual sounds filled the night. A dog barked in a nearby compound out of a sense of duty. In the branches overhead, a bird flapped its wings. Crickets stopped chirping as the men approached, but frogs continued bidding in their nightly auction. Nothing moved except glowflies and the three men.

"You rhinos might want to tread lightly," Wind advised. "The whole world can hear you coming."

"Sorry," Yossou said. Both he and Sande adjusted their stride.

"Much better," Wind said when they picked up again. "If we keep this up we should be there by the time a man's sleep is sweetest." He focused on the track ahead, looking, listening for anything out of the ordinary. After a while, both Yossou and Sande realized why Wind was the greatest hunter in Gololi. He set a punishing pace that he maintained whether they were going through thickets, over rocks or mushy ground. He barely made a sound. They struggled to keep up with him.

Ma'alia knew she had placed herself in a precarious position. She could fall victim to hyenas, leopards, or the occasional lion that attacked villages at night in search of a goat or a sheep. There was also the danger of *Bagondi*. Because they usually carried out their raids by night, she could run into a band on a mission. There was no telling what they could do to a solitary traveler - especially a woman. Ma'alia thought of all these risks, but her desire to flee was inexplicably greater.

Since she had never been far from home alone, she made her way by instinct. The urge that drove her also seemed to guide her, darkness notwithstanding. She was certainly afraid and the shadows took on forms of creatures whose sole intent was to harm her. To keep her spirits up, she said a prayer.

"O Great Father," she whispered. "Please keep me from danger. I am your servant. I have accepted the burden you gave me. Preserve me that your purposes may be fulfilled."

She repeated the prayer several times, but the sense of unease remained, as if another force were working to bring about the very thing against which she prayed. The trees seemed to signal ahead that she was coming. The wind hissed angrily in her ear as it blew past, rushing ahead to conspire with other nefarious agents. The grass rustled menacingly, every blade swaying like a serpent woken by the wind, poised to strike. As her pace increased, so did the rustling. Then the horrifying reality struck her. The rustling to her left had a particular rhythm that made the hair on her neck stand.

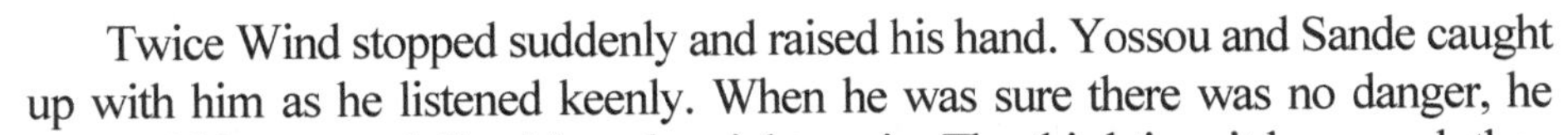

Twice Wind stopped suddenly and raised his hand. Yossou and Sande caught up with him as he listened keenly. When he was sure there was no danger, he lowered his arm and dived into the night again. The third time it happened, they were only a fraction of a day's journey from Ngoma. This time, Wind tipped his head to the wind and sniffed.

"That smell!" he whispered. "Someone's in trouble." He sped into the darkness. Yossou and Sande exchanged puzzled looks and followed as fast as they could. They stumbled through bushes and thorns, barely noticing the cuts and scrapes they suffered. Ahead, they heard a low growl that made them stop in alarm.

Wind heard it too. He weighed his options, concluding that this encounter would require the machete. An arrow released in the dark at a run will very likely miss and he would have no time to reload. His best chance was to anticipate the leopard's lunge, step aside, and slash while it was in mid-air. He could not afford to let the animal knock him to the ground. He braced for what lay ahead. They were running into the wind so the cat might not have caught their scent though it would have heard them by now. This is what Wind was counting on. If it were stalking prey, it would be distracted and try to deal with the new threat.

What followed happened fast. Wind came upon the leopard crouched several paces away with its back to him. About ten paces from the animal stood the shadowy form of a young woman. As he stopped to assess the situation, Sande and Yossou came up behind him.

"Stand back," he ordered and charged the big cat with a loud cry. The leopard, now aware of the intrusion, snapped around quickly. In an instant, it was in the air, lunging at the advancing Wind. He did not have time to step aside completely and the leopard's left paw caught his right shoulder and spun him around. He did however manage to open a gash along its flank with the machete. Man and beast fell to the ground. The leopard got up first and charged at Wind a second time as he scrambled away. The snapping of a bow followed by a brief "*whoosh*" and "*thunk*" indicated an arrow had found its mark. The leopard let out an eerie, almost human scream. It lumbered off into the grass, whining in pain.

For a moment no one moved. Wind was a dark silhouette on the ground, groaning and panting heavily. Sande still held the bow in the delivery position with his gaze fixed in the direction the cat had taken. Yossou looked at Sande then at Wind sprawled on his back. He was still contemplating the fallen Wind when another sound caught his attention.

"*Hmmmh! Hmmmmh!*" It was the sound of a woman moaning softly.

"Ma'alia!" he said, running up to her. "Ma'alia, what are you doing here in the middle of the night?"

She did not answer. She moaned and trembled violently. Yossou could tell she was in shock.

"Ma'alia," he shouted. "It's me, Yossou." He took her by the shoulders and shook her gently but firmly. Since he was getting nowhere, he slapped her with just enough force to bring her back to reality without hurting her too much. This time he met with success and she slowly began to focus.

"Ma'alia, it's me."

She turned toward him. "You came for me," she said. "You came for me, Yossou."

She leaned on him heavily, then passed out. He caught her before she fell, and gently lowered her to the ground. He fought back his own emotions. He did not want to think what would have happened had he not acted on a bizarre premonition. A pained groan made him turn. Wind was trying to get back on his feet using his right arm for support. His left dangled weakly by his side. Sande also snapped out of his trance and ran to help the injured man. He put his arms under his shoulders and helped him up.

"By the Oracle," Sande exclaimed. "You are hurt. We need to patch you up otherwise you'll lose a lot of blood."

Wind could barely stand and Sande caught him as he pitched forward. He would have landed on his face.

Yossou was in a quandary. He held his unconscious wife, but Wind was badly injured and needed help. They had to stem the flow of blood as a matter of urgency. Yossou made a decision.

"Bring him here." Sande helped Wind to where Yossou had sat Ma'alia on the ground. "I'll go look around for *tatula* leaves. For now, press your hand over the wound. And keep an eye on my wife."

"Stop fussing over me," Wind protested. He was barely intelligible. "I'm fine."

"You sit right there and don't move," Yossou ordered.

Tatula leaves, when rubbed together and placed over a wound would stem the bleeding. They were hard to find in daylight, let alone on a moonless night, but he had to try. He was also aware of the danger of snakes and even the injured cat, but he put it out of his mind. He concentrated on finding the special plant.

After an arduous search, Yossou resigned to the fact would not find what he sought. He began to consider the next option, which was to apply soil to the wound. He had just started back when he caught a whiff of something familiar. He stopped, raised his nose, and sniffed. He wondered if his imagination had briefly played into what he desired to find. He took another step… and caught the smell again. He lowered his head and looked around for the dark broad-leafed plants around him. His heart missed a beat. There was no mistaking it. There it was! He bent down and plucked a handful of leaves. *Thank you, Mighty One*. He hurried back to his companions. Ma'alia had come round and was tending to Wind while Sande propped him up. She looked up as he approached.

"Ah! You found *tatula* leaves!" She took some and rubbed them together between her palms. A strong fragrance filled the air as the leaves gave up their potent juices. "That should do it," she said dabbing the wound.

Wind breathed sharply and groaned. She tossed the leaves aside and took the remaining handful from Yossou. She repeated the process and this time she placed what remained on the wound and held it in place with a strip of leather from her pouch.

"I'm thirsty," Wind said weakly. Everyone was silent. Water was the farthest thing from her mind when Ma'alia made her hasty departure from Ngoma. Likewise, none of the men thought of it when they embarked on their impromptu mission.

"We'll find some water soon. Let's start moving at least. We don't know what else lurks in these bushes," Yossou said. "Will you be able to walk by yourself?" he asked Ma'alia.

"Oh, I'm fine now," she answered.

"Good. I'll help Wind along. You lead the way and Sande will guard the rear. Head toward the rising sun and ask if you're not sure which way to go."

"Eh heh."

Silently Yossou prayed Wind would hang on until they came upon one of several streams that flowed around Ronge. The Dzodzo was far from where they were. He placed Wind's right arm over his shoulders, and helped him up. They began their homeward journey just as the sky started to hint at crimson.

Simi always prepared a pot of porridge for her family in the morning. Temin took a gourd to her father before he set about his day's business. He would take it while sitting outside his hut and exchange pleasantries with villagers who made an early start on the day.

This morning however, Temin called out to her father, but did not get a response. A quick inspection of his chambers revealed that he was gone, as were his weapons. The elder Simi was not concerned. She was a little puzzled that he would leave in the middle of the night without letting her know. He had always been good at informing her where he went to avoid causing anxiety.

To his wives, Solena and Aril, Wind was… *Wind.* They knew neither when he went nor came, so when Aril's daughter reported that her father was not in his chamber, she only shrugged and set his gourd aside. She would give the porridge to someone else and prepare some when he showed up.

Of the three missing men, Sande caused the greatest concern. His mother, Alusa, became a widow soon after he was born. Her husband's oldest brother inherited her as tradition demanded, but she was neither accepted nor able to fit in with his family. The only person with whom she could relate was Sande. As her only child, his mother was very protective of him. When he played with friends as a child, she would rush to his side at the slightest fall and carry him off. When he fought with another child over a toy and its ownership was in question, she would take the toy and hand it to him. This aggravated other parents who tried to teach their children to share and play fair. They called Sande "the egg," for the delicate way his mother handled him. Fortunately, he found a surrogate father-figure in Yossou, who noticed his interest in building things. A unique bond developed between them and as he grew older, Yossou took him under his wing as his apprentice.

This morning, Alusa prepared a breakfast of millet porridge and roast cassava. When it was ready, she called out to Sande and got no response. Initially, it did not bother her because he usually answered by the third time. He would often come in while she was preparing breakfast to sit and talk with her. She considered herself blessed to have a son who had not given her much trouble.

When he did not answer on two more attempts, Alusa began to worry and went to his chamber to see if all was well. She did not find him and assumed the worst.

Did a wild animal carry him away? It couldn't be. There were no signs of an animal intruder. Perhaps a band of Vasua had kidnapped him. But it was long since they had engaged the Bagololi in conflict. With the arrival of Xhaka and his governor Tamaa, they had to contend with taxes, restrictions on movement, and other forms of oppression that allowed them little time for conflict. It was therefore unlikely they would come this far to cause trouble.

There was only one person she could ask - Yossou. She went to find him.

"Peace to all who live in this home," Alusa called out as she entered the compound.

A baffled Simi emerged from her kitchen. "Peace," she responded. She would have engaged Alusa in some initial pleasantries, but sensing the tension in the younger woman, she got to the point. "What's wrong, my sister?"

"Sande wasn't at home this morning. It's not like him to leave without letting me know where he's going. Actually, I can't remember if he ever went anywhere so early. I was wondering if Yossou might know where he is."

"*Ee yeh?* This morning, Temin took breakfast to her father, but he wasn't there. I didn't make much of it, but now you say your son is also missing… it must mean they are together, but I have no idea where."

"Well, I feel a little better that he might be with Yossou. Still I wish I could be sure."

"Sande is a strong, intelligent young man and should be fine wherever he is. Now I'm sure they went off together. Like you, I find it odd that Yossou would leave without letting me know.

"Peace!" a high-pitched, sunny voice called from the path. Yaneta, a short rotund woman with an infectious laugh broke from the path to join them.

"Is it well with you, Alusa? You look worried."

Alusa could not help warming up to the ever-jovial Yaneta.

"I came here when I found Sande was gone. My son and hers," she pouted her lips to indicate Simi, "seem to have disappeared in the middle of the night without saying where they were going."

"Hmm," Yaneta remarked. "My husband told me something strange this morning. He said that when he stepped outside to relieve himself last night, he saw four men trotting along. First, he thought they were raiders or scouts, so he stood still and didn't make a sound. For some reason, he didn't challenge them or raise the alarm. Later when he thought about it, he was sure one of them was Wind, the hunter, because of his gait. He thought the second person might have been Yossou, but he wasn't sure. He couldn't make out the third person. Now this is where it gets interesting." Yaneta lowered her voice and looked over her shoulder for effect. Simi and Alusa instinctively craned their necks forward and each cocked an ear toward her. "He said he saw a fourth person who wasn't much more than a lad. He seemed to be part of the group yet not with the group. My husband had the distinct impression the others didn't realize this person was with them. Here's the strangest part. My husband said that though he stood still, the lad saw him and waved."

Simi straightened. "How much did your husband drink last night?"

Yaneta cackled. "He didn't drink. The way he related it to me this morning, he was both puzzled and serious. You know my husband. To him everything is a joke, but this time he was serious."

"*Ei!* Now this is giving me a headache," Alusa said. "I just want my son back."

"He'll be fine," Simi chided again. "Men do strange things, but they come around. It won't do us any good standing here deliberating where they went. We'll see them when we see them."

"That's easy for you to say," Alusa retorted. "You have children and grandchildren. You can even afford to lose some. I can't. If something happens to my boy, your son will have some explaining to do."

Simi was about to respond, but Alusa turned and stormed off. Simi threw her arms up in resignation.

"*Heh!* I didn't expect that." Yaneta said.

"Neither did I."

"I hope I didn't contribute to the situation."

"No, you had nothing to do with it. She probably thinks Yossou talked Sande into something. I doubt it, but I have no way of knowing."

"I wonder who that young lad was."

Simi shot her a glance. "What lad? Oh, the lad your husband says he saw. I wonder too. I've got to go."

"Alright."

"And thanks for the information."

"*Akh!* It was nothing."

The sky turned from gray to crimson as the sun peered over the horizon bringing color to the vast plains and majestic hills. Herds of wildebeest, gazelle, zebra, and other animals made an early start on the tall grass, moist with morning dew. They could graze in relative peace, thanks to some of their number who had given their lives overnight to appease the appetites of their natural predators. A few animals in nearby herds raised their heads to contemplate the little band of humans. Sensing no threat, they went back to grazing.

Yossou and his group had walked for quite some time after their encounter with the leopard. Ma'alia was still in the lead, but she had slowed down due to fatigue. Wind had grown worse. He was delirious, talking to himself incoherently and sometimes shouting at an imaginary person. He could barely stay on his feet. He needed water, but they were a long way from any source. Flies buzzed around his injured shoulder.

"What happened to him?"

The question surprised everyone except Wind who continued to mutter to himself. They all stopped and turned to see a man standing in the grass off the path. He spoke perfect Kigololi, but did not look like he was from the area. Sande would have reached for an arrow, but the speaker's attitude suggested he was not to be intimidated.

"A leopard mauled our friend early this morning," Yossou answered. "He lost a lot of blood and needs water."

The stranger approached and reached for a skin container at his hip.

"I have something he could use." Fearlessly, he came up to them and untied the flask. "Have him sit down."

Yossou and Sande lowered Wind and propped him in a sitting position. The stranger squatted, took Wind's chin, and tilted it upwards. He poured a gray liquid into the open mouth and closed it. Wind swallowed involuntarily with a loud noise, causing Ma'alia to turn aside to hide her smile.

"This should help with the loss of blood and also clear his mind."

The stranger fed Wind more of the liquid until the bottle was almost empty. He untied the strip of skin that held the leaves on Wind's shoulder in place.

"Ah, you did a good job, Ma'alia."

She looked puzzled as if wondering how he knew her name and that she had dressed the wound. He poured what remained in the bottle over the leaves and bound it again. He stood up and replaced the flask. On his left side, he had tucked a sword in the waistband.

"Let him rest a while before you continue. By then, he should be able to walk on his own."

"Who are you? Where are you from?" Yossou finally gathered the courage to ask.

"I come from a distant place. I help men whenever I can."

"That's it?"

"Yes."

"Aren't you afraid traveling alone? As you can see, it's dangerous," Sande nodded toward Wind.

"I serve a Great King. Even in the shadow of death, I have no fear."

Yossou, Ma'alia, and Sande all looked at one another, puzzled at what the man said. However, they did not doubt him because he radiated strength and confidence.

"Well, rest a while then resume your journey. Your friend will make it. I'll see you later."

He set off with the sun to his right. He did not take the path, but cut through the tall grass and bushes and was soon out of sight. Ma'alia, Yossou, and Sande watched him go.

"There's something vaguely familiar about that man, but I can't place it. His voice… it's like I've heard it before," Ma'alia said.

"I don't know. His eyes… there was something about them. I couldn't look into them without feeling dizzy. And when he said, 'I'll see you later," what did he mean?"

"Who knows?"

They heard Wind breathing deeply.

"*Ai!* He's asleep already! Come. Let's move him to the shade under that tree. We could all use some rest." They carried Wind carefully to the spot and sat down.

Ma'alia nestled close to Yossou. "I missed you. I'm glad you came for me." She turned to include Sande. "All of you."

"It's a good thing we did. This man was useless without you," Sande laughed.

"Careful, young man. Remember who you work for."

"Both of you get some rest. We have some more traveling to do," Ma'alia broke in.

Shortly after, they all fell asleep. Some animals looked around whenever the scent of the humans wafted to them, but they went back to grazing. All was quiet on the plains.

Wind stirred first. He squinted to adjust his eyes to the bright sunlight. The sun was almost overhead. He looked around wondering what he was doing out on the plains. As far as he could recall, he had not set out on a hunt. Besides, these were not his hunting grounds. As he grew accustomed to the light, he heard rhythmic breathing around him.

What? Yossou and his new wife? Sande? What are they all doing here? What am I doing here?

A stab of pain reminded him of what had happened. A wad of leaves covered his left shoulder and flies buzzed around it. He remembered his last conscious thought. He was in pain and struggling to get up after a leopard had knocked him down. His thoughts drifted further back to how it all started.

On this night, he had not invited either wife to his hut. He had just fallen asleep when a mysterious force tugged him out of sleep. He opened his eyes and saw the outline of a lad squatting beside him. The hide did not cover the door and pale light filtered in. Strangely, Wind was neither afraid nor irritated at the intrusion.

"Yossou needs you," the lad said in a matter-of- fact way. He paused a moment then straightened and left. He did not replace the hide.

Wind did not think twice about what to do. He took his weapons and made his way to Yossou's boma. He found Sande already waiting by the entrance and suspected this mission had something to do with Ma'alia. He greeted the younger man quietly.

"He sent for you too?"

"Yes," Sande said. "A lad I did not recognize came to tell me Yossou needed me. I came right away."

Just then, Yossou stepped out of his hut. Wind coughed lightly. Yossou appeared surprised to see them. Wind wondered about that.

Now seeing them lying together peacefully, he felt a sense of fulfillment. It was worth the pain. The thought brought a smile to his face.

Sande woke up next. He sat up, locked his arms around his knees, and shook his head vigorously.

"Good morning," Wind greeted him, though it was about midday.

"Good morning. Ah! You can talk! I mean, you can talk sense now."

"What do you mean by that?"

"*Ai, Baba!* A while back you were in a world of your own."

"I don't remember a thing,"

"Exactly!"

Yossou also woke up, looked around, and gently shook the sleeping Ma'alia off his shoulder. She woke up with a groan and an indiscernible comment, but she brightened up on seeing Wind.

"*Chi!* You are sober," she teased.

"I was never drunk," Wind shot back. "You're the ones who must have been drinking."

"And you are the only one among us who had a clear head, eh?" Yossou said. "Well, you are looking better. How's that shoulder?"

"It's throbbing quite a bit, but I can take it. This isn't my first run-in with a wild animal."

"I'm glad to hear it. Are you up to the rest of the journey?"

Wind made exaggerated sweeping gestures of the area. "Unless you're ready to hunt, there's no reason to sit around talking like women."

"And what is that supposed to mean?" Ma'alia demanded.

"Sorry. I just said what everybody says." An awkward silence followed until Yossou spoke.

"Let's get going then. Sande, let's help Wind stand."

"*Akh!* I can take care of myself. I'm not a wo…." Wind caught himself in time.

"You must have a death wish," Yossou said laughing. "By now you ought to know this woman will lop your head off for saying things like that."

"I gathered as much," Wind said, rising unsteadily to his feet. Sande stood close by in case he would need support. A withering look from Wind forced him to step away. Wind righted himself and tested his balance.

"Let's go," he declared and started up the trail with a wobbly, but stubborn gait.

Sande shook his head in admiration. He followed Ma'alia and Yossou as they walked behind Wind.

"They are coming! They are here!" Children shouted when they saw the group from a distance. Soon, excited children and a growing number of adults swamped them.

"Where did you go?"

"Why did you leave like that in the middle of the night?"

"Wind, what happened to your shoulder?"

There was an endless barrage of questions from every direction. As the returnees answered, the crowd relayed the information to those not close enough to hear, and those who later joined the procession.

"What is going on?" one would ask.

"Yossou, Wind, and Sande went to rescue Ma'alia in the middle of the night. They killed a leopard that was about to attack her," another would answer. In this way information passed on through the village.

The villagers paraded Ma'alia, Yossou, Wind, and Sande like warriors returning after a great victory in battle. By the time they got to the square, they had already composed victory songs.

Where did you go, Ma'alia?
Where did you go?
I went to Ngoma, Yossou
I went to Ngoma

Won't you come back, Ma'alia?
Won't you come back?
I come back, Yossou
I come back to you

What do you see, Ma'alia?
What do you see?
I see a leopard, Yossou
I see a big leopard

I come to save you, my love
I come to save you
Please hurry, Yossou!
Please hurry up!

They also sang another song:

Yossou so loved Ma'alia

He set off in the dark to find her
Wind and Sande, such good friends
Would not let him go alone

Ma'alia alone in the night
Afraid, alone, and oh, so lost
Faced a leopard, big and mean
Ready to tear her apart

Wind, swift and strong
Cut the leopard in flight
Sande though, young and brave
Stood firm to save the day

The procession had split into two groups. The advance party sang the victory songs that informed the villagers ahead what had happened. Yossou, Ma'alia, Sande, and Wind were in the second group amidst people singing, ululating, and waving leaves and fronds. Villagers sandwiched each of them with an arm around the waist or shoulder except Wind, who protested claims to his left shoulder. Someone claimed his right arm and he could not object.

The arrival of the group was a welcome break from the monotony of everyday life and gave the villagers an excuse to gather and celebrate. Those working in gardens or fields set aside their tools to join the throng. Mothers left their chores, planted their babies on their hips, and headed to the square. Artisans set aside their projects for later. Old men reminiscing under trees conscripted the nearest boys to carry their stools to the square. The boys grabbed the stools and raced to see who would get there first as the old men hobbled after them.

The impromptu party started with singing and dancing. There was no time to prepare a celebratory meal, so the villagers brought fruits, nuts, boiled and roast cassava, potatoes, and other treats from their stash. A celebration like this would not be complete without wine. A pot somehow materialized for those old enough to drink. The celebrations began in earnest.

A couple of strong women asked the returnees and their families to sit on stools as honored guests. Sitting among them, Sande's mother was bursting with pride. Her son was not only alive, but also the undisputed hero of this bizarre venture. He was now a man. She would have to find him a wife soon.

Solena, Wind's first wife, did not join the euphoria that swept through the village right away. She heard the ululating and shouting and knew her husband had come home. At the square, she picked him out easily. He was a head taller than most men and had a distinct hawk-eyed look. The strain on his face indicated he was hurt. Solena worked her way to him. When she saw his shoulder, she knew it needed attention right away. As she had suspected, he was being brave though clearly he was in pain. She pulled him out to the edge of the crowd.

"Stay here. I'll be right back," she commanded. Wind was too tired to argue and nodded weakly. She went directly to N'ne Shoni for a potion to treat the injury. She came back only to find Wind sucked back into the crowd. Solena dived in to fish him out again. *Senge* M'lola, one of the strong women, rushed at her, protesting that he should remain until the celebrations ended. Solena stared her up and down with disdain.

"Look. Do you see this wound? I have to attend to it. Go back to your silly games and leave us alone."

M'lola muttered invective and stalked off. Solena regarded her receding posterior for a moment then turned aside and spat. Fatigue finally caught up with Wind and he faltered. He was too heavy for Solena to prop up. Sande noticed her predicament and came to help move him to the nearest tree away from the crowd. Curious individuals tried to follow, but when Solena hissed at them venomously they slunk back to the arena. She guided Wind down to the foot of a *dalagua* tree then gave Sande a dismissive, "Thank you." She took off the old binding and was mortified at the sight. There were ugly gashes where the leopard's claws had torn flesh down to the bone. A whiff of something putrid wafted to her nostrils.

"When you left in the middle of the night I didn't know you were planning to get yourself killed, you idiot."

Few people stood up to Wind. Solena was one of them. Though she aggravated him, he loved her for her forthrightness, but up to a point. Taking Aril as a second wife had as much to do with defying her as a desire for someone more feminine in his life. Aril was more docile and unquestioning of his decisions.

"A man who fears a challenge is not worthy to be a hunter," Wind countered.

"Even the greatest hunter is no match for a leopard. They are natural hunters, especially at night when they are in their element."

She took a handful of the potion, gently cleaned the wound, and squeezed some herbs over it. Her rebuke and the concoction she rubbed over the torn flesh both stung. Wind bit on his lower lip to absorb the pain and hold back a rejoinder.

"You would teach me to hunt," he muttered.

"What?" Solena asked.

"Nothing." He paused then spoke again. "A friend sends for help and you expect the great Wind to say, 'Go away! I'm warm and my woman is in my arms!'"

Either by accident or by design - he suspected the latter, Solena pressed a little too hard on the wound, increasing the pain tenfold.

"*Aaai!*" he cried.

"Oh! Sorry," Solena said insincerely. "You were saying…?"

Wind let the pain subside before he answered.

"You know me better than that. I don't turn down a friend or anyone in trouble for that matter. Besides, think what would have happened if we hadn't been there? Yossou would have lost another wife and there'd be no singing and dancing tonight. We'd probably be mourning Ma'alia right now."

"I understand, but I don't know if you realize you're not young anymore. You can't keep gambling with your life." Solena put a fresh batch of herbs over the wound and tied it in place with strips of banana fiber.

"It's not a gamble. I'm a hunter. That's what I do for a living and it involves risk. If I didn't do that, where would my honor be? If someone calls me to go on a mission and I refuse, how will I live with myself? What report would the lad Yossou sent to fetch me give of the great Wind?"

"And who was that by the way? Where is he?"

"Who?"

"*Akh!* The lad you claim called you to help - the one who was with you as you were leaving on your midnight foray."

"He didn't go with us. In fact, I didn't see him again after he stepped out of my hut."

"Really? Yaneta's husband swears he saw four people. One of them was a young man who turned and waved at him. What mushrooms have you been nibbling on?"

Wind looked at his wife baffled and speechless. He did not have the foggiest idea what she was talking about. Just then, several voices started hollering for Wind so they could honor him.

"They are calling for you," she said. "Let's go."

Yossou, Ma'alia, Wind, and Sande sat in the place of honor. They continued to relate their adventure to newcomers. Word of it had spread fast and some people even came from the outskirts to hear it first hand. Yossou and Wind tacitly agreed to push the idea that Sande had dealt the blow that put the leopard away. They said he had saved Wind's life, and indeed, all their lives. Several times, the villagers sang the new song in praise of Sande's prowess. Though the song about Yossou's love for Ma'alia was more emotive, Sande's song made it into village lore and immortalized him. The village of Ronge and the Bagololi had found a new hero.

The dancing and merrymaking continued for a long time. Even Wind joined in, despite the wound. He noticed Sande could not keep the girls away. No doubt, many women had pushed their daughters into the arena, each hoping hers would catch the new hero's attention. Tradition frowned upon marrying a girl from the same village, but with heroes, communities could make exceptions. Wind watched the once shy young man having the time of his life as the center of attention.

Wind remembered his day in the limelight. It was after his first kill many harvests in the past. On his first hunt, he had somehow separated from the rest of the party when he came face to face with a buffalo. He did not know how he did it, but when it charged, he drove his spear deep into the animal's neck, killing it instantly. He suffered several cuts and bruises in the process. When other hunters found him, he was standing over the bull, not knowing what to do next. They immediately hailed him a hero because few encountered a buffalo alone and lived.

That was a long time ago. Solena was right. It was time to move on and let somebody else lead the hunting. He knew the injury would affect the strength of bow and his leadership on a hunt. He had always led by example and never asked his men to do what he himself could not do. He had had his time and had no regrets. He turned away and found Solena in a group of women dancing.

"I'm tired. I'm going home," he said as he passed.

Solena heard more than physical fatigue in those words. She said goodbye to her friends and hurried after the staggering figure. In a gesture of affection rarely seen in the village, she took his hand and they walked home hand-in-hand. No one knew or cared that the wound on his shoulder had played a part in saving the life of a young bride and her unborn child.

The days that followed were relatively quiet for Yossou and Ma'alia. In all, he was a happy man. She had been away almost six moons and Yossou realized how much he loved and missed her. It did not matter that he could not be intimate with her. She was more important to him than his needs.

Ma'alia did not let her pregnancy slow her down either. She still went to the stream to fetch water, performed her chores around the home, and even worked in the field. The one thing Yossou would not let her do was to split firewood. He came home one evening and found her attacking a log with a thick stick and a wedge. He stared at her incredulously. He waited until she had dealt the wedge another blow then came up behind her and took the stick away. The look he gave her said everything.

"Go start the fire with what you have. I'll split the rest of the wood and bring it to you."

She did not split another log as long as she was with child.

Her relationship with her mother-in-law also changed significantly. From the day Ma'alia returned from Ngoma, Simi deferred to her on household matters. Together they decided on what to cook. Simi also held back when giving instructions around the home. Whereas before she would assign duties to Ma'alia and her grandchildren alike, now she gave instructions only to Simi and Temin.

On the matter of discipline, the elder Simi had also changed. Previously, she would correct the children and arbitrate in their squabbles with little regard for Ma'alia. Now, if the girls wanted to do something that called for parental sanction, she would tell them, "Go ask your mother or your father." Initially, the girls were miffed, but they became more accommodating when they realized Ma'alia was not out to make their lives miserable. With subtle backing from her mother-in-law, Ma'alia established a sense of order in the home where everyone had a place and a voice. Many in the village were watching to see how she would take to her new family and were impressed with how she fared. None was happier than Yossou himself. The prospect of becoming a father again, added to the sense of contentment.

"What are you smiling at?"

"Wh… what? Who is smiling?" Yossou asked. He had not heard Ma'alia approach.

"Oh, I'm talking to that rock over there! It's you. I've been watching you for a while. You seem lost in a paradise of your own."

"Well, I am and I've got you to thank for it," Yossou said patting her bulging stomach. "Promise me it's a boy. It would be nice to have another man in the house."

Ma'alia paused a moment before answering. "It's not in my place to make that promise, but I believe you will have a son."

Yossou noted the gravity of her tone. He pulled her down beside him gently and wrapped his arms around her. He did not care that the village was not used to open display of affection. He sighed heavily and Ma'alia responded with a sigh of her own. They sat together for a long time each with his or her private thoughts, yet strangely united. It was dark when Ma'alia broke the embrace and picked up the uneaten food.

"If you want me to warm this food you'll have to help me up."

"I'm not hungry, my love, but I'll help you up."

They stood facing one another after he had helped her to her feet. He truly loved her. And she… he saw that she loved him. What passed between them was more than words could say. Ma'alia backed away and headed to the kitchen.

"You have dinner for tomorrow," she said, turning to his silhouette.

Yossou sat down again and leaned back to look at the night sky. He could sense the ancestors looking down at him. They smiled on him. Then he noticed, as if for the first time, the black canvas against which the stars twinkled. It smiled on him too. Life was good indeed.

Chapter 5

counting the people

The state of bliss did not last long. One morning, the unmistakable voice of Alila, the village crier, cut through the air with his unique call for attention. The cool air carried his voice over a great distance. The villagers would pass the message along and it often preceded him.

"Hear, oh hear, everyone. This is a pronouncement from the great Tamaa bin Tumbo whose word is greater than both the bearer and the hearer. Starting the first day after the harvest and for ten and five days, every member of the Avantu will present himself in the city of Bora-ini for the counting of the people. Hear, oh hear me one more time. This is a pronouncement from the great Tamaa bin Tumbo whose word is greater than the bearer and the hearer. Every member of the Avantu is required to present himself in the city of Bora-ini for the numbering of the people. Everyone must attend personally. Anyone found not to have done so will suffer punishment. The word of Tamaa bin Tumbo, Great Ruler of Kwavantu"

"What ails that madman?" Wiki-Zugu asked.

"It's beyond comprehension," Wind answered.

He had joined Sakul Wiki-Zugu for a calabash of porridge as he did many mornings since his encounter with the leopard. He winced as he shifted on the stool. Solena had done her best to nurse him back to health, but the cat had damaged the muscles and tendons in his shoulder so he could not move his arm without pain. Hunting was out of the question and he had passed the mantle to Sande, who proved to be an able leader and skilled hunter. The villagers thrust Wind into the ranks of the elders who spent their waking hours with chewing sticks in their mouths dispensing unsolicited advice, barking at children, dozing off, and generally solving the problems of the world.

Wiki-Zugu noisily sucked in a mouthful of porridge. "Well, there's nothing we can do about it. Remember Turuki?"

Wind did.

Some harvests back, the Baturuki decided they would no longer pay taxes as Tamaa demanded, and would not show up for the count. To drive their point home, they killed the messengers he had sent to remind them of the outstanding taxes and dumped their dismembered bodies on the Plains of Sacrifice. Though the clans shared the Baturuki's sentiments, they abhorred this last action, which they deemed a desecration of the hallowed grounds. Tamaa's response was vicious.

A few days passed after the slaughter of the messengers. The Baturuki did not hear from Tamaa, so they assumed he would not bother them anymore. However, one night, at that time when sleep is sweetest, all but the heaviest sleepers on the outskirts of some villages woke up to the unmistakable "clop, clop" of people trotting in time. The short guttural, "humm!" that fell on every third step meant it was a raiding party. They knew who would be grieving tonight.

In the morning, a great plume of smoke rising over Turuki greeted the clans. When it cleared, black specks circled above the area. Word of the spectacle spread quickly in surrounding villages.

"The vultures feast today," a villager in Vogol told his neighbor.

"Poor souls," she answered in agreement.

When they were sure no harm would befall them, people from nearby villages went up to what once was Turuki. What they saw was enough to make any man lose hope in life. Bodies lay strewn everywhere amidst the still smoldering chaos of huts and barns. Some of the victims were burned to black lumps with just enough form to identify them as erstwhile humans. From the posture of many girls and women in death, it was clear the assailants had raped or assaulted them. The warriors had also torn babies from their mothers' arms and dashed them against rocks. The men, taken by surprise, must have put up a weak fight. Most had arrows or spears sticking out of their backs, indicating they had tried to flee, but the weapons had sabotaged their attempts. A few bodies had lances shoved up their rear ends and the shaft driven into the ground leaving the unfortunate victim in a profane attitude over the spear. Viscous rivulets of blood and offal had run down the shaft ending in a sickening pile at the bottom.

A few surviving Baturuki cowered in nearby bushes, too terrified to come into the open. They screamed hysterically and struggled against their would-be rescuers. They did not need to say what happened. The carnage Tamaa's boys left behind told the whole story. That was the end of the Baturuki. Other clans got the message.

"If all the Avantu came together, we would be able to stand against these foreigners, but we are too busy with petty grudges to form a united front," Wind lamented.

"Right," Wiki-Zugu agreed. "And I have seen enough to know it won't change. You can never get the clans, let alone all our people, to agree on anything. Some take a different position just to prove their independence. No, I'm afraid we will continue to pay taxes to Tamaa until things change. He is, after all, a man and will pass on some day - soon I hope."

They sat in silence for several moments, each lost in his thoughts.

"So when do we travel, Sakul?"

As Wiki-Zugu was about to answer, a chicken came running round the corner squawking loudly, wings fluttering, and a little boy hot pursuit. He stopped, surprised to see the adults and immediately bolted back out of sight.

"Adolua, I'll knock your head off!" Wiki-Zugu threatened. The chicken slowed down, clucked thankfully, and ducked under a bush. Turning back to Wind, Wiki-Zugu said, "Let's call a meeting of the elders tonight so we can decide how we will travel and then inform the people."

"Good," Wind said rising to his feet. He grimaced again as pain shot through his shoulder.

"Rest that arm, Wind," Wiki-Zugu advised. "Stop those little projects you dig up for yourself. It's not your fault that your arm is injured. And remember it was for a good cause."

"*Akh!*" Wind grunted in agreement. He still felt bad that the women and children had to do most of the work while he scrounged for things to occupy himself. Above all, he missed the freedom to come and go as he pleased and he became a little overbearing. Often, Solena ran him off when she had had enough of his fussing.

"Get out of here!" she would say. "Go find something to do - anything, but get out of here!" Wind would leave, cursing all women and the world. Later as only she knew how, Solena would nurse his pride just as she nursed his wound and he would be man enough to face another day.

Toward evening, Tumba, the village drummer belted out the summons on his drum. It summoned the head of each household to a meeting in the village square at dusk. The meetings usually started when each home had a representative. Wiki-Zugu, as the most senior elder, would moderate the discussions.

Men began to trickle in well before dusk. They sat in a semi-circle, talking and bantering as they waited. When the meeting began, they discussed how they would travel to Bora-ini, concluding that half the village should travel first and the other half seven days later. They also determined which families would go on each trip and which young men would take care of the animals. They also worked out a plan to share with neighboring villages in the unlikely event the village came under attack. The meeting went longer than they anticipated, sometimes getting heated as some individuals took things personally. In the end, they reached a consensus and parted amicably. Each man went home with little enthusiasm for the prospect of a long trek to Bora-ini.

Early on the seventh day after the meeting, Tumba's drums summoned everyone who would be traveling to meet at the village square. Yossou's household was already up when the announcement came. The younger Simi and her sister were sweeping the compound and putting things in order. It was bad luck to leave an untidy compound when going away for an extended period. Temin was obviously having a harder time with the early morning. Barely awake, she had a white streak of dry saliva running from the corner of her mouth to just below her right ear. She ran her broom over the same spot several times until Simi asked her to wake up and move to another spot.

The herdsboys had taken the cows to the communal pastures the previous day. The chickens would roam free since they could fend for themselves and found their way home in the evening. The cat and the two geese would keep serpents and other unwelcome guests away.

"Why are you taking this big pouch M'ma?" Yossou asked when his mother handed him the oversized bag. "You have a smaller one."

"If you won't carry it I'll do so myself. I carried you nine moons so what's a little pouch for a couple of days?"

Yossou bristled at the remark, but he hefted the pouch anyway. Sometimes he did not understand his own mother.

Once again, the village of Kilima asked Zai, his cousins, Amit and Boza, and their friend, Aloni to take the animals to the marshes while their owners prepared for the trip to Bora-ini. Zai prayed that there would be no drama, human or supernatural, while they were at the marshes. He still remembered that day when a small cloud in the shape of a fist let fly a bolt of light. He was still smarting from the embarrassment he felt when they ran into the village inquiring if anyone had seen the bolt fall from the sky and if it had hurt someone.

"What bolt?" Tindi asked.

Zai and the other two boys were confused. They looked at one another.

"Surely, we aren't the only ones who saw it!" Zai protested.

"The bolt hit the ground sometime back! Didn't you see it?" Amit was close to tears.

"No," Mabu, the middle-aged artisan who worked in hides and skins said coldly. "Nobody saw anything. What have you been up to? You're not sucking on zaga stems, are you?"

"No! No!" the boys protested.

"We don't do such things," Zai emphasized. "Still, I'm sure about we saw. It was a cloud shaped like a man's fist and it threw a bolt of light to the ground. What followed was a loud sound like thunder that lifted me off the ground."

Mabu continued to look at him with an expression of disbelief. Tindi chortled in the background. Zai looked from one man to another, totally baffled.

"Basiani, what are you doing here? Who is with the animals?"

It was Kilum, Amit and Boza's father. The boys' hearts sank. Now they were in big trouble.

"No one's with them, Father. We came to see if..." Boza started.

"If what? Your business is to watch the herd. In case you didn't know, we have elders who can take care of anything that comes up."

"Yes, Father."

"Now get your tails back to the marsh. For this, you will stay two extra nights. Now go!"

Everyone knew Kilum drove his sons hard. He had little patience with anyone he thought was a failure. He was concerned about the animals because most belonged to him, which is why he always suggested his sons and nephew should take them to the marshes. The boys knew his animals and were aware of his instructions.

"Don't let anything touch any of my animals," he always warned. "Whatever happens to one of them will happen to you."

Zai turned and trotted back to the marsh without a word. He was seething on the inside at the way his uncle and the other men had treated them. The smell of cooking hung strong in the air, further enraging him. They would have to eat wild strawberries and bitter leaves tonight. They could catch a hare or some other rodent to roast over a fire, but soon it would be too dark to hunt. He braced himself for a cold night on an empty stomach. He heard Amit crying behind him.

"Shut up, you baby! What are the tears for?" Boza shouted.

Amit slowed to a walk and continued to cry. Boza whipped around to face his brother.

"Stop this nonsense! You're behaving worse than a baby! A short scolding from Father and you dissolve into tears! When will you become man enough to take it?"

Amit stopped walking and cried even more. Boza started toward him with clenched fists.

"Leave him alone!" Zai said calmly.

Boza turned to his cousin, pointed at his brother, and attempted to speak, but the words would not come. He threw up his hands in exasperation and walked on, bumping Zai as he passed. Zai walked up to Amit, put his arm round his shoulder, and walked with him. The younger boy stopped crying and was talking animatedly moments later.

Zai was concerned that by now the animals will have drifted far in every direction. They would have to herd them to the usual spot for the night, account for each, and build a fire. He was not looking forward to doing all this in the dark.

"Let's start collecting twigs and branches as we go." Zai told his cousins as they got close to the marshes. They began to gather fuel for the fire. It was already dark when they got to the marsh. To their surprise, the animals appeared to be where they should be for the night.

"Wah!" Zai exclaimed. His surprise turned to fear. Maybe the Vasua had been watching from the ridges and had come to take the animals while they were away. These nomads claimed that all the cattle on the earth were theirs by right. Besides, they were fierce warriors and the Bagololi did their best to avoid conflict with them.

Zai was even more alarmed when he heard the crackling of a fire. Turning in the direction of the sound, he saw a silhouette against the backdrop of flames. He stopped and motioned his cousins to do the same. For some time, they just stood watching the intruder, ready to run if necessary. They could not tell whether he was by himself or if there were others waiting in the shadows.

"Come, basiani. Join me," the figure said without turning around.

No one moved. When he turned and the firelight played on his face, they could tell he was a stranger to the area. In fact, he did not look like a member of the Avantu. The boys were hesitant, but the aroma of meat roasting over the fire made their mouths water.

"You must be hungry. Come. There's enough for all of us," the man urged.

He turned the meat over. Drops of fat fell into the fire causing the flames to flare. The boys could no longer resist. They set their twigs down and approached with caution. The man was roasting a small boar on a spit. Next to the fire were two large yams, roasted and ready to eat. On a broad leaf next to him was an assortment of fruits - wild berries, papaya, guavas, mangos, and passion fruit. This was as good a feast as they had ever seen and would have taken ages for them to put it together. The boys sat down on the opposite side of the fire, watching the stranger. His eyes twinkled and he smiled to reassure them. When he reached for the sword at his hip, all three immediately scurried away.

"Be not afraid, boys. I just want to share this meal with you," he said laughing.

They sat down again. He took the spit and held it over the leaf with the fruit. He curved off several juicy slices of meat onto the leaf and placed the rest back over the fire. Next, he took the yams and cut them into slices. When he finished, he raised his head heavenward.

"O Mighty One, thank you for what you've provided that we may be nourished." He pushed the leaf toward the boys. "Eat."

He wiped the sword on the grass and slid it back in his waistband. On the handle was the carved image of a lion. The boys huddled closer and began to eat. Each remarked on how the meat was full of flavor. The fruits were rich and incredibly juicy. The roots were cooked just right. Everything was delicious and they ate heartily. The man did not eat. Presently, he stood up. They stopped chewing to look up at him with a little apprehension.

"I have work to do," he announced. "Enjoy the food and don't worry about the animals. They grazed well."

With that, he walked away. As the boys watched, he melted into the night as though he walked into another world through a dark door. They looked at each other in amazement. Only then did they notice how quiet and calm the animals were. Some sat, asleep on the ground while others stood, chewing the cud contentedly. The boys shook their heads in amazement and went back to their meal.

"A strange one," Zai said with his mouth full.

"Uh huh," the brothers agreed.

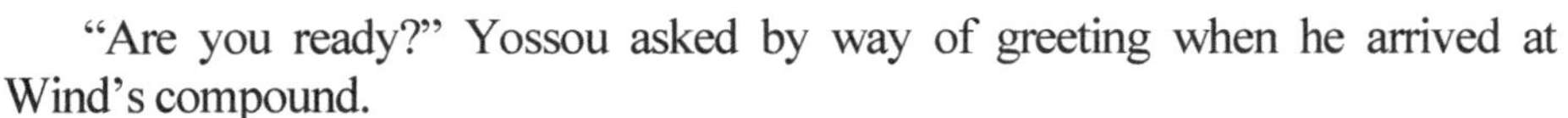

"Are you ready?" Yossou asked by way of greeting when he arrived at Wind's compound.

"As ever," Wind answered placing his machete in its holder at his waist.

"You aren't going to need that, are you?"

"You always have to be prepared, my friend. Always be prepared."

"Ah!" Yossou agreed, his thoughts going back to the night Wind saved Ma'alia.

He was glad he would be traveling with Wind. Though he was still injured, Yossou felt better in his company. Wind was his senior by an age-group, but they were great friends and shared a deep mutual respect that had grown after the incident with the leopard.

"*Vaya!* Hurry up and let's get out of here," Wind shouted. "We have a long trip ahead of us and you are still dawdling. Where's Moni?"

"I'm out here, *Baba*."

Moni, his youngest daughter by Aril, was probably his favorite child. She was the same age as Temin and as soon as Yossou's family arrived, they found each other and were already at play.

When everyone was ready, they headed to the square where the travelers would congregate for final instructions. Other families were already at the square by the time Yossou and Wind arrived. Children were running about and yelling at the top of their voices, excited about the trip to the stone city. The adults had mixed feelings about it. The only good thing about the trip was the opportunity to meet relatives and friends from other villages.

The villagers were never comfortable leaving their possessions and animals behind even with a plan to protect them in case of a raid. The chief concern of any village was the *Bagondi* and the Vasua who were the traditional enemies of the Bagololi. In case of an attack, two columns of smoke from predetermined locations would signal distress to nearby villages. Warriors, hunters, and all able-bodied men from the villages would surround the community under attack, giving the raiders little room to escape. The villagers would cut them down mercilessly.

"Listen! Listen, everyone!" Wiki-Zugu called out. The chatter died down and everyone came closer. "We will be the first group making the journey. Some of us have been to Bora-ini before, while others have never been beyond the hills around us. It will be a new experience, and everyone should be careful. There's danger of wild animals, bandits, and creatures that sting and bite. Parents, keep an eye on all the children. We don't want them wandering off by themselves. See to it that you have enough dried meat to last the time we will be away. I'm sure others will be willing to share with you, but it would be better if you took care of yourself and your family. Also, make sure you have your tribute to Tamaa. It's thirty cowry shells for an adult and twenty for a child. Does everyone have enough? We need to know before we start off." He paused and looked around. The adults inspected their pouches and gourds. All indicated in the affirmative.

"That's good. When we travel, I want the strongest both in front and at the rear because an animal stalking us will pick out the smaller, weaker individuals at the end of the convoy. Let's also pray that the Oracle will spare us an encounter with bandits. We may also meet members of sister villagers along the way. The children will obviously be excited to see their friends and cousins so you will need to know where yours are at every stage of the journey. This is not the same as the Festival of Sacrifice, where only the Bagololi are present."

Wiki-Zugu then selected his front and rear guard. M'mata and three other young men would lead the march. Yossou, Sande, Kofi and Avoga, both hunters, and Juma, the ironmonger, would form the rear guard. Though he made and repaired weapons and tools for Ronge and other villages, Juma was averse to carrying a weapon. It was therefore strange to see the axe that gleamed wickedly on his waistband. Not many had witnessed it, but the story ran that he could hit a target from a distance of a hundred strides with his axe. One could only imagine what damage he could do at close range. The other members of the rearguard were glad to have the soft-spoken ironmonger with them.

Having addressed all possible concerns, Wiki-Zugu sought the blessing of the Oracle and the ancestors on the journey. When he finished, they started down the path leading out of the village. M'mata, the champion wrestler, set a comfortable pace. They would be in Mahu by nightfall and in Bora-ini the following evening.

In spite of her advanced pregnancy, Ma'alia did her best to keep up with everyone. She joined in the song and occasionally turned to Simi and Temin to break up a squabble or admire a flower. Yossou called out often to inquire how she was coping. She assured him she was fine. It did not become a woman from her clan to use pregnancy as an excuse not to work or travel, so she plodded on.

By mid-afternoon, Ma'alia was tired. She felt light-headed and faint, but did not want to show it and hold up the group. They were, after all, only a fraction of a day's walk from completing the first part of their journey. It was all she could do to stay on the path as waves of pain engulfed her with increasing frequency. It was getting harder for her to focus and she began to feel as if she were floating rather than walking.

"M'ma, you are soiling yourself!"

Through the thickening fog in her mind, she could tell Simi had spoken to her, but the import of the words barely squeezed into her consciousness. *Why would I soil myself?* Before the answer came to her, she felt as though her legs had turned into heavy stumps and she could walk no further. Yossou had watched his wife's faltering steps with concern. He pushed past his daughters and was at her side in an instant.

"Are you alright?" he asked. In response, she sagged and he had to hold her to prevent her from falling. He sat her down gently by the path. He held her head up and looked into her eyes. She looked up at him and smiled, but it was not a knowing smile.

"I think her baby's coming." Kofi said calmly. "Her water has broken."

He could see the dust-coated rivulets of fluid that had recently flowed down her legs. Others gathered around the family and the convoy came to a halt as word passed on to the front that Ma'alia was about to deliver. Mideva and a couple of other women were already making their way back.

"Is M'ma going to be fine?" Temin asked tearfully. "Is she going to die?"

"No, child," Yossou assured her.

"I don't want her to die," Temin wailed. "I don't want M'ma to die!"

"Take them away from here." Yossou told Juma.

"I'll take them," Aril, Wind's junior wife said.

Mideva pushed past Yossou so she could assess the situation. She knelt beside Ma'alia and looked disdainfully at the men standing around them.

"Move away. She's about to give birth and that's not a man's business. All you do is cause the problem."

The comment stung Yossou because he felt he had nothing to do with the pregnancy. He nodded to the other men to move on. Wiki-Zugu waited for the men to join him. He saw the strain on Yossou's face and laid a gentle arm on his shoulder. He glanced in Ma'alia's direction.

"We all started like that, and we're here, aren't we?"

Yossou bowed his head and nodded, feeling somewhat comforted by the old man's words, though the children he had lost came to mind.

"She's going to have that baby soon, but darkness will overtake us if we wait." Wiki-Zugu continued. "Some of us will have to stay with her while the rest continue to the wayfarer's camp in Mahu. There are caves around here where one can take refuge from bandits and wild animals for the night. I want to know who's willing to remain. We should be back by the third day. Yossou, naturally you'll stay with your wife."

There was a brief pause while the other men weighed the matter on hand.

"I'll stay," Juma said.

"Me too," Sande offered. Yossou raised his head and looked at him gratefully. He also turned to Juma and gave him an imperceptible nod.

Kofi started to speak, but Wiki-Zugu cut him off.

"No, Kofi. You're coming with us."

Kofi shrugged. Yossou looked at him and smiled.

"Thank you."

"We need two more men." Wiki-Zugu continued.

"What's the hold up? It will be dark soon," someone shouted from the group that waited up ahead.

"You want to proceed? Go on by yourself. See if you'll make it," Kofi hollered back.

"Just ignore them. You don't need two other men. Already, Mideva and Simi will remain with Ma'alia. All you need is one other man just for numbers. I'll stay."

Everyone turned to the speaker in surprise. None of them had thought to ask if he would stay and Wind had remained silent up to this point. They all presumed he would proceed with the rest of the party.

Kofi was first to speak again after the initial surprise. His eyes glanced involuntarily at Wind's shoulder before he started.

"But you…"

"But what?" Wind cut in. "What are you trying to say? Am I no longer useful because I can't go hunting anymore? You think I can't handle a little rabbit-hunt like this one." He glared at Kofi who stared back and appeared to resent the way Wind interpreted his concern.

"Alright, men. Let's not get testy," Wiki-Zugu intervened. "This is a simple matter. If Wind wants to stay, he'll stay. Now we have everybody we need, is there anything else we should consider before the rest of us move on?"

"You say you might find us here when you return, right?" Sande asked.

"Oh, yes. You'll have to complete the trip to Bora-ini. That monster Tamaa wants to count every head in these lands and he'll cause trouble if he learns some of us did not show up. If a group from another village comes along, join it. If not, we will come by here tomorrow and some of us will turn around and go back to Bora-ini with you. The only concern is that you'll have enough food since you will have an extended stay from the village."

"Oh, we'll improvise," Wind said. "We can always catch small game and pick wild fruit to supplement what we have."

"But this is not a hunting trip." Kofi pointed out. "You want to avoid drawing attention to yourselves while you are here."

Wind threw Kofi a fierce look and his right hand instinctively went for the machete at his hip. Kofi braced for an assault.

Yossou stepped between the men, arms outstretched to separate them.

"That's enough! We'll take care of ourselves while we are here." He turned to Kofi, "You should go now."

"That's right. And you need to attend to that woman over there," Wiki-Zugu nodded toward Ma'alia. "Stay well, son. You'll have a fine boy. He'll be a great leader someday."

"Thank you, *Baba*."

"Let's go! Move!" Wiki-Zugu called out to those who waited.

"Stay well," the men who would proceed said to Yossou and those who remained with him. The others who had been waiting for the deliberations to end shouted the same prayer and then proceeded toward Mahu. The tension that had built up earlier gradually dissipated as the parties separated, but Wind was still smarting from the exchange with Kofi.

"More of that and I'll have his head," he said watching Kofi who waited to take his place at the rear of the convoy.

"No, Wind," Yossou said. "He didn't mean to upset you or to look down on you. I think it was a misunderstanding. He's a good hunter, and I know he admires you as others do. Your injury has done nothing to diminish that."

"*Eesh!* He needs to learn how to talk to his seniors. As if I don't know the difference between a major hunt and hunting small prey!"

"That was unfortunate. But you know…"

"*Vaya!* Whose wife is about to have a baby?" Mideva hollered sarcastically. "Do you want the child to become *enzira*?"

She was massaging Ma'alia's distended belly while the elder Simi propped her up from behind and rubbed her lower back. They shared the task of shooing away the flies that took a keen interest in the areas around Ma'alia's legs. The object of their attention was unconcerned and sat with her legs far apart with little regard for modesty. The men averted their eyes and maintained a respectable distance.

Mideva looked up when Yossou joined them. "Where is this child going to be born? Here?" she asked, taking in the expanse of the path with her upturned hand. She taunted him with both her tone and body language.

"But you are the one who chased us off a while ago, Mideva. Give us a little time. We'll have to scout those ridges for a suitable cave or enclosed area."

"Tell that to your son. I cannot speak for him as to whether or not he'll wait."

She assumed, as most people did, that the child was a boy. Yossou walked away to rejoin the men. He did not want to butt heads with Mideva who could be overbearing when she took matters upon herself.

"Sande, Juma, do me a favor. Scout those ridges for a place where Ma'alia can have her baby. Wind and I will stay here with the women."

"Sure," said Sande. He turned round to give Juma a somewhat patronizing glance. "Come on!"

"Juma," Wind said, briefly halting their departure. "You'll want to look around that area first." He pointed to a section where the ridge was higher. "You're likely to find larger caves over there."

Juma knew what Wind was doing and he nodded in acknowledgment. He turned to Sande.

"Lead on." He had little interest in jockeying for importance.

Yossou and Wind watched them go.

"He's a fine lad. He'll make a great leader if he doesn't let it go to his head," Wind observed. They sat down.

"Yes indeed. I miss working with him. He is hardworking and quick to learn."

With nothing else to do, Yossou could only watch his wife moan as wave after wave of pain washed over her. Simi and Mideva did their best to soothe her.

"She's close," Mideva said.

"I know," Simi answered. "I don't know if she'll make it to those ridges. We might as well prepare to deliver the child right here." She looked up toward the two men sitting silently at a distance. "Yossou, where's my pouch?"

For a moment, Yossou could not gather his wits. He had been carrying it for his mother, but he could not recollect where he had placed it when all the excitement with Ma'alia started. He got up and started looking around him.

"You can't remember where you placed it?" Wind asked.

"No." Yossou strained to remember.

"Where were you standing when we first stopped?"

"Maybe it was over there, but I don't remember. So much has happened in between."

"Where did you put it?" his mother called out again.

"That's what I'm trying to figure out, M'ma," he hollered back.

Mideva snickered.

"That dark line over there – those are ants. A line of ants leads to food," Wind told him. Yossou looked, but did not see anything out of the ordinary. "You don't see it? Well, back that way then. I believe you'll find what you're looking for."

"Eh heh."

Yossou made his way back along the narrow path. Halfway between Wind and the women was a thick black line of ants. They were the medium-sized variety, but they could cause much havoc for sheer number. The pouch lay in the grass off the path. Yossou picked it up. The tiny creatures reacted to the interruption with consternation. Yossou shook the pouch vigorously. The ants that were unprepared for the disruption fell off in a spell of black hail. The few that survived the initial shock clung to the leather with their strong mandibles and he could not dislodge them even when he slammed the pouch repeatedly on the ground. He resorted to scraping them off with a twig.

Mideva stopped him for a moment and dug into the pouch to empty its contents. She yelped when the agitated ants bit her. She dropped everything on the ground and brushed off the ants that clung to her hand. They covered what was left of the pieces of dried meat. One by one, Mideva scraped them off, setting aside the pieces she had scraped clear.

"Yossou, bring me that small pouch," Simi called out.

Mideva handed Yossou the pouch, which he took to his mother. She dug into it and found a fatty ointment that she proceeded to rub onto her daughter-in-law's belly. Ma'alia looked at Yossou and smiled weakly.

"You will soon have a son," she said.

"Thank you," Yossou answered. "Just don't leave me when you are having him," he added. I've lost every son I've ever had. I don't want to lose this one… and I don't want to lose you either."

"I'll be fine," Ma'alia answered, smiling before a stab of pain shot through her body. *"Woi!"* she cried out as a contraction rippled through her. Simi held her hand and rubbed her back. She felt better.

Just then Sande and Juma appeared.

"What did you find, boys?" Wind inquired, turning from clearing the ants from the pouch.

"Ah, we found the perfect spot," Sande answered. He turned and pointed. "You remember the section you showed us? Just to the left of it is a cave whose opening is large enough for a man to enter without bending. Inside, it is larger than a small hut."

"Good. Let's go." Mideva gave the items in her hand a final shake. She took the pouch and restored its contents. She started toward Yossou, Simi, and Ma'alia. "It would be good to get to the cave while it's still light so we know what it's like inside. Yossou, help me with Ma'alia. M'ma you can carry your pouch since we are not going a long way and I don't trust some people." She glanced sideways at Yossou as she spoke.

Mideva and Yossou helped Ma'alia along. Sande and Wind led the way to the cave. Juma at the rear said little, minding his own business.

Chapter 6

a child is born

For Sujia and the *Bagondi*, this was their "harvest" season. Tamaa's call for a count of the inhabitants of territories under his control would disrupt each village's routine for several days. Through a growing network of spies, Sujia and her deputies knew which villages had already sent parties to the count and which ones still planned to travel. They would be vulnerable to attack as they traveled and their tax cowry shells would make decent bounty along with the women and children they would capture. The villages were also vulnerable to attack with the reduced numbers that remained, but that was a problem because most had a contingency plan in place.

This time, the *Bagondi* had two choices. They could attack either the convoy from Ronge or the one from Ngoma. They chose the one from Ngoma. The spies reported that the travelers from Ngoma were fewer and less disciplined. To waylay the villagers, the *Bagondi* had to travel by night. A keen eye could easily make out the topographic anomaly of a band of humans traveling by day. The villagers would warn their neighbors using drums, smoke signals, or by runner. As evening approached, Sujia led her band to the upper edges of the hill country to survey the land below. When night fell, they would descend to the lower hills.

By the time they got to the cave, Ma'alia was utterly exhausted. She had become dead weight between her husband and Mideva. Sweat glistened on their faces and necks and they too, were out of breath. At the entrance, Simi halted.

"Stop. I want to see the inside. Wind, come with me."

Yossou and Mideva eased Ma'alia to the ground. Yossou turned aside and pinching his nose between thumb and index finger, he blew out of one nostril then the other, expelling a white blur each time. He flicked his fingers then rubbed his hands together to clear what clung to his digits.

The entrance of the cave was just high enough for the average adult to enter by stooping slightly. Wind stepped into the cave and Simi followed closely. It took some time for their eyes to adjust to the darkness. Simi noted the dampness and other clues to its suitability as accommodation for the night. It had as much room as a big hut. For the most part, the roof was high enough for a person to stand upright. A musky smell hung in the air.

"What do you think?" she inquired of Wind.

"An animal may have used this place as its lair. By the faint spoor, it hasn't been here for some time. However, there's no telling when it will be back. I doubt it will attack us. We should be safe here for the night."

"Good. I want to clear that spot over there while it's still light so Ma'alia can have her baby. Mideva, come help me."

Mideva stumbled into the cave. She would have fallen had Wind not held her.

"*Ei!* It's dark in here," she commented.

"Your eyes will get used to it," Simi pointed out. "Get some twigs and sweep this area. I have to prepare a little portion for Ma'alia to help the baby along."

The normally assertive Mideva recognized the authority with which Simi spoke and had little choice but to comply. She went back outside and gathered a handful of leafy twigs to serve as a broom. Wind and Sande, meanwhile, climbed up the rocky ledges to hunt small animals for the evening meal. Yossou and Juma collected twigs and branches with which they would build a fire.

Ma'alia breathed heavily as she waited for the next volley of contractions. Simi sat beside her daughter-in-law and pulled out a small package wrapped in banana leaves and tipped the contents into a small calabash. She added water and a little ash from another pouch, stirred the mixture, and handed it to Ma'alia.

"Here. Drink this."

Ma'alia put the concoction to her lips and grimaced.

"Finish it all."

Ma'alia put the calabash to her lips and tipped it. She drank and swallowed in one noisy gulp then wiped her mouth. The concoction left a strong aftertaste. She felt a slight giddiness first then a sense of calm.

"I've finished sweeping in there," Mideva announced. "The dust!" A red coat of dust around her legs explained her remark. "I pushed the loose dirt to a section of the cave, but we'll have to wait for the dust to settle."

"That's all right."

After some time, Simi took a roll of soft hide and handed it to Mideva.

"Place this on the floor then come help me with this pregnant woman."

Mideva chuckled and ducked into the cave with the hide. She came back out and they helped Ma'alia to her feet and up to the cave entrance. Simi went in first.

"Come on," she urged.

"What is this place?" Ma'alia asked leaning with one hand on the wall of the entrance. She held her belly with the other.

"Just get yourself in there. This is not the time to fuss," Mideva said.

Ma'alia took a couple of hesitant steps into the cave. Mideva gently but firmly edged her in and guided her to the soft hide. Simi called Yossou and handed him a wick lamp that burned animal fat and asked him to light it. She rested Ma'alia's head on her lap. Instinctively, Ma'alia threw her legs apart as her time of delivery approached.

The evening was not cold, so Zai wondered why he shivered so. He sat by himself at his favorite spot on the slope from where he could see the herd below and the village in the distance. He was bored with looking after animals. He had been looking forward to the trip to Bora-ini so it was a major vexation for him to be in the marshes again. He was also starting to resent having to look after the herd on these "special" occasions. He looked forward to the day he would join the ranks of young men to hunt, build structures, drink wine, and take a wife.

They had started the day with a breakfast of roast meat left over from the previous evening. Afterwards they played a game of *visala* to see who could flick a short stick and hit it farthest with a longer one. Later, Zai made a spinning top from the stem of a small bush using an old spearhead he always carried. On it, he carved various patterns and shapes.

Early in the afternoon, he and Aloni watched the animals while his cousins took naps. His turn came when the day was warmest. He slept fitfully and woke up feeling groggy and ill tempered. His cousins usually left him alone until he descended from his lofty perch. He would sit brooding for sometime until his ugly mood uncoiled and slithered off. He would then join them in conversation or a game.

He looked over to the village and remembered the day the sky "struck the earth." The Avantu as a whole, considered the "red rooster," or a lightning strike, as the most common manifestation of the wrath of the spirits. The memory sent a chill down his spine and he shivered involuntarily. He still wondered what it meant. *Was the Great Spirit upset with someone in the village?* That could not be the case because no one had died, gone blind, or been crippled. The people viewed these as punishment for those who upset the Oracle. No one had gone mad either. That would indicate a person had offended the spirits or the ancestors. It was strange. There had to be a reason for that event several moons back. Suddenly, he heard it as clearly, as if someone whispered in his ear.

"Soon you will know."

Zai looked around wondering who had spoken. He had the distinct feeling the voice brushed over him when he heard it, but he saw no one nearby. His cousins and their friend, Aloni, were talking below. He shook his head to make sure he was not hallucinating then picked up his spear and spinning top. He descended the slope to join the other boys. They were busy talking and paid him scant attention. Zai preferred it that way. He stayed with them the rest of the evening.

Sujia and her band had walked part of the afternoon until they came to the upper ridges of the hills. Provided they stayed low, no one in the valley below would notice them. Still, she took precautions and invited only Jambazi to the edge overlooking the plains.

"I see the villagers have put their animals out tonight."

"Yes. They'll be there overnight," Jambazi replied.

"How many herdsboys do you think there might be?"

"Usually three or four - rarely more than that."

"You think we can persuade them to let us have one of the bulls? It's been a while since we've had fresh meat."

"I don't see why not. That might jeopardize our plans for the other village, though. What they'll be carrying is worth more than a meal."

The comment irritated Sujia slightly though it made sense.

"What do you suggest?"

"We wait until nightfall and make our way to the lower ridges as planned. Three or four of us should overpower the boys easily. Then it will be a matter of choosing a cow to slaughter and eat. We'll tell them to stay put for at least a day or we'll be back for them and their families. Then we'll attack the convoy tomorrow and by evening we should be back in the hills. They can go crying to their mothers after that."

The plan satisfied Sujia. "Good. We'll do that."

She stretched on the ground, crossed her arms, and rested her head on them. In moments, she was fast asleep.

Jambazi was amazed she could fall asleep so quickly. She looked vulnerable lying there, but he knew better. The evening sun played on her features accentuating the youthful beauty. When she was upset, one could forget she was barely a woman. Life among the *Bagondi* had hardened her to the point that she could cut down anyone who crossed her as easily as she trod on an ant. The man who recently contradicted her did not know what surprised him more - her marksmanship, or seeing his entrails slip between his fingers where the arrow found its mark. He died before he could figure it out. She could be cunning too. Asai had underestimated her and paid for it. After she had killed him, the men whispered among themselves she had magical powers. Now they regarded her more as a leader than a mere woman and her word was law.

Jambazi also realized something else and was at pains to acknowledge it. He had developed strong feelings for her. He would do anything for her and she knew it. That annoyed him somewhat. It was a sign of weakness that did not become a man of his stature. At the same time, he felt liberated by the thought. He became aware he had been staring at Sujia for a long time when he heard snickering. He looked up and saw some of the men grinning at him. His expression changed to murder and the grins vanished.

Light was fading fast. The men had moved a distance from the entrance of the cave and were talking in low tones. Yossou was anxious, but he tried not to show it. He had lost one wife and could not bear the thought of losing another. He did his best to appear interested in the conversation, but his attention was on the sounds that still carried from the cave. He could hear Ma'alia moaning, huffing, and puffing as the labor intensified. Simi and Mideva offered encouragement and urged her to push. As he grew more anxious, he became more animated. Noticing this, Wind led him further away. *At least she isn't cursing me*, Yossou thought. He was not the father so she could not hold him responsible for her misery. Memories of the conception came rushing back. He remembered the pain he felt when he thought she had fooled around, leading to the incident with the powerful man at the river. He also recalled the dream about the birds attacking Ma'alia and the adventure that followed. *This was no ordinary child.*

"Son of the Oracle," he muttered.

"What?" Wind asked.

In that moment, Yossou perceived the awesome majesty of something far greater than himself. He raised his head to the sky in reverence. In the depths of the night sky, he sensed the power that prevented it from crashing down on them. The shadows of the mountains with their quiet majesty and their peaks pointed to The One who carved them out of the earth. The young moon, tucked in a corner of the sky, smiled on them. He wondered about the myriad of stars and the hand that had cast them like seed across the sky. He saw a star - brighter than any he had ever seen and it seemed to travel slowly against the dark canvas. Yossou was mystified.

"Do you see that?" he asked Wind without taking his eyes off the star.

"You see it too?"

"Yes. Bright, isn't it?"

"Yes, *they* are." Wind sounded tense.

"And it's coming our way."

"I don't know. I wonder if we haven't seen it before."

"We have? When?"

Wind gave Yossou a puzzled look. “You forget so soon? Let’s join the others. Stay close to me. Walk slowly and make no sudden movement!”

Yossou found this a strange reaction to what he saw. They joined Sande and Juma who both trained their eyes skyward.”

“That’s a strange star.” Sande said when he heard them approach.

“Star?” Wind tapped Sande on the shoulder and pointed. “Is that your star?”

Sande’s blood went cold.

Ma’alia was drenched in sweat. She felt hot and disoriented yet the cave was cold and musty. She lay flat on the soft hide. Simi held her hand and massaged her oily belly with the other hand. Mideva was on her knees poised to receive the baby.

“Right. Push now!” Mideva urged. Ma’alia pushed with all her might. She gasped at the end of the effort.

“You are doing just fine,” Simi encouraged.

“Yes. You are a brave woman. Take a deep breath and push.”

“I’m tired,” Ma’alia said. “I have no strength left.”

“You are almost there, child. Just one more push.”

“You can’t go back now, Ma’alia. I can see the head already. You’ve got to…”

Right then, pain shot through Ma’alia’s lower back. For a moment, she was too shocked to react. She snatched her hand from Simi’s and sat up looking down between her legs. She inhaled sharply, held her breath, and pushed. There was a squelching sound as she expelled the child unceremoniously. The hasty birth caught Mideva off-guard. She barely managed to catch the baby before he hit the ground.

“The baby! The baby has come!” was all she could say. She cleaned him with a handful of soft leaves dabbed in water. All the while, she uttered words of thanksgiving.

Ma’alia sat breathing heavily. Sweat glistened on her forehead and she wore a glazed expression. Simi pushed her gently down onto her back then severed the cord that tied the child to the mother. Moments later, Ma’alia expelled another spurt of blood.

“Just one more push now,” Simi encouraged. Ma’alia pushed and this time a bloody mass came out easily.

“Good. Very good,” Simi said. She took the mass, set it aside, and cleaned her daughter-in-law with water and soft leaves from her pouch. She also girdled her with a fresh modesty patch and helped her sit up.

Mideva handed her the baby. "Here's your baby, little mother. What a beautiful child he is!"

"Thank you." Ma'alia took the child and held him to her bosom. Though Simi had severed the physical bond between them, this simple action established another one, deeper than any physical bond.

"I'll go tell the father," Simi said.

She scooped the mass of tissue, rose, and stepped out of the cave. Night had already fallen. They had been inside a long time.

A draught of crisp evening air woke Sujia. She rolled to her side and looked around in the fading light. Jambazi sat next to her with arms locked around his knees.

"Good morning!" he mocked.

She only grunted. "Are the men ready? We need to move. You'll be able to guide us to the herd below, right?" She stood up.

"Of all the raids we've undertaken, who has led us? What is it to find something I can hear and smell?"

"*Eesh!* I was just asking!"

Since Jambazi said nothing further, she ordered the men to start the tricky descent. In the growing darkness, other men would have slipped and rolled down the steep incline but the *Bagondi* had adapted to life in the harsh conditions and had even come to love it. Soon, they were at the top of an embankment overlooking the pasture.

Amit had shot a hare that afternoon so they were sure to have dinner. They built a fire at their customary spot. Boza skewered the hare and held it over the flames to burn off the hairs. Once it blackened, he scraped off the burned skin then began to roast it in earnest. Aloni fed twigs to the fire to keep it going. Zai hardly said a word. He kept his eyes on the fire and his thoughts to himself.

When they heard the good news of Ma'alia's delivery, the men congratulated Yossou and drifted closer to the cave. He was all over Simi as soon as she stepped outside.

"How is Ma'alia? How is the baby?"

"They are both well. Ma'alia delivered the child without a problem. You've given me another wonderful grandchild. Go in and see him."

Yossou did not need further urging. He rushed into the cave.

Simi looked at the other men and sensed tension. Wind held his machete in his hand. Sande had notched an arrow.

"What's the problem?" she asked.

"Nothing," Wind lied. His eyes continued to scan the area around the cave as he spoke.

"Really?" Simi said skeptically. "Let me borrow your machete. I want to dig a hole near one of those shrubs over there."

"I have to hang on to it for a while, M'ma," Wind said, still abstracted.

"I'll help you dig the hole." Juma offered. "Where do you say you want it?"

"I just said over there," she pointed. "What's wrong with you men?"

"Be careful Juma," Wind warned without turning his head.

"It won't take long," Juma promised.

He followed Simi to a spot next to a thick shrub and began to dig. It was a little awkward digging with an axe, but Juma was adept at it. He cut into the earth and scooped out the soil with his hands.

"Is that what comes out after a baby is born?" he nodded toward the bundle Simi held.

"Yes," Simi replied. "She did well for a first child. She's very strong."

"I'm glad to hear it," Juma continued. "When the mother and child are safe it is always good."

Though he worked calmly, Simi observed that he kept an eye on his surroundings.

"That's good enough," Simi said after some time.

She went down on her knees, laid the bundle in the hole, and pushed the soil back over it. When it was all covered, she packed it tight by stomping on it. Burying the tissue seemed a futile effort because wild animals usually dug it up and ate it. However, it was tradition, and everybody did it without question. When she finished, they started back toward the cave. Simi noticed the men's highly defined shadows. She looked up and saw, directly above her, the brightest star she had ever seen.

"*Wah!*" she exclaimed.

"What? The star?" Juma inquired. "We saw it travel from the direction of the setting sun until it came to rest above us. We've been wondering what it means."

"Something of great significance must have taken place somewhere tonight. Sakul Wiki-Zugu would probably know."

"M'losi would know too. He is always consulting the Oracle and the spirits."

They resumed walking with Simi still looking at the mysterious star. They rejoined a tense Wind and Sande who still stood back to back.

"M'ma, get back in there now!" Wind commanded. "There's an animal stalking us. It can pounce any time. Juma, come stand with us and remain alert."

Winds eyes never left the rocks above the cave. The intensity of his gaze and the tension in his voice said it all. Simi entered the cave quickly.

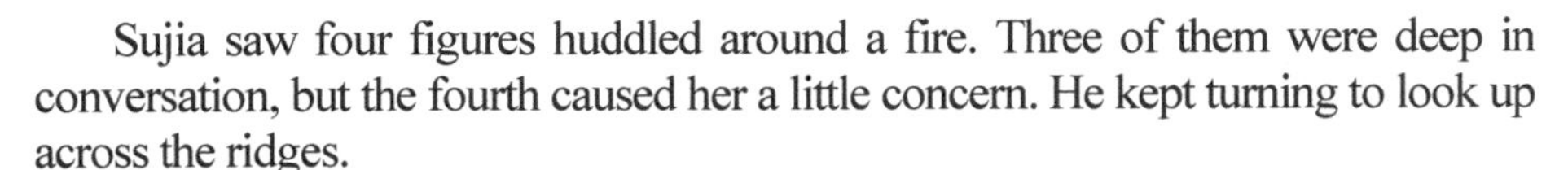

Sujia saw four figures huddled around a fire. Three of them were deep in conversation, but the fourth caused her a little concern. He kept turning to look up across the ridges.

"That one there - the one to the right. Do you think he suspects something?" she asked Jambazi.

"How would he know? He's probably just afraid of the night."

"I don't think so. He seems older and more cautious than the others. I'm sure he has a spear or a bow. Here's what we'll do. You and I will go down with two men first. We'll descend further to our right then come up from behind him. As soon as we are within range, I'll take him out with an arrow. The other three shouldn't be a problem. We'll order them to the ground so we can spare them. If they don't cooperate, they're dead."

Sujia paused to study the situation one more time and concluded it was time to move. She was about to give the order when the wind suddenly picked up, whipping erratically across the hills and the valley below. It grew in strength and sound until it roared like a mighty gathering of warriors. The sound reached its climax in an ear-piercing ululation behind them. Sujia turned and saw a most spectacular sight. A mighty spirit-warrior stood at the top of a nearby ridge, his arms raised as if he had just overcome a foe. In his right hand, he held a heavy spear. In his left, he raised a powerful shield. Around him was an ethereal brilliance that lit up the night. He let out another cry before descending the ridge. Sujia and her men were rooted to the spot in great fear. The spirit-warrior leaped from one crest to the next without effort. No ordinary man would have cleared the distance with such ease.

By this time, Zai and his companions had fallen to the ground, petrified at the sight of the warrior who now trotted down the embankment toward them. He was a tall imposing presence with features that seemed paradoxically familiar and foreign at the same time. He stopped a few paces from them, and spoke in Kigololi.

"Peace!" he declared raising his spear. Zai and his friends were too scared to respond. "Do not be afraid, young men of Kilima. Lift up your faces for I do not seek to harm you. I bring good news instead. This night, a child is born who will be called King of the Avantu. He will heal the hearts of the people and bring freedom to the land. This is a night of great joy, and the Oracle has appointed you, O young men, to receive the news of this great happening and see it for yourselves. This will be the sign. Follow the star. It will lead you to the child."

The spirit-warrior paused and looked at the boys with a benign expression. Suddenly, the surrounding terrain filled with a mighty army of spirit-warriors covering every ridge all the way down to the pasture. Each had the same brilliant aura. Together, they lit up the hills and marshes with incredible beauty. They raised their voices as one and sang the popular song, *Mwana wa Mberi*, in praise of the firstborn child. Their voices resonated from hill to hill and filled the entire marshland with its joyous melody. As they sang, the leading warrior began to rise. The others followed, ascending steadily in a canopy of radiant bodies. As they rose, they merged into a single bright light high up above. The song and the wind faded with them, leaving a deafening silence below.

The boys looked at each other and up at the light. It stood above them like a benign spirit and began moving slowly in the direction of the rising sun.

"Let's go and see this amazing thing that has happened," Amit, the most impetuous of the boys said.

Without waiting to see if the other boys agreed, he started in the direction the star indicated. The others scrambled after him. Zai picked up his spear and followed. As he ran, he heard heavy footsteps gaining on him. He turned to see who it was. A man with a hideous shock of hair and hard chiseled features smiled and caught up with him.

"Who are you?"

"I'm Jambazi. We were going to kill you, but now I want to see what the spirit-warrior was talking about."

"*Ai?* Alright."

The gravity of the confession did not register with Zai immediately. They trotted side-by-side behind the younger boys. Moments later when it did, Zai looked at the man running alongside him and stopped. Jambazi also stopped and patted him on the shoulder.

"I said we were going to, but not any more. Let's go see this child."

Zai left it at that. Neither said much the rest of the way.

Sujia and her band were all too shocked to move or speak even after the spirit-warriors had ascended. The scene had moved her deeply and she wondered what she should do. *What manner of child was this? Who is his mother? Who is his father?* Then she remembered a conversation she had overheard one afternoon several moons back the day she had killed Asai. *The man and young woman at the creek were the parents of the child!* She had been angry with the Spirit-Father for imposing himself on a woman. Now she felt another surge of anger she could not explain.

After the spirit-warriors had risen skyward merging to become a star, Jambazi stood up as if in a trance and started toward the boys. Sujia had tried to hold him back, but he shook her off and continued in spite of her harsh order. For a moment, she thought of putting an arrow in his back, but for once, her usually suppressed morals would not allow it. She watched him catch up with the oldest boy. She noticed the brief exchange with the older boy, and then he was gone. She had lost her deputy. She still had the rest of the band and they now looked at her for guidance. She wished she did not have to make a decision, but she had to. She vaguely remembered the animals cowering at the sight of the spirit-beings all around them, but she had no further interest in them. They would come back another day. Tonight she was tired and just wanted to go back home.

"We go back," she told her recovering band.

"But I thought we…" The dissenter, a short man with a wicked gleam in his eye, pointed at the unattended livestock.

"We go back!"

The man thought better of pursuing his case. Sujia stalked past him and made for the slope that marked the ascent to the hill country. The men followed grudgingly.

Just as Wind, Sande, and Juma were getting ready to relax their defensive stance, they heard a low growl from the direction in which Wind was facing. Sande and Juma turned around. Wind tightened his grip on his machete. The animal was a dark silhouette with a pair of bright yellow eyes. Against conventional wisdom, he stared the animal down. He knew instinctively it was the same one they had encountered almost eight moons ago. Man and beast locked eyes for what felt like eternity. Sande slowly raised his bow, but did not pull back. For Juma, the encounter was more fascinating than frightening. He had never been this close to a wild animal before. Its eyes hypnotized him, but he also sensed the tension in the confrontation.

The cat was the first to move. It barely inched forward. Sande's bow creaked as he pulled on the string. One more move, and he would release the arrow.

"Step back," Wind ordered softly.

"What?" Sande whispered in surprise.

"Step back, both of you." They did.

Wind took one stride forward and stood still. The cat took another step, all the while never taking its eyes off Wind. A mysterious understanding seemed to have developed between them. Finally, the cat abandoned the charade. It approached Wind and rubbed itself against his legs circling him once. Wind experienced conflicting emotions at that time. The fear against which he had fought gave way to exhilaration. When the leopard stopped, it looked at Sande and Juma as if to ask, "And who are these?" Wind turned to Sande and Juma.

"Put your weapons away. I think he wants to be our friend."

Juma lowered his axe. Sande was more wary and eased his bow down reluctantly. He watched with fascination as Wind dug into his pouch for a piece of dried meat, which he offered the leopard. The animal took it in his teeth and settled on the ground to gnaw on it. When it finished, it stood up and faced the entrance of the cave. It let out another low growl. When he did not seem to understand, it growled softly and inched toward the entrance. Once again, Sande raised his bow, but Wind waved at him to put away his weapon.

"This may surprise you, but I think he wants to see the child," Wind said.

"And you will let him?" Sande asked incredulously.

"Sande, of all the things that have happened today, what has made sense? Here I am standing next to an animal that would have killed me and which you thought you had killed. In that cave is a woman it would have killed. Not only is she alive, but she has also brought another life into the world the very night we all meet again. Don't tell me that's coincidence. The Great Spirit is doing things we'll never understand. Perhaps he is showing us he can do things beyond what we believe is the natural order of life. That child in the cave is born in strange circumstances. This animal's desire to see him is only part of the mystery." His eyes drifted to its paw. It triggered a recollection of the spoor he had seen when he first inspected the cave. "*Mwaza!* That cave is this animal's lair. The spoor in the cave is this leopard's. We are his guests!"

Sande shook his head in utter disbelief. He regarded Wind as if he had gone mad.

Wind turned to Juma.

"Don't look at me!"

Wind sighed before he called out to those in the cave.

"*Enzi!* There's a visitor here to see the child. I warn you he's not the regular type."

"Who is he?" Mideva asked.

"Why don't you wait and see. May we come in?"

Wind heard her consulting the others before she answered.

"You may enter."

Wind ducked into the cave and turned to invite the cat to follow. Though forewarned, none of those inside were prepared for what they saw. Mideva, because she had given the go ahead, was watching the entrance and was therefore first to see the strange guest. With a sharp cry and hitherto unseen agility, she was at the furthest end of the cave in an instant.

"Get that thing out of here, you wizard!" she shouted.

Yossou and his mother likewise, were pushing themselves backwards with their heels. Only Ma'alia remained where she lay. She raised her head lethargically to see the cause of commotion. Wind patted the leopard to calm it.

"Oh! It's *that* leopard," was all Ma'alia said.

For its part, the cat stared at the baby and purred. It approached the baby, eliciting panicked cries from Mideva and Simi. It stopped and turned toward the panicked women. Wind, who had become an interpreter of sorts for the cat, assured them that it meant no harm. He too, approached the child and patted him on the head. The cat, taking the cue, nuzzled the child's side and purred with its eyes closed. Ma'alia showed no fear at all. Satisfied, the cat backed away, went up to Wind, rubbed its flank against his leg, and exited the cave.

"What were you doing with that creature?" Mideva demanded after the cat had left.

"I don't know how to explain that to you," Wind responded, "but we come a long way. Maybe Yossou can explain."

"What are you talking about?" a mystified Yossou asked.

"That, Yossou, is the leopard that almost killed your wife and her unborn child and this, I believe, is its lair. I was going to kill it when I saw it earlier, but something held me back. The rest you have seen for yourselves."

"Are you saying that is the same leopard that mauled you that night?"

"Yes."

"But are you sure..."

"I'm sure it's the same animal and it came back to see the child."

"Great Spirit!" Yossou exclaimed.

"Then there's this thing about the star above us," Simi added. "What does this all mean?"

Ma'alia listened, silently recalling the stranger who called on her nine moons ago and what he had said about the child. His birth in the world of mortals was of great significance. Only time would reveal how and why.

The herdsboys and the stranger had been running for a long time, but felt neither time, distance, nor fatigue. Amit led the way. His brother, Boza, and their friend, Aloni followed closely. Zai and Jambazi, running side by side, came up last. They constantly looked at the star to be sure they were still on course. At one point Zai had called for a halt so he could answer the call of nature. That is when they noticed that the star appeared not to move when they stopped. When they resumed, the star moved again. They figured as long as they were moving, the star would lead them to their destination.

Sujia started back to the hills at a brisk pace. She admitted to herself the brutal pace was a form of self-flagellation. Various scenes of what she had witnessed this evening flashed randomly in her mind. The more vivid the scene, the faster she walked.

After they had established a rhythm, the men started discussing it animatedly and speculating on its significance.

"Did you all see what I saw or was I dreaming?" a man asked.

"No. It wasn't a dream. The leader of spirit warriors and his army descended into the world of men today," another answered.

"All because of a little baby?"

Different men joined the exchange.

"*Ai!* What kind of child is he?"

"You were there, weren't you? Didn't you hear the spirit warrior say the child will bring healing to the land?"

"Apart from the lepers and dogs like us who have been driven to the hills, who needs healing?" the man who had spoken first asked.

"Everybody needs healing," the second man said angrily. "We are all sick in one way or another. I am here because I killed my brother for the simple reason that his cows crossed into my field. Those who sent me here are sick because they do not understand what it feels like to have your mother openly favor your brother. You need healing because you are here for whatever reason your village expelled you. Think about it. Why are we marching in the middle of the night, instead of lying on our bedrolls with our wives, eh? And why are we…"

"Amadi! Amadi! Stop it!" a man shouted. He pointed heavenward. "Listen all of you. The star still beckons. You may follow it if you choose. You saw Jambazi's brain become porridge and he started running with little boys. Go now if that's what you want! Otherwise, shut up and let's go home!"

Sujia also stopped and watched this exchange with tired interest. She watched how the man named Muzo resolved the discussion. She knew he had strong feelings for her but she always kept him at bay. She had noticed his open jealousy when she gave Jambazi or any other man attention. He was clearly a strong leader, but she could control him. She had just found a new deputy. It was time to break him in.

Back in camp, she went straight to her hut and dropped on her bedroll in a tired heap. She kept her knife, bow, and arrows close. She had learned to sleep lightly and still benefit from the rest. By attuning herself to sounds, smells, and everything around her, she could tell when people approached, their manner of approach, and to an extent, their intentions. Some time after she had lain down, she heard a faint rustling close to the door. She grabbed the bow and an arrow.

She listened a little longer, but heard nothing further. Still, she knew someone was still out there.

"Who's there?" she demanded.

"Muzo."

"What do you want?"

"I'm keeping guard out here," he said. "I heard grumbling among the men."

"Go away. I can take care of myself."

She lay back on her bedroll. She did not sleep, but continued to listen to the occasional rustling of her self-appointed bodyguard. Finally, she knew it was useless trying to sleep with all the tension and pent-up emotions. She stood up and went to the entrance of her chamber. The night was relatively light due to the star. She saw Muzo with his spear, seated on his haunches a few paces from the hut. He did not notice her until she called out softly.

"*Weh!*"

He turned to her shadowy form.

"Come," she said.

He hesitated a moment, looked around then and rose to join her at the entrance. She looked up at him. Her eyes were like smooth, dark pebbles. She drew him into the chamber and onto the bedroll. Her hands worked all over his body in slow deliberate patterns. Soon he was breathing heavily with the urgency of desire, but she pushed his hands away each time he tried to advance his intentions. In time, she too was working over him feverishly and the urgency increased until she finally yielded. In frenzied passion, they tore at each other in the heat of desire. When they finished, they were spent.

Not long after, Muzo was snoring heavily. Sujia listened to the thunderous sounds for a while then turned aside and allowed herself to cry. She cried from pain, loneliness, and self-loathing. She would have wanted to see the child about whom the spirit-warrior spoke, but felt she had gone too far, done too much wrong to merit a visit to this child. She had hoped, foolishly, that by indulging herself this way, she would somehow dispel the guilt. Instead, she felt worse. Having so judged herself, she refused to feel anything further. Just before dawn, she fell into troubled sleep unlike the man who snored beside her. *So much for protecting me*. Her last waking thought was how she despised him, all men, and all things spiritual!

About the time a person starts dreaming, the four men sat outside the entrance of the cave talking quietly about the events of the day. Wind asked Yossou about the unusual circumstances of his son's birth. Without divulging such details as his encounter with the man with the strong hand, he admitted that he knew the child would be unique in many ways. He also admitted that he had not expected it would be on such an extent.

"Never in our people's lore did we hear of a star standing above the place where a child was born," Wind said.

"And who ever heard of an animal coming to pay homage to a baby! That is the most incredible thing I have ever witnessed," Sande added.

"Wind, when you first befriended the leopard, how certain were you he wouldn't turn on you?" Juma asked.

Wind raised his chin and thought for a moment.

"I wasn't. At first, I was apprehensive too. I was sure we had encountered the animal earlier. These creatures are not stupid. Once they have suffered at the hand of man, they are unlikely to repeat the mistake. Something else drove it here. Most of all, I saw something in its eyes that was not menacing. Am I making sense?"

"No, but I believe you," Juma admitted.

"That's why I hesitate to talk about how this child came about. It's unfathomable," Yossou added.

"You mean there's more to it?" Juma asked.

"Yes. Even Wind and Sande can tell you… Wind? Wind, what is it?"

Wind had fallen silent and seemed to be listening intently. Suddenly he got down on his hands and knees and put his right ear to the ground. After listening briefly, he raised his head and spoke urgently.

"Get your weapons ready! There're people coming this way. Yossou - back in the cave and make sure everyone remains very quiet. Sande - to the left behind those rocks. Juma, follow me. We may have to fight protect the child. Go now!" He jumped behind a rock to the right. Juma followed closely.

They did not have to wait long. They heard them before the newcomers came into view. Obviously, stealth was not a priority for them. A young boy led the group and two other boys followed. At the rear, an older boy walked alongside a man about Wind's age. This last individual was clearly out of place in the company of the boys. He wore his hair in long unkempt locks and had the rugged features of a hill-dweller. They all kept looking up.

"I think it is somewhere here," the youngest boy said. "If I move this way and that, it doesn't seem to move. If I move this way… Ah! It moves!" he said excitedly as he tested different directions. "It's that way - and very close," he said pointing.

Wind saw the boy make straight for the cave. For the second time in one night, he had to determine whether the approaching party was friend or foe. He had to decide quickly, realizing they had not designated someone to make the call to strike. By the apparent reference to the star, he was certain they would not have to, but he would still have to be careful when revealing his position. The younger boys carried only sticks. The older boy and the man both had spears. Wind was concerned about the wild-looking man. He felt the ground for a small rock, found one and threw it over the intruders' so that it fell behind them. They all turned. Wind decided to take a chance.

"Peace, my friends," he called out from behind the rock. Had there not been the inherent danger in what he was doing, he would have found it funny to see how they all whipped around again. He especially noted the older man's crouching stance. He had pinpointed Wind's voice and both he and the older boy held their spears in an attack posture.

"Friends," Wind said, "you have found what you seek. The star has led you to the child. My friends and I are here to protect the mother and child. If you will lower your weapons, I will show myself. I will not have any in my hands."

The five huddled in a tight group. The man and older boy hesitated briefly before standing straight and lowering their weapons. They appeared to believe Wind because he mentioned the star leading them to the child. There was no way he would have known this detail.

Wind stood up slowly with hands raised high.

"Good evening friends," he said. "We have seen many strange things this night and you have just added to them. Juma, Sande, these are not enemies. The Mighty One has led them here."

Juma stood up beside him, as did Sande on the other side. Wind approached the newcomers. He shook hands with all of them. Sande and Juma did the same.

"Welcome. This is our home for the time being so we welcome you. Come see the child."

He led them toward the cave. At the entrance, he called out for the second time this evening.

"Yossou, if you can believe it, we have more visitors to see the child."

"Woi, Mwaza! What have you brought this time?" Mideva lamented.

Yossou appeared at the entrance and was surprised to see a group of boys and a rough looking man. The boys appeared even more surprised to see him.

"Chi! Are you not Yossou, the man who married Egadwa's niece? I recognize you!" the older boy said.

"Yes indeed. And who are you?"

"I'm Zai. These are my cousins, Boza and Amit and this is our friend, Aloni. We are from Kilima. We just met this man tonight." He addressed the wild-looking man. "I've forgotten your name."

"Jambazi."

"And you've traveled this far so quickly! *Weeh iyah!* Come in! Come in! Your kinswoman, Ma'alia, is the mother of the child you seek."

Yossou led them into the cave. The lamp still burned next to Ma'alia.

Inside, they all fell on their knees before mother and child. Ma'alia sat, her legs crossed in front of her, and the baby in her arms. With the arrival of the four herdsboys and the former bandit, a warm sensation filled the room, engulfing everyone. They broke into songs of praise to the great Oracle - songs that villagers sang during the Feast of Sacrifice.

The offering of praise affected the wild-looking man the most. He broke down, confessing he was bitter and did not deserve to live among decent human beings. He added that he had not valued life. He had accidentally killed his neighbor when they got into a dispute over their children. His village expelled him without listening to what happened. In his bitterness, he said, he had subsequently destroyed other lives. Now he felt his own life was worthless. He cried some more until a long string of snot dangled from his nostrils. Mideva came up to the man put an arm around him and wiped away the snot with some soft leaves they had used earlier. As soon as she placed her hand on him, he started to shake uncontrollably and to groan in an unearthly voice. Mideva jumped back. Suddenly, his demeanor changed. He became belligerent, thrashing around violently on the floor and not allowing anyone to touch him. The room, which only a while ago had been warm and blissful, became cold and oppressive. The man's maniacal shrieking and moaning replaced the singing and praise. The young men who came with him cowered in a corner, eyes wide with fear and disbelief. Simi and Yossou began to entreat The Mighty One on behalf of the stranger.

"Great Oracle, you see the heart of this man. Set his spirit free from the wicked spirits that have taken over his heart," Simi cried out.

"Let it be so!" Yossou agreed.

"Remove the restless spirits that have refused to enter the land of the departed, but cause mischief in the realm of the living."

"Remove them!"

"Set this man free!"

"Set him free!" Simi cried out harder and Yossou echoed her call.

Mideva and Wind, Sande were emboldened as the invocation progressed and they joined Yossou in the response. Even Ma'alia added her voice to the intercession. Meanwhile, Jambazi kicked, shrieked, and cried one moment, then laughed and mocked them the next. His eyes took on a wild look. Thick yellow mucus mixed with dust and plastered his face. As the prayer grew more fervent, his screaming and thrashing became more violent. An unseen force picked him off the ground, and threw him back down, but Simi persisted in prayer and the others responded. Finally, they all noticed something that they had missed with all the noise they made. It was the baby.

"*Aah! Aah!*" he cried.

He seemed to look at the pathetic form on the ground and reach out to him with his left hand. A hush fell over the group. Even the wild man lay still before slowly turning toward the child. The expression that followed - absolute terror and panic, was beyond description.

"No!" He sat up pushing himself backward with his heels. "No! Leave us alone."

The wild-looking man shielded his eyes, but still looked at the baby through his fingers. Finally, his panic was absolute and he let out an ear-piercing, heart-wrenching cry.

"*Nooooo!*"

His body jerked and convulsed like a man who had taken an arrow in the heart. The last convulsion was the most violent, contorting his body and threatening to snap his back. That very instant they all heard a loud *"whoosh!"* like a mighty wind rushing out of the cave. It was so violent it kicked up a cloud of dust and knocked chunks of rock from the entrance. The man lay twisted on the ground. His eyelids flickered rapidly and his breathing gradually became normal. Mucus, sweat, and dirt covered his body. When his eyelids stopped flickering and he opened them, they were no longer wild-looking. Through the grime and sweat, one could tell his skin had lost the leathery sheen and taken on a baby-soft tone, making him look much younger.

He looked up at Simi and said, "Thank you for praying for me, M'ma. Thank you - all of you."

Turning to Ma'alia he said, "You, young lady, are privileged to be the mother of this child. The Mighty One sent him. I saw it with the eyes of my spirit. Because of him, I am free. I now understand what the spirit-warrior meant when he told these boys, 'He will heal the hearts of the people and bring freedom to the land.'"

"What spirit-warrior?" Mideva asked, handing him more straw to clean his nose and face.

"And who are you?" Simi inquired.

"I am Jambazi, originally from Zaniga," he said wiping his nose. "I have dwelt in the hill country for more than seven harvests now. If it were not for the spirit-warrior's words about this child, I might have killed these boys. They can tell you what happened and how we ended up here."

The boys looked at one another and tacitly agreed Zai would tell the story.

"Now that I think about it, this whole thing must have started perhaps nine moons back. Just like today, my cousins and I had taken the animals to the marshes. I saw a cloud in the sky in the shape of a man's fist and wondered..."

Chapter 7

the road to bora-ini

After the better part of a day's march, the stone city of Bora-ini gradually came into view as a cluster of earth colored buildings in the distance. The name *Bora-ini* could mean two things. The most accepted translation was "the place in the rain." This was because the city sat on rolling green hills and valleys and received plenty of precipitation for much of the year. The name also loosely alluded to "goodness of quality." The impressive homes of the elite with whom Tamaa consorted sat at the top of every hill as a testament to quality workmanship. On the tallest hill was Tamaa's palace - an imposing structure even from such a great distance. Around Bora-ini, the landscape was a patchwork of fields of different crops that grew year-round due to plentiful rainfall.

The villagers from Ronge were glad that their destination was in sight. The worst part of the journey, ascending the escarpment, was over. The paths to the city became more defined as they drew closer, indicating heavier human traffic. The vegetation was thick and richer because it rained often in these highlands. The greenery also provided robbers with good hideouts. Due to safety concerns, if even one person stopped, everyone else had to. Early in the journey, Kofi had assumed the task of assigning "relief" zones. It was only mid-morning and already they had stopped five times. The cold seemed to increase frequency of stops.

"Why can't you do it all at once, you people," Avoga complained.

"Men on this side – to my right; women, this side," Kofi called out. "If you're not sure what you are, ask me and I'll squeeze something that will remind you. You hear me Kapsi?"

Laughter followed this last comment. Kapsi, just entering puberty, was guilty of having trespassed into the women's zone on an earlier stop. He surprised Selima and her daughter right in the middle of their business, causing the older woman to soil herself in her hasty rise to preserve modesty. She unleashed a string of epithets that quickly sent him across the gender line. The other males who heard his undignified expulsion, laughed at him mercilessly.

"Did he not hear which way males should go? Or did he not know what he was," they laughed. He bore the brunt of their jokes whenever the issue of nature's call came up.

The rest of the afternoon was uneventful though there was much that was fascinating around them. They marveled at the variety of plant life. This place had more fruit species than the most fertile areas in Gololi. If one did not crave meat, a person could easily live on plants that grew wild. Since most of them had never traveled far from Gololi, they were surprised that a place could get this cold. Children complained the most and clung to their mothers for warmth.

After recounting the events leading up to their visit to the child, the herdsboys answered many questions from Yossou and the other men as they roasted and ate small game Wind and Sande had caught. They boys had many questions of their own and the discussion continued deep into the night. The women had already fallen asleep. Finally, Yossou suggested that they should also go to sleep because they would all leave early in the morning.

The sense of peace had returned to the cave after the heart-rending session with Jambazi. Little else seemed to matter. No one even suggested posting a guard to look out for wild animals, though they lit a fire by the cave entrance. Soon, all were fast asleep.

Some time in the night, Amit woke up to relieve himself. It was still dark, but he knew it would not be long before the sun chased the darkness away. He heard breathing and snoring all around him, and after working out his bearings to avoid treading on anyone, he gingerly picked his way over bodies. At the entrance, he stepped on a hot ember.

"*Ai yah!*" he sucked air through clenched teeth and hopped back clutching his foot. Now aware of the fire, Amit exited the cave to the welcome of a crisp, gentle breeze. He yawned, twisting his body and stretching, enjoying the sensation as his muscles loosened. He observed that the light that had led them to the cave was no longer in the sky. He dropped his eyes concluding his yawn with a contented, "*Aakhhh!*" He rubbed his arms to blunt the chill of the air. As he did so, a slight movement caught his eye. When he realized what he beheld, he jumped back terrified. A pair of yellow eyes moved slightly when he jumped. Amit inched back, feeling his way and quickly ducked inside. He stepped on the embers again, but this time it was the least of his concerns. His sudden entry woke the others.

"What is it?" Wind asked.

"There's an animal outside." Wind felt for his machete and was already at the entrance. He heard movements behind him. Carefully, he stepped outside the cave, weapon ready. He was looking for a pair of bright eyes. And there they were. They looked at each other for a moment.

"Good morning brother," Wind said. Sande and Juma also emerged from the cave. He spread his arms to prevent them from getting past him or taking any rash action. The cat picked up the carcass of a small antelope and laid it at Wind's feet. In what was now becoming a ritual, it rubbed its length against his leg. In turn, he patted its flanks.

"I guess our friend has brought us something to eat. Thank you, friend."

"How did you do that?" Amit asked from behind Juma.

"Do what?"

"Make friends with the leopard just like that?"

Wind spoke as he patted the leopard's neck. "Let's not try to make sense of what the Oracle has ordained. *Enzi!* Since we are already up, let's get a fire going. We travel today."

"We also need to get back to our herd," Zai added.

"And I need to go somewhere," Jambazi said pensively.

"Where will you go?" Zai asked.

"I don't know."

"Come with us. You can live in our village."

"No. I'll only bring you trouble. Even as I shed my past, the consequences of my actions will always follow me. Thank you for the offer, though."

"My father has much land and many animals. If you change your mind, look us up in Kilima," Amit offered.

"Thank you."

Jambazi noticed Wind struggling to remove the hide from the carcass of the antelope.

"Wind, it's no shame to ask for help. Let me help you skin that animal."

Juma had dug up the embers from the ashes of the fire and thrown a few dry twigs and grass onto it. He blew over it a few times and the embers glowed red. With a little more coaxing, the flames caught. He added larger twigs and soon the fire crackled happily as it mocked the morning chill. Wind and Jambazi drained the animal's blood into every horn available. As they did so, they talked about trapping, hunting, weapons, game, and a host of other things. In Jambazi, Wind found a kindred spirit. Together, they skinned the animal, gutted it, and laid the intestines and internal organs on the hide.

"Keep the liver and kidneys for the young mother," Jambazi said. "She will need the strength in them to make the baby's milk."

"Good idea. We'll have the innards first and dry out what meat is left for the journey." He cut off a thigh and offered it to the leopard, which lay on the ground casually observing them. The cat just sniffed it and looked away.

"Oh, you are full already," Wind said. "You are a kind, clever cat." He cut the intestines into segments roughly equal to the number of the men present.

"*Oi!* Each of you fetch a stick and come roast your own strip of intestines," he told the men. He proceeded to roast strips for himself and the women.

"Don't eat the entire animal by yourselves. We have mouths too," a voice shouted from the cave.

Yossou clicked his tongue in annoyance. Only Mideva could put a damper on a person's best intentions. He soon forgot about it as they roasted a skewered strip of intestines. Whatever the antelope had last eaten provided additional nutrition. Nothing was wasted. The brain, the tongue, and even the eyes and snout were much loved delicacies. They would crush the bones to get to the marrow. The bones would make handles and small implements. Its hide would make modesty patches or breast coverings for married women. The tail would become a flywhisk for an elder while the hooves could form part of a necklace, or an amulet. The Oracle was good to send them food by way of the leopard.

When the strips were ready, Yossou took them to the women. Wind gave the head to the boys. They stuffed it into the fire and carefully controlled the roasting to burn off the skin and still cook the brain and tissue. Wind and Jambazi continued to cut the meat into portions, which they handed to Sande and Juma to roast. Everyone would have enough for the journey. With little else happening, the leopard got bored. It stood up, stretched, yawned, and wandered off to the rocks beyond the cave.

Yossou skewered the liver and kidneys and held them over the fire just enough to cook them without drying them. He found three smooth stones and stuck them in the fire. When they were hot, he took them out and put them in the drinking horns full of blood. They sizzled briefly and submerged. He let them sit until the blood was hot enough to scald the unwary drinker. He then fished them out and took the food to the women. Ma'alia sat up, holding the baby in her right arm as he suckled noisily. With her left hand, she accepted the kidney. She muttered a prayer and began to eat. A strange sensation welled inside Yossou's stomach when he looked at the boy. He swallowed hard. All the women caught the moment and understood instinctively.

"Do you want to hold your son?" Ma'alia asked, smiling.

"Only briefly," Yossou said sheepishly. "I haven't handled anything so delicate in a while."

"He may be delicate, but he's not an egg. Here." Yossou handed the horn to his mother before taking the child.

The baby just stretched and yawned with clenched fists and legs constantly in motion. The women all looked on, smiling at the tender moment between father and son. Simi handed the horn to Ma'alia.

While the women ate, Yossou said, "We have to get moving soon, but we have to decide whether to continue the journey to Bora-ini or go back home. If we go back, we'll have to make this journey again - even you Ma'alia. Tamaa does not accept excuses from his subjects. On the other hand, if we continue, we'll do so as a much smaller group and bandits or animals could easily attack us. We have to decide one way or another."

"I'd rather do it now and get over with it," Mideva said. "After all, it only takes place once every five harvests.

"If Ma'alia is able to walk to Bora-ini then I would rather travel today," Simi said. "I'm too old to start this journey over."

"I'll be able to walk M'ma," Ma'alia said with her mouth full.

"The only thing you'll need is plenty of water so you can have enough milk for the baby," Mideva pointed out.

"I have a little left in my gourd. I'm sure there are streams along the way where we can refill," Simi said.

"Good. Let me check with the men. I'm sure they feel the same way." Yossou handed the baby back to Ma'alia and went outside where the men were still roasting meat.

"I was talking to the ladies about continuing to Bora-ini or returning to start over with the second group."

"By the Oracle, no! Who wants to do this again?" Sande blurted out.

"Slow down, son. Listen. The women would rather complete the journey since it takes place every five harvests. The only concern I have is for our safety since we are a smaller group. Remember there are bandits and wild animals along the way."

"And we have to get back to the animals in the marshes. My uncle will not be happy to learn that we left them alone all night." Zai jumped in and turned to his cousins. He was surprised at their calm demeanor.

Amit smiled and said, "I don't know what will happen, but I'm glad we came."

"This child is wise beyond his years," Wind observed of Amit. He turned to Yossou. "We'll just have to take our chances. I'd be more worried about bandits than wild animals. Besides, the others should be starting back tomorrow. I'm sure some of them would be willing to wait for us on the return journey, and if they won't... well... The Mighty One is with us."

This last statement closed the argument. All were quiet for some time, pondering what he said. Yossou broke the silence.

"All right. Once you finish roasting the meat, we leave. We want to travel as far as possible while it's still cool."

About mid-afternoon, the group from Ronge began to encounter more people traveling alone or in small groups, meaning they were probably making short local trips. To the Baronge, they were a little strange, because they stepped off the path completely to stand several paces away when the group approached. They stared at the travelers from the time they appeared to the time they disappeared from view. They also did not return greetings. However, nothing could have prepared them for what they witnessed next.

Approaching a small outpost known as Matunda, they came upon a scene that they could not figure out at first. Realization came upon all of them at the same time. The macabre sight made mothers shield their children's eyes so they would see no more. Queasy villagers vomited. Most though, were fascinated and kept looking, trying to make sense of it.

No. That's not a human being. No one would do that to fellow man. Wiki-Zugu could not turn away as he debated with himself. Like him, the rest, were petrified and for some time no one moved. Finally, he overcame his revulsion and called out.

"Come on. Let's get out of here. Move!"

The spectacle rattled even the normally confident Kofi. He remained rooted to the spot, shaking his head.

"Great Father!" he said repeatedly.

The man who hung on the tree was completely naked. His crumpled body leaned forward, his hands nailed to branches spread out in opposing directions. The downward draw of his weight had torn his blackened hands. Jagged lines traced their way across his chest from his back. Whatever drew those lines had broken skin and come away with chunks of flesh. Powerful blows with a blunt object had shattered both his legs, the lower portions of which had pierced the skin and stuck out like stumps of small trees. Even in death, the agony he had undergone still showed on his face. His deeply furrowed brow, open mouth, and the dried tears, mucus, and dust that caked his face all froze his dying moments. Flies buzzed around the cadaver in a muted high-pitch *sostenuto* - a fitting accompaniment to his silent scream. Ants completed the grisly picture, almost obliterating him from view as they crawled in and out of every orifice to make the most of the tissue.

"That shocks you, eh?"

The speaker was a powerfully built warrior. The Baronge were surprised he spoke Kigololi.

"Yes," Wiki-Zugu spoke finally. "We've never seen anything like it. What did he do?"

"We caught him stealing from a group like yours on its way to the count," the warrior explained. "Nobody touches Great Tamaa's treasures and lives. Who are you? I take it you are going to the count."

"Yes. I am Wiki-Zugu, son of Oungouk, from the village of Ronge. We started our journey yesterday morning. We're hoping to make it to Bora-ini by nightfall."

"You don't have much further to go. If you don't stop too often, you'll be there before dark. Be careful of the likes of him when you get there," he added. "They are always trying to take advantage of strangers. That's why we make an example of them whenever we catch one."

"Thank you for the advice. We'll be going now. Stay well."

"Travel well."

The Baronge began to leave. A band of warriors sitting in the shade of a large tree heckled them as they moved on. They made lewd suggestions to the women and a few who spoke Kigololi ridiculed the men, calling them shepherds of women who could not fight.

After shaking hands with the men, the herdsboys went into the cave to bid the women farewell. Each bowed in reverence before the baby, uttering blessings upon him. Then they began the trek back to the marshes at a trot. With time, the confidence Amit felt about the venture began to wane as apprehension as to what may have befallen the animals in their absence grew. He knew how his father felt about his livestock. The others also shared the same concerns and the pace increased rapidly.

"Come on! Hurry up!" Amit urged. "We've got to get back soon. Father will be mad to know we left the animals by themselves all night."

"Oh, stop it," Boza cut in. "Aren't you the one who said nothing could take what you witnessed away from you? In any case, it doesn't matter how fast we run now. If anything were to happen to the animals, it has already happened and rushing won't make a difference."

Aloni added, "It's true nothing can compare to what we saw." He stopped running and walked. The others slowed down too. "You know, I think we are greatly privileged that the spirit-warriors chose us to receive the message of the star and to see the child. I think we ought to tell everyone about it."

"Will they believe us?" Zai asked. "Many older folk have never seen a spirit-warrior except in visions and dreams. They'll ask how the Oracle would reveal such things to mere herdsboys like us."

"Whether or not they believe us is not our problem. We can only tell them what the spirit warrior said about the child and what we saw. We owe them at least that much. Besides, the people at the cave are our witnesses."

"You're right, Aloni," Zai agreed. "This night we've seen a great thing. It will always stay with me."

"Me too," Boza said. "I believe the One who made us follow the star is watching over the animals in our absence too."

"Yes."

They continued at a less frantic pace.

After the boys had left, Wind turned to Jambazi. "We'll continue to Bora-ini. What are you going to do? Will you go back to the hill country or would you like to come with us?"

"No. I cannot go back to the hill country. That life is now behind me, but I'm still a marked man. I can go with you as far as the escarpment, but not beyond that. My people banished me for life. With the clans going to the count, someone may recognize me and raise a cry. They will kill me on sight and perhaps all of you as well. No. I'll try to find a new life beyond the lands of the Avantu."

"You are going to wander these plains alone?" Wind asked incredulously. "You're a dead man if I knew one."

"If I die on the way, so be it. I will have died trying."

"Do what you must. We understand," Wind conceded. He turned to Yossou. "Are we ready to move on then?"

"Yes. Let's go."

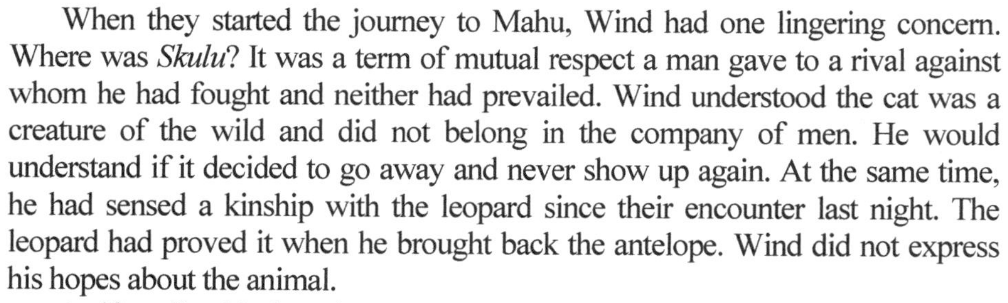

When they started the journey to Mahu, Wind had one lingering concern. Where was *Skulu*? It was a term of mutual respect a man gave to a rival against whom he had fought and neither had prevailed. Wind understood the cat was a creature of the wild and did not belong in the company of men. He would understand if it decided to go away and never show up again. At the same time, he had sensed a kinship with the leopard since their encounter last night. The leopard had proved it when he brought back the antelope. Wind did not express his hopes about the animal.

As if reading his thoughts, Sande asked, "Wind, where's your new friend?"

"I don't know. He's probably found a better way to spend his time rather than consort with stupid humans with nothing better to do than travel four days back and forth to have their heads counted."

Everybody chuckled at Wind's response.

"Or maybe he has already seen what he had to see, just like me and the herdsboys - that baby," Jambazi pointed to the infant in Simi's arms.

"You are probably right. Just like the boys and yourself, the spirits must have led him to the baby just for that purpose."

The day grew warmer as the Baronge descended to the lower lands away from the escarpment. The thick vegetation played host to all kinds of insects that harassed them at every opportunity. They each had a halo of hundreds of tiny bugs flying just above their heads. It would have been funny except the little creatures never left them alone. Water was the one thing about which they did not have to worry. Streams of cool, sweet water snaked all the valleys. They also ate of the abundant wild fruits and plants along the way to supplement the dried meat.

By the time Wiki-Zugu and his people reached the environs of Bora-ini, everyone was tired and irritable. All they wanted was to sit down and rest. They could see the camps the authorities had set up around the city and were amazed at how crowded the streets were. The people spoke different languages, reflecting the expanse of Tamaa's jurisdiction and Xhaka's empire.

As they approached the camps, a group of hawkish individuals rushed up to them, all talking at once. The people of Baronge were confused and uncertain what to do.

"What do these men want?" a woman asked.

"Ah! You are Bagololi," one of the men said, sensing linguistic advantage. "Do you need a place to stay tonight? I have just the place for you. Come with me. Are these your children? Let's go." He attempted to drag the woman, Adisa, away by the arm.

"*Weh!* Let me go," she cried, pulling away her arm. It was disrespectful for a man to touch a woman in front of her husband. Shimei, the husband, reached for his machete and advanced on the offender. Avoga rushed forward and stayed Shimei's hand while pushing the other man away.

"No," he told Shimei. "Not here. We are not in our land."

Wiki-Zugu spoke next. "Be very careful. Don't let someone drag you off otherwise we won't be able to find you." He turned to the touts. "We are all together. We need a place to spend the night before we go to the count tomorrow."

A tall thin man stepped out of the group and took Wiki-Zugu's arm.

"Yes, yes. I have a place for you. How many people do you have? A hundred, maybe?"

"*Eh heh,*" Wiki-Zugu agreed. "A handful stayed behind with a woman who was about to give birth on the way."

"Really? I hope she's fine. I know our women are of hardy stock, but it's still difficult to give birth away from home. So he will be another *Enzira*, eh?"

He steered Wiki-Zugu and the Baronge to a patchwork of fenced sections, some of which other travelers already occupied. Wiki-Zugu laughed softly, glad for the chance to talk to an outsider.

"I don't know. There's a bit of a story about him - something about a spirit-being appearing to the mother, saying he should have a different name from that of his lineage. She said the spirit-being mentioned something like he will be king of the Avantu."

The hawkish man stiffened for just an instant.

"King of the Avantu, eh?" He laughed, but there was no mirth in his voice. "Well, his parents certainly have high expectations for him already. Ah, here we are." He led them to a vacant enclosure. "How long will you be staying?"

"Just one night," answered Wiki-Zugu. "We travel back home tomorrow after we've been counted."

"That's fine. For this place I normally take three hundred cowry shells, but because you've come a long way, I'll take two hundred and fifty."

"How then, have you helped us? I thought it goes for a hundred only. We paid fifty when I was here for the last count."

"That was five harvests back. Things have since changed. Tamaa is demanding more taxes from us, so we ask a little more from you. Make it two hundred. I won't take less than that."

"A hundred and fifty?"

"I won't do it. You'll have to go elsewhere."

Wiki-Zugu saw the pained expressions on the faces of his people gathered around him. He understood how they felt. Like them, he was tired and the haggling was sapping his last reserve of energy.

"Fine. We'll take it for two hundred."

"Good," the man said.

Wiki-Zugu nodded to Anaya who was the keeper of the purse on the journey. He counted out ten leather strings each bearing twenty shells and gave them to the hawkish man.

"And your friends - the ones who are having a baby, when do they plan to get here?" he asked as he placed the shells in a leather pouch.

"I don't know. We didn't talk about that when we parted. I assumed they would continue, but they may decide to go back home and start over with the next group.

"Well, if you run into them, tell them to ask for Salit and I'll take care of them. I thank you. Have a good visit and I hope the count goes well for you tomorrow."

"Thank you."

Wiki-Zugu turned to acquaint himself with his surroundings and to find a spot where he could sit down.

"Over here, Baba," Kofi waved at him from a spot next to a tree.

Wiki-Zugu hobbled over and sat down, sighing heavily.

"*Woi!* These old bones!" he said when he realized how tired he was.

The villagers had spread out over the enclosure. Children had already found sticks and stones with which they could play. Adults either sat or lay down. Some were already snoring. In the neighboring enclosure, the occupants had two fires going. Over one, men roasted a portion of a cow while on another, a heavyset woman wrestled with *chima* in a large pot. The aroma wafted across to the Baronge and made their stomachs growl.

Seeing their eyes rove hungrily toward their neighbors' cooking, a man with a toothy smile sauntered to the fence and beckoned Kofi over. Avoga joined them.

"*Lo!* You people look very hungry," he piped. "I am sure you'd all love a hot meal after a long day of travel. Not so?" He laughed as if it was the funniest thing he had heard.

"Correct," Kofi said hesitantly.

The man leaned forward, speaking in a conspiratorial voice with rather exaggerated gestures.

"The name is Bongo. Bongo can get you everything you need - firewood, pots, water, flour, and meat.

"What's the fee?" asked Kofi.

"Three hundred cowry shells for a half a cow or two goats, two hundred for vegetables, a hundred and fifty for the meal and water. You will find it easier if you let Bongo provide everything. You can't trust everyone on an occasion like this with so many people. Not so?"

"And we should trust you?" Avoga asked.

Irritation flashed in the man's eyes for an instant.

"That's up to you. If you think you can find your way in this confusion by yourselves you're welcome to it."

"Let's confer among ourselves then we'll let you know," Kofi said.

They went to consult Wiki-Zugu under the tree. Other men and women gathered around them. After a brief discussion, Kofi and Avoga called the man over.

"We'll take the offer. Bring us the half cow."

"Good," he said, smiling to reveal discolored, misshapen teeth. "That will be six hundred shells altogether. Now, if you'll just hand it to me, I'll go order your food."

"Shouldn't we wait until you've brought the food before we pay you?" Anaya asked.

"Oh, I have to pay the livestock traders and the farmers before they can let me have the produce. That's why I need to go with the payment. Don't worry. This is what Bongo does for a living. I'm here everyday taking care of people from all over the land for the count, to trade, to pay taxes - whatever. Any of the people you see here can tell you where to find me, so don't worry about anything. Trust Bongo."

Wiki-Zugu hesitated, but Bongo flashed another smile and tapped him lightly on the shoulder.

"Look. See over there?" He pointed to what looked like a collection of small buildings with a large animal pen behind them. "That's where I buy meat for travelers like you. I have a group of women who bring water, flour, and firewood to my customers every day. As I said, this is what I do for a living. Why would Bongo want to destroy his livelihood?"

Wiki-Zugu relented.

"Alright." He looked up at Anaya. "Give him the money. He knows his way around here better than we do."

"Uh… Right," Anaya said hesitantly. He counted out the shells and handed them to the smiling Bongo.

"Good. Bongo will be back with your food soon."

With that, he made his way toward the buildings he had indicated.

Wiki-Zugu settled himself more comfortably against the tree. Anaya squatted beside him. Avoga, Kofi, and a few other men joined them. They talked about all that had transpired along the way and what they thought about Bora-ini. The sun was setting and the light fading. The group in the enclosure next to them had finished cooking and settled down to eat. The Baronge children went up to the fence and stared shamelessly while their neighbors ate.

"You'll give us the big eye," some men told the children in Kigololi, alluding to the belief that if a person ate while another watched, the eye of the person who ate without sharing would swell to a hideous size.

"Surely our food should be here by now," Anaya commented after a while.

"You'd think so," Avoga agreed.

Wiki-Zugu did not say anything. A sense of disquiet began to grow in him. He recalled a nagging doubt he had felt about Bongo, the overly friendly broker, and wondered if he should have heeded his instincts then.

"Let's give him time. He should be back soon," he said, ignoring the snide remarks some women made about food and hunger. Though seemingly random, Wiki-Zugu knew the comments were for his benefit.

"I'm going to find that fellow," Kofi said, picking up his spear.

Avoga also took his weapon. "I'm coming with you.

"Be careful," Wiki-Zugu warned again.

Kofi and Avoga started their search in the direction the vendor had said he obtained his supplies. After a long search, they failed to see a face they recognized as Bongo. As the sun went down, they were wandering among the stalls at the trading square as it emptied of people. Most merchants were in the process of packing their wares. Porters carried the bulky *junzi* sacks on their backs to nearby warehouses. Kofi stopped to talk to a couple of merchants who were piling wares into sacks. He chose the pair because they could make out much of what the vendors said.

"Peace!" he saluted them, raising his right hand while holding his spear upright in his left. Avoga stood behind him in the same posture. One man righted himself and grunted a response. His friend also stopped what he was doing and regarded the visitors.

"We hope your day has gone well and the Oracle has blessed your efforts," Kofi continued.

In halting Kigololi interspersed with words they did not know, the man responded.

"Oh, it was not a good day. We sat here all day and barely traded anything. Look at all the items we have to take back."

Vendors in adjacent stalls also stopped their work and watched. After the perfunctory exchange of civilities, Kofi broached the purpose of their visit.

"Friend, as you can tell, we are not from here. We have come for the count. We've traveled two days from the village of Ronge in the lands back that way," he pointed toward the setting sun.

"You've come far indeed."

"Yes. We've eaten nothing but the dried meat we carried and the wild fruits we picked along the way. Our women and children are hungry. This evening we wanted a hot meal so we may regain our strength for the journey back tomorrow."

"*Ei!* Even a mighty warrior needs to get his strength back after such a journey."

"*Eh heh!* When we got here, we paid Bongo for food. He said he would bring us meal, a goat, water, a pot, and firewood. Quite some time has passed and we haven't seen him. Where can we find him?"

The merchants looked bemused.

"We don't know who Bongo is. There are all sorts of traders, brokers, and touts in this city. But you say you paid the man already?"

"Yes."

By now, a crowd had gathered.

"You say you paid the man in advance and he promised to return with the things you requested, eh?"

"Yes." Kofi did not like where this was going.

The merchant looked askance at the visitors. He scratched his beard and it rasped loudly erupting in a cloud of tiny flakes visible against the sunset. By his demeanor, it was clear he was trying to decide whether the men before him were naïve or plain stupid. Finally he spoke.

"The man has swindled you, my friend. Bongo may not even be his name. No one in his right mind pays another before he holds what he is buying in his hand. Not in Bora-ini."

There was a snicker from the crowd, which quickly grew into open laughter, finger pointing, and comments. The man with whom they talked laughed too, though a little more sympathetically. But he switched to a rapid exchange in vernacular with his colleague so the visitors would not understand what they said.

"Let's get out of here," Kofi told Avoga. He did not know whether to be angry or disappointed. They left amidst laughter. Back on the dusty street, they stopped to ponder the next step.

"What now?" Avoga asked.

"I think those merchants are right. That rat conned us. I had a bad feeling about him anyway."

Avoga saw a group of men under a large tree taking down chunks of dried game meat displayed on metal hooks, hefting them onto their backs and carrying them toward a line of buildings.

"Let's look over there one last time," he suggested.

Halfway there, something did not quite feel right. The laughter stopped and people now looked at them with foreboding. Kofi and Avoga looked at one another in puzzlement. They saw shadowy movements on the fringes of the crowd. That signaled trouble. Instinctively, they stopped and stood back-to-back with spears ready. It was pointless. Ten warriors surrounded them and approached with slow, menacing strides, shields raised, and spears pointing at them. With each step they took, the warriors tapped their shields with their spears. The circle grew smaller until the warriors were only a few paces away. Their leader barked an order. One of the words he uttered was akin to the Kigololi word for "spear." The pair hesitated. The warrior repeated the order this time shaking his spear and pointing to the ground.

"Lay down your spear," Avoga told Kofi.

They simultaneously bent their knees and laid their spears on the ground, keeping their eyes on the warriors. As soon as they were upright, the lead warrior shouted.

"*Hiiyah!*"

Immediately, four warriors charged Avoga and Kofi at full speed. They slammed into the pair with their shields, knocking the wind out of them. The attackers gingerly stepped back after impact, leaving the men wobbly and in great pain.

"*Hiiyah!*"

Another quartet ran into Kofi and Avoga. They took the blows on their heads, the force of which drove them into each other. The shield-bearing warriors, propelled by their own momentum, slammed into the men once more. This time neither could stay up. They fell to the ground, their noses bleeding and with cuts to their heads and forearms. A curtain of blackness, spotted by tiny capricious lights, overcame each man and they passed out before strong hands dragged them off.

Mahu had developed naturally as the point of intersection of three trade routes to the land of the Vasua, to Bora-ini facing the rising sun, and to Gololi and other lands, facing the setting sun. Late that afternoon, Wind could make out the outpost, which showed up as a dark streak on the landscape at the base of the escarpment. Wisps of smoke rising skyward marked it as a place of human habitation.

He led the way as they walked single file, bantering, and occasionally breaking into song. Jambazi grew increasingly pensive. The others did not try to draw him out. Soon, they would have to face the inevitable. Jambazi would be leaving. He had made it clear other communities of the Avantu should not see him. When they got to a fork on the trail with one part leading in the direction of the upper plains, he stopped.

"Friends, this is where we part. I'll take this trail to wherever it leads."

Like the rest, his eyes were red from squinting against the sun. Beads of sweat clung to his forehead, nose, and upper lip, which quivered slightly as he spoke. Everyone was sad that this moment had come. They felt that together they had all experienced something beautiful, something that linked them inextricably.

"We'll miss you," Yossou said.

"Yes, we will," Sande agreed.

Wind put his left hand on Jambazi's right shoulder.

"Brother, there's a reason why the Oracle brought you out of the hills. Perhaps it is to share this marvelous story with people in distant lands. May the Oracle be with you. I know he will keep you, even in the valley of death."

"Thank you," Jambazi said.

He wiped his eyes with the back of his hand. Wind patted him on the shoulder twice then moved on. Yossou, Sande, and Juma came up and did the same. Mideva took her turn and bowed before him with hands clasped together. When Ma'alia tried to bow, Jambazi stepped back in near panic.

"No. I'll not allow you, the mother of this child, to bow before me."

He fell to his knees then prostrated himself with his forehead to the ground. He remained prone for a while. Simi and the rest of the party did not dare to interrupt the deeply intimate and personal act of worship. Finally, he stood and touched the baby briefly.

"My Lord and Master." He stepped back and raised his right hand. "Go in peace, friends."

"Peace be with you, too," they all answered.

Jambazi switched the spear to his right hand and hit the trail. After several paces, he turned round and stopped, raised his spear high and jabbed the air three times - the sign of victory in battle. The radiance that suffused his countenance completely erased the furrows of bitterness and hard living he had born when they first met him. They saw a changed man. He turned to resume his journey with purposeful stride.

Wind nodded slowly.

"He has seen the Oracle."

Chapter 8

tough encounters

Late that afternoon, they got to the outskirts of Mahu. The small but important center was a cluster of mud huts with an open section in the middle where its leaders made pronouncements. On a rare visit from one of Tamaa's lackeys, this too, is where he would make known the Governor's edicts. Here, traders from all corners gathered to sell and barter their goods. This season, though, commerce was down due to the count. Most traders had gone to Bora-ini to take advantage of the increased number of visitors.

With their destination in sight, the pace and energy of the little band picked up a notch as they became confident no harm would come upon them by way of a surprise attack. The path had widened to allow two or three adults to walk side-by-side. All the men were in front. Ma'alia, now carrying the baby, walked side by side with Mideva. Simi brought up at the rear. They all looked forward to a solid meal of *chima* with vegetables and stew, and rest.

Thunk! An arrow whizzed over their heads and lodged in the trunk of an acacia tree. The men were first to react. They ducked and stayed low.

"Down!" Wind shouted to the women. "Get down!" Looking at the arrow, he tried to determine its point of origin. He looked toward the slightly higher elevations beyond the path. He did not see anyone, but he knew that their assailants were hiding in the bushes further up. He was also sure there was more than one attacker.

"Do you see anything?" Sande asked as he peered in the distance.

"No, but they are up there," Wind indicated with a nod.

"What shall we do?" Yossou asked.

"We don't know who they are and how many. These bushes won't provide enough protection. We can't fight, so we'll just have to show them we have no ill-intent," Wind said.

"Meaning?"

"I don't know yet. That arrow may have been a warning. They would have taken all of us out by now if they wanted to finish us. Let's wait a little and see."

After a long time, Wind stood up, still looking at the foliage from where the arrow came. He hoped by this time those who shot at them would realize they came in peace.

"Stand up. Let's start walking," he urged.

They all stood and took tentative strides to continue their journey. Wind saw a slight movement behind some bushes and rocks from where the first arrow had come.

"Down!" he shouted and hit the ground hard just as a second arrow found its mark below the first. Everyone went down once more.

"What is going on?" Yossou asked in irritation. "What have we done?"

"I don't know, Yossou," Wind said, wincing. He had aggravated the injury when he ducked. "They don't want us to move. The sun will soon set and they will surround us under cover of darkness. We'll have nowhere to go. I think they are toying with us. Let's hope they'll let us live."

"Can we get away when it gets dark?"

"And go where? Those men are skilled with bow and arrow." He jabbed his thumb toward the arrows in the tree. "Besides they have the patience of a python. They'll wait us out as long as they have to."

"Why don't we just surrender?"

"I'm not sure how we do that. Their intentions are unclear. From how they have behaved so far, this is pure sport to them."

"So we just sit here and wait?"

"Yes." Wind stiffened. "I think there are people coming our way."

"People coming this way?" Yossou asked.

In response, Wind turned to face the direction from which they had come. Soon, against the rays of the tired afternoon sun, they saw a cloud of dust. They watched and waited to see who was coming and how it would affect their situation. By the time the shadows increased by the length of arm, they could make out a group of people, but without detail. The people disappeared from view where the land dipped, later reappearing like shimmering apparitions against the horizon. The group from Ronge watched in anticipation as the larger group approached. A familiar figure led the company.

"Lemba!" Ma'alia exclaimed on recognizing the group from Ngoma. She was about to get up to greet her kinsman when she remembered the arrows that pinned them down. She stayed put.

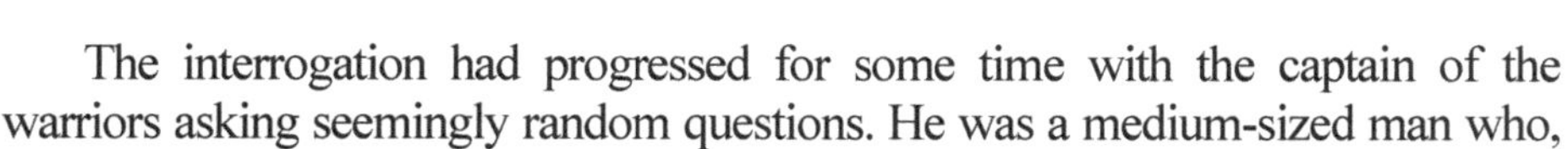

The interrogation had progressed for some time with the captain of the warriors asking seemingly random questions. He was a medium-sized man who, by the scars on his face and body, had seen many battles. A hideous scar ran from the corner of his right eye down the cheekbone, tapering a short distance from the mouth. Other scars embossed on his powerful chest and muscular arms. His voice, though not deep, bore the timbre of authority. Two of his deputies stood behind Kofi in the dimly lit room. The single fat-burning lamp fixed on one wall threw eerie shadows against opposing walls.

"Who is King of the Avantu?" he asked Avoga.

"Xhaka."

"Xhaka," the captain sneered. He paused a moment then turned to Kofi.

"Hit him!"

Kofi looked confused.

"Did you hear what I said? Hit him."

Still confused, Kofi asked, "Why?"

"Why? Because I said so, that's why. Hit him!"

"I can't. He has done no wrong."

The captain spoke slowly and softly, but the voice carried the undertone of a deadly threat.

"No? That's fine. I'll just send for that old man leading your group. Then perhaps you'll stop asking questions and do as I tell you."

"No, no! Don't harm Sakul Wiki-Zugu!"

"Well, then…?"

Kofi made a half-hearted show of hitting Avoga on the chest. It was more of a shove than a blow and it caused him no discomfort.

"*Hah!*" the captain laughed scornfully. "I asked you to hit him, not fondle him. Kato, show this peasant what I mean."

The blow took Kofi completely by surprise, sending fiery waves of pain through his entire body. He fell to his knees, holding the left side of his back just below the ribs. Whoever hit him did it with the express intention of hurting the unprotected organs inside the body.

"*Hakhhh! Woooi!*" he gasped.

"*Eh heh!* I think you get the idea. Get up!" Kofi rose using his right hand for support. With his left, he soothed his injured side.

"*Bas!* Let's try again. Hit him"

This time, Kofi delivered a more telling blow. Avoga fell to the ground groaning in pain. Kofi looked away and continued to nurse his side.

"Very good," the captain said nodding. "Now we are having fun!" He said to Avoga. "Get up on your knees. Again, who is King of the Avantu?"

"The Great Xhaka."

"Oh, you learn fast!" He paused. "Now, I hear in your dunghill of a village you've declared some obscure infant to be King of the Avantu. Who is this child?"

"Sir, I have no idea of what you speak."

The captain motioned to Kofi who shook his head pleadingly. The captain merely furrowed his brow in a subtle signal to the shadow.

This time Kofi's right side exploded. He fell forward taking Avoga down with him. As if that was not enough, he vomited on his friend's neck and shoulder. The warrior's blow impressed the captain.

"Wah! Very nice!"

"Thank you, *Afande*."

"Get up! I need answers. I don't have all night."

At that moment, they heard scuffing in an adjacent chamber. A man was pleading as he was bundled into the chamber unceremoniously. The second voice belonged to a terrified woman who whimpered constantly. A third voice demanded something of the couple. Kofi and Avoga did not understand what they said, but from the context, it had something to do with taxes. In the ensuing exchange, they figured that the two had not paid their taxes and were here to answer for it. The man was either pleading for more time or promising he would make good on his debt. It seemed the interrogator would have none of it.

The captain apparently thought what was going on next door might enlighten present company because he crossed his arms and listened with his eyes on the two villagers and a smirk on his face. In the period that followed, the interrogator next door asked the man a series of questions punctuated with beatings. At times the man howled horribly, and Kofi and Avoga could only imagine what part of his anatomy they were squeezing. The woman's wailing rose with his cries of agony. A relatively quiet period followed when the punishment subsided.

But there was worse to come. The questions continued and the man still pleaded his case. Then the interrogator made a suggestion that drew the most earnest pleas yet. The man begged desperately.

"No, please! No!"

A new level of panic entered the woman's voice as she too, joined in. Now both man and wife cried shamelessly, begged, made promises, and pleaded against whatever the interrogator had just threatened. He disregarded their pleas and called out.

"Afande!" several distant voices shouted back in response.

He rattled off another order and from their tone, the respondents sounded eager to comply and approached. By this time, the man was talking hysterically. The interrogator tried to shut him up, but he pleaded even more. On another order, they heard urgent shuffling and remarks from an eager, gruff voice. Men whooped and hollered as a man began to grunt and breathe heavily to the pulse of a smacking sound. The husband howled pitifully. The woman's voice sounded pained and traumatized. Kofi and Avoga looked down and covered their ears. They could not bear to listen. It ended in an explosive, gasping cry. Another heavy breather took over and it went on for a long time. When it was all over, the man was babbling like an infant and the woman whined at a strained high pitch, calling repeatedly for her mother.

"That was interesting, wasn't it?" The captain said finally. "Now, where were we?"

Having heard what happened in the adjacent chamber, Kofi realized the futility of attempting to be heroic or smart. He struck Avoga hard when ordered. He too, did not escape the blows that the shadow behind him administered whenever he did something that displeased the captain. For his part, Avoga strove to give the captain what he thought the man wanted to hear, but was never enough. He eventually passed out from the beating. Kofi too, was barely conscious. It was late in the night when the captain finished with them.

"Take them back. This will serve as a warning to the rest who'll be more compliant in case we need to talk to one of them."

The people from Ngoma slowed down several paces from the travelers from Ronge obviously wondering why they sat on the ground in the middle of the *bundu*. At first, Lemba wondered who called him by name.

"Ma'alia. What's going on? What are you all doing here?"

He took a few steps toward her. In his confusion, he failed to understand the desperate gestures she and other Baronge made. He stopped when he realized they were asking him to back away. There was a crush of bodies behind him as his people surged forward to look at the Baronge.

An arrow struck the ground a few paces away from Lemba causing all of them to jump back.

"That's why we can't move." Yossou shouted. "Someone keeps shooting at us whenever we try to."

Then the drama took another odd turn. An elderly woman with a leathery, deeply lined face broke through the wall of bodies. When she saw Ma'alia, she came unhinged.

"What are you doing here you witch? You took my son's life and now you've come to torment me!" She started angrily toward Ma'alia.

"M'ma, stop! Get back! They'll kill you!" Wind cried.

In her rage, the woman did not heed the warning. Another arrow struck the ground in front of her and ricocheted, barely missing her shin, but her hatred for Ma'alia so consumed her she did not notice. Ma'alia had seen that face before. The image of a wild-eyed woman cursing her flashed in her mind. She remembered a young man named Edoni who had died suddenly in Ngoma. This woman was his mother. As Ma'alia watched, an arrow whizzed by, and she saw the shock on the older woman's face. A pink line formed on the woman's left upper arm. It slowly turned red as the blood rose to the surface and trickled down. Ma'alia reacted as soon as she realized what had just happened. The next arrow would not miss. With her baby in her arms, she stood and ran toward the petrified woman.

"Ma'alia, what are you doing?" Yossou cried. "Get down!"

He could feel an arrow going through his wife and the searing pain at the thought of it. He tried to get up to wrestle her to the ground, but he could not move. He willed himself to stand, but his body would not obey. For the first time in his life, he understood that there was a link between willing and the body's ability to comply. This time, he could will all he wanted, but his body would not move.

The most fascinating perception while this was going on was the sense that time slowed almost to a standstill and he saw everything with amazing clarity. His wife ran in slow motion toward the woman who slowly, very slowly, turned her hate filled face from Ma'alia to the injury on her own arm. He saw Ma'alia reach the woman then turn around, shielding her with her own body and exposing the baby to danger!

Most intriguing, though, was the demeanor of the child. He first gazed at Ma'alia. Yossou could have sworn he deliberately lifted his left hand to touch her bosom. Next, he turned to the bushes from where the arrows came. The child raised his right hand in a gesture that clearly said, "Stop!" Though Yossou did not look in the direction of the attackers, he saw, as if in a dream, six nude armed men crouched in the bushes. With the same mysterious faculty, he knew they were a rogue outfit of Bagondi who had planned to rob and kill his party. Their eyes were wide and filled with terror. They trembled like frightened puppies, paralyzed where they hid and did not take their eyes off the baby.

Finally, the child gave Yossou a penetrating look. It melted his heart and his will collapsed, bringing down with it the effort to stand. It also burned through the scaffolding that supported the sliver of eternity in which time had slowed to a crawl. Time moved on again.

Ma'alia stood with her back to the woman and stared defiantly toward the unseen assailants. The bushes ahead exploded. There was fierce growling, shaking of bushes, and a flurry of arms and legs. Men screamed horribly as a powerful animal struck and tossed them in the air. Two stark-naked men were already running to get away. One stood and raised his spear to strike, but the leopard was too quick for him. In one bound, it caught his arm before he could release it. The man disappeared in the bushes as he fell. Surprisingly, he was up in a moment and running for his life, as did the other three who had remained. The leopard faced the travelers and was visible for only a moment before it too, ducked low and disappeared. Only a keen observer could trace the subtle movements of the shrubs that tracked the leopard's path. Wind watched it go, knowing the leopard, his friend, had saved their lives. *But who sent it? How did it know?*

The villagers had watched it all in shock. No one spoke. No one moved. When it was over, Ma'alia turned to the confused woman behind her. She had placed a hand on the cut on her arm, but the blood still flowed through her fingers. Ma'alia moved the hand away and touched the wound. The bleeding stopped instantly and the wound looked as if it had healed for a week. All that remained was a faint, slightly embossed line.

The baby... as soon as she looked at him, Ma Edoni felt as if a gale started to blow through her. Its powerful gusts blew away the huge boulders that had weighed her spirit down for years. The sharp, cutting wind unraveled the cords that had bound her. The noose that choked her every night when those evil forms came upon her loosened and blew away. As suddenly as the gale started, it stopped. What remained was a calm, fresh breeze. She inhaled deeply, held her breath, and exhaled. Everything was pure and fresh! She felt alive... so alive!

Ma Edoni looked at Ma'alia and let out a joyful, hearty laugh. Both women hugged spontaneously. When they broke the embrace, Ma Edoni's face had a youthful freshness that made her look a generation younger. Both the Bangoma and Baronge burst into applause. People came to hug them, having seen the transformation in Ma Edoni take place right before their eyes. They had seen how Ma'alia had risked her life for the older woman and how the leopard had routed their attackers.

"Let's go M'ma," Ma'alia said.

"Yes, let's go," Ma Edoni agreed.

Without asking, she took the child from Ma'alia and held him to her bosom. They walked up to Yossou and Wind.

"Lead us into the center," Ma'alia said to them.

Wind struggled to his feet. Yossou hesitated, unsure his body would cooperate. *Yes. He could stand.* When he did, he looked at his wife for a moment and returned her smile. He was still very emotional, and fought the urge to embrace her. He looked at the infant in Ma Edoni's arms. He seemed oblivious to what was going on around him. Yossou was still entranced and did not know what to make of anything they had witnessed.

"Yossou!"

He realized everybody was looking at him. He cleared his head and moved past Ma'alia to follow Wind. No one said much. No one sang. In solemn silence, they marched into Mahu. Only Sotsi, a hollow-eyed thin man ventured to ask the question on everyone's mind.

"Where did that leopard come from? What did those attackers want?" he asked loudly. No one answered. "*Akh!* I need some wine," he concluded.

A short while later, they arrived in Mahu. A warm-hearted couple led them to the enclosure where they would spend the night. With the provisions they bought from their hosts, they prepared the meal as the sun set. All went to sleep early, tired from the journey and the recent drama.

In addition to his position as Chief Administrator of Bora-ini and its environs, Stimela was a prominent businessman, landowner, and perhaps the most influential leader after Tamaa. He made a point of knowing what was going on in the city and what the people were thinking. In so doing, he made himself one of Tamaa's most trusted confidants, though "trust" was a loose term with the governor. Through his spies, Stimela knew when the peasants were planning a riot or a boycott. He knew who was disgruntled and who was speaking out against the leadership. When visitors came from foreign lands, he heard about it. From them, he learned of events in the world beyond Kwavantu. When the Great Xhaka conquered new territory and brought it under his vast empire, Stimela made it his business to know because he admired Xhaka greatly. In his eyes, there was no leader like him - fearless in battle, a great strategist, manipulative, and authoritative. Stimela always listened to reports of Xhaka's exploits with deep reverence.

On a smaller scale, Stimela tried to emulate his idol by acquiring as much land as he could. As Chief Administrator and Tamaa's confidant, he wielded a lot of power and influence over the general population and people had learned not to cross him. Whenever someone did, the offender would learn he somehow had unpaid taxes or had offended Tamaa in some way. The person would also learn he had to make reparations immediately. To Stimela, anything was fair game if the person could not pay. He confiscated land, took wives, children, livestock, or whatever he desired as compensation. Though he turned many of the assets he collected over to Tamaa's coffers, he always kept a token for himself. Over the years, it grew to a sizeable fortune.

Like his employer, Tamaa, Stimela's list of enemies grew with time, but by studying, both Tamaa and Xhaka, he learned the value of intimidation, bribery, blackmail, and spying to control his detractors. Often, this meant dealing with lowly characters such as the thin man standing before him. Salit had a knack for sniffing out useful information. His front as an accommodations broker for visitors to the city was perfect for this purpose. However, this story about a child born by the wayside to parents from an obscure village becoming King of the Avantu seemed a little far-fetched.

"Look, Salit, everybody dreams of becoming something someday. Perhaps the parents, having failed to achieve their own dreams, want to live them out through their child. All parents think their children are special and destined for great things. You know how it is with our people. We attach great significance to everything that happens at birth as if it has a bearing on what they will become. Therefore, if one or two odd things happen by coincidence, we take it as a sign from The Mighty One. These parents are probably just hallucinating like many others before and after them."

"I know how Tamaa hates dissent so I didn't take chances. I told the captain of the guard at the trading center to pick up some members of their group for interrogation. He picked up two last night."

"What did he learn from them?"

"Apparently, they were not sure of the story. Though he pressed them hard, he didn't squeeze much out of them. At best, they admitted hearing a rumor about a young bride who conceived out of wedlock. She and her husband tried to cover it up by claiming the pregnancy was the work of some spirit. Other than that, she's an ordinary woman."

"And you trouble me with this tonight? Salit, you have generally supplied me with good information and I have rewarded you generously for it. Let's keep it that way."

"I thought I would report it since up to now I've never heard anyone lay claim to the throne of the Avantu. I've heard people claim to be prophets, mystics, military leaders with supernatural power, and the like. Not this."

"I know. Consider it a first. Now you've heard it all. Come back when you have something important to report. I can't go to Tamaa with this."

Stimela rose, indicating the meeting was over. The spy hesitated as if he wanted to say more, but thought better of it. He bowed and left.

Alone in the dimly lit room at the back of his house, which also served as an office, Stimela replayed the conversation with Salit in his mind. He felt the spy might indeed be onto something. In spite of the lack of sufficient information about this "King," he was a little disquieted about dismissing it, which he pretended to do to avoid paying for the information. *What if Salit were right?* He, Stimela would be a dead man. Tamaa had no loyalties. Anyone who stood in his way or presented a threat, however remote, fell off the earth mysteriously. So too, did the person who failed him in any way.

On the off-chance there was something to this claim, Stimela decided to take preemptive measures. He walked to the door leading in to his living quarters, opened it, and called out.

"Bobo!"

A short, stocky man came running in near panic. He bowed and kept his head down, awaiting instructions.

"Run to Mattu's house and tell him I want to see him immediately."

"Yes, my Lord." Bobo was out like a bolt.

While he waited, Stimela pondered what he should do with this child and his parents. He could easily order their deaths and not feel a thing. However, he was curious to see how it would turn out. Apparently, the parents did not make much of the child's future aspirations. If he did not bring it to Tamaa's attention, the governor would be none the wiser. He would wait this one out.

Presently he heard a knock on the outer door.

"What!" he barked.

"Mattu is here to see you, Master," one of his guards announced.

"Let him in."

Mattu was half a generation younger than Stimela. He was hard working and trustworthy. He was also wealthy by local standards and most of his wealth came through his work and business ventures. Stimela learned this from spies like Salit who kept an eye on key figures in the city. Mattu was married to a beautiful young woman and much of his success and wealth, Stimela knew, was due to her wisdom and sound judgment. While Mattu worked hard, Fanta managed his personal affairs astutely. They had a son and a daughter. Unlike other prosperous men who married a second wife at the faintest whiff of success, Fanta was Mattu's only bride.

"Ah, Mattu. I'm happy to see you."

"I'm happy to see you too, my Lord," Mattu responded. He knew this was not an invitation to socialize, but he went along until Stimela was ready to disclose the reason for the summons. There was a tap on the inside door and after a brief pause, Bobo pushed it open. He carried a metal tray on which sat two goblets of special tea and a plate of exotic snacks from distant lands. Bobo set the tray down and shot a nervous glance at his master in case there was coded communication in his eyes. Seeing none, he fled.

"How is your family?" Stimela handed Mattu a goblet as he spoke.

"Oh, they are very well, thank you. They spent the day at my parents' house. They just got back this evening. The children love visiting their grandparents."

"You are blessed with a good family. Not many daughters-in-law enjoy the kind of relationship Fanta has with your parents. I'm sure it's because of her excellent attitude."

"I cannot deny Fanta makes life easy for me in many ways."

They dwelled briefly on Mattu's marital bliss then talked about events in the land, and politics, both local and global. They also touched on the different groups of people who were in town for the count. The topic gave Stimela a perfect segue.

"How is the count going?"

"It is going well in spite of the organizational problems we've been having. It has certainly boosted business in the city and we should have a good year."

Mattu did not want to go into details because he sensed Stimela was not actually interested in them.

"Do you have all the people you need?"

"I could have used a few more people in the beginning, but we now have a system in place and it's working well. I have five stations where we count people by region every day. The warriors have done a good job keeping the crowds under control. We've not had any serious incidents since the chaos of the first few days."

"I'm happy to hear it," Stimela said and paused. "I want you to do something for me. There's a family coming to the count tomorrow. I want to see them. All I know is that they are from a village called Ronge and have a newborn baby. When their turn comes, detain them and send me word."

Stimela's request upset Mattu visibly. Little good came out of such a request - especially for the party in question.

"On what grounds will I hold them?"

"*Akh*, Mattu! That's your business! Just make it happen."

"As you wish, my Lord."

"Good."

They sat in awkward silence for a while and Stimela switched to other mundane matters. It was late when Mattu rose to return to his house. Stimela asked two of his guards to see him home.

Wiki-Zugu could not stand it anymore. He sensed hostility all around him. As the evening wore on with neither food nor any sign of Kofi and Avoga, he became increasingly isolated. Hungry children cried. Nursing mothers offered their breasts to older children long weaned, all the while cursing "some stupid men with goat droppings for brain." M'mata and a small group of men sat apart, talking in low tones, frustrated that they were unable to provide for their families in this strange city. They could not be sure what awaited them beyond the confines of the enclosure. They were now sure the man who was supposed to bring provisions had swindled them. They were also concerned that Kofi and

Avoga had not returned. Unfortunately, they could do nothing but wait. They had seen enough along the way to convince them of the low currency of life in this region. It would be inexpedient to venture into the dark alleys of closely packed buildings in search of their fellow villagers.

Approaching footsteps interrupted their muted conversations. They could make out shadowy figures of six to eight warriors by their demeanor and weapons. As they neared, the people of Ronge noticed they were dragging two men. The villagers gasped collectively when they realized who the men were. Unsure of the consequences of any reaction, they remained in place until the warriors came up to them. Without a word, the warriors tossed Avoga into the enclosure. He crashed on the fence and lay immobile. Next, they shoved Kofi forward. He stayed on his feet for two or three wobbly steps before the fence compromised his balance and he fell, bringing another section of it down with him. He groaned and tried to raise himself. The warriors, visible only as silhouettes, waited briefly, perhaps to gauge the visitors' reaction or to ensure that they had made their point. Then they walked away casually. Only when their steps had faded did the visitors approach their fallen comrades.

"Mwaza!" Anaya lamented when he got to Kofi. "Who did this?"

"By the spirits!" M'mata swore.

He stared at his uncle, Avoga, for a moment, turned him over, then stood suddenly. His head struck the chin of a girl who was looking over his shoulder. She yipped and walked a short distance away in tears, holding her chin. M'mata ignored her and glared in the direction the warriors had taken.

"Easy, M'mata. Easy," Wiki-Zugu put a hand on his shoulder. M'mata pushed it away. Those who had formed a circle around the injured men saw M'mata's reaction. It was an act of extreme disrespect. Heavy silence followed, thickened by the odor of unwashed bodies and the foul breath of hungry stomachs. Wiki-Zugu turned away slowly and went to sit under the tree - crushed.

By now, the commotion had disturbed even the groups in neighboring enclosures, some of whom had come to look over shoulders at the men on the ground.

"*Weh!* Step back, everybody!" Anaya shouted at the people crowding him. "Step back, all of you! I can't see! You're blocking what little light there is!"

Siga fetched a gourd of water she had saved. She forced her way through the onlookers and yelled at them to disperse. They moved away reluctantly. She asked the men around her to carry the unconscious Avoga to a place close to the tree. They also brought Kofi over and laid him next to Avoga. Siga dug into her pouch and pulled out a handful of herbs. She added a little water to the leaves and ground them to a paste, which she rubbed into Avoga's wounds.

"This person really worked him over," she said. "Just about every bone on his face is broken."

Kofi stirred when he heard what she said. "I killed him," he said feebly.

"What?" Anaya asked. He turned to Siga. "What did he say?"

"He said, 'I killed him.' I don't know what he means."

"They made me hit him until he collapsed. I killed him," Kofi whispered. "I killed him." He raised his voice. "I killed him." He repeated the words, getting louder and more hysterical each time. He sat up.

"Killed who?" Anaya demanded.

For a moment, lucidity returned to Kofi's face. The poor light accentuated the terror in his eyes. His breath reeked of blood, hunger, and vomit, making Anaya draw back in revulsion.

"They were asking about a child who would be King of the Avantu. Avoga did not know of such a child - and neither did I. They made me beat him when he said that. If I didn't, they beat me too. I killed him!" He became hysterical again. "I killed him! I killed my kinsman!"

He was screaming, fighting those who tried to restrain him, and tearing at himself badly enough to draw blood. He lunged at a man's machete, but the man stepped aside just in time.

"Don't let him get to your weapons. He might hurt himself or someone else." Anaya warned those around him.

A man from the adjacent enclosure approached with several strands of twine in his hand. In sketchy Kigololi, he said had worked with extremely agitated people with a measure of success. He suggested they should restrain Kofi, adding that he will eventually stop fighting and calm down. The villagers were willing to try anything and they agreed. Hearing what was about to happen, Kofi became even more violent and it took six or seven men to hold him down while two others bound his hands and legs. Sweat glistened on their backs due to the effort. Dust and a fresh burst of body odor filled the air. The man from Wasu pulled out a pipe, filled it with herbs, and lit it with an ember. It gave out strong acrid smoke that overpowered the pervasive odor around them. He asked them to sit Kofi up. The man sucked on the pipe deeply. He blew a huge cloud of smoke in Kofi's face. Kofi coughed lightly. The man repeated the process a few times and Kofi suddenly relaxed. He inhaled deeply and let the air out in a long odorous breath. His demeanor also changed and his focus adjusted to infinity. He smiled to himself and began to rock back and forth.

"Give him some water. It will help him. He should soon fall asleep." The man from Wasu said. He rose and returned to his enclosure.

He was right. Kofi drank some of Siga's water and promptly fell asleep, snoring loudly. Only the perceptive listener could tell the cadence of his breathing was not normal. The villagers left the injured men who up to this time had been the focus of attention. Siga finished administering the medication on Avoga and went back to care for her two children and Yossou's. M'mata sat near Avoga while Anaya and a few men stayed close to Kofi. It would not be long before morning came. Everyone was tired, but most could not sleep. One of them was a lonely old man who sat at the foot of a tree watching everything. It grieved him to learn the assault on the two men was because the warriors wanted learn out about the coming King of the Avantu. He remembered mentioning to the friendly man what Ma'alia and Yossou had said about the child's conception. The old man felt he had betrayed his friends. Though Kofi cried that he had killed Avoga, he did not know who had actually sentenced him to death. *No, I killed him Kofi,* the old man whispered to himself. *I killed him.* He bowed his head in shame and guilt.

Days in Mahu were warm and comfortable all year round. Acacia trees provided plenty of shade when the sun was hottest. Being on the leeward side of the escarpment, Mahu did not receive much rain except what trickled over after the clouds had given themselves to the lands on the other side. As if to make up for denying her rain, every night the uplands rolled sheets of cold air down the escarpment in spells lasting late into the morning.

One such draft woke Ma'alia well before the rooster crowed. She felt refreshed after the night's sleep though her feet, nose, and cheeks were cold. A stab of pain in her lower back reminded her she had just become a mother. She lay on her side with the baby's body against her bosom to keep him warm. He slept with both fists clenched close to his cheeks. She cracked open the bedroll that she had folded over to cover herself and the baby against the cold of the night and brushed a hand over his head. He stirred and grimaced, making Ma'alia smile as she looked on his fresh features.

Simi who was sleeping beside her stirred and woke up too. She grunted and yawned. Ma'alia also yawned reflexively.

"Did you sleep at all?" Simi asked.

"Oh, I slept like the dead. The cold woke me, otherwise I could have slept longer."

"And the baby, how did he sleep?" Simi whispered, leaning over and pulling back Ma'alia's bedroll a little in order to steal a peek at the child.

"He suckled for part of the night then fell asleep. He hasn't stirred since."

"You're fortunate he's not like his father. That man slept very little as a baby. He was either suckling or crying. Even with the teat in his mouth, he would still squawk. I'm surprised he turned out the way he did."

"Yes. People change,"

"Where is he, by the way?"

"Who?"

"Your husband."

"I don't know. I just woke up."

"Never mind. I'll find him."

Simi stood up, folded her bedroll, and placed it beside Ma'alia. The sounds from the square indicated some people were already up. She walked to an open area where a group of women huddled around two large fires whose shimmering flames gave them the appearance of witches concocting an arcane brew. Over the fires, two huge pots bubbled with morning porridge. Simi greeted the women and they returned her greeting. Yossou heard her and called out to her. He was squatting over some water in a calabash.

"Chi! This is the coldest water I have ever touched. I can't feel my fingers after just one swish."

"Then why go through with it. You don't have to wash everyday. You're traveling, remember?"

"I couldn't stand myself walking around feeling dirty all day."

Simi watched him grit his teeth in preparation for the shock that was to come. He cupped his hands and scooped some water, which he swung to his chest. When the water hit his body, Yossou gasped sharply and nearly rose to his feet. At this reaction, Simi doubled over with laughter and could barely speak for some time.

"Good morning, Ma Yossou. What makes you laugh so?" It was Lemba.

"*Ah ah!*" was all she said, still sniffling from mirth. Another splash and sharp intake of breath behind her indicated that Yossou was continuing his self-inflicted punishment. She waved a hand over her shoulder.

"I don't know why he does that to himself."

Lemba smiled.

"He insisted. The women won't heat water for anyone to take a bath, so he has to deal with the cold water. Now, to change the subject, I've paid the women for porridge, potatoes, and cassava. There should be enough for everyone. They need to get up so we can make an early start on the journey, though. Would you like some water to wash your face?"

Simi laughed again and turned to look at her son who now shivered as he danced around in an effort to dry off.

"That's why I came here in the first place, but after watching him… No! I'll go rouse the others."

Lemba went to see how much water Yossou had left. He found enough to wash his face.

"*Ei!*" he exclaimed when he felt the water. "You are a hard man to take this to your body."

"To be clean, it's worth the trouble. How long do you think it will take us to get to the top of the escarpment?" Yossou asked as he regarded the forbidding rock face that loomed over them.

"Typically, it takes the better part of the morning. We should be at the top before the sun sits on our heads. It's a tough climb, but our people can do it. God forbid it should rain. That would spell all kinds of trouble."

"Does it rain here at this time of year?"

"Does it *ever* rain here? I was just saying. This is one of the driest places in the land. Rain? *Hah!*"

Chapter 9

strange intervention

The people of Ronge woke up tired, hungry, and depressed. They had eaten only the meat they carried from the village, wild fruits, and leaves they picked along the way. Everyone craved a hot meal of *chima*, vegetables, and meat. The children were first to declare their hunger, though occasionally, an adult would echo their sentiments and curse the man who had tricked them.

With Kofi out of his mind and Avoga unconscious, the people of Ronge faced a dilemma. By Tamaa's directive, everybody had to be personally present for the count and his officials did not accept excuses. This meant no one got the benefit of doubt. When the officials went round villages for a post-count survey, anyone without the special metal disc that served as a certificate for having been personally present at the count had some explaining to do. The officials were always on a tight schedule and had little patience for inadequate explanations. They imposed huge fines and if individuals were unable to pay, they would seize whatever they deemed appropriate, including family members. Kofi and Avoga were in no shape to attend the count and the people of Ronge wondered what to do.

"Let's ask Sakul Wiki-Zugu for advice," Imbaze said.

"Do we have to?" M'mata retorted.

Anaya turned to him sharply.

"Look. What you did last night was wrong. You disrespected an elder in front of everyone. Even if you are the strongest man in the village, it's no reason to treat a man old enough to be your grandfather that way. First, you owe him an apology. Second, it's only proper that a man of his standing should sanction such a decision."

"You want me to apologize to him when he's the one who led Kofi and Avoga to their fate?"

"He did what anyone in his position would do. How was he to know what mischief the rat that took the payment was up to? How could he have known that our friends would fall into the hands of those thugs?"

"Forget it. I'm upset at what happened to my uncle and Kofi. What's wrong with that?"

"And Wiki-Zugu was just trying to calm you down. Did you have to react that way?"

Imbaze sensed M'mata was getting angrier the longer the argument went, and it would soon get out of hand. Besides, they were drawing the attention of other villagers who would take sides and exacerbate an already volatile situation.

"*Enza! Enza!* Do what you want," he told M'mata. We have a decision to make and the proper thing to do is to consult an elder. But hear this, M'mata. We shall relate what you did to the village and all Gololi. You'll be famous, not for your prowess as a wrestler, but as one who urinates on the head of an elder." Imbaze stood up. "Anaya, let's go talk to Wiki-Zugu."

Wiki-Zugu had watched the exchange from his post under the *M'kuyu* tree knowing he was the topic of discussion. He continued to clean his teeth. Years of experience had taught him to read lips and body language as well as he could hear words. He would find an opportune time to talk with M'mata. Though the young man had acted disrespectfully, he would reach out to him. He could not afford to spend what little was left of his life in bitterness. Presently, Anaya and Imbaze came up to him and each dropped on one knee before him.

"*Baba*, we know things have not gone well so far and we don't know what foul spirit possessed our people to cause such rancor. Some among us have spoken rashly and acted inappropriately. On behalf of your people, we want to say we are sorry and that not every one feels that way."

Imbaze punctuated the speech with sounds of agreement. When Anaya finished, both men bowed their heads as a further sign of respect. Wiki-Zugu listened until he was sure they were through speaking. He stopped cleaning his teeth, turned aside, and let out a thin stream of spit through the gap in his teeth. He cleared his throat.

"Young men, I thank you for the honor you bestow upon me. In turn, I honor you. We've gone through much and I, as a leader, take responsibility for what happened. Last night I should have listened to my heart when it whispered to me not to trust that smooth-talking trickster. I should have warned Kofi and Avoga not to venture out in a place of which they know so little. I could have prevented all this pain and animosity. I have failed the people and lost the moral authority to lead them. They *have* to want me to lead and offer advice. At this time, I don't think they want to listen to anything I say."

"With all due respect, *Baba*, I beg to differ. What you see there," he nodded back to where M'mata sat in a smoldering heap, "is the reaction of one, maybe two immature individuals. At this time, we don't need heroism. We need cooler heads to prevail in this place where life means little. We cannot overlook your wisdom and counsel. There may be dissenters, but we want you to lead."

Wiki-Zugu stuck his chewing stick back into his mouth and adjusted his gaze beyond the present into his heart. The men had a point. He could not continue to ignore the growing tension in the group. He had listened to arguments, conversations, and comments, both loud and whispered, and realized that the stress of travel, hunger, and fatigue, lay behind the bickering. M'mata's actions obviously hurt him, but it would not be right to deny the people guidance because of one man's actions. If they sought it, he would give it to them. Once more, the chewing stick came out and the spit followed.

"I gather the question at present is, 'What do we do about Kofi and Avoga?'"

"Yes. We need to make a decision soon because we travel back today don't we?" Anaya asked.

"Yes. We can't afford another day here. Our farms and gardens are waiting for us. Besides, the village is less safe with so many people gone. This is what I advise. Leave both men here with me as you go to the counting station. They'll ask which village you come from and who is your elder. Give them my name and tell them I remained at the camp with these men. Tell them their warriors beat them severely to the point they cannot walk. If they want, they can come back for me. I'm not afraid of what they'll do to me."

While they were talking, three local women came along, each balancing a large pot on her head. A young boy and girl accompanied them carrying several gourds. They stopped at the first enclosure and had a brief exchange with the occupants. They lowered their pots and doled out porridge into gourds, and handed out boiled cassava and sweet potatoes from large pots. The people of Ronge, seeing this, could barely contain themselves. They descended on Wiki-Zugu and the younger men.

"Will we get something to eat now?" There was still a hint of bitterness in the speakers' tone.

"So you will. So you will," Wiki-Zugu said patiently. He turned to Anaya. "You have the purse. Take care of it."

Anaya rose and pushed back against the group that surged around them.

"Be patient. Those women will soon be here. We have enough to pay for all of you. Stand back and wait."

Finally, the vendors came to their enclosure. Anaya stepped forward to negotiate with the women. They settled on a price and the women lowered their pots and started to serve the Baronge, amidst pushing, shoving, and an occasional slap. Wiki-Zugu waited until everybody had received a portion of food. Only then did he accept a gourd of porridge and a stick of cassava. No one talked much as they relished the long anticipated meal.

After they had eaten, conversation resumed. It was more cordial and even-tempered. Wiki-Zugu asked Anaya and Imbaze to get the people ready to go to the count. He instructed them to repair the broken fence to avoid further expenses and the ire of the owner. After the repairs, he asked the people to gather around him. He pointed out that what had happened so far was a test that the spirits and ancestors had brought upon them. He urged them to rebuke the foul spirits that were playing havoc with their unity and to call upon the Great Oracle to bless them. He asked their forgiveness for having failed them the previous night by allowing the thief to trick him. The people all said they forgave him. Wiki-Zugu then told them he would remain with Kofi and Avoga while the rest went to the count.

In closing, he raised a bony hand and a strong voice and brought all these matters before the Oracle and the ancestors. He was especially passionate when he prayed for Kofi and Avoga. The crowd responded with much feeling. He then gave Anaya final instructions. He reminded heads of households to make sure they had enough to pay the taxes for their families. With that, he asked volunteers to place Kofi and Avoga beside him and loosen Kofi's restraints. Wiki-Zugu settled back against the tree with his chewing stick in his mouth, hoping he had seen the last of the excitement.

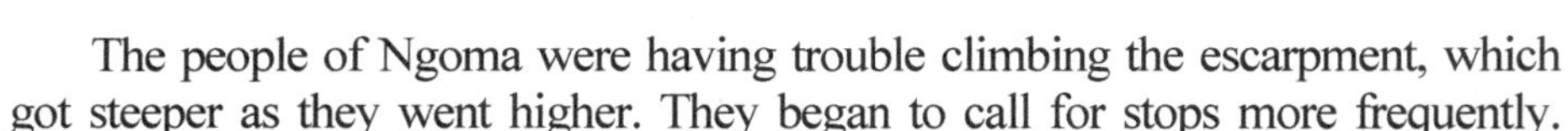

The people of Ngoma were having trouble climbing the escarpment, which got steeper as they went higher. They began to call for stops more frequently. Lemba became concerned that some would not make it to the top. To his dismay, the clouds began to gather rapidly.

"I did not expect it would rain at all," he told Yossou with whom he trudged at the head of the convoy. "Fate is determined to prove me wrong."

"So it would seem. This is not good. Not good at all."

"I know. I must have jinxed us."

"*Woi!* Please stop! I have to rest!" A woman called out.

"Who is it this time?" Lemba asked irritably.

It was Didi, usually a jovial, funny woman. Today she was having no fun at all. She was tired and short of breath.

"Do you realize the rain may catch us if we don't hurry up to the top?" Lemba asked.

"How much faster can you make us climb? If we are tired, we are tired." Several voices agreed with Didi. Everybody felt the strain from climbing and tempers were short. Even the few who had previously made the climb thought it was inexplicably harder this time. Lemba stopped reluctantly and waited a few moments.

"We have to move on now otherwise we'll be on the wrong side of the escarpment when the rain starts and that could be very dangerous."

The clouds grew thicker and more ominous until they completely blocked out the sun. It became almost dark as night. A single drop of rain hit the ground with a distinct "*thop!*" as if to herald what was to come. Moments later, intermittent drops began to fall, sounding like the patter of ghostly feet around them. Lemba was very worried. There was no way they could continue. But they had climbed too far to turn back. They were stuck.

The rain now came down in drops that hit the people with a degree of malice.

"Let's keep going," Lemba urged, but in his heart, he panicked. He knew once the clouds let fall, the people were doomed.

In its second phase, the rain was a steady drizzle, falling to the accompaniment of low rumblings of thunder and flashes of lightning. It made the narrow trail slippery, especially for those who followed the leaders. As more people trod on it, the loose earth and rocks became muddy and slick. Already, there had been a few narrow escapes. If it were not for the firmly rooted shrubs onto which they held, many would have tumbled all the way to the bottom.

The rain increased to a full-fledged downpour, forcing Lemba to call for a halt. Attempting to keep going only increased the risk of a fall. Besides, they could not see well in the near darkness and rain. While they stood, a brilliant flash lit the sky, revealing the wonder and majesty of the escarpment and surrounding lands for a moment. But Lemba had no interest in the eerie beauty around him. He knew what was coming and he put his hands to his ears and shouted frantically.

"Find a plant - hang onto . . ."

RRRRR-BOOOOOM!!

People screamed. Though he had anticipated the thunderclap, the sound, which seemed to rend the sky, still made him jump. He heard what sounded like the tumbling of bodies receding down the mountain. *No!* He held onto a sturdy shrub, praying, and hoping. To contradict his prayer, rain came down in massive sheets as if they were standing under a large waterfall. Above the sound of the rain, Lemba heard wailing. He knew they had lost some people and prayed no one would become so desperate as to throw himself down after those fallen when the thunder struck. He too, felt hopeless and ready to throw himself to his death on the rocks and bushes below. Only the thought that his people looked up to him prevented him from letting go of his little shrub.

As the conflicting thoughts played in his mind, the lightning flashed revealing a strange sight. He was not sure whether it was just the lightning, or his mind playing tricks on him. In that moment, he saw Ma'alia and the baby. The momentary image was so vivid it caught his attention immediately. Some of the most hideous creatures he had ever seen flashed in the darkness, poised wickedly over mother and child. They seemed to struggle against an unseen force in an attempt to get to her. The darkness swallowed the vision. He peered into the rain and darkness hoping to confirm what he saw. It happened again. This time the flash shimmered a little longer and Lemba knew he was not dreaming. While others around her clung to plants or to one another, she stood straight, her head lifted heavenward. He thought she was praying, but he was not sure. The nefarious creatures still struggled to get to the child, but something prevented them. A single strong spirit warrior stood before Ma'alia and the child, his sword pointing at the creatures. They could not get past the sword-wielding spirit-being and could only swirl around him like thick dark clouds. The child was a study in contrast. He was fast asleep. Nothing seemed to bother him - not the thunder, lightning, or even the rain that fell on his face. The placid scene quieted Lemba's heart. Then in a flash, it was gone and darkness returned.

The lightning flashed again. This time he saw several spirit-warriors who seemed to stand on air in a defensive stance. They faced a horde of wicked beings that lurked in the churning darkness of clouds and rain. Smaller flashes of lightning snaked from the darkness and attempted to snatch a villager from the face of the mountain. Each time, a spirit-warrior repelled the attempt. This vision of opposing forces also disappeared though the flashes continued. Lemba had barely processed what he had seen when he noticed movement downhill. The fear returned. With the intermittent flashes, he made out figures coming straight up the rock face toward them. *Spirit-beings!* The steep climb and the rain presented them no challenge. There were two females and four males. A female spirit-warrior and a male each carried the limp form of a person who had tumbled to the bottom after the huge thunderclap. By now, all had noticed the strange group coming up toward them, and they feared greatly. Panicked cries replaced the wailing.

As if sensing their fear, a female spirit-being raised her head to the villagers. In the intermittent light, she looked on them benevolently and raised her hand in a gesture of peace before closing the distance. Her companions followed closely. The two who carried the villagers who had fallen gently stood them beside their fellow travelers. The young woman and the man who had fallen mysteriously regained consciousness and showed no signs of injury.

"Take my hand and that of the person next to you," the female leader ordered.

Lemba took her hand and turned to take the hand of the young woman they had retrieved after her fall. They formed a chain with a spirit-being at each end and the other four evenly spaced in among the villagers.

"Let's go," the leader shouted.

The spirit-beings attacked the steep hillside, walking straight up instead of zigzagging across its face as people normally would. In a short time, they had made it to the top and the angle reduced rapidly. Here, the vegetation was greener and thicker with more trees. They still had some climbing to do, but it was not as bad as what they had just been through. The villagers realized were it not for the woman and her strange band, they would not have survived. She led them along a trail for some time before she stopped and turned to Lemba.

"That way to Bora-ini," she pointed. "You'll be there before nightfall. The Oracle *is with you.*" Walking up to the baby, she bowed lightly before him and whispered to Ma'alia, "Take care of my Lord."

Following her example, the rest of her group came up and bowed before the child. When they had all observed this ritual, the leader raised her hand to the people of Ngoma, wished them a safe journey, and walked off. The villagers watched in amazement until they disappeared in the bush and rain. Lemba called out to resume the journey.

The Bangoma were soaked through, but it did not matter since they were uplifted in spirit after the strange encounter. They wondered why the Oracle would care so much for them as to send a band of spirit-warriors to intervene on their behalf. They also tried to understand the significance of the spirit warriors' action when they bowed before Ma'alia's child. None gave voice to these questions lest they upset the spirits and the Oracle.

The people of Ronge walked out of their enclosure to join the throng making its way to the counting center. They walked down a tree-lined arcade past several stone and brick structures to the right. These were storage sheds for vendors who sold their wares at the open-air stands to the left. On verandahs, men sat taking in the morning sun and cleaning their teeth with chewing sticks. On the street, porters carrying *junzi* sacks full of merchandise, each weighing more than the bearer, assumed the right of way and never yielded to anyone. When they came up behind someone, they whistled or hissed sharply and simply ran into the unwary or unyielding. If someone made an issue of it, the men dumped their load and swung the first blow. After a couple of confrontations, visitors quickly attuned to the signals and stepped aside at the first call.

The Baronge merged with other tributary groups into the river of humanity that flowed to the counting center.

"Stay together! Parents, hold your children!" Anaya shouted. He was now the leader in Wiki-Zugu's absence. When the crush of bodies increased, parents had to pick up the little children, otherwise the crowd would trample them underfoot. Outside the center, the fence gradually funneled to a gate under the guard of four warriors. Two of them carried rhino skin whips with which to control the jostling crowd. They asked for group leaders and directed them to respective stations in a large open field.

"Where are you from?" one asked Anaya impatiently when he came to the front of the line.

"We're from Ronge in the lands beyond the great escarpment."

"Which people?" His eyes shifted constantly, always scanning the crowd.

"We are Bagololi."

"You go over there," he pointed to a station. Like others, it already had a line of people stretching halfway to where they stood.

"Stand aside and make sure all your people come through before any one else does. Have in your hands what you need to pay the Great Tamaa's taxes," he added.

The Baronge started to filter through. Occasionally both Anaya and a guard had to bark at a child who held up traffic when he stopped to stare at the warriors.

"*Weh!* Move!" The command and a look from the red-eyed warrior quickly jarred the dreamy child into motion.

"That's everyone for me," Anaya said, sticking out an arm to stop a boy from another community.

"*Bas*. Take your riffraff to where I showed you."

"Thank you," Anaya said, but the warrior had already turned to the next group. "Let's go. Move, you people!" They lined up at their respective station.

Their turn came and they stood before two men seated on tree stumps behind a rickety hide table. Atop the table sat two small clay jars into which a frazzled little man dipped and then meticulously inscribed on large parchments. He ignored Anaya and the others while his companion studied the villagers with bored interest. The little man finished and looked up.

"Which village?" he asked in perfect Kigololi.

"Ronge."

"Are you the village headman?"

"Sakul Wiki-Zugu is the village elder. He's in town, but he stayed behind with two of our men who were hurt last night."

He's supposed to be here, isn't he?"

"As the elder, he felt he had to stay with the injured men."

The other man spoke saying, "He felt he had to stay with them? What about his duty to the Great Xhaka? Doesn't he know he disrespects our leader when he does not appear for the count?"

"He said he would come by later after we had finished."

The little man resumed his complaint. "Do you see all those people behind you? We have no time to deal with an individual who thinks he can pick his own time to come for the count."

Anaya and his fellow villagers stood speechless, stunned by the logic of the clerks. At that point, a man who had been pacing back and forth behind the counting stations came and stood behind the clerks. Apparently, he was above them in rank because the clerks addressed him with deference.

"What's the problem here?"

"These peasants have come here without their elder and they expect me to count them first and then count him later. He's playing nurse to some weaklings from their village."

"Where is he?" the man asked.

"Back at the camp where we spent the night," Anaya responded.

"And where are you from?"

"Ronge. In the lands beyond the escarpment." The man frowned as if searching his mind for something. He spoke after a short pause.

"Apart from the elder and the injured men, is this everyone who came with you?"

"No. One of our young women was going to have a baby on the way here. It was in the middle of the wilderness so her husband, her mother, and a few friends stayed behind with her."

"I see. You know it's an offense for someone not to present himself at the count, eh?" Turning to the clerk he said, "Sabu, go ahead and count those who are here. I'm going to see Mattu about this matter."

He walked toward the stone buildings up the hill.

"Well, your elder's in a lot of trouble, I can tell you that," the little clerk said. "Let's continue. I'll start with you since you'll be the new elder. I need your taxes."

Anaya laid his strings of shells on the table. The little man picked them up and counted them. Satisfied, he pushed them over to his colleague who also counted then nodded. He placed them in a sack by his side. The little man began his annotations while the second clerk finished processing Anaya.

"Dip you right forefinger in the dye."

After Anaya had done so, the man picked up from a pile on the table, a thin metallic disc with inscriptions on one face and handed it to him.

"Keep this safe. It shows you were present at the count and paid your taxes. Show it to the authorities when they come to your village to verify the count."

With that, he motioned Anaya to step aside while the little man completed his annotations. The second clerk looked down the line absently and started to pick his nose. He dug deep and twisted, his face contorted, until it came away with the trophy. He scrutinized the flake carefully, turning the finger this way and that before deftly flicking it off. He launched an assault on the other nostril just as the little man finished making his entries and turned to Imbaze.

"Taxes?"

Locho tapped lightly on Mattu's door.

"Enter."

"My Lord, I think the people from that village you talked about are here. I don't know whether the baby and his parents will be coming or not. But the village elder is at the visitors' camp with two villagers who were beaten up badly."

Mattu thought for a moment.

"Send some men to bring them here. Tell your people to be careful with the injured men. I want them all alive."

"Yes, my lord."

Wiki-Zugu was tending to Avoga when an ear-piercing scream jolted him upright. Kofi, with a look of absolute terror, was pointing at the object of his fear.

"No! Stay away from me! Leave me alone! I can't take it anymore!" he pleaded. Wiki-Zugu turned and saw six warriors coming straight at them. Before he could collect his thoughts, the warriors were upon him and yanked him to his feet. A crowd formed as people came to see what was going on.

"Let's go, old man. You have some explaining to do," a warrior told Wiki-Zugu gruffly.

Kofi was already getting hoarse from screaming. A dark patch began to spread on the ground where he sat. Steam rose from it briefly before the ground lapped it up. One of the warriors approached the terrified man and struck the side of his neck in two staccato jabs with straight fingers. Kofi went limp and tipped to one side, hitting the ground like a sack. The warrior tucked his hands under Kofi's arms while another took him by the ankles and they carried him off. Two other warriors took hold of Avoga in the same fashion and started after Kofi's bearers. The last two shoved Wiki-Zugu along.

"Are you going to nail them to a tree?" someone in the crowd asked. The warriors shot him a withering look. The one who held Kofi's ankles let go, but did not take his eyes off the questioner, a lanky youth.

"Come here!"

The youth tried to slink away, but when the warrior raised his spear, he reconsidered.

"You carry him since you are keen to know what's going to happen to him. And you," he pointed at another man. "Take over from him." He indicated his colleague who let go of Kofi's arms unceremoniously. The warriors recruited another unwilling pair to carry Avoga before they continued toward the town square.

Mattu was perusing the previous day's records when he heard the knock.

"Yes?"

A servant slipped into the room and closed the door carefully behind him. He stepped no further.

"My Lord, Lagat has brought the three peasants."

"Good. How are they?"

"They look a little roughed up, Master."

"*Akh!* Idiots! I'll be right out."

The servant left. Mattu took his time before stepping outside. Two men lay unmoving on the ground. Off to the side, a slightly stooped old man stood looking at Mattu.

"This one's almost dead," the warrior said, digging a toe into Avoga's side.

The sight made Mattu sick. He had never seen a person so beaten up. The eyes were swollen to mere slits. His cheeks and lips were bruised and puffy and lacerations covered his body. Mattu turned away to look at the second man whose face was also bruised, though not as much as the first man. Mattu's stomach heaved and only the thought of appearing weak before the warriors prevented him from vomiting.

"Didn't I say I wanted them alive? I need information from them and you've all but killed them."

"But that's how we found them. This one was lying on the ground, completely unresponsive. That one screamed like a maniac when he saw us so we silenced him. The old man is fine, though."

"Lock them up until I decide what to do with them."

Mattu felt the old man's eyes on him and he looked up. He was either brave or foolhardy, for no one dared to look at a man of greater stature straight in the eye. *He's probably beyond caring.* Mattu refused to answer the man's questioning eyes and went back into his office. He sat at his desk and looked at the parchments before him but was in no frame of mind to continue working. He loved his work though he thought Tamaa and his henchmen treated ordinary people unfairly and placed a huge burden on them. They had few rights and little say over their own affairs. For example, it did not make sense that entire villages had to make the two or three-day trek for the count. He had formulated a simpler, more effective way to achieve the same objective, but presenting it to Tamaa was a delicate matter. Suggesting change could mean death and Mattu felt he was more useful alive than dead. Someday, when the time was right, he might suggest it. For the present, he had to deal with the tired, smelly villagers from all over the region. He rose and stood in the middle of the room wondering what was so important about a little baby whose misguided parents had probably spoken out of turn. *Kings did not rise from uneducated peasants in remote villages.* He did not want to get back to his work because the thought of the three men he had just locked up bothered him. Worse still, he did not know what to do when this little king showed up. He rose and paced the room in frustration.

On the other side of town, Stimela was finishing a late breakfast when someone knocked impatiently on the door. He rose to answer it himself, intending to rip the offender apart. His irritation turned to trepidation when he opened the door and saw who stood before him.

"I bear a message from the Great Tamaa, Governor of Kwavantu and citizen of Azania," the man started without waiting for Stimela to speak. "The Great Tamaa wants to know how many kings shall rule this land. You will personally deliver the answer on the third day at a sitting of the ruling council. Have a good day, my Lord."

His mission accomplished, the messenger spun around and left, guards in tow.

Stimela stood rooted to the spot and watched them go. The message matched the morning perfectly. Heavy dark clouds brooded over the city, occasionally grumbling to one another in low rumblings. The air was humid and oppressive. He wondered what someone had said to Tamaa about him, or what he might have done to elicit this message. Maybe it was another of Tamaa's shake-ups. The governor owed his success and longevity in part to the fact he trusted no one - not even his closest family. He constantly shuffled friends, pitting them against each other as they scurried for his favor. When they fell out, they fell hard and no one wanted to be the victim. Competition was stiff - just the way Tamaa liked it.

Stimela turned, shut the door slowly, and began to think back to everything he had said and done in the last few days. He could not nail down anything for which he was culpable. Whatever unscrupulous things he did were standard practice among the elite in Bora-ini. Tamaa himself was guilty of many of them so it was unlikely that was the problem. Perhaps he just wanted to shake things up a little to see where his friends' loyalties lay - if indeed Tamaa had any real friends. Whatever the case, Stimela considered the message a warning and he would find out what was going on. If he went down, he would not go down alone. He knew too much to be the sole sacrifice at the altar of egotistic ambition.

"Bobo!"

The servant materialized through the inside door.

"My Lord?"

"Get Tsuma and Stombi."

"Yes, my Lord."

Bobo left to find the bodyguards. By the time Stimela was ready to leave, Tsuma and Stombi were already standing by the door with their weapons. They fell in step behind him as he started down the hill toward the middle of town. People he met along the way stepped aside and bowed as he passed. He neither glanced at them nor acknowledged their show of subservience. Soon he arrived at the town square, which was busy as usual with people from all over Kwavantu bartering their wares. He could pick out the visitors by their lost looks and fascination with everything. As he cut through the pedestrians, he became the focus of their attention. Tsuma took up position at the front to clear a path, surprising the unwary with a painful jab with the butt of his spear. Their protests died when they realized whose progress they impeded.

At the counting center, Stimela walked up to Mattu's chambers, knocked twice, and let himself in.

"Now what?" Mattu asked irritably before he realized it was Stimela.

"Good morning, Mattu."

"Stimela! G… good morning. What brings you here so early?" Mattu was standing in the middle of the room looking agitated though he tried to hide it.

"*Akh!* It's that future king thing. It seems Tamaa got wind of the tale and wants to know what's going on. What have you heard about it so far?"

Mattu went to sit at his desk while Stimela settled himself in one of the beautifully crafted chairs along the wall.

"I have three men from that village who did not personally appear for the count. Actually, city guards beat two of them so severely one of them can barely walk while the other has not regained consciousness. The third is the elder who stayed with the men while the rest came up for the count. I asked the warriors to bring them here so I could learn more from them. I still haven't decided what to do with them. The injured men will certainly need treatment and I've asked Lukalo, the physician, to check on them later."

"Honestly, I don't care what happens to these men. I just want to see this controversial child. Who are his parents and where do they come from? We cannot afford an insurrection should these peasants get it into their heads they can rule the land. Tamaa is not happy with this information. I'm not happy either. By the way, have the members of that village left yet?"

"I don't know. I don't think so."

"Find out quickly. Keep the men you are holding. Send someone to find whoever is now leading this group of peasants and bring him back. Let him know his friends' lives are in his hands. If the parents of this king-child don't show up the men will die and I will make sure the rest of the village suffers."

Mattu looked dismayed.

"I'll send my men to bring the leader back."

"Do that. I have to report to Tamaa in three days. I'll be going now."

Mattu saw Stimela out then called for his servant. The sky had darkened from the time he was last outside. Something bothered him, but he did not want to dwell on it. When the servant came, Mattu instructed him to find a couple of warriors.

Two of the six warriors who had brought Kofi, Avoga, and Wiki-Zugu appeared shortly after.

"Have the people from that village beyond the escarpment left?"

"Yes, they left a short while ago. They said they were going to come back with their elder and the injured men so they can be counted."

"I have another mission for you, then. Bring their leaders back here."

"That might not be necessary," the other warrior said. "I think they are bringing themselves to us."

They all turned in the direction the warrior was facing. Three men, obviously visitors to the city, approached timidly. They stopped several strides away, unsure and afraid to come any closer. Mattu eyed them then waved them over. They approached cautiously and still stopped at a distance but within earshot.

"Does any one of you speak their tongue?" Mattu asked the warriors.

"I speak a little Kigololi," one warrior answered.

"Ask what they want?"

The warrior asked the question and one of the villagers responded in a hesitant shaky voice.

"He says they are looking for their elder and two injured comrades. The men were not at the camp where they left them this morning," the warrior interpreted for Mattu. The nervous man spoke again.

"What did he say?" Mattu asked.

"He says they were told your warriors had taken their fellow villagers away. He has come here to beg you to release them. He says the elder and the two men have done nothing wrong and they just want to take them home to care for them."

"Tell them there's one condition for getting their friends back." Mattu spoke looking sternly at the villagers. "There's talk about a woman from their village who gave birth on her way here. These stories could cause a lot of trouble in the city. The child's family must come to the count and see me. If they don't, then tell these men they will not see their comrades again and we will hunt them down and burn their village."

As the warrior translated his words, Mattu saw the horror on the villagers' faces and he felt sorry for them. However, he kept up appearances because force and fear were an essential part of Tamaa's leadership style. As part of the system, he played according to its rules.

"Ask him if what I said is clear."

The warrior interpreted back and forth.

"He says it is. They will inform the parents of the child to present themselves to you personally."

"Tell them not to fail. They may go."

The villagers turned and left despondently. Mattu watched them and shook his head. He despised himself for what he had just done.

"Thank you boys," he told the warriors. He went back inside and threw himself into his work.

"They have Kofi, Avoga, and Wiki-Zugu," Anaya reported morosely to the people of Ronge when he returned to the campgrounds. "They are holding them until Ma'alia appears before them with her baby. I don't know where they got the notion her child will be king one day. The leaders in Bora-ini are consumed with it."

"What shall we do?" Siga asked.

"I can only hope Ma'alia and the others chose to travel to Bora-ini after the baby was born."

"Do you think she'll be able to travel so far right after giving birth?" another woman asked.

Siga jumped at her. "Maybe you women from Ronge cannot travel after giving birth. Ma'alia and I are Bakilima. We give birth to a child the size of a calf and go right back to work unlike you who are pampered for days after dropping a lizard."

"That depends on the type of lizard!" The woman retorted.

"Enough!" Anaya cut in. "We won't solve anything arguing like this. Let's pray Ma'alia and the rest decided to travel to Bora-ini. Right now, we need to make sure we have everybody who's supposed to be here, and you all have whatever possessions you brought and all your cowry shells."

All took inventory of their possessions and were satisfied they had everything. Anaya advised them that they would not be having a formal meal since they had a late start on the journey.

"We are starting right away. As you might have realized by now, life is easier in the village than in this confounded city."

"There's one more thing," Dube, Avoga's middle son, said. "We've not sought the blessing of the Oracle. Perhaps it's the reason we're having trouble again."

Silence followed the young man's sobering pronouncement.

"He's right," Anaya conceded. "We've acted as if we're in control of our destiny forgetting there's one greater than us."

There was silence at first, but gradually, heads began to nod in agreement.

"Well then, let's bring our petitions before the Oracle," Imbaze said.

"How can we do that when Wiki-Zugu is not here? Is it not an elder who voices our petitions?" Siga pointed out.

"Are we to stand around with our thumbs in our mouths because one man is not here to do what we can do ourselves? *Chi!* It's good we honor the elders, but when they are not present we have to do what we have to do," Anaya said firmly. "Now who will lift our cries to the Oracle and the ancestors?"

There was another spell of silence.

"I will."

"Heads turned toward the speaker, many registering surprise that he would volunteer. By his gaze, M'mata challenged them to turn him down. They saw he was serious.

"His father," he pointed at Dube then pounded his chest with his fist, "my uncle is lying there half-dead. I don't need someone else to invoke the Mighty One on his behalf. I will."

With that, he lifted his eyes to heaven, saying nothing for a long time, but intense emotion was evident on his uplifted face. He clenched his jaw and his eyes blazed. The tension built up in him, rippled through his taut muscles, and charged the air around him. He started to shake. A tear formed at the corner of his right eye, growing larger by the moment until it broke free and rolled down his cheek and onto his thick neck. Almost everybody thought the same thing - he was challenging the Oracle and the spirits. *He should be careful*. Before anyone could act according to these thoughts, M'mata let out a short guttural cry and collapsed onto his knees with his head bowed. That very instant, a jagged bolt of lightning rent the sky and a short, sharp report followed. While the noise startled those around him, M'mata stayed on his knees, arms hanging limply by his sides. Nobody said it, but they all wondered why the lightning fell so far away instead of turning him into a pile of ash.

"I'm sorry," he cried. "I was a fool to speak to an elder the way I did last night. I displeased the ancestors and now Kofi and my uncle will die because of what I did."

Dube put a hand on his shoulder. "They will not die. You acted in anger because of what the warriors had done to him. The Oracle forgives you and they will not die."

The villagers looked on, amazed that the erstwhile reticent youth suddenly spoke with such maturity and conviction when even adults felt helpless.

"May it be so, son. May it be so," Anaya said. He helped M'mata to his feet. "Well, there's nothing more to do. Let's start our journey and pray we run into Ma'alia and the others for the sake of our kinsmen."

They picked up their pouches and weapons, took the children's hands, and started the first part of the journey back home. It would be dark by the time they got to Mahu.

Mattu barely noticed the lightning, but the report startled him. It did not sound right. A thunderclap had a broader tone. This one sounded distinct and localized. The sound of items falling followed it. He heard a crowd gathering and exclaiming. A while later, they cheered and then jeered. Mattu wondered what was happening. A sharp rap on the door brought the answer.

Wiki-Zugu sat wondering what he and the two men in the in the dark little room had done to deserve this treatment. As far as he could recall, he had heard details about Ma'alia's baby from Yossou's relatives as they related the events surrounding his conception. He heard that the Oracle designated Ma'alia as the mother of the child and that she was still a virgin - something he could not quite grasp even with his superstitious mind. He heard very little about the child becoming king, so he wondered why the furor.

He was still thinking about these things when a brilliant flash lit the chamber. The roof and the door both disappeared as if a mighty man had kicked them out. Avoga, who had been unconscious since last night, sat up and uttered only one thing.

"*Mwaza!*"

Kofi also sat up startled. Though he did not say anything, his expression said it all.

"What am I doing here?" Avoga asked. He looked himself over, smelled himself, and grimaced.

"*Chi!* I stink. Where am I?"

Kofi, on the other hand, had the appearance of one who had just emerged from a deep trance. Wiki-Zugu noted that the earlier signs of abuse on the men's faces had faded somewhat.

"I wish I could answer you," Kofi said, "but I feel as if I've just crawled out of a deep, dark hole myself."

"This is not the time for explanations. Let's go," Wiki-Zugu ordered. He rose and made for the door.

Outside, city folk gathered to gape at the tiny chamber where the lightning had struck. Amidst expressions of amazement, they cheered when the three men stepped into the open.

"I wish someone would tell me what's going on," Avoga lamented.

"Later," Wiki-Zugu told him. "For now, we have to find our people. We also need to let our captors know that we're leaving."

While he was talking, a band of warriors stopped them, but they seemed nervous and uncertain. The crowd jeered.

"Not again," Kofi moaned. He appeared to be on the verge of becoming hysterical again.

"This time no one's going to touch you. You are not staying," Wiki-Zugu declared. He stared the warriors down. "Get out of my way. You don't know who you're dealing with."

The warriors looked at one another indecisively, realizing the crowd was waiting to see what they would do.

"We are going home and you're not stopping us," Wiki-Zugu told the warriors when they did not move. He was not sure if they failed to understand his language or if the just wanted to prevent him from leaving. Whatever the case, he was having none of it. He pushed the spears pointed at him aside. Kofi and Avoga followed. The warriors remained where they stood, paralyzed with indecision. A cheer rose from the crowd and they followed the three who made their way to Mattu's door. Wiki-Zugu knocked.

Mattu flung his door open and stepped back in surprise. The three men he intended to hold stood before him, all apparently in full control of their faculties. Behind them, a crowd surged. Guards raised their spears to keep it at bay.

"My Lord, we are leaving," the old man said unequivocally. "The Mighty One stretched his arm from heaven in brilliant light to set us free. We are here to let you know so you do not wonder where we've gone and cause someone else trouble. Stay well, my Lord." The old man bowed.

Mattu was dumbstruck. Even if he had wanted to, he could not detain them without causing a riot. He sensed they had the sympathy of the crowd and he did not wish to aggravate them. He was glad be get rid of the headache these men presented anyway.

"Farewell, my father," he said finally. It did not occur to him until much later they did not need an interpreter

The old man and his friends bowed one last time and left. The crowd erupted and danced alongside them. They improvised words of praise to The Mighty One for the amazing thing they had just witnessed.

The people of Ronge were barely beyond the environs of the city when they heard singing behind them.

"What's going on back there?" someone asked. "That city doesn't seem like a place where there'd be much singing and dancing."

"It must be something really big because I don't see the leaders tolerating any sort of merriment," another added.

"Whatever it is we are not going back to find out," Anaya said. "We have to get to Mahu before it's too late. Besides, the risk of running into bandits and wild animals increases with the dark."

They pressed on, but the singing did not diminish. If anything, the singers seemed to gain on them.

"Perhaps it's a wedding party heading to a village in this direction," Siga suggested.

Since it had rained recently, there was no cloud of dust by which they could gauge how far the singers were. They agreed what they heard were not war chants, so it could not be that Tamaa had set his warriors on them. It could not be a wedding party either for there had been no signs of festivity in the city. They would have to wait and see.

When they realized the singers would overtake them, the Baronge decided to let the party pass. Many admitted they were curious to find out who it was. A short while later, a large group of men and women decorated in leaves and feathers broke through the foliage. They waved twigs and branches as they sang and danced. The Baronge could make out a few words of the song, which was in praise of The Mighty One. Then they saw, to their astonishment, who the crowd was escorting.

"Wiki-Zugu!"

"*Wah! Wah!* Avoga!"

"Kofi! By the Oracle! Kofi!"

The people of Ronge ran to embrace their fellow villagers. Avoga got the most attention. Everybody wanted to touch him as if to confirm he was indeed alive and sound of mind.

"We had lost hope with you," Anaya told him. "We thought you'd never wake up."

When the initial joy of meeting their kinsmen passed, the questions began in earnest. *Did a medicine man pray over them? Was it a spell? Who broke the spell? How was it that the city leaders released them so soon after taking them hostage?* Wiki-Zugu surprised them when he answered the last question first.

"It was a bolt of lightning that set us free."

The Baronge gasped and turned to M'mata who looked surprised himself.

"The Mighty One heard your cry, M'mata! He heard our cry!" Anaya said. "I am amazed!"

The residents of Bora-ini, not to be outdone, gave an account of what they too had witnessed, emphasizing how they had rejoiced when Wiki-Zugu had stood his ground first with the warriors then with the tax collector. One after another, individuals related their particular spin on the events of the morning until Anaya pointed out they would have liked to talk some more, but were still on a journey. He bowed slightly toward Wiki-Zugu.

"We are happy to have you back, Sakul."

"Thank you," Wiki-Zugu said. He turned to the people of Bora-ini. "We thank you people of Bora-ini, for the love you've shown us. Should any of you get the chance, come see us in Ronge. Thank you for everything. We may have another group coming this way tonight. We ask that you take care of them too so they do not suffer what we've been through. May the Oracle be with you. Again, thank you."

The two groups parted.

Chapter 10

the king child

Fatigue and cold had taken their toll on the good humor of the travelers from Ngoma. Someone would utter a harsh word to which another would respond with equal venom. Only the firm intervention of a few elders prevented fights from breaking out. The elders knew that one of the reasons the people were short on temper was the lack of wine. The troublemakers had not been sober in a long time and were not handling it well. When they set off, they had filled their gourds with beer instead of water and had run out.

Sotsi, a young man, was suffering the worst. As the day progressed, he became sluggish and disoriented. The only thing he said that made sense was, "Beer. I need beer." He had already broken his gourd and licked it dry. Soon, he was unable to walk on his own. Two of his comrades carried him between them and cursed him as they walked. His ranting grew increasingly incoherent and sweat poured down his face and body. White froth ringed his mouth and dangled in foamy strings whose ends broke off periodically. His friends grew tired and dumped him by the wayside. They moved on. Sande and Juma, witnessing this senseless act, stopped to attend to the disabled man. Sande took out his gourd, forced the crazed man's mouth open, and poured some water into it. Sotsi swallowed automatically. Sande did this a few more times. Sotsi's ranting decreased, though he maintained an incoherent commentary of his hallucination. Sande and Juma helped him to his feet between them and they continued.

By mid-afternoon, it was clear that Sotsi was in no condition to travel further. He had been talking so long he had lost his voice. He had also become too heavy for Sande and Juma.

"Do you think he's going to make it?" Sande asked.

Juma only made a wry face and said nothing. Just then, Sotsi's head dropped, he sagged, and became dead weight between them. Sande and Juma exchanged glances and laid him down on the ground. Others also stopped and surrounded the three. Lemba and Wind made their way back to the ailing man. Wind went down on one knee and felt for Sotsi's vital signs. There was a pulse, but it was very faint. He looked into the man's eyes and did not like what he saw. The life had gone out of them - a sure sign the man himself was not far behind.

"What's his name?" Wind asked.

"Sotsi."

"Sotsi," Wind called. "Sotsi, can you hear me?"

The man did not respond. Wind looked up at Lemba and shook his head. Sotsi shuddered briefly then lay still. With one hand, Wind closed the dead man's eyes and stood up.

The villagers looked at Wind and Lemba as if waiting for either one to say something that would contradict what they feared, but the two merely stood over the body with their heads bowed. When it finally registered Sotsi was dead, there was an uncontrolled explosion of grief. Sotsi's younger married sister, Thalla wailed the loudest. Two women restrained her from climbing up a tree with the possible intent of harming herself. Her husband followed her weakly, absent-mindedly holding their two children. Other villagers ran around with hands on their heads, wailing loudly. One would think they had just lost a model member of the community.

The Avantu treated a death in the course of a long journey differently. They truncated the mourning process due to the practical aspects of transporting the dead. When he felt that they had mourned enough, Lemba administered last rights. He asked one of the relatives to break Sotsi's legs to prevent his spirit from making its way back into the land of the living. The brother-in-law was too queasy to do it and other relatives unwilling. Lemba therefore declared should his spirit drift back to the realm of men it should go directly to his family because they refused to do what would guarantee it rest. Sande and Juma to carried the body for disposal far from the path.

After his role as *m'sali,* Lemba was drained physically and emotionally. The day had started in most dramatic fashion and he began to wonder if the excitement would ever end. He recalled their predicament on the escarpment and the image of the spirit-warriors making a stand against the dark forces. He was sure the child somehow played a role in their deliverance. *How is it he could not save Sotsi?* Lemba was not angry, but only wondered why the child, if indeed it was in his power to save, had let the man die.

The travelers sat in groups, talking quietly as they waited for Sande and Juma to return. Ma'alia, Simi, Mideva, and Ma Edoni comforted the sister while the men from Ngoma consoled her husband. Wind, Lemba, and Yossou sat with the older men from Ngoma bemoaning a life cut short. Wind suddenly held up his hand. Yossou and Lemba exchanged puzzled glances when Wind got on his knees and put his ear to the ground.

"A party approaches," he announced, raising his head.

"Who could it be?" Lemba asked. "I can't hear a thing."

"I can't tell until they get closer."

They all fell silent, each straining to hear who was coming. All they heard was the occasional bird, the flutter of a butterfly and the incessant buzzing of an insect that had elected to fill the air with an eternal monotone. Presently Sande and Juma returned looking glum and tired. Intense but muted conversation resumed in all the groups. Lemba rose and started to speak, but Wind held up his arm once more.

"Again?" Lemba said looking at Wind.

Wind neither answered nor lowered his arm.

"People?" Sande asked. "From the rising sun?"

Wind smiled. Finally, someone else had keen senses like his.

"Yes," he said.

"Baronge?" Sande asked.

"I think so. By their footsteps they are not trained warriors, but it could be a raiding party."

"I think I hear men, women, and children also. It can't be a hostile group."

"You're probably right, son. You have a good ear," he smiled again. He addressed the rest.

"There's a large group of people approaching and we can't hide - at least not for long. I don't think they are hostile, but we should still be prepared. Men, if you have weapons, have them ready. We'll stay on this side of the trail and fight if we have to. Women and children move to that side as far as you can. If they overcome us, run and scatter. That way some of you may avoid death, captivity, or assault. From this moment, everyone must remain quiet. Watch and listen for my instructions. Now move!"

The women scampered. A little girl started to cry for her father, but the mother quickly hushed her. Wind shook his head when he saw some men retreating with the women. He concluded he was better off without them in a skirmish.

"Sande, up that tree! See who is coming and how they approach," Wind said as he led the men to the other side of the trail. "Come! Take cover and remain quiet. I'll give the word if we have to fight."

The men took their positions and waited. Each moment felt like an agonizing eternity. Soon they all could hear the sound of people approaching. Wind had a feeling he knew who they were, but he preferred to err on the side of caution. He continued to listen and watch Sande concentrate his gaze in the distance.

"Baronge!" Sande exclaimed and dropped to the base of the tree like a plumbline.

"You're sure?"

"Either it's them or whoever taught me to observe the land did not know what he was doing."

Wind chuckled at the mild rebuke. "Good. We can relax a little. Keep your positions a while longer men. Sande, climb back up the tree and give me a signal when they are within the strike of an arrow."

Wiki-Zugu and his people had made good time from Bora-ini up to this point. They would get to the escarpment at twilight, which was good because to attempt the steep descent in total darkness would be unwise. He was no longer the young man who had trekked for miles in search of a bride. He was not the warrior who had participated in two major battles until Xhaka pummeled the land into submission. He was tired but kept pace with Anaya who now led the way.

The exhilaration of the morning wore off as the day progressed and the monotony of the trek set in. It was a miracle that Kofi and Avoga kept pace with everyone. Their injuries were healing faster than Wiki-Zugu had ever seen. Avoga's face, which had been puffy and swollen in the morning, looked normal except for faint cuts and bruises. Kofi too, was clear-headed and coherent.

Wiki-Zugu was so preoccupied with his thoughts he almost bumped into Anaya who had stopped abruptly.

"What is it?" he asked.

Looking past Anaya, he saw a solitary figure on the trail about a stone's throw away. For his poor sight, he could not tell whether he was friend or foe.

"Who's that?"

"Wind!" Anaya exclaimed as he ran toward his kinsman. They embraced. Wind gave the signal and other figures emerged from the foliage. The next moment, they drowned in the confluence of bodies as members of the two villages came together. Wind was glad to see fellow Baronge. It was a welcome break from the complaining and sniping of the Bangoma. Simi and Temin ran to Ma'alia and their grandmother and hugged them while laughing and crying at the same time.

"I'm very happy to see you my babies," the elder Simi said. "Girls, remember your mother couldn't come with you the other day?"

"Yes, N'ne."

"Come. I'll show you why."

She led the girls to a group of women who were ogling over Ma'alia's baby.

"Look!" she said parting the women. "Your little brother!"

"Oh! He's beautiful!" said the younger Simi. "Can I hold him?"

"Of course!"

The woman holding the baby handed him to Simi and showed her how to cradle him properly. Temin and Moni touched the baby's hair and giggled.

"Do you girls care for your father?" Mideva asked after a while.

"It's not their fault," the elder Simi said. "They're excited to see their brother. They will greet their father shortly."

Meanwhile, the rest of the Baronge learnt the reason for the crestfallen faces among the Bangoma. A few who had known the dead man mourned him, lamenting the passing of one so young.

When they felt that a suitable period of meeting, catching up, and mourning had passed, Anaya and Wiki-Zugu sought out Ma'alia, Yossou, Wind, and Lemba.

"There's a grave matter of which you need to be aware. It involves you, Ma'alia, but your husband and other leaders should know about it too," Wiki-Zugu started. "I feel somewhat responsible for it and for all the trouble we experienced in Bora-ini."

He related how he had casually mentioned to a vendor that some of the party had remained behind with a woman about to give birth.

"I don't know what possessed me to talk about the child." He choked for a moment.

Ma'alia touched his arm lightly. "It's alright, Baba."

Sensing Wiki-Zugu might find it difficult to relate the rest of the story, Anaya took over. He told them how Avoga and Kofi had gone to look for their food when warriors plucked them off the streets and beat them. He related the previous evening's conflict among the villagers, the harrowing experience of the morning where the warriors also took Wiki-Zugu and the injured men, and their miraculous deliverance.

Wiki-Zugu picked it up again. "They intended to hold us to ransom until you showed up. They had warned us earlier that if we did not make it happen, they would attack the entire village."

"Yes," Anaya said. "That is the dilemma. You and the baby can present yourselves to the authorities, but there's some risk to it because we don't know what they are planning. The decision is yours, Ma'alia, and we'll respect it either way."

Ma'alia looked at Yossou, her eyes betraying her inner struggle. He held her gaze for a moment then looked at the ground. They all stood in a circle, sensing the couple's anguish as they pondered the difficult choice.

After some time, Yossou spoke.

"Ma'alia, you know I love you and I would hate for something to happen to you. And God knows I also love my son." He touched the baby's soft hair, "But it would be selfish of me to sacrifice the whole village for my happiness." He looked at all the others around him. "We have done no wrong. My son is only a day old, so we cannot claim to know his future. However, if the leaders want us to show up and Ma'alia agrees, we will."

Tension filled the air as the villagers waited for Ma'alia to speak.

"I agree. I do not fear for my husband, my child, or myself. The Mighty One who gave me the child will protect us all. We will present ourselves before the leaders of Bora-ini."

They all relaxed.

"Thank you," those who stood around them said. There was an awkward silence before Wiki-Zugu spoke again.

"The Oracle will surely keep you. You have greater faith than I do. For now, we all need to get going. Gather the people together so we may seek the blessing of the Oracle."

Yossou and Lemba called the two villages into a tight group. Wiki-Zugu first advised them on what to do for provisions for the evening.

"There's a group of women who prepared our food this morning. Ask for Ma Pishi. I told them you'd be arriving this evening so they'll be waiting for you. Don't trust anybody else. We've also told the owners of the camp to expect you so other touts won't pull you this way and that."

Wiki-Zugu then asked Lemba to bless the gathering. Lemba lifted his hand and voice to heaven. When he finished, members of the two groups embraced and parted. Wiki-Zugu sought out Yossou and Ma'alia and embraced them.

"I will see you back in Ronge."

"Yes," they answered together.

"Go well, my children."

"Thank you, Baba."

The hardest part was dealing with Simi and Temin who wanted to be with their parents and grandmother.

"No. It will be too much of a journey for you, girls. Stay with *Senge* Siga. We will see you in two days."

Both girls cried. Temin was most inconsolable. Eventually, a stern word from Yossou and a mushy banana wangled from some thrifty soul placated her.

"Look after my babies," Yossou whispered to Wiki-Zugu. "You know what to do if something happens to us."

In Bora-ini, Mattu wondered what to do, having lost bargaining power with the release of the villagers. He did not even know what he would tell Stimela should the child's parents fail to present themselves. The way the warriors had treated the now free villagers, he would not be surprised if the family did not show up at all. He asked his servant to fetch Locho, the man who managed the counting center. It was a long time before he knocked on the door and entered, his face glistening with sweat.

"Where have you been? I called for you ages ago."

"Forgive me Master. This has been a trying day. I don't know what got into the guards. I think they're upset over what happened this morning. They feel they lost face in the eyes of the people and have been taking it out on anyone they come across. I've already had to deal with cases where warriors beat up some villagers and a local woman. I had to invoke Stimela's name to get them to stop."

"Why didn't you tell me about this? The warriors can only act on orders from their commanders." Mattu said this knowing they often acted as they pleased. They beat people and sometimes killed them with impunity. Rarely did they suffer repercussions. When they did, it was usually because they had upset a superior.

"Feelings are running high, but things have quieted down a little. I just fear if something should happen, there could be bloodshed."

"No, we don't want that. Let me know whenever things threaten to get out of control. Now, I called you here concerning that family we've been talking about - the one from Ronge. We were holding three of their fellow villagers hoping it would guarantee that they come, but you know what happened. Make sure, and I repeat, make sure you identify them. Look for a young mother with a day-old baby. I don't know anything about the husband, but we have enough to go with already. Use any means to identify the woman and child. Let me know when you find her. Is that clear?"

"Yes, Master."

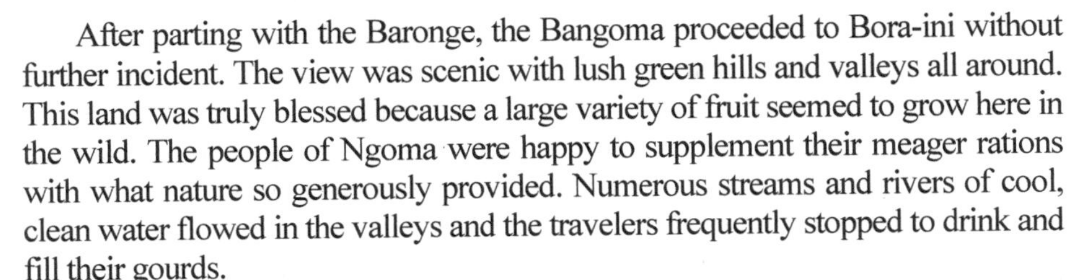

After parting with the Baronge, the Bangoma proceeded to Bora-ini without further incident. The view was scenic with lush green hills and valleys all around. This land was truly blessed because a large variety of fruit seemed to grow here in the wild. The people of Ngoma were happy to supplement their meager rations with what nature so generously provided. Numerous streams and rivers of cool, clean water flowed in the valleys and the travelers frequently stopped to drink and fill their gourds.

"*Wah!*" Sande exclaimed after slurping in a mouthful from cupped hands. "Who said water has no taste? This is the sweetest water I have ever drunk."

"Oh, that's so true," Mideva said throwing some over her face.

"Pity it's not beer."

Heads turned to see who had made the twisted remark. It was Shuma, one of two men who had dumped their friend, Sotsi, by the wayside.

"Is that all you think about?" Mideva chided as she took Yssa from Wacu. "Your friend's body has barely cooled and here you are talking about the very thing that killed him."

Shuma clicked and stalked off. Sande and Mideva looked at one another and shook their heads. She squatted and opened the soft hide that kept the baby warm from the highland cold. The baby breathed in sharply when the cold air hit him. Mideva dipped her hand in the water and ran it over his body. This time he lodged his complaint by way of a heartfelt cry.

"Sorry, child. A spell of cold air and water is good for you. You'll be clean of all the sweat and dust." When she finished, she covered him again and stood only to give him up to yet another woman. They hurried to catch up with the rest who were already climbing out of the valley to get back on the trail.

At twilight, the Bangoma came to the outskirts of Bora-ini. They noticed a marked difference in the construction of homes. Though mud and thatch huts were still in evidence, they began to see more stone structures, which mesmerized the villagers.

"How many people live in that thing?" they asked one another. "It's like a temple."

"Wait till you see some of the houses the wealthy have built in the city. I'm told Tamaa's palace can easily hold our entire village and more."

"That is madness. I prefer my hut in the open country," another man said.

"You say so only because you don't have the opportunity to live in a place like that. I'd love to live there myself," a third man countered.

At this time, they were making their way down the road leading to the campgrounds on the outskirts of the city. As the Bangoma neared, they noticed a crowd ahead of them. They slowed down and approached carefully, given the recent experiences of the Baronge in the city.

"Don't get lost in that crowd," Lemba reminded them. "Keep walking."

Curiosity, however, got the better of them and they merged with the crowd, craning their necks for a better view. Even Lemba stopped to watch.

In the middle of the road, five warriors stood over two men and a woman who were on their knees with their hands tied behind their backs. The three were scraped, dirty, bleeding, and begging for mercy. Two warriors were asking questions to which they never seemed to get satisfactory responses. A vicious jab with the butt of the spear to whatever part of the anatomy presented itself followed each answer.

Lemba interpreted for Wind. He understood Wahsil, a unique blend of local and foreign languages. It was the language of trade in coastal cities and Bora-ini, and fast becoming *lingua franca* in Kwavantu

"They are supposed to have danced and escorted a group of villagers who caused trouble this morning. They are, therefore, guilty of disrespecting Tamaa."

Wind gave him a look that asked if he was thinking the same thing.

"I know," Lemba said. They watched the proceedings in silence. One of the warriors, having questioned the three to exhaustion, turned to the crowd.

"Let this be a warning to all of you. You will not mock the Great Tamaa, or his warriors and get away with it. These three shall die tonight." He turned to his comrades. "The woman first."

"My children!" she implored. "Please don't kill me. I have five children who need me. Have mercy on them."

"You should have thought of that before you went dancing with people who insult our leader."

"I'm sorry. I will be Tamaa's slave for the rest of my life. Just let me live for the sake of my children."

She saw no mercy. A warrior plunged his spear deep down the side of her neck. Blood spurted from the wound in a deep, red fountain that sprayed the warrior when he pulled out the spear. He stepped back with a look of utmost glee. The woman fell and lay still. Wind was horrified that some viewed the execution as they would a wrestling match. A few squeamish individuals looked away when the warrior struck, but still turned back to stare at her body. Others even laughed and made obscene remarks about it.

Wind had seen enough and made his way out of the crowd. He saw Ma'alia and Yossou waiting at the back. He shook his head as he joined them.

The first man met the same fate despite his pleas. The second man, knowing he would die anyway, chose to make a statement in his final moments. He cursed the warriors and said things about their mothers that would have made a hyena weep. His defiance won him the sympathy of the crowd and they egged him on. The warriors decided to make him pay for it. Even with his hands tied, it still took all five to hold him down. He kicked, bit, cursed, and spat as they cut off the small finger of his left hand. He screamed in pain, but still cursed. The crowd jeered the warriors who became agitated and cut off two more fingers. Now the victim became as one possessed. He was beyond pain and goaded them to do more. They did. A warrior tore away his modesty patch, and cut off his genitals. He let out a blood-curdling howl, but still managed to turn it into a string of obscenities. The warrior held the bleeding member for the crowd to see before throwing it in the man's face.

This time Lemba also made his way out of the mob. "Let's get our people out of here," he told Wind.

They wrested their fellow travelers from the macabre theater and moved on after they had accounted for each head. The man was still screaming and cursing and the crowd roaring when they got to the camping area.

Almost everybody had gone to the execution. However, a man approached and asked the Baronge if they were from the lands beyond the escarpment. Lemba responded in the affirmative, adding that they were looking for a place to camp for the night.

"I've been expecting you," the man said. He led them to an enclosure among some trees. "This is one of my better spots. There's no other large group in town tonight so you should be comfortable here. I usually charge three hundred cowry shells, but I'll take two hundred from you, which I think is a fair price."

"We'll take it. We are all tired so we won't waste your time bargaining."

"I understand. I promised your fellow villagers I'd take care of you."

"There's also the matter of food," Wind pointed out. "Our people who left this morning told us someone cheated them out of their payment for food. That led to all kinds of problems. We just want to complete the count and go home. A group of women catered to them this morning. We'd like to use them tonight and tomorrow morning to keep things simple."

"Oh, you must be talking about Ma Pishi. Yes, I can find her and let her know you need her services."

"That would be very kind of you." Lemba dug in his pouch and pulled out a set of leather strings with cowry shells attached. He counted aloud eight strings of twenty five and handed them to the vendor.

"Thank you, my friend. To relieve yourselves, use the stalls by those buildings. Tamaa does not take kindly to people ducking into bushes or watering trees within the city. I'll send Ma Pishi your way. Welcome to Bora-ini and sleep well tonight."

"Thank you."

The travelers from Ngoma spread out across the enclosure to rest. A few energetic children chased each other around, but most sat with their parents.

After a long wait, Ma Pishi and her women appeared with large pots of food. Lemba negotiated and agreed on a price with them, after which they handed out gourds of *chima*, green vegetables, and meat stew. This was different from what the Baronge had experienced earlier. The villagers settled down to enjoy the meal.

While collecting gourds after all had eaten, one of the women casually spoke to Lemba.

"By the way, three of your young men just sneaked off. There's plenty to tempt a young man in this city."

"Idiots!" Lemba swore.

He thought of going after them, but remembered Kofi and Avoga. He was not going to risk his own well-being or that of someone else for the indiscretions of a few.

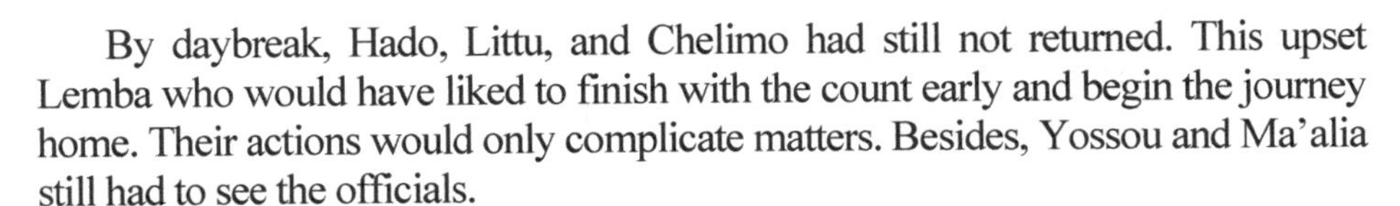

By daybreak, Hado, Littu, and Chelimo had still not returned. This upset Lemba who would have liked to finish with the count early and begin the journey home. Their actions would only complicate matters. Besides, Yossou and Ma'alia still had to see the officials.

Ma Pishi brought a breakfast of porridge and boiled roots. As he paid, Lemba asked if she had any news of Ngoma's wayward sons.

"Oh, I was going to tell you they were at Ma Kadogo's last night. That's a brothel in town. Typically, those who patronize it run a high tab so you might want to prepare accordingly." She gave him directions to Ma Kadogo's.

After breakfast, Lemba asked Wind and two other men to go in search of the youths. He furnished them with resources to cover any expenses, but told them to call it off if they ran into any trouble. With or without the young men, they would meet at the counting center. They all left the campgrounds and headed to the count.

Ma'alia and Yossou were nervous about their visit with the authorities. They neither noticed the impressive stonework of buildings lining the main street nor paid attention to the folk who sat in front of them, soaking in the morning sun. Ma'alia thought of that day, many moons back, when the strange man said her baby would one day be great and deliver his people. She admitted to herself she had witnessed some amazing things she could only describe as miraculous. All she wanted, however, was to raise her son in peace, whatever he was to become.

"Here we are," Lemba said when they were close to the counting center. "You are to report to the Chief Collector. I think you'll find him over there."

He pointed to a cluster of buildings up a slight hill. A little way from it, a small crowd stared at a section of a building whose roof appeared to have blown off.

"The Oracle be with you. Meet us at the campground when you finish. We'll wait for you."

"Alright."

Yossou and Ma'alia went up the hill to the building that served as the taxman's chambers. They walked past the people looking at the small building with the roof blown off. As they neared the chambers looking nervous and uncertain, a warrior stopped them.

"What do you want here? You go over there to be counted." The onlookers turned their attention to them.

Yossou stammered, "We... we were told uh... we have come to present ourselves to the big taxman. All three of us." He included the baby.

"Ah! Bagololi."

The warrior spoke Kigololi himself. "Locho!" he called out.

A man who was engaged in conversation with two other men looked over his shoulder in response. The warrior waved him over. The man did not appear to be a warrior though he was tall and muscular. He ambled over. The warrior spoke to him in Wahsil.

"Aha!" he said, looking at the family. He looked at the baby and laughed lightly before he spoke to the warrior. He gave the family another look before he returned to his friend. Yossou and Ma'alia knew he was talking about them because the men turned simultaneously toward them.

"Mattu is not in, but he'll be here soon. Wait for him over there," the warrior pointed to the side of the building.

The baby was getting restless. Ma'alia sat down and thrust a breast in his mouth. Yossou squatted beside her, picked up a stick, and doodled on the ground. Onlookers divided their attention between the damaged building and the family. The building got the last look before individuals moved on.

The baby was still suckling when an important-looking man, dressed in the strange garb city folk favored, walked up to the building where they waited. Locho broke away and ran up to him. He whispered to the man who looked at Ma'alia and Yossou before he entered the chamber.

It would be some time before Locho summoned them. The warrior who had been hovering around also joined them. Yossou and Ma'alia had never been inside a stone building and they were awestruck by how spacious it was. The man sat in a large chair behind a table overflowing with parchments with strange inscriptions that made no sense to them. Hides and skins of beautiful animals like zebra, giraffe, and leopard covered the walls. There were masks and figures whose workmanship they did not recognize. They stared open-mouthed at everything.

Mattu noticed how enthralled they were. He studied the couple. As best he could tell, he did not perceive any inkling of kingly aspiration in either of them. The man was an ordinary villager who had probably never fought a day in his life. That certainly was not a regal quality. The woman was much younger -

possibly a second or third wife. She seemed alert, intelligent, and independent. She reminded Mattu of Fanta. Of the two, she might harbor great ambitions for her child, but he doubted that was the case. As for the infant, he had never seen anything more ordinary. His mother continued to nurse him after they entered and he suckled away, oblivious of his surroundings. *King? Maybe. Anyone can be king given the right circumstances.* Mattu did not see anything that would concern him about this family. Having come to this conclusion, he drew their attention. He spoke and the warrior interpreted.

"The man before whom you stand is Mattu. He is the Chief Tax Collector of Kwavantu. He has a few questions he'd like to ask you."

Yossou and Ma'alia waited. The warrior listened to a question from his superior who pointed at the child as he spoke.

"My master would like to know if that is your child."

Yossou hesitated. Ma'alia saved him from his predicament with a class response.

"Yes. This is my baby. This is my husband. This is our child."

Yossou thanked her inwardly that he did not have to lie. The man asked another question through the interpreter.

"What do you know about the child becoming King? Did either of you say such a thing or hear anyone say such a thing?"

This time the man looked directly at Yossou.

"No, my Lord. I have said no such thing, neither has my wife. Our child is barely two days old. Ever since King Adu's empire fell and the alliance of the people scattered, a council of elders has led each village. Our elder is Wiki-Zugu, whom you met yesterday. We have no kingdom to which we aspire and don't know what the future holds for our child. That is in the hands of the Oracle."

The words seemed to confirm the man's thoughts and he sat back.

"So neither you nor your people have any plans to make your son a king of some sort?"

"No, Master."

The important man said a few things to Locho in Wahsil. Locho opened the door and escorted them out. He guided them back to the side of the building, away from the door.

"Wait here," he said and went back into the chamber.

Mattu turned to Locho when he returned.

"You heard everything they said. Go to Stimela right away and tell him the child who is at the center of this problem is here with his parents. Relate this conversation to him and ask what he wants me to do with them. Get the word to me as soon as he gives it to you."

"So they came in last night, eh? Did you learn anything more about their claim to the throne?"

"Well my Lord, I must admit that after seeing the parents and the child, there's nothing kingly about him. He's just another infant with two ordinary parents. I don't think Tamaa should expect any trouble from that quarter. The Vasua and *Bagondi* are trouble enough for now."

"I don't recall who appointed you tactical analyst."

"Sorry, my Lord."

There was a light knock on the door.

"Well, thank you, Salit. I appreciate the information you have brought and I'll see to it you are rewarded for your work."

"Thank you, Master."

As Salit left, he threw a puzzled look at the man at the door. He recognized him from the counting center.

"Ah, Locho. Come in." Stimela closed the door behind him. "Well, what did you learn?"

"I sat through the interview with the family."

Locho related the interview exactly as it went.

"So you would have no concerns about the child, his parents, or his people?" Stimela asked.

"From my impressions - none. I think whoever brought up this matter was being over-enthusiastic in his spying. There's nothing to it."

"Good. I'll give that report to Tamaa tomorrow. And how's my boy doing?"

"Clean as ever. Everything he collects, he reports. No problem there either."

"Very good. I think this has been a fruitful morning." Stimela dug into a pouch on his waistband and pulled out two gold coins, which he handed Locho. "Let me know if you learn anything else."

Locho hid the gold in a pouch in his waistband. "Thank you. I'm your eyes and ears. Master, uh . . . what should Mattu do with the child and his parents?"

"Send them away. I have greater matters to which I must attend. You may go now."

"Thank you, Master."

Stimela reflected on what he had learned so far. All his sources agreed there was nothing of concern about the child. He would give Tamaa the report the following day. It was a double-edged sword to be a part of Tamaa's inner circle.

You were never sure if you were an asset and he valued your advice, or you were a threat and he kept you close in order to watch you. So far, all was well.

Locho returned directly to the counting center. Mattu was eager to hear the verdict.

"What did he say?"

"Master, he says you can let the child and his parents go."

"Good. Now I can continue with my work without worrying about kings and minions. Tell the family they can go to the count and on home. See to it they are cleared at their station immediately."

"Yes, Master."

Locho went outside to inform Ma'alia and Yossou. They were relieved to learn they would not have to go through more grilling. Locho escorted them to the counting center. The group from Ngoma was just finishing. They were all equally relieved that the issue had finally ended. Locho guided Yossou and Ma'alia to the desk and told the clerks to process them right away. They were all happy to start the journey back home as soon as they finished their business in the city.

The only blight on the day was two of their young men had disappeared. Wind and his men had found Littu sitting outside Ma Kadogo's as Ma Pishi had said. The establishment had thrown them out during the night. Through slurred speech from an equally foggy mind, he told them Hado and Chelimo had left him where he sat. He thought he heard them say they would not be going back to the village. Lemba told the Bangoma the young men had made their choice and he would not risk the lives of other villagers trying to find them.

When Wiki-Zugu led his group into the village, those who had remained welcomed them joyfully. They were ready to celebrate, but Wiki-Zugu urged them to wait another day when they would have greater reason to do so. They all knew Ma'alia had given birth on the way. Some said they had seen a bright star in the sky two days earlier. They were yet to verify the account of herdsboys from Kilima who claimed on that night, a strange star had led them to the place where the child was born.

On the journey home, only the descent at the escarpment presented a problem for the Bangoma because of their experience the previous day. Fortunately, no rain had fallen since and the ground, though not entirely dry, was firm. Many still needed encouragement, especially the two who had tumbled to the bottom. Everyone made it down safely. The hardest part now over, the villagers spent a quiet evening in Mahu before continuing the following day. By mid-afternoon, they got to the point where the Baronge branched off. The Bangoma would continue and get to their village when it was dark. They had the benefit of numbers and were therefore, not too concerned about the dangers of the night.

Ma'alia hugged a few women from Ngoma farewell and shook hands with Lemba. When she asked for her baby, but no one came up with him. Several voices picked up the question.

"Who's got Ma'alia's baby? We are parting ways here."

Still no one answered. Ma'alia got a little concerned. A baby could pass from one person to another, and, eventually, someone will have passed the baby to another without paying attention. Finally, after a number of people had shouted the question, they saw two girls at the very back, deep in conversation. One of them had the baby. They were so busy talking they did not hear people hollering for him. Deeply embarrassed and apologetic, the girl handed the child to Ma'alia who was more amused than angry. She thanked the girl and joined fellow villagers for the short trek to Ronge.

By the time Ma'alia's group arrived, the feast was ready. Villagers met them from afar, singing and dancing not only to welcome them home, but also to receive her newborn child into the community. Women relieved her of the baby immediately and took turns carrying him back to the village. At the square, they had spread different dishes on banana leaves. They had also roasted a bull - the highest honor one could accord a special guest. They deemed Ma'alia's child a very special guest.

The celebration started with singing and dancing which Chizi and Ziki orchestrated with skill born of the need to improvise at the last moment. They picked lively tunes that spoke of the love of life and living, to which the drummers belted out a brisk rhythm. Chizi and Ziki blended their voices as they led the call, and the crowd responded on the chorus. When they had worked the villagers to fever pitch, they delivered the climax. They sang *Mwana wa Mberi*, a song of praise and gratitude for the first-born child.

Sakul Wiki-Zugu knew that if allowed, the people would sing and dance all night, so he stood up and motioned to Ziki to wind it down. When they did, he cleared his throat to speak.

"Friends, I don't have much to say other than we are indeed touched by what you are doing for us. How you received this child is more important. When we think about it seriously, we can only conclude he is no ordinary child. I know many of you may have whispered, wondering about his conception and if it happened before his parents came together. Well, if you had any doubts, the events of the last two days should show the Mighty One can do anything.

As we traveled to Bora-ini for the count, the time for Ma'alia's delivery came suddenly. She could not continue the rest of the way up to Mahu, so Sande and Juma found a cave where she could spend the night and continue the following day. That's when amazing things started to happen. Spirit-beings appeared to a group of boys from Kilima, who were looking after their village's herds. They declared to the boys the birth of this child, and when they ascended to the heavens as one, they became the star that led the boys to where he was born. The leopard that nearly killed Ma'alia several moons past also came to see the child. It actually came to see the child! And not only that. It also saved them when they came under attack from unseen assailants. How can you explain that?

The most wonderful thing is because of this child, many who might have perished at the escarpment survived. Even the authorities in Bora-ini, through a mistake on my part, heard that this child would be King of the Avantu. They became agitated and put some of us through a lot of trouble. Kofi and Avoga would not be here if it were not for events that can only be the work of The Mighty One on their behalf. Today, we have much to celebrate and much for which to be thankful. Therefore as we sing, dance, and eat, let us honor The One who has done all this. He has enabled us to have a glimpse of the spirit world by giving us a son. We celebrate him this day."

After he had spoken, the villagers clapped and cheered for a long time. They lifted up their voices, praised The Mighty One, and gave thanks for the safe return of their friends and kinsmen, for the safety of their village, for their animals, for their families and friends, and for life. As spontaneously as it started, the outpouring of praise quieted to a murmur. They shared what each person had brought to the feast.

A number of moons passed and the village put the count and the events surrounding it behind them. With the new addition to the family, Ma'alia had enough to keep her busy. She had a close relationship with her mother-in-law who was like a mother to her. She also regarded Simi as a friend in whom she could confide and count on for advice. When they worked together, whether pounding maize or tilling the land, they talked, laughed, and shared their hearts.

They also helped the younger Simi and Temin to learn their roles in the home and the community. They taught them to pick vegetables from the garden and cook them. The girls also learned how to save a fire from the previous night's embers and to light it for the next use. Ma'alia went with them to the river to draw water and taught them to balance the pot on the head without holding it. They showed the girls the proper way to greet visitors and serve guests. Ma'alia and Simi also mentored scores of other girls who were in and out of the home, which had become a favorite meeting point for village girls. The greatest attraction was Yssa, for whom competition was always fierce. Ma'alia was never short of help when she needed someone to watch the child.

Yossou continued his work, building and repairing huts, thatching roofs, and making beautiful wicker chairs and baskets. He exchanged his services for items they needed in the home - a clay pot, a new axe-head, or a garment. He sometimes took payment in cowry shells. His services were in demand in all the villages.

As a new father, no one could be prouder than Yossou. In the evening, when his work was over and the girls otherwise occupied, he would sit outside his hut holding his son - something most men did not do. To them, caring for a baby was a woman's work. His mother and his wife admired him for it. People treated him with more respect now that he was the father of a man-child. He became influential in village governance as Wiki-Zugu and other elders grafted him into their circle. Things went back to normal in Ronge and the surrounding villages as people went on with the activities of life. But it all changed when a group of strangers walked into the village with animals they had never seen before.

Son of the Oracle

Part Two

Chapter 11

the restless

Rasul was born to privilege in Laksh, the capital of Nagar Province, Chandustan. His father, Dev Seth, was a prominent businessman who traded in spices. For over two decades, he built his business to become the largest retailer and wholesaler of spices in the province.

Like other children of wealthy families, Rasul received the best education under the tutelage of highly esteemed scholars in the city. When he was older, his curriculum included mathematics, astronomy, astrology, architecture, and medicine. He also took courses in swordsmanship, horse riding, and public speaking. One subject that his parents emphasized was religion. They were devout Mahanassa, a faith whose core teaching said man found inner peace by tapping into the divine within himself.

Rasul was a congenial, intelligent student, though not outstanding in any respect. He frustrated his tutors by doing just enough to avoid uncomfortable discussions with his parents. His tutors pointed out he had great potential if only he should apply himself. However, he had a propensity for religious and philosophical studies where he was wont to ask questions that reflected profundity of thought and a personality deeper than the casual youth he pretended.

When he completed his formal education, Rasul eased into the family business, joining his older brother who was already a manager. Dev raised his sons to understand they were not entitled to anything in the world, so Rasul joined the company as a clerk where he proved himself a hard-worker. He got along with his father's employees and treated them fairly. After a number of promotions, he took charge of local distribution while his brother ran the import and export department. For their work, the sons received a decent stipend.

Rasul married Kulsam, a beautiful girl three years his junior, in a wedding so lavish all Laksh would talk about it for a long time. Like him, Kulsam was from a wealthy family, the daughter of Rai Bhapu, a retired army lieutenant and the deputy governor of Nagar Province. The families had been friends a long time and it only made sense to seal the friendship with the union of their children.

Kulsam joined her husband and in-laws in their large house in the affluent section of the city. The house had several rooms. Adjacent rooms had interconnecting doors. A third door opened into a corridor that ran all the way round the house. There was a common kitchen where all the women worked together, and two common shower stalls, and two toilets outside the house. Also living in the house was Rasul's older brother, Prankaj, his wife, Sonal, and their three children. The paternal grandparents made the third generation of the extended family as was typical in Chandustan.

Rasul and Kulsam were relatively happy and grew to like, if not love each other despite their arranged marriage. Within the first year, Kulsam gave birth to a girl named Pritti. Two years later, she had a boy whom they called Sankar. They loved their children and doted on them. With Rasul's allowance, they lacked nothing. While he worked, Kulsam looked after the children.

Three years into their marriage, things began to unravel. Rasul became increasingly distant and gradually lost interest in everything, including his family. He was irritable and unapproachable. The frequency of their moments of intimacy so decreased that he went weeks without touching her. He continued to function in the family business, but he was rapidly losing passion for it. After work, he would often wander the streets and get home just in time for dinner. He seemed to eat out of a sense of duty to the women who invested a lot of time preparing the elaborate dishes.

When she started to notice the change, Kulsam tried to find out what was bothering her husband. One evening she snuggled close to him in an attempt to get him to respond, but he brushed her off and turned his back to her. Shut out in this manner, she did not sleep, but lay staring in the darkness. She tried again a few weeks later after they had gone to bed - the only time they had any sort of privacy.

"Rasul, I'm worried about you. Lately you've become so withdrawn I don't know you anymore. I don't know if I'm the problem and whether or not you are happy with me."

"There's nothing wrong. Can't a man just have a moment of peace by himself?"

"Yes, but everyday for weeks? Honestly, when was the last time you knew me as your wife? We are literally living like brother and sister. Tell me what's going on Rasul. I'm your wife and I want to help."

"Why are you making such a fuss? I said there's nothing wrong. Leave it at that!"

Kulsam could hold it back no longer. She broke down and cried inconsolably. Rasul got out of bed and left the chamber. He did not return until it was almost morning. Neither spoke, though each knew the other was awake. She got up early as usual and washed her face with cold water so her mother-in-law,

Bilqis, would not notice the puffy eyes. She went about her chores as if nothing was wrong, but she could not hide the pain that seeped out of her breaking heart.

"Is everything well, my child?" Bilqis asked.

"Everything's fine, Mama" she answered unconvincingly.

When Rasul walked into the kitchen for breakfast, her in-laws could sense the wall of ice between them. They neither looked at one another nor addressed each other directly. When he left, Kulsam attacked her chores.

"They are having serious problems," Sonal whispered to her mother-in-law. "We should try to help them."

"We can't help her if she doesn't want to talk about it," Bilqis said.

That evening, the subject left work at the usual time and took one of his meandering routes home. As he turned the corner from the family business, a shadow detached itself from the wall of an adjoining building and followed him along the main street toward the center of town. About halfway, the subject turned onto a narrow dusty street.

"Hah!" the shadow thought. He knew there was a brothel on that street. He took the corner and had no trouble identifying the young man. The street served as a playground for urchins and a place for animals to lounge rather than a thoroughfare. A group of half-clad children played noisily with a dog. A dirty-white cow sat in the middle of the road, with an expression of utter disdain for the wretched mortals who considered her a deity. A nanny goat and her two kids dug through a pile of garbage. Women set their wares on the ground on both sides, selling everything from spices and sweets, to incense and textile. A man whose peripheral vision must have served him well, jumped in time to avoid a sheet of dirty water chucked out of a doorway. In turn, he spewed colorful epithets whence it came. A shrill female voice rewarded him with a matching response setting off a shouting match between the two. The subject walked right over the wet ground, seemingly unaware of the profane intercourse. A few strides later, the shadow jumped over the muddy patch past the irate man.

Noticing the subject approach the whorehouse, the shadow hastened to catch up so he could observe what would transpire. As luck would have it, a slender young woman stood in the doorway, batting her eyes at every man who approached. She was very attractive, but the heavy makeup, cherry red lips, and dark eye shadow gave her the appearance of a life-size waxen doll. Every now and then, she wiggled her limber midriff as a foretaste of what she offered.

The shadow's heart raced when the subject stopped in front of the seductress. In search of an excuse to stop, he went to the corner of a building and urinated while observing them discreetly. Their conversation seemed halting at first with the seductress acting coy. The subject maintained a serious demeanor and appeared to engage the woman. The shadow groaned when the subject, perhaps at her invitation, sat down in the lotus position by the door. Likewise, she slid down the doorpost, against which she leaned, to sit facing him. The shadow drifted back down the street and merged with pedestrians in order not to blow his cover. He walked slowly, looking back frequently in case the situation changed. He turned back when he felt he had gone far enough not to draw attention. He walked back and forth a few times, wondering when the subject would go in with the woman. Finally, as he approached the whorehouse once more, he saw the subject reach under his *kanzu*, take out a pouch, and hand it to her. *Hah! This is it!* But the subject stood up, bowed, and moved on. The shadow was disappointed because he would have to submit a mundane report. He was still curious about their conversation so he approached the woman who now sat bemused with the pouch in her laps. She was young, fair skinned, with a strong, supple body. The ravages of her profession, which circumstances had probably foisted on her, were yet to catch up with her.

"I'm sorry to bother you sweet lady," the shadow said insincerely. He sat on his haunches uninvited. "I know you are working, but I'm curious - what did that man just say to you?"

She looked up at him with black doe-eyes she obviously used effectively to mesmerize men. This time though, there was only sadness in them.

"He's a very sad man."

Her soft rasping voice complemented her perfectly sensuous lips despite the overdone lipstick. The shadow struggled to remain focused under the allure of her perfectly formed breasts and exposed flat belly. He forced himself to keep an eye on the subject, who trudged along. He did not want to lose him.

"I thought he wanted me, but he just wanted to talk," she continued

"What did he say to you?" the shadow asked, barely controlling his impatience. "What did he give you?"

"He asked me if I was happy. I tried to pretend as I usually do, but somehow, I could not pull it off with him. I told him I'm not happy. I told him I had nothing of my own and that's why I do what I do. He told me he has everything he could want - health, wealth, a lovely wife and children, but he isn't happy either. He feels empty and wants more. He gave me all the money he had. It's more than I could make in a month. Poor man," she added pensively.

As she was speaking, a thin woman with hard features came to the door from the inside. Without a word, she slapped the girl across the face.

"You are supposed to be working, not talking." She reached down and took the pouch from the girl's lap. "I'll take that. Stand up and get to work."

The thin woman went back inside. The girl stood up and struck her customary pose. She pasted a sweet smile on her face and jiggled her midsection for the shadow's benefit. The only incongruity was a single tear that squeezed out of her left eye and scurried down her red cheek like a squirrel that had barely escaped a tree snake.

The shadow was completely nonplussed and felt guilty for getting the girl in trouble. He rose hastily to run after the subject who was talking to himself and gesticulating. He turned left, toward the Mahanassa temple and the shadow followed. A group of *bhageli* - wise men and devotees of Lord Mahan, sat by the temple gate. The shadow saw him pass three wise men and then a fourth one rather hurriedly. He passed the entrance and stopped in front of a fifth holy man. He lingered until the priest was ready to attend to him. The shadow used the cover of approaching darkness to drift in closer. What he heard confirmed what the harlot's account. The subject was pouring his tormented soul before the priest. The shadow had seen enough. He made his way to the affluent section of town to report his findings.

The first three wise men that Rasul approached had taken vows of silence and shut themselves from the world by sitting stoically in the lotus position with eyes closed and hands clasped together. He bowed before each as he passed. The fourth man must have taken a vow rejecting physical indulgence in any form. By his awful odor, he must have rejected personal hygiene as well. Though he venerated the wise, Rasul could not bear the smell, and quickly moved to another one on the other side of the entrance. He felt he could talk to this particular wise man, so he sat down before him and waited until the man acknowledged him.

It was almost dark when the sage finally turned his attention to Rasul.

"What do you seek, my son?"

"I don't know, wise Master. I have everything most men desire yet I feel empty. I don't understand it and I don't know how to fill it. Perhaps from years of listening to people and teaching them you will tell me what I need to do. I want to be free," Rasul said desperately.

When he finished, the holy man looked him over for a while as if trying to read into his soul.

"Young man, I don't have an answer for your troubled heart. If I did, I'd have one for my own. For years, I have sat here, watched people, listened to their problems, and given advice. I sense you have a good heart. Nonetheless, you have a unique problem and it is this - you have everything yet have nothing. You have what the ordinary man pursues in hope of finding happiness. Your source of happiness or contentment is not in these things. Neither is it in you."

He stopped and held Rasul's gaze to make sure the younger man was listening to what he was going to say next.

"I have one suggestion. It is only a suggestion. Think hard about it before you act - especially if you might rue it later. This is what I suggest. Give up everything you have. Give it up completely and see if you'll find *all* you need in having nothing. Make this your quest and see where it leads you. May The Lord be with you. May you find what you seek."

With that, the wise man adjusted his focus inward, signaling he had said enough.

"Thank you, wise Master," Rasul said rising.

Rasul had never opened up to anybody about how he felt until today. The irony was things he had never shared with his family - not even his wife, he had shared this day with persons on opposite ends of the moral spectrum - a prostitute and a priest. Neither had condemned him, but his heart was none the lighter for it. It was already dark as he made his way home thinking about what the priest had just told him. *Give up everything you have… and see if you'll find all you need in having nothing.*

He dreaded going home and facing his family and their questioning looks. He thought about his wife and children, especially his children, and felt tortured beyond measure. He knew that he had not been a good husband or father lately and felt he had nothing to offer his family anymore. He hesitated before making his way through the garden and into the house.

His wife, his mother, and sister-in-law were in the inner courtyard preparing the ingredients for the next day's dishes. Kulsam caught his eyes for an instant before he averted them. He slunk into their bedchamber, where he sat in the dark. He could hear his children playing with their cousins in the yard and it made him feel worse. After a long period in which he allowed morbid thoughts to wander unsupervised in the corridors of his mind, the door opened quietly and Kulsam slipped into the room with a tray of food. She placed it on the floor and slipped out without a word, leaving the door ajar so he could see the tray and have the option of lighting the torch on the wall. He did not, preferring to sit in the near darkness. Even the sweet aroma of chicken pulau rice and rich chili sauce did not work up an appetite in him. He nibbled on the food, drank some mango juice, and set the tray in the hallway by the door.

He had just lain down and returned to his random thoughts when he heard footsteps approach then a tap on the door. His father strode into the room with his mother right behind, bearing a torch. Dev sat on the floor while his mother stuck the torch in a cradle in the wall. Rasul sat up, leaned on his elbow, and waited for them to speak. When his mother had sat down, his father began.

"Son, we are worried about you. Over the last several months, you have changed a lot. You are not the Rasul we've always known. As I understand it, you are not even taking care of your wife as you ought. That concerns me because her family and ours go back a long way. What's going on? What's bothering you?"

"Why is everybody so concerned about me? Just because I do not sit around making empty talk does not mean I have a problem. Why can't I just be?"

His mother spoke. "No, Son. You're trying to make this appear simpler than it really is. You come home late, you're always moody, you hardly talk to your wife or children, you hardly eat... Why shouldn't we be concerned?"

"And for that I have a problem?"

"Rasul," his father said. "You cannot continue like this. You have a duty to your wife, children, this family, and work. What will people think when my son wanders the streets aimlessly like a *vadaka*, the lowliest of beggars. What will they say when my son sits with harlots in front of a whorehouse and throws my hard earned money at them? Can you imagine...?"

"What? You followed me today? Your hard-earned money, is that right?" Rasul became animated.

"Well, then what were you doing...?"

Bilqis interrupted her husband and tried to calm both men down. "Dev, no!" she pleaded, but Rasul was ready to explode.

He stood up and looked down at his father, his face red as *pili pili,* and the veins on his temples and neck sticking out.

"What was I doing at the whorehouse? I'll tell you!"

"Rasul. Don't shout at your..."

"Shut up!" He snapped at his mother.

Bilqis had never seen her son like this. In shock, she gathered her dress, stood up, and fled the room. Dev was livid. In an instant, he also stood up and swung a vicious backhand striking his son across the mouth.

"How dare you talk to your mother like that?"

The blow checked Rasul. He put a hand to his lips and saw blood on his fingers as the warm salty taste filled his mouth. What he did next surprised his father. He went down on his knees, took his father's hand in both of his, and kissed it, leaving a red smear on it. He stood up.

"Tell Mama I'm sorry, and I love her. Tell Kulsam and the children I love them. I love you all."

He strode out of the room.

Dev clutched his chest and winced. He crumpled to his knees, leaning against the wall with his left hand. The pain in his heart was emotional as it was physical.

He had never told his sons he loved them or encouraged them to express affection. This was a cruel way to hear of his son's love for him.

"Andhia mahga!" It was the first profanity to escape Dev's lips in a long time. He directed it at himself.

In their lush, ornately adorned bedchamber, Bilqis buried her head in a cushion and sobbed, not so much for her own pain, as that of her son and daughter-in-law. She had dreaded this day. She had seen it coming, but she could not have prepared for it and the bitter heartache it brought.

Kulsam could hear the exchange in her bedchamber. She left the house when it got louder and angrier. She went outside, through the garden, and out of the compound where she sat on the ground her back against the wall. She rested her head on her knees, trying not to feel anything. A short while later, she heard footsteps and looked up. Rasul walked through the gate and was about to walk away when he noticed her. His upper lip was swollen and bleeding. Their eyes held for a moment. In his, she saw the torment in his soul - something she could neither question nor understand. He was as much the victim as the perpetrator. He turned and walked down the street as if desperate to get away. They had been married almost five years and it came down to this. He had turned his back on her and walked away. She knew he was not coming back. She buried her head in her knees and cried hot tears as though someone had driven a searing lance through her heart.

Hammoun was a popular physician in the ancient garden city of Bhustan, capital of Senna, during the reign of King Be'el-Sherrazz. He treated ailments of every kind. Rich and poor, he treated them all. If some needy soul could not come up with the fee, he would waive it and even give the person some *fezzah,* a silver coin or two, to buy food. What he charged the wealthy was more than enough to make up for his generosity. With his reputation, he had no shortage of clients. He was not a royal physician, but among his clients were men and women in high places from all across the land.

Hammoun's wife, Shiroz, bore him only one child, a feisty boy named Rezan. By the time he was a toddler, he was already a handful, managing to get into all manner trouble from which he was not always successful at extricating himself. In one instance, as a two-year old, he was at home with his mother while she picked sand out of grain. She did not notice him slip out of the kitchen. What alerted her was the silence that always prevailed when he was up to mischief. She set the tray aside and went to look for him. She searched all the rooms in the house. When she did not find him, she went out into the front yard, calling his name. Still there was no answer.

"Have you seen Rezan out here?" she asked a neighbor who was winnowing grain outside her house.

"No. I've been here a while. I haven't seen him."

Shiroz went back to the house and climbed up the steps to the roof calling his name. He did not answer. She looked in every chamber of the house again with no success. With mounting fear, she went out to the backyard. As she looked around and called out, a sound caught her attention. She stood still and listened. The muffled sound came from a section of the yard where they stored wood and other materials not in immediate use. She raced to the source and what she saw drained the blood from her head. Behind a number of thin logs leaning against the wall was a large round earthen pot with a small neck at the top. She saw his little body, bottoms in the air and legs frantically scuffing the side of the vessel. She barely heard the sounds coming from within it. His head was stuck in the neck of the pot and no matter how much he struggled, he could not work himself free. Shiroz ran to her child, lifted his body, and tried to pull him free. Holding him suspended in the air only increased his panic. He started to kick and scream. She realized that the more she pulled, the more she hurt him. She gently placed him back on the vessel and looked for something - anything she could use to ply him loose, but there was nothing suitable.

She finally decided on a drastic course of action. Picking up one of the logs, she swung at the side of the pot. The vessel shattered, releasing a large amount of water and the boy toppled over onto his side his head still stuck to a section of the broken pot. Carefully, Shiroz broke shards from the pot until all that remained was a clay necklace around his neck. She found a rock and broke it off. When at last he was free, she sat in the pool of water, holding him tight. The pot had filled up due to recent rains and she realized had been full, the boy would have drowned. With this sobering thought in mind, she refrained from reprimanding him, but was careful to keep a close eye on him in future. He still managed to get into sticky situations, though they were not as serious as the pot incident.

At the appropriate age, Hammoun placed Rezan under Maalim Shoopav, the Grand Master who tutored children of the affluent to prepare them for specialized fields such as medicine, astronomy, astrology, mathematics, and architecture. Hammoun hoped his son would follow in the medical profession, and took every opportunity to expose him to his work. In time, it became clear the boy had little interest in medicine, preferring to play with the abacus by day and spend evenings on the roof, gazing at the stars. His favorite game, which would have frustrated most children his age, was attempting to count them. Rezan found a way to try to accomplish this by picking out the brightest stars and mentally making them the pinpoints of a grid. Then he tried to count the stars within each grid, tallying them with a piece of charcoal on the floor of the roof. When he did not finish, he made a mental picture of where he left off by relating the particular grid to a pattern of stars. Realizing this, Shoopav pointed out to Hammoun that his son was highly gifted in mathematics and astronomy and he should encourage the boy to pursue that line of study.

Working his connections at the palace and calling in favors, Hammoun secured an apprenticeship for Rezan with Mursal, one of the king's counselors. It was not long before Mursal also noticed the lad's knack for numbers and astronomy. What had once been a game soon proved useful in the King's service.

Mursal introduced Rezan to charts and diagrams dating back centuries, in which his predecessors had recorded the relative positions and movement of the sun, moon, and stars. Almost immediately, Rezan identified on the charts, patterns that he had observed from his parent's rooftop. By applying his grid system to the charts, he refined his observations and inferences. Superimposing them on a time-line and using mathematical models, he found relationships between the movements of the celestial bodies and particular occurrences such as solar eclipses, lunar eclipses, and meteoric sightings. Mursal used this information to make predictions and advice the King. He was so impressed with the young man that he recommended him to the King for a position. The King approved Rezan's appointment as a junior advisor in his court. He moved out of his parents' house and went to live in special quarters in the palace. For his convenience, the king provided Rezan with a horse for travel on special assignments and general use. For his age, he had progressed rapidly in the sphere of political influence.

Hammoun died of breathing complications shortly after Rezan moved into the palace, leaving his Shiroz and Mursal as primary influences in the boy's life. From the tales she had heard, Shiroz was concerned for her son's well-being in the palace. She begged Mursal to watch over him and protect him from political intrigues and infighting. She also arranged for Rezan to marry her niece, Rukia, an unsophisticated but intelligent girl. Unlike her compatriots who grew up in Bhustan with its corrupting influences, Rukia had a strict upbringing. Shiroz had seen many city girls succumb to the enticement of wealth and the good life traders and merchants who came through town promised. None of these girls, she thought, were worthy of Rezan. She took Rukia under her wing to help her become a good wife. She also prevailed upon Mursal to give Rezan two days off each week so he could be home with his wife. On one of those days, Shiroz found things to do away from the house to afford the couple as much time and freedom as possible.

Rasul took to the road like a man possessed, completely unaware of people around him. A few neighbors out in the early evening recognized him, but his expression had a blankness indicating an attempt at conversation would meet with little success. He trudged on, mindlessly placing one foot before the other.

The crunching of his footsteps on the ground became an urgent cadence to which his spirit marched into another realm. His mind seemed to detach itself from his body. Now he heard his steps as if he were walking alongside himself. He heard his own heavy breathing overlay his footsteps.

He was in a sublime state of heightened perception. He sensed every blade of grass that swayed in the wind. Every tree was a solemn presence along the path, wondering whither he strode with such purposeless determination. He felt the chill in the air as the wind wafted across the path, but he did not feel cold. The entire universe took on the form of a celestial blanket that began to wrap itself tightly around him. It restrained and dragged him along.

Time lost its rigidity and space collapsed and their march to eternity vaporized into swirling nebulous ether. He was in the past, standing in the Mahanassa temple in the middle of town. His cousin, Subina, and his childhood friend, Anish, were there too. They gazed at him curiously.

"Rasul, what's wrong? Are you alright?" Subina asked.

They approached and caught him. They started to drag him toward his parents' house in the future.

"No! No! I don't want to go back there!" He cried and struggled free only to be sucked into a star-spangled void.

After timeless swelling, he stood in the infinite before a most brilliant light. It did not actually radiate, but rather suffused him and everything around. He experienced a strange feeling standing in the light. It was not fear, but a profound sense of unworthiness. He felt lost – damned. Yet he yearned to remain in the presence. He raised his voice and cried out. Then the light spoke.

"Why are you here, Rasul? I did not send for you."

Rasul was speechless. His voice stuck in his throat and his tongue felt like a slab of marble. He gasped and struggled to breath. He started to slip from the light. He tried to reach out and hang on, but he could not. He plummeted faster, falling past lost souls in the nebula hopelessly calling on him to save them. Even with the rushing sound of his fall in space, he could still hear his own breathing... and footsteps approaching, marching in time. Whoever approached was breathing as heavily as he was and soon caught up with time. The footsteps faltered. He groaned when he slammed through a wall of darkness into oblivion.

After serving for five years in the palace, Rezan did not have much about which to complain. It did not bother him that he and Rukia still did not have children. In a way, he was glad because they would have distracted him away from his beloved study of mathematics and astronomy. Except for the passing of his father, which left a huge vacuum in his life, everything was going well.

From his understanding of the movements of the sun, moon, and stars, Rezan predicted a solar eclipse and three lunar eclipses. He left the divination to Mursal who wove the phenomena into his counsel to the King. These prophecies, for or against certain courses of action, were highly speculative, but Mursal had a lot of experience spinning them favorably. Fortunately, Mursal's pronouncements had worked out favorably so far.

As one who recognized talent, Rezan asked Mursal to petition the King to establish a university dedicated to the study of mathematics and astronomy. The king consented and Rezan became the first chair of the institution. He sought out young, talented individuals with an interest in these fields thereby ensuring a constant flow of fresh ideas and research. He developed an extensive curriculum that led to the design and refinement of several mathematical and astronomical tools and models, including a lunar calendar, various number systems, and a system used to tell the time. In appreciation of the meticulous records his predecessors kept, upon which he built his knowledge, Rezan insisted students and tutors also keep precise, clear records of their research and findings. As his fame spread across the region, rulers and scholars from other lands consulted him frequently.

Rasul woke to the sensation of something cold and moist on his face. He opened his eyes to see a scruffy dog sniffing cheek. When he stirred, the dog retreated to a safe distance from where it regarded him with its head hanging low and its tail between its legs. Rasul squinted as his eyes adjusted to the morning light. He could make out men, women, and children standing in a circle, observing him silently. Only the dog ran back and forth within the ring of humans. Rasul rolled over and sat up, but he raised himself too quickly because the blood drained out of his head and blackness flooded in. He fell back and there was an explosion of lights when his head hit the ground.

When he came to, someone was propping him up and holding a steaming metal cup of spiced herbal tea to his lips. He drank gratefully. His head gradually cleared and pain began to register. Its epicenter was a sizeable mound on his forehead.

"Where am I?" he asked. His breath misted as he spoke.

"This is the village of Tandoon. I am Bhundia," the man answered as he fed him tea. He was about the same age as Rasul's father, but looked more haggard from a hard life and long hours in the sun. "You are a stranger to these parts. Are you a holy man?"

Despite his melancholy disposition, Rasul could not help chuckling at the question but he realized the man spoke in earnest.

"Me? No! I'm just a lost soul trying to find myself in the cycle of life."

"A *bhageli*," people whispered they heard his response.

"Lord Mahan must have sent you to us. Just this week we scattered the ashes of our priest on the river. His dog," he pointed at the wretched creature that ran indecisive rings around him, "found you this morning. That is one sign. The other is *Gulbit* did not carry you off."

"*Gulbit*?" Rasul asked, gently taking the man's arm off his shoulders now that he felt strong enough to sit up by himself.

There was palpable fear among the villagers at the mention of the name. Even as he answered, the man whispered as if this Gulbit would hear.

"We are not sure whether it's a lion, tiger, or leopard, but it's certainly a big cat. It has terrorized us for six months now, attacking at night when no one can see it. It has carried off five goats, seven sheep, and killed two cows. That's not the worst of it. It has even broken into homes and carried off three children at different times, the last attack coming just six days ago when it snatched an eight-year-old boy. We've sent out search parties to find the victims, but have found nothing - not even the bones. He's very clever this Gulbit. For you to have traveled this far in his territory and to have lain there as long you did without coming to harm is a divine omen."

"I'll tell you the truth. I left my father's house in Laksh, my wife, children, and wealth last night. I don't know where I'm going or what I am going to do. I just left it all behind."

This comment set off a murmur in the crowd. The dog, recently distracted to chase an itch on its rump, also reacted to the buzz with renewed running back and forth.

"You left Laksh last night and you are here this morning? It takes at least three days to walk from the city to our village! How did you do it overnight?" someone asked.

Rasul, not knowing where he was in the first place, could not educate them.

The man who fed him tea thought for a moment then said, "I think it is a good sign that you came to our village. Stay with us a while. We have a small temple where you can stay, study holy writings, and teach the people." He turned to the crowd. "What do you say, my friends?"

"Yes, let him stay with us. The gods sent him to us."

"Please stay. We beg you, stay."

Sensing their desperation, Rasul hesitated a moment then agreed almost impulsively. He had nothing to lose after all. In any case, he had been honest about his situation and they still wanted him.

"I will stay," he said.

They raised a cheer and danced around him. Some men picked him up, and carried him shoulder high to the temple as they chanted praise to Lord Mahan. The dog, not to be left out, ran around erratically, looking up at the stranger, and yipping frantically.

At the temple, they installed Rasul on a cushion at the top of a flight of chipped, worn steps. Bhundia and others then lined up to pay him homage. They praised the gods for bringing him to them. This change in fortunes left Rasul dumbfounded. Just yesterday, he had a job in his father's business, a wife, and a home. When he left, he neither knew where he went nor cared whether he lived or died. He had pushed himself ruthlessly to get away from all the things that bound him until he collapsed. According to the villagers, he had walked a three-day journey overnight. Now this group of villagers looked up to him as their spiritual leader when he could have used some wisdom and guidance himself.

Maybe the gods are trying to tell me something. He put his hands together and uttered a blessing upon the villagers as they came up to him, noting how satisfied they all seemed after meeting with him.

Rasul's stay in Tandoon turned out to be an enlightening experience. Having grown up wealthy, he had no concept of poverty. Now he saw people who breathed the same air he did, but struggled to put a single meal on the table. He often felt guilty that these poor folk made sure he had something to eat so he could concentrate on the pursuit of holiness. They depended entirely on what they grew on their tiny plots of land. Many who did not have land had to travel a long way to work the fields of wealthy landowners for a pittance.

Life was hardest between harvests. If the previous season's rains came late or failed, they starved. The villagers told him of a time in the past when famine almost wiped out the village. Were it not for their last holy man who encouraged them to stay, they would have abandoned the village. Gulbit made a bad situation worse by reducing the time within which they could work safely. They could not risk being out of their homes after dark or before dawn.

Realizing the people ascribed divine attributes to him, Rasul did his best to meet their needs by giving them hope. In the morning, he read and memorized the holy books. In the afternoon, he meditated on the ideas he read and formulated a philosophy of life based on them. He encouraged the Tandooni to aspire for the best while remaining circumspect. Above all, because the villagers bore the yoke of poverty, he taught them to look on challenges as opportunities. The villagers gradually responded to his teaching with subtle changes in attitude, increase in productivity, and decrease in crime and other social ills.

There was, however, one dark moment in his time in Tandoon. Just ten days after his arrival, Gulbit struck again. Pinita, a petite mother of four, had stepped out of her house early in the evening to relieve herself before going to bed. According to her husband, she could not stand the idea of relieving herself in a pot in the house. She chose to take her chances and sneak just outside the door for a quick answer to nature's call. By all indications, that is precisely where she was when the animal pounced. This latest incident rattled the villagers because it confirmed Gulbit was smarter than they thought. He (everyone assumed the animal was male) chose and stalked his prey carefully. With the same precision, he picked the time and place to strike.

The screams of the unfortunate woman haunted Rasul. Her shrill voice carried the full weight of terror in the face of death. She screamed her husband's name before her voice cut off, probably as the animal broke her neck. Rasul was angry because the entire village was at the mercy of this beast and none one knew what to do about it. As they had come to expect, a search for the remains of the victim were fruitless. Feeling he had to do something, Rasul decided on a radical course of action. It was a gamble that could go horribly wrong for him and the village he hoped to save. He would start tonight.

Pandip lived across from the temple. He liked the new holy man and the fresh, positive outlook he had brought to the village. The evening after the attack, he looked over to the temple and saw both the entrance and the temple door left wide open. It bothered him, but he did not dwell on it. The following day, however, he observed the same thing. As darkness fell, he saw no attempt on the part of the holy man to close these entrances. Pandip got concerned. It was unlikely Gulbit would strike again after two days, but it was unwise to give him the opportunity to identify likely prey. Pandip was tempted to run across at least to shut the gates, but decided against it. He went to bed ill at ease. In the morning, he was relieved to see the holy man at the top of the steps, reading the ancient writings. Later that day he mentioned his observations to Bhundia. They agreed to pass the word around for all the Tandooni to close the gates of the temple compound while it was still safe. They implemented their plan and closed the gates that evening. To his dismay, Pandip saw the holy man descend the steps and throw the gates open again. When he went back up to the temple, he also left the door wide open. Pandip went to see Bhundia about it the following day.

"I don't know what he's doing, but clearly it's deliberate." Bhundia said.

"It is. He knows the risk he's taking, especially now that Gulbit is ready to attack again."

"I like him. I would hate for something to happen to him."

The fifth night after Gulbit took Pinita, Rasul lay awake looking at the stars through the small window in the sleeping quarters of the temple. Every night since his decision to leave the gates and the door open, he went to bed with deep apprehension. When Pandip and Bhundia confronted him about it, he simply told them to leave the matter alone.

Why am I doing this? Is it out of a sense of guilt because I could not save the poor woman? Do I want to punish myself for leaving my wife, effectively making her a pariah? My children are without a father. I don't deserve to live.

These people have nothing yet they make the best of it. They love their husbands, their wives, and their children. Even that woman's last utterance was her husband's name. But if I die, then what? If Gulbit drags me to the forest, where no one will find my bones, then what? He'll just come back and take someone else. What will I have achieved?

He was still debating with himself on the merits of placing himself in harm's way without fully knowing the consequences when he felt an odd sensation on his skin as though something repulsive crawled on it. He turned away from the window. The feeling crept over his entire body from the scalp down to the toes again. The reason was right there - literally staring at him. The shiny yellow eyes did not move.

Gulbit!

By the silhouette, it was a lioness - a big one. Rasul did not dare move lest he upset the creature. He knew the light from the stars lit his face slightly, but for the animal, it might as well be day. It crouched, took three strides, and stopped. Rasul was so terrified he could hardly breathe. A foul odor filled the chamber and only later did he realize it was his own smell of fear. Just as the cold terror had engulfed him, a calm wave swept in, washing out the fear. At that precise instant, Rasul imagined he saw the silhouette of the animal back up just a fraction and its stance became defensive rather than aggressive. It seemed ready to run, but Rasul was not about to test this possibility. Slowly, he sat up. His eyes never left the animal and the yellow eyes never left his either. He felt a connection with the animal - two beings, each looking deep into the other. Neither had the advantage as both ascended to a plane where natural law did not apply. In this realm, Rasul addressed the cat. He did not know where the words came from.

Why, my sister, do you consume what you were never meant to eat? Why do you visit such misery upon men?"

The animal relayed the answer, which he understood without the need for a physical medium. What came through was that she had been the matriarch of her pride until a younger, stronger female took over and ran her off. Other lions had ostracized her and she could not go into their territories. Her sole sanctuary was a small corner of the jungle, not far from the village, with very little room to hunt. But she had to survive, and the village provided the solution, albeit one she would not have taken if she had a choice. Therefore, she applied her skills to finding prey in the village and taking it back to her territory away from other predators.

Rasul's heart was heavy when he perceived what had driven her to eat human flesh, but he understood. Once more, he felt the warm glow coursing through his body. The words came unbidden.

"Sister, you are free from the taste of human flesh from this night. You will find food on your hunting grounds until the day you return to the soil."

After this proclamation, they both descended from the cosmic plane as it morphed into the present. The animal came up to him, licked his face twice and left. Rasul was exhausted and remained staring at the door for a long time. He then fell back, his emotions in a whirl. Strangely, he was not elated that he had encountered the dreaded Gulbit up close and lived.

Pandip got up in the middle of the night to use the night pot. He was still concerned for the holy man's safety, so on impulse, he opened the window facing the temple just a crack. He was not sure what he expected to see, but nothing seemed out of place at first. He was about to close the window when he noticed a movement at the temple door. Utter panic came over him when he saw the dark form slip silently down the steps, out of the gate, and disappear from view. From its attitude, it carried nothing but images of the badly mauled holy man's body filled his mind. He closed the window quickly in case the animal detected him. His hands were shaking. He was sweating and breathing heavily. As he regained his composure, he felt his bladder pulsating and a warm wetness running down his legs. He quickly found the night pot before his organs gave out altogether. He did not go back to sleep, but waited in agony for morning when he would collect the holy man's body.

He was both mystified and overjoyed when day broke and he saw the holy man outside the temple studying the sacred writings. No one had delivered breakfast to him, so Pandip asked his wife to brew a cup of tea and make some flat bread and spiced goat cheese. He delivered them personally so he could look for evidence of an attack on and around the holy man.

"Good morning, Holy Master."

"Good morning, Pandip. Did you have a good night?"

"I had a good night, Master. And you?"

"I had a wonderful night, thank you."

You must have, Pandip thought. Aloud, he said, "I bring you something to eat."

He observed a glow around the man that he had not seen up to this day. There was neither a sign of a struggle around the temple nor an assault on his person.

"Thank you, Pandip. You are always very kind."

He left the holy man's presence wondering if last night was just a bad dream. But he was absolutely certain about what he had seen. As he headed back to his house, right there on the ground by the gate, he saw the fresh print of a big cat's paw in the loose soil. He looked back at the holy man who had gone back to his books. Pandip shook his head and went to prepare for the day. He mentioned his bafflement only to his wife and Bhundia.

Days passed without another attack. Even more days passed. The villagers began to wonder what had happened to Gulbit, whispering the question lest they jinx themselves. They were sure something had happened. Most thought he had died. Others thought he had moved to another area, or someone had captured him. The important thing was they grew less fearful of the big cat coming to snatch a person or livestock. Life was much better and the mood much lighter. People started their days earlier and finished later. Parents could now sit outside their houses and tell their children stories in the evening. They even developed legends about the dreaded Gulbit with different theories about what became of him. Only two men knew Gulbit had not died. One could not explain why the attacks had stopped despite this fact. The other could, but he did not talk about it.

Chapter 12

seeing the light

As life became more bearable for Tandoon, Rasul started to get restless. He felt fulfilled in having taught the people to look at life differently. He had read the holy writings several times and woven them into his thoughts and teachings, but he still wanted more. Because he could not find what he sought, he was often frustrated with himself, the world, and the divine being - if there was one out there. The restiveness that had driven him from his wife and family reemerged. Unlike his predecessor who stayed within the confines of the temple, he started taking walks around the village, acknowledging the villagers who bowed before him as he passed. He would sit on the ground to teach the children who often followed him on his walks. His favorite spot was at the edge of the village where he sat facing the hills and valleys to the west.

One morning, while seated at this spot, he tried to meditate, but the question kept coming back to him. *What is the meaning of life - my life in particular?* In desperation, he opened his eyes hoping to see the face of The One in the heavens or a sign of some sort. Instead, he saw a light. He had seen bright stars at dusk or dawn, but never this late in the morning and certainly not this bright. The light grew brighter as it slowly inched across the sky. It seemed to beckon. His heart quickened.

Arise! Go west!

He heard it, but it was neither a sound nor a voice in his head. It was as if the words brushed over him. That was all the urging he needed. Without going back to the village to bid the people farewell, he rose and took the road. The people he met wondered what was wrong. He walked with urgency, barely acknowledging their greetings. He looked up frequently to see the star. It sat there for the better part of the morning before fading away. He walked the rest of that day, stopping only to chew on wild berries and nuts. By nightfall, he was exhausted and could push himself no further. He sought shelter among some rocks in a field where he promptly fell asleep.

Because of his research in celestial bodies, Rezan was used to staying up late at night. On his days off away from the palace, he often went up to the roof of his mother's house to enjoy the evening breeze and gaze at the stars. Rukia usually joined him to make the most of their time together. He had long given up trying to interest her in the stars and their movements. She grew up under the open sky and took their presence for granted - much like her own existence. She saw no need to expend time and energy trying to explain it.

"They are there because they are there," was her simple philosophy.

Rezan had liked her right from the start. She did not have lofty goals in life, but she was intelligent in her own way and was a good listener. She especially loved to hear about the students from other lands and their experiences. When he fell silent while trying to figure out something he had noticed, she did not nag him. She would lie beside him until he disengaged from the problem and came down to earth.

One such night, they lay on the roof enjoying each other's company. She draped an arm over his chest, her fingers alternately doodling on his skin and pulling on his chest hairs. He lay on his back, fingers interlocked behind his head, eyes lazily caressing the sky. Suddenly he stiffened. Rukia opened one eye and looked at him, wondering what had caught his attention this time. Off to the south and west, he saw a faint heavenly body creeping upward in the sky. He sat up, watching it grow perceptibly brighter as it rose. Rukia also sat up and looked.

"What's that?" she asked.

"I don't know. That's never happened before. It formed out of nowhere and is now as bright as a star - and getting brighter by the moment."

They watched it a little longer.

"I'm going to the palace to record it. It might be of significance to the king."

He rose, went down the steps, and gathered a few things he would take back to the palace, loading them on the steed the King had provided. Rukia came down and talked with him as he packed. He bid her goodnight and rode to the palace, his eyes on the strange light.

The banner on the horse identified him as a man of standing in royal service. The guards at the priests' annex recognized him easily and let him in. He went straight to the observatory where he hurriedly pulled out recent charts. He perused them to see if there was an antecedent to tonight's occurrence. All the data and calculations showed nothing strange in the offing. He then took a fresh chart and wrote down the day and the hour before he began to record his observations. When he had written all he had observed, Rezan continued to watch the light, which now shone brighter than all the stars. Unlike Mursal, he was not one to ascribe spiritual or political significance to such phenomena, but he was certain this event had meaning beyond the natural. Out of curiosity, he estimated its land position based on its elevation, time of appearance, and relation to other celestial bodies. He looked over a map of the land masses and factored in the coordinates.

By his calculations, the light stood over a position somewhere in Nubia, a land with which his people had a little contact. After some time, the light faded. Rezan did not go back to his wife. He completed the entries in his journal then went to his sleeping quarters. As morning approached, he was still thinking about what he had witnessed.

At daybreak, he related what he had seen to Mursal, showing him the journal entries and charts. The older man listened keenly, occasionally asking for clarification. When Rezan finished, Mursal thought for a long time. He was grave when he spoke.

"A light usually indicates a god or a king. The rising star could mean a new king arises in the lands to the south and west, but I don't know what it means to us. Say nothing of this to anyone until I hear what the other advisors make of it. We don't want to upset the king."

"It's you who speak to the king of such matters. All I do is observe and record," Rezan said, but his mind and his heart were wide open to the numerous questions regarding the strange sighting. The matter would gnaw on him for many days.

The rains were upon them. It was time for Abena to move his animals from low-lying areas, which receive a large amount of rain, to higher ground on the leeward side of the Enjere Mountain Range. Here, the rain fell sparsely and because of the higher altitude and rocky soil, it did not soak in and turn the land to bog. Better still, what little rain fell magically transformed the jaundiced scrubland into a lush green paradise. The rocky terrain also allowed the rain to collect in several pools and small lakes that provided sweet, fresh water.

Like other livestock owners, Abena took advantage of the wet season to calf his animals. Cows that had their calves in this season had plenty of milk as they did not have to travel long distances to find food. The growth of the herd, and its concentration over a smaller area, made keeping the animals a labor-intensive occupation during the rains. Nonetheless, it was perhaps the best time of year because the weather was cooler and everyone benefited from increased milk production and the slaughter of older animals for meat and hide. It was the time the herder actually enjoyed the fruit of his labor.

Early one evening, after a hard day of tending to the animals, Abena relaxed outside his *manyatta* - a simple dome-shaped structure made of thin, sturdy branches covered with hides, while his children played in the moist soil. The women sat near the kitchen with their youngest ones. At one point in the evening, the children approached him with a request that seemed out of turn in itself.

"*Abo*, tell us again how the stars came to be."

Abena smiled and wondered how many times he would have to tell the same story. He remembered as a child, he too, had asked Disana to tell it several times.

"Well, children, this is how it happened…

Many, many harvests in the past, there was a great famine in the land. There was nothing to eat and many animals died. A father saw his children starving and could not bear it, so he went into the wilderness in search of food. Unfortunately, he walked too far and got lost. He wandered all over the land trying to find his way home, but he always found himself back where he started. This continued for a long time and he grew tired. It was getting dark and there was no moon in the sky. He knew his friends would be looking for him. So he lit a fire and when he got it going, he took some embers and tossed them to the wind, which caught them and lifted them…"

"Higher and higher, brighter and brighter," his son finished, his gaze fixed to the sky.

Abena wondered why the story so captivated him today. The boy's face was growing radiant right before his eyes, and he had the appearance of one deep in a trance. Abena noticed a reflection in his eyes. He turned to the sky and could not believe what he saw - a light, brighter than any star. It rose in the heavens, getting brighter by the moment. He sat with his children and together they watched it rise. It stopped and stood in the sky for a long time. His wives, also seeing the strange phenomenon, called out asking what it meant. He said he had never seen anything like it before and could not hazard a guess as to its meaning. Shortly, the children all fell asleep. Their mothers came and peeled them from him one by one, leaving him to stare in wonder until the star faded.

Sometime in the night, Rasul woke up wondering what smelly creature nestled close to him. He recognized the mangy dog that had woken him when he arrived in Tandoon. The animal had tracked him down and probably helped by snuggling up to him and keeping him warm. It got up and seemed to apologize for taking the liberty to follow. Rasul smiled and stroked the dog's muzzle. Still exhausted, he went back to sleep until the light of dawn woke him again. The dog was already up and pacing with his snout to the ground in search of something to eat. It occasionally pulled on a clump of grass and chewed on it. Rasul shook his head clear of sleep, yawned and stretched, then got up to continue his journey.

From his work at his father's business, he had an idea which way to go. He had to find the Great Trade Highway that linked the mighty North Kingdom's capital, Fong Hu, in the mountains further east, to the lands in the west. The highway would take him towards his destination. The voice had clearly said, "Go west!" He, therefore, took every step with this purpose in mind. He braved the cold of the mountainous terrain for the next five days, taking shelter behind rocks when the wind became violent and bitterly cold. At such times, he was thankful for Sibi, as he named the dog, which helped keep him warm by laying his bony body beside him. They stopped in two small villages along the way where Rasul set himself up at the temple. Most mountain communities held holy men in high regard and rarely did them harm. A few residents left donations of food wrapped in rough cloth at his feet. By the sixth day, he had cleared the highest section of the mountains and started the descent to the lowlands. He could see the city of Doyath through the mountain ranges. He was close to the trade highway.

In Doyath the following afternoon, Rasul found the city a little smaller than Laksh. He was, however, amazed at its cosmopolitan atmosphere because there were people from every known nation - Sirim, Ghalan, Guandong, Maghden, Chechin, and Li Ngu, to name a few. Along the main street, there were businesses on both sides with people buying and selling, and trading in everything from spices, silk, pottery, and glassware to herbs, hides, skins, and ivory.

Rasul had neither money nor means to buy anything to eat. Sibi took care of himself by rummaging through garbage and coming away with a bone or offal. Rasul walked on, leaving him to catch up when he finished foraging. Hoping to get some food himself, Rasul approached a temple at the corner of a street, but the cold expression of the priests at the gates discouraged him. He experienced the same thing at another temple further down the road. Apparently, the priests in this area did not take kindly to perceived competition. People also stopped what they were doing and looked at him strangely. He felt unwelcome and made his way as far out of the city in a hurry. In the evening, he ate wild fruits and berries before lying down to sleep in an old granary in an abandoned field. The weather was perfect and he did not need to cover himself to stay warm. For five more days, he drove himself hard, avoiding towns and villages and living only on fruits and herbs he picked along the way.

Presently, the mountains gave way to the fertile lowlands of northern Chandustan where numerous rivers flowed providing plenty of water for irrigation. The natives grew rice, peas, beans, wheat, sorghum, and a variety of other crops. Rasul took the liberty to pull on an ear of grain or pluck a few pods of beans to supplement his diet of wild fruits and herbs. He had decided to forgo the assumed advantage of priesthood to obtain food and found the decision highly liberating. He came upon many streams from which he could drink, bathe, and wash his worn out garments. He walked three more days in these farmlands before he came to a road that led to the great highway.

Finally, after almost two weeks since setting off from Tandoon, he arrived in the city of Janshin at the junction of the Great Trade Highway. He was weary, but found a renewed sense of purpose just by setting foot on the famous highway. As usual, he kept walking until he was beyond the city limits. Only then did he try to find a place to spend the night. He had become adept at identifying edible plants and fruits for food, and finding abandoned structures for overnight shelter. He was not afraid of wild animals, but he took precautions to make it harder for them to make a meal of himself or Sibi.

The next day, Rasul took to the road in earnest. Men and women traveled on mules or donkeys on the busy highway. Swift emissaries rode on horseback and large caravans, consisting mostly of camels, carried goods and wares. Occasionally, there was an oddity - an individual with nothing to trade and bearing no message for distant royalty. Such was Rasul.

By the third day, the terrain began to change. The vegetation thinned rapidly, becoming drier and offering less to eat. Fortunately, the states that benefited from the highway mandated the construction of wells at regular intervals along the highway so travelers always had fresh water for themselves and their animals. He also knew the long trek took its toll on life and limb and caravans often had to replace individuals who took ill or died. He therefore inquired of each caravan, or group of travelers heading his direction, if they needed an extra hand in exchange for food for himself and his dog. On the fifth day, a trader from Mae Ting, a city in the northern kingdom of Li Ngu, finally agreed to hire him.

Hsun Wang, his new employer, traded primarily in silk, which was highly valued by the rich in lands far to the west. Along the way, he picked up spices, hides, and skins of rare animals favored by the ruling class in the near West. He turned Rasul over to a dour character called Zhe Dong who trained him on how to handle camels. Dong also taught Rasul how to load and unload the animals without damaging the goods and, most important of all, how to guard the property. Rasul proved to be a quick study and soon took charge of five camels. By watching and listening carefully, he began to pick up their languages, which were vastly different from Nagrani. In the evenings when they stopped to rest, the workers sat in groups, depending on the region from which they came. Rasul, the only Chandustani, sat by himself looking at the stars and reciting verses he had memorized from the holy writings in Tandoon. This practice kept his mission alive in his heart in spite of the loneliness.

Over the next six weeks of travel, the landscape gradually changed for the worse. The scrublands gave way to desert with nothing but sand and sky. It would have been a beautiful sight except that walking in sand was especially arduous. Just when everybody hoped it would not get worse, it did. They came to a wind corridor where the wind whipped sand in the air and obliterated the sun for days.

Rasul begged his employer for a piece of cloth to cover his mouth and nose. He cut a small portion with which he covered Sibi's snout. These were among the most miserable days he had ever experienced. The constant darkness, the incessant howling of the wind, and inability to eat because the wind would cover the food with sand, was enough to drive a person insane. Wang pushed them hard, but it was often impossible to keep moving. Even the most experienced guide would have trouble finding his way in the near darkness and constantly shifting sandscape.

After four days of driving wind, the nightmare ended as the wind died down. They lost a camel and two men in the sandstorm. They dragged the camel to the side of the road where it would rot. They interred the men in shallow graves. Wang pushed on for five more days, trying to make up for lost time.

In all this, there was good news and bad news. The good news was the wind and sand were behind them. The bad news was the mountains stood ahead of them. From what he could pick out from fellow travelers, one could travel through the entire mountain range without having to ascend to high ground. Over centuries, caravans had identified areas where they could travel in the valleys going round the mountains that towered over them like sheer walls. Rivers and streams flowed on the lush green valley floors, herds of deer grazed unconcerned, and mountain goats frolicked with incredible agility on the mountainsides. The breathtaking scene made him reflect on the creative power of The One.

With the beauty of creation came the ugliness of the human heart. Rasul noticed his companions had become tense and constantly scanned the mountainsides. He surmised that bandits attacked convoys as they traveled through passes where they were most vulnerable. They could shoot arrows from vantage points on the hillsides with little chance the caravan would counter effectively. In an attack, caravan drivers did not expect to repel an attack. They strove only to minimize material losses. Human life was expendable, so they concentrated their efforts on keeping the caravan moving.

As chance would have it, the bandits chose to attack this particular convoy. It happened as they approached a narrow pass between two craggy mountain walls. The bandits released a volley of arrows, killing several men instantly. Though the rest fought back gallantly, they could not repel the bandits.

"Keep moving!" Dong, who was behind Rasul shouted. As soon as the words were out of his mouth, he took an arrow to the chest and fell. Rasul tried to turn around and run, but the dying man's camels ran him over and sent him crashing on a rock. The impact opened a deep gash in his temple and knocked him out.

When he came to, it was cold and dark. He shivered uncontrollably. Rasul tried to remember where he was, but could not, though he had a feeling that something traumatic had happened. His head ached so badly he felt it would explode. His tongue was thick in his mouth and he had a raging thirst. He looked around, trying to gather his wits when he saw the dog at his feet. The animal seemed happy to see him alive. It stood up, wagged its tail vigorously. Rasul took great comfort in the gesture. He wanted to get away from this place, but was too weak to rise. The dog, as if sensing his predicament, started to sniff around amidst the chaos. He came back carrying a leather canister full of water in his mouth. Rasul opened it and drank thirstily. The dog searched again and returned with something else. Rasul took it and tasted dry spiced meat. He ate gratefully. He did not feel inclined to travel in the dark so he fell asleep again.

The dog's barking woke him. It chased off big birds investigating the possibility of gaining nutrition from his still form. The sun had just started to paint the tops of the mountains red and yellow. Flies buzzed around him, but he was too weak to fight them off. He looked around and could not believe the carnage. Bodies lay strewn around him. The sight jolted his memory and he now recalled Dong shouting before an arrow cut him down. The caravan had come under attack and his fall had probably spared him from witnessing the massacre as it happened.

Apparently, the bandits had shaken them down and taken all valuables. How they had spared him, he did not know, but he had seen enough and he wanted to get out of this valley of death. The vultures were already fighting over bodies. Rasul watched with disgust as a bird dug its beak into a man's eye socket and plucked out the organ with the vein still attached. He looked away as the bird wrestled the eye free. Mustering all his strength, he rose, taking the canister with him. He staggered, stepping over bodies in an effort to get out of the pass. Sibi followed closely. The giant birds bobbed out of his way, each turning an eye toward him, miffed that a possible meal should be perambulating.

Just before he exited the pass, he saw a black pouch partially hidden in the grass. He picked it up and found it full of gold coins. A fleeing survivor must have dropped it. Rasul wondered how he would get the gold back to Wang. For the present though, he had to make it out of the mountain range alive. He knew it was not going to be easy given the way he felt.

He made it out of the narrow pass to an open area with a creek flowing a little way from the trail. Not having the energy to go all the way to it, Rasul chanced on the dog. He put the canister in its mouth and pointed toward the creek. Sibi immediately bounded through the grass in the direction Rasul indicated. He returned a short while later with a good amount of water in the container. Rasul patted it and drank once more. He felt better and took to the road resolutely.

On one of his days off, Rezan came home to find a stranger in the guest chamber of his mother's house. The young man appeared Panjuri or of similar extraction from the east. He slept fitfully, his face twitching sporadically as if he was reliving a traumatic experience.

"Some travelers found him on the Great Trade Highway a half a day's ride from here." Shiroz explained. "They said he would have died if he had stayed out there another day. You remember three days ago a caravan came into town with many injured, saying bandits had waylaid them at the Ordum Pass? They said many died in that attack and they lost much property. He must have been one of those left for dead. His rescuers came into town asking for a physician and the townspeople directed them to us. I know enough from helping your father to help him pull through. See here," she pointed at the bandaged head. Blood seeped through the dressing at the temple. "He probably lost a lot of blood and did not have enough water, food, and rest."

"You did well, Mother. Father would have been proud of you."

"Thank you. Your wife and I worked on him together." Rukia smiled, blushing slightly.

"I'll move him to the palace and into the care of the King's physicians. We might learn something from him."

"Good. We'll let him rest for now."

As Rezan turned to leave, a scrawny dog slunk from the door.

"What's that thing?" he asked Rukia.

"That's his dog. His rescuers him said it followed them all the way here."

"*Lo!*" he exclaimed.

Rezan went into the family room and poured himself a cup of pomegranate juice. He thought of the injured man and wondered in passing who might be able to interpret what he said to him. Dusk was approaching and he decided to go spend some time at the town square, a place he did not frequent because he could not stand the smoke from the communal pipes. He thought the men wasted time, sparring with one another on various issues. He suspected that they talked so they would appear intelligent and avoid taking concrete action or standing up for a cause. Nevertheless, when he wanted to know what was going on in the city, the town square was the place to glean information. Here, he learned that a few other people had seen that star. From the discussions, the consensus was it might have been the soul of a great king moving from one celestial palace to another.

"Ah, Rezan," the men hailed him when he arrived. "We're glad you could join us today."

"How's your guest?" someone asked.

"I don't know yet, but I think he'll make it."

"That's good to hear," another said. "Someone needs to do something about those bandits in the mountains. They wiped out a third of the caravan from Li Ngu."

"The states that benefit from the highway should do more to protect caravans from attack. The loss of life and property is ridiculous."

"Who's to say government officials aren't involved in the attacks? They must be getting a cut of the loot. Maybe they own the bandits even."

Someone must have jabbed the speaker in the ribs because he looked at Rezan sheepishly. Rezan smiled to assure him he would not make an issue of it. From the conversation that followed, he got a clearer picture of the attack on the caravan based on second hand accounts from survivors who were now in the care of various physicians across the city. The discussion moved to other subjects from which Rezan did not think he would benefit. He bade them good night and left.

Back at home, the guest was awake, but still incoherent. The evening was not warm enough to warrant such profusion of sweat, indicating he was feverish. When Rezan talked to him, he only blabbered, sometimes with a smile that did not reflect in the eyes. Rezan went back into the main house, leaving the visitor to rest. The women said they had fed him and cleaned the wound. When Rezan expressed concern about the man's state of mind, Shiroz said incoherence was typical of a person fighting severe infection or trauma. She was sure he would be better in the morning. They would check on him periodically because in his present condition, he could accidentally hurt himself.

The next day Rezan went to check on his visitor and saw the dog in the room. When he approached, it slipped out to watch from a distance. The stranger appeared to sleep better than the previous night. He breathed evenly and looked like he was actually resting, rather than fighting unseen demons. Rukia and Shiroz were already preparing the day's meals. The aroma wafted from the kitchen and made Rezan hungry. He patted the ailing man's arm and went back into the main house. Rukia brought him a cup of strong hot coffee, sweet deep-fried pastries, strips of roast lamb, and dates. She retired into the kitchen and he ate in silence. When he finished, he informed the women he would return to move the guest to the palace. He saddled the horse and left.

By the fifth hour of the day, Rezan had settled the injured man in one of the commuter chambers at the palace. He made a few quick inquiries of fellow staffers and learned that the man was actually from Chandustan, one of the nations to the east. Fortunately, Rezan found a palace assistant, Mastaf, who spoke some Nagrani - the man's native tongue. That evening with the assistant's help, Rezan carried out an exploratory interview with the guest who seemed much improved.

"Ask him how he is feeling." Rezan told Mastaf.

"He feels much better," the assistant interpreted.

"Where is he from, and how did he end up on the highway with a caravan from Su Ching?"

For some reason, the question disturbed the injured man. He did not respond immediately. He averted his gaze and looked uncomfortable. When he found his voice, it was tremulous and full of emotion.

"He says it's hard to talk about it and you may not understand."

"Tell him I'm not asking to pass judgment on him. I only want to help him continue to his destination. It always helps to know a person's name and where he comes from. If he had died, we wouldn't know who he was and where to send his remains."

As the assistant interpreted, the traveler's eyes misted and he took some time before he spoke.

"He's Rasul, son of Dev Seth from the city of Laksh in Chandustan. His father owns the largest spice business in the city."

Rasul spoke again, becoming agitated with each statement, until he was stumbling over the assistant's words. It had the effect of intensifying the emotions that bubbled to the surface. He told of the sense of emptiness in spite of all he had and of his last day with the family.

"He says he'll always regret shouting at his mother and he's not sure if he'll ever forgive himself for walking out on his wife."

Rezan nodded in sympathy. Rasul related how he lived in Tandoon for seven months, of his priestly duties in the village, and how the restlessness returned. Then he mentioned something that cut across Rezan's gut.

"He says one morning as he sat in meditation, he saw a strange light rise up to a point in the sky. He left the village right away and embarked on a journey to find where it had stood and that's why he's here today."

"And how did this star behave?" Rezan asked trying to sound casual though his heart raced.

The stranger spoke again, raising his arm to point.

"He says it started like a faint dot in the sky about over there." Mastaf pointed like the stranger had done moments earlier. "It rose, gradually getting brighter until it stopped. He says that at that point, he heard a voice clearly tell him to go west."

"Tell him that's enough. I know how he ended up here anyway. He should rest. See to it he has everything he needs."

The following day, Rezan told Mursal what he had learned from Rasul.

"Hmm. It looks like there's more to this than I thought. I still hesitate to take it to the King as I have yet to make a decisive reading of the event. Like I said before, it might have to do with the rise of a King in another land. Such tidings may not please His Majesty."

Rezan did not have new data and there had been no new phenomena in the heavens to shed fresh light on the sighting. They could not dismiss it as coincidence or collusion because Rasul, a man who did not speak their language, had observed the event in a far off land. The only coincidence was he should end up in the home of another man who had witnessed the same thing.

Over the next few days, Rasul made a complete recovery and the only evidence of the ill-fated journey was an angry scar on his temple. Rezan had already told Rasul he had seen the same star and showed him the charts on which he recorded the event. Rezan also sought permission for Rasul to stay a little longer as a guest of the palace in which time Rezan learned of his new friend's education, work, and the life he left behind. Rezan could only imagine his pain and wished he could help the tortured man in some way. As he thought about it, Rezan became aware of his own restiveness. He believed they had seen the star for a reason and it bothered him that time passed and he knew so little. He even presented the problem to his students, some of whom said they had seen the star. None could offer a plausible explanation for it.

This mystery so consumed him he started losing sleep over it. Shiroz noted the change in her son and confronted him a few days later. She already knew the same thing had led Rasul to her door. Knowing he could not hide anything from her, he confessed that the sighting several weeks earlier still troubled him.

"Son, follow that star if you must. Just be sure you have your wife's consent. I don't want to sit here with a woman who feels slighted because her husband left to chase after an illusion."

"It's not an illusion, Mother," Rezan said defensively. "What I saw was real. Rukia and I both saw it."

"I understand. It is your work to observe and explain things. But remember it's a woman's nature to feel things and not necessarily explain them. Whereas your quest may make sense to you, you'll do wise to find out how your wife feels about it."

That evening as he lay with Rukia on the roof as was now customary, Rezan struggled to find a way to broach the subject. The words he rehearsed in his mind did not sound right so he did not dare say anything. He was still pondering how to frame his request when she surprised him. She lay on her back looking at the sky.

"Go," she said evenly.

"What?" he turned to her sharply.

"Go."

"Go where? What are you talking about?" He suspected she alluded to what was bothering him, but he wanted her to say it herself.

"Go find your star. I knew from the day we saw it you would eventually want to know its meaning. I've watched you look to the sky in search of an explanation for it. Rasul's arrival only served to increase your restlessness. What drove him here? The star. I know you'll not rest until you know what it means. Therefore, I won't stand in your way. I give you my blessing. Go find your star."

Rezan was surprised that she understood so much.

"Well… see, I really don't have to…"

"Go! I know how much you love your work. You've also treated me better than most men treat their wives and your mother accepts me as her own daughter. I'm a lucky woman. I can do it because I love you, Rezan."

Rezan had never heard those words from anyone but his mother. A quick examination of his own feelings led him to conclude he was very fond of Rukia though he did not verbalize it. Indeed, he loved her. He ran a hand through her hair.

"I love you too. And you are right. I'd like to know the significance of the star. It's strange someone else should see it, embark on a journey to understand its meaning, and end up at my door. I have felt the same urge and I'm glad you understand."

Rukia became serious and turned, supporting herself on an elbow to face him.

"I want you to promise me two things."

"What would they be, my dear?" he asked guardedly, fearing that she would cumber him with impossible conditions.

"First, come back to me. Second, come back to me alive."

Rezan laughed. "That's a promise I plan to keep." He drew her close and held her for a long time.

Rezan had the following day off, but he still went to the palace. He wanted to talk to Rasul and Mursal to let them know he would like to go on an expedition to the land of the star, as he now thought of it. He found Rasul in the middle of a lesson with Mastaf, the young assistant. They had become good friends.

"Ah, good. You're both here," he said to Mastaf.

"*Aktha*," he greeted Rasul.

"*Muktha naba*." Rasul smiled at the attempt at Nagrani.

He rattled off another string of words in his native tongue to which Rezan could only smile, shoulders raised and hands spread out in the universal gesture of ignorance.

Through Mastaf, Rezan asked Rasul what his immediate plans were regarding his mission. Rasul informed him that despite the danger and hardship he had experienced, he planned to continue. He felt strong enough to travel but he was not sure how he would proceed. He planned to continue by offering his services to caravans headed in his direction.

"Ask him if he would like company on his mission."

Mastaf, understanding the implication, looked at his superior curiously until he realized Rezan was serious. Still confounded, Mastaf interpreted the request. When he finished, Rasul appeared equally baffled. Rezan only smiled and nodded.

"He says he would be delighted," Mastaf interpreted when Rasul answered.

"Wonderful! Tell him I'll need to get Mursal's blessing first then I'll let him know how we'll proceed."

The prospect of having someone else on the mission clearly delighted Rasul. He beamed and thanked Rezan.

"Are you sure you want to do this or are you just getting caught in the emotion of the moment?" Mursal asked Rezan.

"I couldn't be more certain. I think the sighting of the star is of greater significance than we imagine. If that's the case, wouldn't the King want to know what it means?"

"You're right." Mursal was glad that Rezan wanted go on this journey. He had come close to suggesting it himself, but hesitated because he did not fully understand what it would entail. Now he could go before the King and tell him he planned to send an expedition to discover the significance of the phenomenon to the kingdom. Put that way, the King would probably be more amenable to funding the trip, therefore lending it legitimacy. That is what Mursal counted on.

In the days that followed, Rezan went through a series of emotions, sometimes ready to give up the whole thing and at other times telling himself he would go through it with or without the King's consent. But since the matter was now before the King, he had to await the verdict. If he acted on his own, he would most likely end up without work or in prison. It would be ten anxious days before Mursal summoned him.

"I have good news and even better news for you. The good news is the King thinks it is important to find out the meaning of the star's appearing. The better news is he has agreed to underwrite the expedition. This is now a royal venture and *you* are representatives of the King. You travel in ten days. Serve His Majesty well. He has granted you audience in a week - three days before you leave. Until then, you will determine your route, work out an itinerary, assemble a caravan, and identify the equipment and supplies you'll need. Start right away so by the time you meet him, you have a specific plan and list of requirements."

"That's already done. While waiting for His Majesty's approval, we put together the list. Here." Rezan handed Mursal a scroll, which he opened and read.

"This is a rather small convoy for a royal expedition."

"I want to travel light, taking only what's essential for the trip. We'll report to the King if future trips are necessary."

"No warriors?"

"No. This is a peaceful venture. We'll count on the goodwill of all the people we encounter."

Mursal frowned. "Right. I'll brief the King before you meet him."

As the time for his audience drew nigh, Rezan grew increasingly nervous. His mother and Rukia encouraged him, saying it was a good omen and an honor to appear before the King.

"Since the King himself grants you audience, you'll succeed in this venture. The gods smile upon you Rezan," his mother pointed out. "As we've said many times before, this is not a coincidence. It's a sign the gods have something to reveal to men and you're going to play an important part in it. Therefore, face your King with confidence because he's counting on you."

The words emboldened Rezan. On the eve of the meeting, he went over charts and reviewed calculations and annotations of stellar movements, especially those of a star that did not fit the general pattern.

Rezan was a frequent visitor to the priestly and ministerial quarters of the palace where they often requested his input on weather conditions, celestial sightings, and conclusions they could draw from them. He had never gone beyond that to the King's Court. The morning of his audience, Mursal led the way as they went through three different chambers with four guards at the entrance of each chamber. These warriors checked each person's credentials - even Mursal's despite the fact he met with the King at least once a week. He presented the gold ring on his right middle finger. The guards gave Rasul and Rezan armbands with inscriptions to serve as passes. The last door stood almost twice the height of the average person. Eight soldiers stood on guard outside and inspected their credentials one last time. They would have to wait until the King was ready to receive them.

After a while, the large double doors opened to reveal an expansive hall, with scores of statues lining the walls. Large pillars topped off into beautiful arches on the ceiling. High windows between the arches allowed the morning sun to filter through, throwing a surreal golden aura on everything. Inside, by the massive doors were members of the King's elite brigade. They wore red tunics, bronze breastplates, helmets, and protective armbands and shin guards. Each had a spear in one hand and a shield in the other. A mighty sword rested in the waistband of each guard. They were the best-trained warriors in the land, fiercely loyal to the King, and conditioned to do anything to protect him. Many warriors aspired for a place in this much-envied unit. Few attained this goal.

Beyond the soldiers sat the King's ministers, high priests, and consultants. They were a fascinating assortment of characters whose primary shortcoming, at first glance, would appear to be the lack of humor. They all turned grave faces toward Mursal and the young men when they entered.

Most impressive was the King - an imposing figure seated on golden throne at the top of a series of steps. On his hoary head sat a beautiful gold crown, studded with rubies and other precious stones. Even through his long, white beard, one could see his beatific smile, which also played in his keen black eyes. He wore a gold necklace and gold earrings. On his arms, he also wore gold bracelets. He had a ring on every finger. His purple silk robe embroidered in gold set him apart from everyone else in the room. In his right hand, he held and ivory scepter with a gold knob and tip. On the left side of the throne was the sculpted image of a lion and, on the right, a bear. Next to each image stood a strong youthful warrior. Shadows behind the King indicated the presence of more guards.

At the bottom of the steps and off to one side, stood the King's spokesman, an elegant man in a white flowing robe. He bid them to approach. Just before he got to the steps, Mursal went down on his knee and bowed his head. Rezan and Rasul prostrated themselves as Mursal had instructed. Slowly, with infinite grace, the King raised his right hand and pointed at the group with his scepter. The spokesman told them to rise.

"Why seek ye the presence of the King?" he asked.

The King had already received details about the expedition from a prior meeting with Mursal. This session served as an official endorsement of the matter.

"I, Mursal, Senior Advisor and Member of the King's Court, come into the presence of the Great King Be'el-Sharrazz because of a wonderful sign that appeared in our skies almost three months ago. The wise men and priests sought to know its meaning, but found it shrouded in mystery. About a month ago, a man came into our city, and by the will of the gods, to the home of our esteemed scholar, Rezan, who had also seen the sign. The gods moved the hearts of both men to find the truth behind the sign. These men stand before the King and before this court to seek your permission and blessing to undertake this venture. I Mursal, stand before you, O Great King, to present this request."

The King listened in silence. Once again he raised his scepter slowly toward the three.

"Na'am! The King gives his blessing. Let the records say so!" the spokesman declared.

The men seated on both sides of the aisle grunted in approval. A scribe seated off to the side recorded the decision on a scroll. Mursal and the young men bowed, turned, and left the court. It was a much shorter meeting than Rezan had anticipated. He was prepared to answer several questions regarding the sighting and the prospective journey. He was a little baffled, but not disappointed. Past the last guard station, Mursal stopped to shake hands with Rezan and Rasul who were obviously relieved it was over. They turned in their armbands.

"Congratulations! Go finish preparing for the journey. I'll see you later. I still have business in the court."

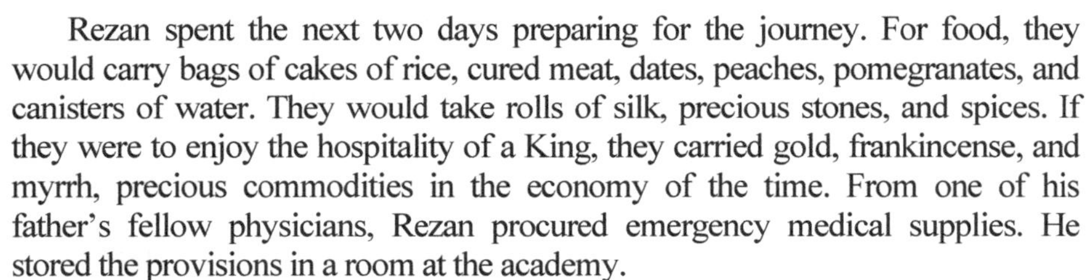

Rezan spent the next two days preparing for the journey. For food, they would carry bags of cakes of rice, cured meat, dates, peaches, pomegranates, and canisters of water. They would take rolls of silk, precious stones, and spices. If they were to enjoy the hospitality of a King, they carried gold, frankincense, and myrrh, precious commodities in the economy of the time. From one of his father's fellow physicians, Rezan procured emergency medical supplies. He stored the provisions in a room at the academy.

A small caravan would be more manageable and less likely to attract serious attention from bandits who would use intimidation rather than an outright attack to divest them of property. Rezan asked for only five men. First was Mastaf, whose interest in the expedition increased as he interpreted for Rezan. On Mursal's recommendation, he picked Shebazz, a camel driver, who had been on several trade missions. He was a somewhat intransigent character, but his experience would prove very useful. As a condition to his going on the trip, Shebazz insisted his cousin, Irzik, and his friend, Fouad, join him. Rezan agreed. Last to join was Ebram, one of Rezan's foreign students. Though Rezan had some reservations with respect to Ebram's ability to withstand the rigors of the journey, his enthusiasm, and easy manner won him over.

Except for Rezan and Ebram, all were skilled swordsmen. From his father's patients, Rezan had seen enough blood and wounds from sword fights and he did not want to be party to spilling more. He therefore never learned how to handle the weapon. Nonetheless, he wore one. He was glad to have men who, unlike him, could wield a sword without putting themselves and others at risk. They also carried bows and arrows.

In all, they would take four camels and two horses for supplies and gifts. The horses were the desert variety, known for their stamina and agility. They would handle the long trek across the Djanguan desert and provide quick transportation in an emergency. Satisfied that everything was ready, Rezan went home to spend a final night with his wife and mother. He tried to ignore the thought it would be a long time before he saw them again - assuming he made it back alive.

After breakfast the following day, he kissed Rukia and his mother goodbye. He also bade the dog, Sibi, goodbye. With Rasul intent on traveling, Rukia had since adopted him. Rezan rode to the palace and found Shebazz conducting last minute inspections.

"Mursal asks you to see him as soon as you arrive," Mastaf told Rezan.

Rezan was surprised to find almost the entire council of advisors in Mursal's chambers.

"Do not be surprised we are all here," Mursal started. "We believe the journey upon which you embark is of utmost importance. We have studied the charts, looked at past events, and have not seen anything like the sighting of the star. The matter had also come to the King's attention and he was demanding answers. We did not have anything substantial to tell him until you came up with this expedition. We are therefore counting on you to view this journey with utmost seriousness. Observe and record everything and bring a concise record of your observations. You have our blessing."

"Thank you," Rezan said. Observing custom, he went around the group, bowing before each priest who extended his hand to touch his head in blessing.

"The gods be with you, son. I will miss you," Mursal said.

"I'll miss you too, Master," Rezan said sincerely. With a final bow, he left to join his party.

Chapter 13

the quest begins

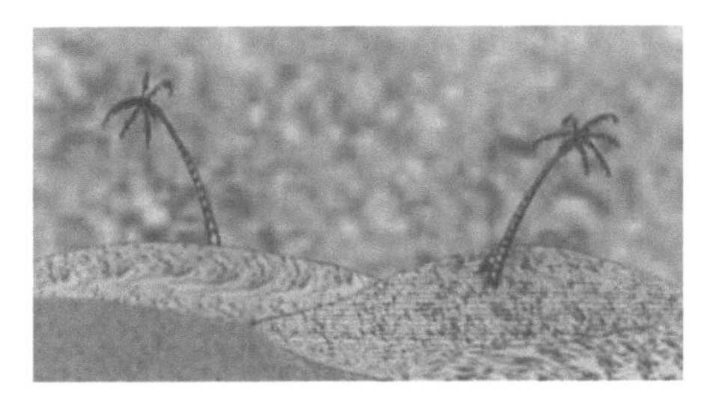

When they set off in the morning, they did not expect the crowd that lined the road to bid them farewell. As they passed, people cheered them on like warriors off to battle.

"The gods be with you!" some shouted.

Others called out, "Come back safely to us, Rezan!"

"See you soon, brave children," an elderly woman told them.

Children walked alongside the small caravan, peering into the men's faces as if they would somehow discern what possessed them to undertake this mission.

They were well out of town before the crowd thinned and their journey began in earnest. Barring incident, Rezan had calculated they would cross the desert and be in the port city of Qumz in two weeks. After that, they would take a ship for a four or five-day trip down the Sea of Aldam to the Port of Xalis on the land mass of dark-skinned people. From that point, they would be in uncharted territory.

Trouble began the very first day. At about midday, Fouad, who was walking behind the second horse, noticed the animal favoring its front left leg. He called out to Shebazz to halt the party. Neither Shebazz nor Irzik could see what was causing it discomfort. However, Shebazz thought it could still travel. They took some of its load and redistributed it among the other animals to take the pressure off the injured leg. The horse fared better, but they had lost time in the process.

Some time after they resumed, a headwind blew sand in their faces, making it difficult to see. It gradually gained strength until they could no longer travel. Shebazz brought the convoy to a halt and since there was no shelter, they huddled together to take the edge off the wind. They had no choice but to wait it out. The wind gave no sign of abating soon. Rasul, who had recently been through similar situations, took advantage of it to get some sleep.

Rezan and Ebram, both novices in the open desert, could not help looking around when they heard what they thought was someone calling for help. It did not seem to bother the others. Irzik and Fouad resigned themselves to their fate, but Shebazz glared at the wind from behind the scarf that covered all his face but the angry eyes.

After blowing continuously for hours, the wind died down late in the night. With it, the sand cleared to reveal a slice of the moon sitting above the western horizon, lending a haunting beauty to the landscape. A deep blue halo enveloped the moon. The stars, big and small, bright and faint, speckled the rest of the dark canopy. The ground was a mesmerizing study in design. Rippling waves of sand sat frozen on the curvaceous dunes, drawn with the bold extravagance of a master artist who executed his stroke without a hint of imperfection. The interaction of light areas and shadows gave it a sense of something powerful, swelling, yet calm - a complete antithesis of the angry assault that had formed it.

Shebazz suggested they travel part of the night to redeem some of the time they had lost. No one objected so he roused the animals and they took to the road. The night grew chilly and they were glad to be moving as it worked against the cold. Initially, Rezan kept an eye on the stars to ensure they were on course but was impressed that Shebazz maintained course even after the wind had wiped out the trail. He concluded Shebazz knew what he was doing.

For the next four days, they observed the same routine. The wind picked up around midday and would not relent until late in the evening. They would huddle under any available shelter until it spent itself. They would then travel until mid-morning when they unburdened the animals to give them some rest. The greatest blessing came on the third day when they came upon an oasis with plenty of shade and some muddy water. The animals were grateful for it and grazed on whatever greenery grew around the oasis. On the fifth and sixth days, they crossed the desert basin where the heat was extremely oppressive during the day. It took its toll on their energy and they made little progress. Shebazz guided them to a shade where they rested when the day was hottest and made up for it in the evenings and early mornings.

On the morning of the seventh day, Shebazz mentioned to Rezan he had an uncomfortable feeling someone was watching them. Rezan had no idea what he was talking about and ascribed it to heat-induced imagination. However, even during the rest period, Shebazz was still on edge, standing up every so often to scan the surrounding dunes.

"There's someone out there," he said with certainty.

Rezan looked at him and said nothing. He covered his face to get some sleep. He did not know how long he dozed, but an elbow to the ribs scuttled any further aspirations to this end.

"What?" he asked irritably. Ebram, the offender, only stared ahead.

When Rezan looked, he almost soiled himself. A large swarthy man in a black beard stood before them with a wicked-looking scimitar in his hand. All around them atop the dunes, other men stood, arrows pointing at the band of travelers. The big man spoke rapidly in a strange tongue. Shebazz answered, and he fired another question. This time Rezan figured he was asking what they carried because in his answer, Shebazz sounded off a list, which included words similar to Shastani. He stole a glance at Rezan. Noticing this, the big stranger approached Rezan, stuck the scimitar under his chin, and spoke again.

"What's he saying?" Rezan asked Shebazz. He was sure the man would not hesitate to drive the weapon into his throat.

"He's asking if you're the leader of this convoy," Shebazz interpreted. The others watched apprehensively.

"Tell him it is so. Ask what he wants."

When Shebazz interpreted, the big man laughed mirthlessly and rattled off a response.

"He says it's not a matter of what he wants. We are in his territory so he's taking everything."

"Let him know we are emissaries of the King of Senna. We can give him a gift if this is his territory. But he cannot have the King's property."

Shebazz hesitated before turning to the glaring bandit. When he finished interpreting, the bandit laughed aloud before he gave his answer.

"He says he can finish us off right now and there's not a thing the King can do about it. Out here, he is king and all who wander into these lands must pay tribute to him."

The man shouted a series of commands and some of his men descended the dunes toward them. He spoke to Shebazz one more time.

"He says he'll spare our lives so we can go back and tell our King what a good man he is and maybe our King will come and thank him one day. He wants all our weapons."

"He might as well kill us," Mastaf lamented.

They all tossed their weapons in a pile on the ground. Two bandits collected them while others kicked the travelers away from the animals, reloaded them, and drove them off. As they left, the big man shouted to Shebazz.

"He tells us not to think of following. He says they own the desert."

The bandits disappeared over the dunes leaving the dispirited group. No one said anything for some time.

"What shall we do now?" Ebram asked. The encounter left him most shaken.

Rezan thought for a moment then looked up at the sky.

"We will continue."

"Wait!" Shebazz said sharply. "You want us to continue with no provisions, no weapons, no food, and no animals? Are you out of your mind? We barely have a chance of making it back to the city alive, what makes you think we'll make it to Qumz?"

"We set out on a mission. We are halfway there and still alive. That means we still have a chance to accomplish it even if we do not see how."

"Rubbish! You rich boys have lived in the luxury of the palace all your lives while we slaved away to make the wealth you enjoy. What do you know about life and death? You don't even know where you're going and what you'll find along the way. Now you want to try it empty-handed!"

Fouad joined in. "He's right. It's best to turn back now. Besides, if we run into another band of thieves, they'll kill us for the mere fact we have nothing and will have wasted their time."

"What about honor and commitment? Doesn't it mean anything to you when you take up a cause that you do everything in your power to succeed?" Rezan asked looking at each person in turn.

"This is no longer in our power. If you choose to continue, I'll not be part of it," Fouad said.

Rezan lost his temper.

"Fine! I was not sure of your commitment to this venture in the first place. If that's how you feel, leave now!" He looked around at the rest. "Does anyone else want to go back? Speak up! Let's settle it right now! Irzik? Ebram? Rasul? Mastaf?"

Rasul, knowing what he asked, thumbed his chest then pointed in the direction of their destination.

"I'm with you," Mastaf said.

Ebram seemed undecided and looked pleadingly at Rezan and Shebazz. Both gave him impassive looks that did not help him decide one way or another.

Shebazz glared at Irzik.

"Well?"

Irzik looked at the ground, avoiding the look.

"Are you going to stand there doodling with your toes like a virgin or will you make a decision?"

Irzik was clearly in an awkward position and struggled with the choice. He remained silent.

Rezan turned to Ebram who averted his eyes. "I'll go back," he said so softly one could hardly hear it.

"What?"

"I said I'll go back!" Ebram shouted this time. "I've had enough of wind, sand, and bandits. I can't do this any more!" He turned away.

"Great Abil! Now I have a baby to look after," Shebazz said spitefully. He turned to Irzik. "Well, what are you going to do? You can't have it both ways."

"I'll continue with the journey."

Shebazz was stunned. He assumed both his friends would side with him.

"You what?"

"You heard me. I'll continue."

Shebazz looked Irzik up and down like some despicable creature.

"Well then, we don't want to remain in each other's company any longer, do we? We are turning back right now. Good luck," he told Rezan. To those who elected to return, he said, "Let's go!"

Rezan, Rasul, Mastaf, and Irzik watched sadly as they left.

Rezan faced those who remained. "Thank you for staying with me… I mean… with Rasul and me. This is as much your mission as it is ours. I know it was not an easy decision for you to make, but I believe what lies ahead is of great significance and it is our privilege to be part of it. Now, if we just sit here, we get no closer to our objective. I suggest we start walking so we can make some headway."

The four resumed the journey.

"Do you know the way?" Mastaf asked Rezan.

"No, but we're going that way," he said pointing in the general direction they were heading. Mastaf shrugged and followed. It was mid-afternoon, the hottest part of the day when they set off, and there was no shade in sight. Soon they even had difficulty swallowing saliva for the dryness in their mouths.

"Is that water I see over there?" Mastaf asked squinting at the shimmering in the distance. He stepped off the trail to investigate. "Water! I see water!" He ran unsteadily toward the perceived body of water.

"No! Come back." Irzik ran after the young man and tackled him to the ground. "If you follow what you think you're seeing, it will be the death of you."

Mastaf looked as though he were slipping into delirium. Irzik looked into his eyes. "Stay with us. We will keep you alive. Don't do anything you don't see us do. Understand?"

Mastaf nodded. They went back to join the others.

By late afternoon, they were all frustrated, tired, thirsty, and hungry. Without weapons, they could not hunt even if an animal crossed their path. Irzik informed them the only recourse would be to dig up scorpions, snakes, or lizards for the little water they provided and sustenance. Out of desperation, they all turned their attention to looking for signs of earthbound creatures. At dusk, they had still caught nothing when they came upon a set of footsteps.

"These are fresh prints," Rezan said. "Someone's going our way ahead of us."

"Four people," Rasul said in halting Shastani, pointing out four distinct sets of prints.

Irzik did not like what he was thinking, but kept walking. He confirmed his fears when he noticed that two sets of footprints broke off and another two sets came back to the path at about the same place. He followed the prints and they led to a point where the individuals had disturbed the sand heavily.

"My friends, these are our footsteps," Irzik announced despondently when he returned. "We've gone round in a circle and are back right where Mastaf saw a mirage."

Rasul threw up his hands in despair and cursed in Nagrani. Tears formed rapidly in Mastaf's eyes. Rezan dropped to his knees, grabbed a fistful of sand, and threw it angrily to the ground. He did not notice the rock he had just slammed into the sand. Irzik, still upset at having gone round in a circle, watched everyone's reaction with detached resignation. He was about to walk away when he saw Rezan stiffen and point wordlessly in front of him. Irzik turned and saw six beautiful oryx traversing a dune. There was no wind to speak of, so it was unlikely the animals would pick up their scent. Irzik motioned his friends to keep still. He carefully reached down and picked the rock Rezan had just thrown to the ground. He took off the scarf around his neck, gingerly twisting it into a tight strip as he crept stealthily toward the animals. They stopped and looked around. He froze.

Not perceiving the danger, the oryx continued and the leading animals dipped below the dune. Irzik loaded the rock, knowing he had only one chance to hit his target. The odds were against him, but he had to try. He made a quick assessment and picked the fourth animal. He swung the improvised sling over his head three times and released on the fourth. The animals stopped again. They realized the danger and sprang into action, but it was too late for Irzik's target. The missile found its mark with a resounding "*thonk!*" The animal finished its jump out of reflex, but landed clumsily on wobbly legs. The others bounded off. The injured animal attempted to run, but it could not coordinate its movements. It still managed to hobble below the dune. Irzik sank to his knees, drained from the intense concentration he had invested in the effort. His friends, seeing him collapse ran to help him. Rezan put his arm around his shoulder.

"I think you got him," he told Irzik who only nodded. Sweat streamed down his temples and his hair was damp and matted.

"We have food!" Mastaf shouted. "You got him, Irzik."

This time Irzik smiled. Rezan helped him up. They found Mastaf prancing around the animal like an excited child, while Rasul just stood over it shaking his head in amazement. He uttered a phrase repeatedly in his native tongue.

When Rezan and Irzik came up to the animal, Rasul put an arm around Irzik's shoulder and continued talking in his language. They all understood that he marveled at the accuracy of the shot that would most likely save their lives. Irzik did not believe it himself. Even seeing the animal's cracked skull did not make it any more credible. The rock had struck just below the left ear shattering the skull. Deep red blood oozed from the wound. The animal had stood no chance and was breathing its last.

The ever-practical Rezan saw that they were wasting precious daylight.

"Let's eat before competition gets wind of the kill. We must assume there are other predators in the desert." With a couple of bracelets, he improvised a knife and sharpened it on the rock in order to skin the oryx. They slit the side of its neck. Blood and what little life remained oozed out.

Irzik, who had recovered, knelt down and sucked on the dark blood. Mastaf turned away in disgust.

"I suggest you do the same because you don't know when you'll get your next drink." Rezan said as he took his turn.

Rasul gagged on the first attempt, but thirst and survival instinct prevailed. Nothing would bring Mastaf to partake of the macabre ritual especially when each of his friends raised his head with gore dripping down the chin. They skinned the animal and gutted it. They shared the internal organs equally, eating them raw. Even Mastaf ate his share, albeit under duress.

Having eaten, they worked quickly using their improvised knives to divide the carcass into four parts. They cut the lower legs stripping away the meat. They would use the bones as clubs, to fend off small animals like foxes, which could be vexatious when they smelled meat. Rezan cut off the long sharp horn and tied it with strip of the animal's hide to a one of the bones forming a crude thrusting weapon. Now they had some sort of protection.

"Each of you, pick a section of meat and I'll show you what to do. Irzik, you go first since you are the eldest and you slew the animal."

He picked a section of the front end. Mastaf and Rasul picked their portions as well. The last portion being his, Rezan cut deep slits all along its length and placed it on the hide. Next, he lifted his robe and the *kamsi* underneath and urinated on the meat. This time Mastaf could not hold it and he vomited.

"What are you doing?" Irzik asked in shock.

"Preserving my meat, and curing the animal hide," Rezan answered nonchalantly. "We have neither salt nor fire. I don't know where I heard that when neither is available, urine works fine as a preservative. I also heard that a predator might not eat meat another creature has marked. Meat will attract predators, but the urine might repel them."

The argument made sense and reluctantly they all administered the unusual preservative on their chunks. The sun had set by now and they were all ready for some rest. They all felt much better now they at least had crude weapons. As an extra measure of security, Rezan assigned guard duties. He took the first shift. The others stretched out on the sand and were soon fast asleep. He took the time to continue curing the hide and studying the skies for a better sense of his bearings. Without the charts, he would have to rely on his knowledge from years of study and research to determine their route. He still did not know how they would pay for the passage across the land masses. He decided to set aside those concerns for the time being. First, they had to get to Qumz.

Irzik had the last shift. He roused his friends when sleep was deepest.

"Time to get going, Master," he said, shaking Rezan.

They woke up shivering from the cold. They all ate some meat, then stripped the rest from the bones. Each wrapped his portion in a section of hide. They set off in the relative cool of the early morning. They were all in high spirits as they crossed dune after dune with Rezan in the lead. Rasul and Mastaf walked together so Mastaf could teach Rasul Shastani. This was their way of breaking the monotony of travel.

About mid-morning, they came upon what looked like a distinct trail with signs of recent use. They decided to take it since it pointed their direction. Rezan called a halt just past midday at which time they ate of the meat, which was still fresh. For the remainder of the afternoon they rested under young palm trees that now dotted the landscape.

As the sun began to set, they beheld a most unexpected sight. A small caravan approached. Other than the bandits who robbed them the previous day, they had encountered no one else. They ducked below a dune to watch the caravan's approach. With two horses and four camels, there was something familiar about it.

"Aren't those our animals?" Rezan asked incredulously. "Where are they taking them?"

"I would think they would have split the loot by now," Irzik said.

As the caravan neared, they recognized the big black-bearded bandit at the head with one of the camels. A bandit led each of the other animals. They all looked disheveled and distressed.

"They are going to walk right over our tracks," Irzik said.

He was right. They came up to the tracks and stopped to inspect them. The big bandit raised his head and looked directly where Rezan and his friends hid. He called out. They did not move. He shouted again, gesturing wildly to the animals. He shouted at one of his bandits who brought to him the weapons they had confiscated from the travelers. The big man took them and called out a third time. He raised the weapons, threw them on the ground and kicked the pile. Rezan figured something must have upset him recently. He stood up, descended the dune, and stopped a short distance from the bandit who started talking animatedly again. Irzik and the others also rose and came to stand behind Rezan.

"I think I have an idea what he's saying," Irzik whispered. "He's telling you to take your animals and goods. He doesn't want to deal with those people you sent to harass him any more. He asks you to take your animals and magic away from here. He hopes never to see you again."

"What people? I didn't send anyone to harass him," Rezan protested softly. "I know nothing about magic."

The man tossed the camel's reins in a final act of frustration then walked away still ranting. His companions followed. This incident was the latest in a series of events Rezan and his party could not explain. That a bandit would return loot was unthinkable. They watched the bandits go past a couple of dunes before they went up to their animals. Everything was intact - the supplies, the food, and even the gifts. This was to be the last major incident on the journey until they got to Qumz. They continued the routine of traveling after dark by moonlight, resting just past midnight, then resuming in the wee hours of the morning until midmorning. After six more days of travel, they arrived in the coastal city.

In Qumz, they learned that one of the ships that plied their route would sail in two days. In this time, Rasul came into his element. First, he secured accommodations for the party for the duration of their stay. Then he wandered the commercial district, getting to understand what was available for barter. He tapped into his experience with vendors in his father's business to tip the balance of the exchange in his favor. He impressed Rezan and Mastaf with the items he obtained in the trades. In turn, he traded the items for gold. By the time they were ready to sail, he had collected a sizeable bundle of gold and precious stones, which he recorded and turned over to Rezan. He also convinced Rezan to sell the ailing horse and two camels. Rezan saw the sense in it because they were down three people and did not need all the supplies. It turned out to be a good decision because the captain of the ship charged a considerable amount for animals, since his was a goods ship.

After a few hitches with sailing conditions and personnel, the ship set sail on the third day. The trip took fifteen days with stops at various ports, big and small, to pick up or drop off merchandise. Rasul always took advantage of the time to go ashore and trade - something at which he became adept. They were all glad when they landed in Xalis across the sea.

Xalis, the most important city on the Nubian coast, served as a trade center for goods from the interior for export and those shipped from other lands for distribution inland. Merchants concentrated their business close to the harbor. From centuries-old stone buildings, they traded in textile, jewelry, spices, exotic foods, and sea produce. Like the major cities in Senna, people of all tongues and nationalities worked and lived together.

The ship's captain, with whom Rezan had struck a friendship, spoke passable Shastani. He arranged for their accommodation with a trader named Zakhan who, as luck would have it, was originally from southern Senna. They stored their goods in one of Zakhan's warehouses before he led them to his residence behind the beachfront shops. The trader was happy to have people from his homeland and suggested they wait a couple of days to get their land legs back. Later, while Rezan and Mastaf spent the evening observing and charting the stars, Rasul joined Zakhan in his store for a firsthand look at local business. He was amazed at how much trade this small city handled. Caravans came from the interior every other day and a merchant ship docked in the harbor twice a week. The city was always abuzz.

On the third day, they were ready to leave. Rezan spoke to Zakhan about their mission. Zakhan told him he had heard from traders about a strange event in a province under a king named Xhaka and suggested this might be the land they sought. Zakhan recommended the better-kept southwesterly route to the mining town of Ormin - a five-day trek. From there, locals could direct them to their destination. Zakhan provided them with water, dried meat, fruits, and fish to last the trip to Ormin.

"If you have a bow and can use it well and your palate is not discriminating, you will find plenty of fresh meat along the way," he told them.

"That sounds better than our experience in the desert," Mastaf said.

"How long do you think you'll be away?"

"We don't know. That depends on the will of the gods. Should they lead us back this way, then you will see us."

They bade Zakhan goodbye and started for Ormin.

Though the region was hot and humid, it did not compare with the Djanguan desert. Therefore, Rezan pushed the men hard the first day. At day's end, he judged they had made good progress. He allowed the animals to nibble on the small leaves of the sturdy shrubs. Unlike the other side of the sea, there were no wells or watering holes along the way. They found twigs, branches, and the occasional dry cake of dung, and lit a fire. They took turns keeping watch overnight. They traveled for the next three days, encountering two trading parties heading for Xalis.

They arrived in Ormin the afternoon of the fourth day. In this town, they realized their appearance was different from much of the town's population. Most were dark skinned with a lean frame and curly hair. The majority worked in the mines or provided services to the industry. They were rather aloof and did not venture to interact with the travelers. For a roll of cloth and a few pieces of glassware, a rancher allowed them to spend the night in a run-down shack. It was a very uncomfortable night. The air was oppressively hot and the mosquitoes unrelenting. Rezan woke in the middle of the night to find Mastaf sitting up slapping himself to ward off the annoying insects.

"How do people live in this place?" Mastaf whispered.

"They must have thick skins. How long have you been up?"

"I barely slept. I can't sleep with insects buzzing around me."

They stayed up the rest of the night. After breakfast, they loaded the animals, thanked the rancher, and headed out of town. The road quickly narrowed to a mere trail, as the bushes grew taller and closer together. The soil took on a red hue. Irzik urged them to have their bows and arrows ready, since they could not tell what danger lay in the vegetation. The day was hot and cloudless and the surroundings filled with all kinds of sounds. Occasionally, a squirrel would cut across the trail, spooking the horse. Of them all, the camels showed the least concern, plodding away with bored expressions. Rezan told them to keep their eyes open for a clearing where they could set up camp. He did not relish the idea of spending the night with bushes so close. They found one late in the afternoon and Rezan called for a halt. The animals fed on the plants before they settled down for the night.

They departed at first light because Rezan wanted to get out of the area as soon as possible. He was glad when the bushes started to thin out. By mid-afternoon, the sparse vegetation and sandy soil had returned. They traveled under these conditions for five more days. On the morning of the sixth, they saw a light cloud of dust on the horizon.

"That can only mean livestock," Irzik said.

"Let's keep going," Rezan urged. "If they are herders, they will have useful information."

Soon they were in the midst of hundreds of animals - cows, goats, sheep, and camels, but not a herdsman in sight. They suspected the animals could not be here completely unattended. Unsure of what to expect, they kept walking. For a long time nothing happened. Suddenly, the bushes came alive with men and boys with arrows trained on them. For Rezan, resisting was out of the question.

"Listen, everyone. Slowly, carefully throw down your weapons. Let's make it clear we come in peace. I'll start," he said.

They raised their arms and Rezan slowly reached over his shoulder and signaled he was going to drop his bow. There was a tense moment when one of the men shouted at him, and he stopped. He signaled again and this time pulled the bow over his head and dropped it. In the same non-threatening manner, he reached for his sword and dropped it. The others also disarmed in the same manner. Their captors seemed uncertain what to do next. The lack of a common language did not help. In the end, one of the men motioned toward the travelers' weapons, upon which a young lad stepped forward and collected them. The self-designated leader then gestured to Rezan's party to start moving. His colleagues, their arrows still ready, flanked the captives. After a long walk, they came to a clearing with several dome-shaped structures constructed from sticks and hides. A man of about Irzik's age sat in the lotus position under a small tree, watching their approach keenly.

When they were a few paces from the seated man, the presumed leader of the herdsmen spoke to him. The man raised his hand, cutting him off mid-sentence, and continued to regard the captives. He uttered what must have been a question because the lad who carried the captives' weapons deposited them at his feet. The man picked up Rezan's sword and inspected it. He spoke in a strange tongue and nodded approvingly. He was clearly impressed. He replaced the weapon and asked another question to which the herdsboy spoke, gesturing with his thumb in apparent reference to the animals and goods of the captives. Rezan and the rest watched the exchange with increasing optimism. There was no hint of hostility in the man's attitude, a position he must have come to in his appraisal as they approached. He gave another order and all the herdsmen left except the man who had acted as leader. The man on the ground indicated they could have their weapons back. Initially the travelers hesitated, but when he repeated the gesture, they picked up their weapons, stepped back, and waited.

The man was tall and lean. He wore his hair short and kept a small beard. Like the herdsboys, he was bare above the waist except for a shawl draped over his shoulders. He wore a plaid skirt made of coarse fabric. He smiled and invited them to sit. They sat with him in a circle. He called out while looking askance at the ground. A woman, whom he had apparently addressed, answered from one of the structures behind him. She appeared shortly with a large skin container. A naked little girl, wearing only bracelets, a beaded necklace, and a beaded string around her waist, followed with a stack of metal cups. Her mother asked her to hand a cup to each visitor and to the man, presumably her father. He held out his cup and the woman poured brownish water into it. She filled each visitor's cup and retreated with the child. In observance of etiquette, the visitors waited for the host to take his drink. He took a long swig and belched loudly, wiping his mouth with the back of his hand. This was the signal for the visitors to drink. The water was refreshing and a welcome relief after the heat and dust. They all relaxed, though they looked at one another awkwardly as their host sipped his water while looking pensively to the horizon.

He finished his drink and smiled at his guests. He pointed at Rezan and gestured with upturned palms. Rezan understood the gesture to mean, "Who are you?" He thumbed himself and said, "Rezan." The man went around pointing at each guest who said his name. Then the man smiled and nodded. He tapped his chest and said, "Abena." Then in sweeping motions of his hand, he indicated everything around him ending the gesture by jabbing his chest with his index finger. "All this is mine," he seemed to indicate.

With no grounds to dispute his claim, the visitors nodded.

A different woman appeared with a platter of dried snacks, which she laid in the middle of the group and withdrew. There were dried dates, cactus fruit, chunks of meat, and a bowl of roasted maggots. Abena picked a piece of meat and popped it into his mouth. He invited the guests to help themselves to what was before them. When they had all taken something off the platter, he posed another question in what had become their method of communication.

"Where are you from? Why are you here?" seemed to be the question.

Rezan looked at his friends wondering how to address this particular question. He presumed him to be a simple herdsman though he indicated ownership of huge tracts of land and many animals. Rezan chose not to mention their search for the star. Instead, he gestured and said, "Xhaka," hoping to convey the idea that they were looking for Xhaka's territories.

"Xhaka?" Abena asked.

Rezan tried to communicate he wanted to go to the land of the great King, Xhaka. Abena could not understand and finally waved his hands in resignation. He called one of his men and pointed out a spot to which the men led the visitor's animals. Mastaf and Irzik went to help unload the animals and store the goods. With a constant rattle of instructions from Abena, the herdsmen unloaded and watered the travelers' animals. With another group of servants, Abena began to build a new *manyatta*.

"Let's go help instead of just sitting here," Rezan said after some time.

They approached Abena and offered to help, but he declined. Before the sun went down, they had completed the simple structure. One of his wives brought four rolls of hide and placed them inside the new *manyatta*. Abena gestured, and they understood these would be their accommodations for the night. Rezan and his company bowed in thanks.

Though tired from the day's trek, the travelers stayed up with their host while the aroma of cooking teased their nostrils. Later, the women placed two huge platters of tender roast lamb, thick blood stew, and soft *falafel* bread before the men. One of the women took a pitcher of water and approached Abena. He washed his hands under a steady stream of water she poured out. The guests washed their hands in the same manner. Abena took the first bite, therefore opening the way for his guests to eat. They were glad for a hot meal and ate heartily. While they ate, the herdsmen brought the livestock back from grazing and grouped them by kind.

After the meal, one of Abena's workers called him to attend to an injured animal. While he was gone, Rezan consulted his companions on what gift they should give their host. They still reserved the gifts intended for the king of the land of the star. Taking into account his family's lifestyle, they agreed on a roll of fabric, some metal tools, and jewelry. While they waited for him to return, Rezan pulled out his charts to log of their position and the movement of the stars.

One year, there was a severe drought in Nubia and they lost many animals. The people were in danger of starving to death. His father, Malik, decided to move his family, servants, and livestock to Zimri. Initially, the denizens were not keen to receive them, but after protracted negotiations, they agreed to allow Malik's people to stay in a part of the land where there was sufficient vegetation for the animals. If the animals lived, the people would live.

The drought had affected other communities from distant lands as well. Among them were the Houdin from Qazzam. The leaders of Zimri put Malik's people and the Houdin together in a narrow strip of land in the flood plains for the duration of the drought. The Zimrians did not make it their business to know how the various groups got along with each other. There was only one stipulation; if there was trouble, they would expel all involved. The refugees therefore made every effort to keep peace with one another.

Malik was by nature a peace-loving man. He had not always been that way. As a young man, he had fought with his father and grandfather to protect their territories from invading hordes of Samaal, Mozran, and Wezzim. Even when they prevailed against their foes, they lost kinsmen in each skirmish and would never again see the women and children the enemy captured. When he took over leadership, Malik always strove for peaceful solutions before taking to the battlefield.

Not knowing how long the drought would last or how long they would be welcome in Zimri, Malik set about fostering good relations with his neighbors right away. To this end, he took a wife from the Houdin. Nelia was a divorced mother of four and the niece of a Houdini elder. When Malik offered dowry for the bride, her uncle asked him if he were possessed.

"Even if you were to give me a thousand goats, what will I feed them? Keep your livestock and look after my niece. That's all I ask."

Nelia was an independent, hard-working woman. She was also very domineering and it was not hard to see why her husband had put her away. From the start, there was friction with her co-wives. They joined forces to make her life as miserable as possible, leaving Malik to wonder what he had brought upon himself. However, he recognized her desire and ability to organize and take charge. He, therefore, assigned her the most difficult servants and left her to handle matters as she wished. She was up to the challenge and accomplished a lot, though she was the least popular of his wives. What aggravated all who worked with her was her insistence on speaking Houdini, though it was no secret she understood Shamaric.

The one person to whom Nelia took a liking was Abena. He was the same age as her youngest son, Fashan. They became inseparable from the day they met. Abena split his time between his mother's manyatta and Nelia's. When his mother complained to Malik about her son spending so much time with her co-wife, Malik told her to let him be. That was the end of that discussion. As a result, Abena spent the better part of two seasons speaking Houdini with Fashan and Nelia. He often mixed up the two languages to his father's amusement and his mother's chagrin.

The rains finally fell in Nubia and quenched the land of its fierce thirst. Malik was eager to move his people back to his territories. Nelia, however, refused to go with him. He pleaded with her and sought her uncle's support to no avail. She was determined to stay with her people and travel back to Qazzam when the time came. Malik gave up. No one was more devastated than Abena. He did not understand why Fashan could not come with them. When they started the trek back to Nubia, he sulked for days, refusing to eat or speak to anyone. When he did, he spoke only Houdini and demanded they bring his friend to him. Fortunately, this phase did not last long and he soon forgot about Fashan and Houdini - until now.

Listening to the strangers stirred up long forgotten memories of Fashan. Some of the words they spoke sounded familiar. Abena also noticed Rezan looking up at the stars. His mind went back to the time when a bright star graced the night sky. He finished putting a splint on the injured calf and settled it. Then he approached Rezan and Mastaf, who both looked up and smiled. Abena looked at the charts and could make no sense of them, but he noticed that Rezan kept looking up at the sky. His actions also fascinated Abena's son and daughter. They looked at him when he studied the charts and at the sky when he looked up, their heads moving at the same time.

Abena waited for the appropriate moment to get Rezan's attention. When he did, he thumbed himself, pointed to the sky, and gestured in a swelling motion. He was talking all the while. Rezan smiled, but something clicked in this odd exchange. He stood up, faced Abena and, on impulse, spoke Shastani. Abena nodded and confirmed by repeating the gestures. Further, he tapped his temple with his index finger and shook his head to show that he did not understand what he had seen. Then the impact of what he had just said hit Rezan. He ran to the new *manyatta,* leaving Abena to wonder what excited him so.

"Rasul! Rasul!"

Rasul woke up. "What now, Rezan?" He grimaced, slightly disoriented from the disturbance.

"You won't believe what our host just told me."

Speaking rapidly in Shastani, Rezan related what Abena described to him. Rasul looked puzzled.

"He says Abena also seems to have seen the same star you both saw months ago," Mastaf interpreted.

Rasul's head cleared immediately.

"He did?" he asked in Shastani.

"Yes. Come. See if you understand his gestures as I do."

They went back to Abena, and with gestures, Rezan asked him to repeat what he had related earlier. When their host finished, Rasul looked at a beaming Rezan and nodded in understanding. Rezan then pointed to himself and to Rasul, indicating that they too had seen the star. At the mention of the word "star," Abena stopped him. He repeated the word, and pointed to the sky, then used his fingers to simulate the twinkling of a star.

"*Aaah!*" Rezan nodded smiling.

Abena launched into a language that Rezan noticed was distinctly different from the one he spoke with his people. Several words sounded similar to Shastani. By listening carefully, Rezan could understand the context of what Abena said. Likewise, when Rezan responded in Shastani, occasionally complementing speech with gestures, Abena seemed to make out what he said. They were both delighted at this discovery and laughed like little boys. It soon became their mode of conversation, and over the next several days, they became adept at understanding one another.

Later in the evening, over hot coffee, Abena turned grave and told Rezan he wanted to join them on the journey. Rezan was amazed to have met a second person who shared the same experience and was willing to give up normal life to embark on this quest. He pointed out to Abena it would be a long and dangerous journey.

In his mild manner, Abena said, "You have acquired this understanding in a few days of travel. I have lived it all my life. Travel and danger are not strangers to me. This thing has troubled me for many days. The fact that you are here, and we can talk about it in similar tongues means the gods sent you. Why shouldn't I obey what the gods have ordained?"

So chastened, Rezan stood up and bowed before Abena. He placed a hand on the host's shoulder and pointed to the distance. The message was clear. A common quest knit their hearts together.

Having decided to join the expedition, Abena wanted to leave his family and herds in secure circumstances. He called his wives to inform them of his decision to join his visitors on their quest. He warned them he did not know when he would return.

"Just like that, you wake up and decide to go?" Isnin asked incredulously.

"And who will look after the home while you're gone? You don't even know when you're coming back," Selwa added.

"*Yakhai*, women! Stop! Tomorrow, we set off to join Tekele and his herd. You will stay with him while I'm gone. You'll also be close to my brother's grazing grounds."

He went on to assign them tasks to handle while he was away. With calves recently born, there was much to do just to keep them alive. He similarly informed the servants of their duties.

The following morning, Rezan woke to find only he and Mastaf in the shelter. Rasul and Irzik sat with Abena and two of his children his favorite spot under the tree. On seeing Rasul, Abena smiled. His son fired off a barrage of questions in his vernacular, but the girl ducked shyly behind her father. Abena poured Rasul a cup of steaming coffee. He pushed the coffee and a plate of dates toward him.

After breakfast, they were ready to break camp, but Mastaf was still asleep. When Rasul woke him, he complained of a headache.

"It's probably from sleeping too much," Irzik joked. "Come on now. Get your behind out of here before we roll you up in these hides."

They stripped the hides off the manyattas, pulled the sticks that formed the shell apart and tied them in bundles. They also packed utensils, tools, and supplies, loading everything onto camels. The visitors also loaded their animals. By mid-morning, they were on their way. Abena and his guests led the convoy. Somewhere in the middle, in the dust and among the animals, were the women and children. The servants brought up the rear.

Sometime in the afternoon of the second day, Abena told Rezan his other herd must be close. He stopped and gave instructions to his young men. They began cutting branches from bushes and placing them in an area they had just cleared. When they had collected a large pile, they set it ablaze. The branches emitted thick white smoke. They all drank some water and waited. Soon they saw what they were looking for. An answering pillar of smoke rose straight up in the distance.

"Ah!" exclaimed Abena. "The camp is not far. We'll join them before the day is over." To his people he hollered, "Come! Let's get going!"

They put out the fire by tossing handfuls of soil over it so the wind would not cause a glowing ember to flare up again. In the past, such negligence had wrought great havoc, destroying lives and livestock.

They resumed the journey. By evening, they started to come across animals in the brush. Abena identified them as part of his other herd by the "X" on the left rump. He stopped the convoy, pointing out that they would set up camp where they stood so the animals from the two camps did not mingle too much. A young man holding a staff across his shoulders sauntered out of the bushes and walked toward them. He exchanged greetings with Abena, and they talked briefly before he disappeared back in the bushes. A while later, an older man, about Abena's age appeared from the same direction. He hugged and kissed Abena.

"Tekele!" Abena introduced the newcomer.

From earlier discussions, they recognized Abena's childhood friend and faithful servant. His intelligent dark eyes and easy disposition explained the long friendship.

With formalities over, Abena sat down for an update on the animals in Tekele's care. It had been over two weeks since they had seen each other, and Abena was keen to know how the calves had fared. He was glad to learn that Tekele had lost only three over the entire calving season. For a nomad, each loss made him that much poorer. Abena released his servant to go back to his animals while he oversaw the grouping of his herd - a process that also served as taking inventory. The sun had long set when they finished and sat down to eat. There was not much conversation this evening since everybody was tired. Because they would be moving again the following day, they all slept under the open sky.

In the morning, Rezan woke to find Abena already up, making the final inspection of his estate. By the time he finished, his visitors were ready and waiting next to their camels. They departed before the sun came up. Abena was glad his children, especially Fados and Malik, were still asleep. They would be inconsolable if they saw him leave without them. Still, it was hard to bid his wives farewell. They stood side-by-side watching him go.

Rezan ceded his place at the head of the convoy to Abena because the nomad knew the area well. Without realizing it, Abena set a punishing pace, which was a challenge for the visitors. After struggling for some time, Mastaf complained.

"*Ayeh!* Slow down. You're going to kill us," he shouted.

Abena recognized the words "slow" and "kill us" for they were similar in Houdini. In this context, he understood what the young man meant. For the nomad, walking was a normal part of living in the wilderness. Not realizing the advantage of his height and lean frame, he did not understand why anyone would complain. Nonetheless, he slowed the pace so they could all keep up. Mastaf resumed his favorite activity on the road - giving Rasul lessons in Shastani.

As the afternoon wore on, the terrain began to change drastically. The vegetation grew sparse and the air became hot and dry. Rivulets of sweat flowed down their faces and stung their eyes. Their clothes were so wet they clung obscenely to their bodies. They sipped water frequently, being careful not to drink it all at once.

Abena maintained a steady pace. He wanted to get to Lefela's territory before dark. But it was not to be. Rasul noticed that Mastaf lapsed into silence after some time. He thought it was merely a pause in their lesson, but shortly after, he got concerned when the young assistant started to walk with a drunken gait.

"Are you well?" Rasul asked in his best Shastani.

Mastaf did not answer. Rasul went up to walk beside him. What he saw alarmed him. Mastaf looked straight ahead, barely acknowledging him. His skin was waxen and streaked with the powdery white of dried sweat, but he was not sweating anymore. Right before Rasul's eyes, Mastaf's face took on a deep hue and he stumbled. Rasul held his arm to steady him. Through the sleeve of Mastaf's gown, Rasul noticed how hot the young man felt.

"What's going on over there?" Irzik asked. "What's wrong with him?"

"I don't think he's well," Rasul said.

Mastaf stumbled again and this time he folded. Rasul had to hold him and gently lower him to the ground. Irzik called out to Abena and Rezan to stop. He also brought both his camel and Mastaf's to a halt. Abena and Rezan stopped their animals and walked back to where Rasul and Irzik stood over Mastaf. He lay on the ground and his eyes started to roll. Abena took one glance at him and knew what the problem was right away. He undid the scarf from his head. He poured some water onto it, and wiped Mastaf's face. He also took off the ailing man's robe, leaving him bare to the waist. He wiped Mastaf's torso with the damp cloth, and then fanned him with the robe. It seemed to work as he reacted to the draft and inhaled deeply. He focused for a moment, but his eyes glazed over again. His mouth moved wordlessly with his swollen tongue sticking out like a mango seed.

Unfortunately, in the salt lake area, there were no trees or bushes. Nothing could survive the scorching heat or the saliferous soil. Abena asked Rezan to fan Mastaf while Irzik stood over him to provide some shade. Abena poured a little water in his mouth from time to time. He asked for more water. Rezan pulled out his canister and handed it to Abena, who continued to wipe Mastaf down. Finally, he looked up at the others and shook his head.

As if in answer to this gesture, Mastaf's eyes rolled again, his body stiffened, and his hands jerked back and forth looking for something to latch onto. His right hand clawed the parched earth, breaking skin. His left hand found Abena's ankle and the fingers locked on it like a vice. Abena screamed in pain and tried to ply the fingers loose, but he could not break the grip. Even when Rasul, Irzik, and Rezan joined in to help, they were still unsuccessful. Abena continued to cry out. Rigid as a board, Mastaf raised himself off the ground with one hand around Abena's ankle and the other bleeding at the tips and clawing the ground. He gritted his teeth and his neck and face strained as if he pulled on something with all his might. The veins on his temples and neck bulged grotesquely. The wide open eyes showing only the whites completed the frightening picture.

As suddenly as it started, it ended. Mastaf coughed once and his body sagged, dropping to the ground. The hand that had locked on Abena's ankle fell away limp. Abena hopped back, rubbing his leg, which broke out in a dark welt. Rezan talked frantically to Mastaf while Rasul knelt beside him, his chin in one hand, silently looking at the assistant who had become a close friend. Abena hobbled back and knelt between Rezan and Rasul. He put a hand on Mastaf's neck looking for a pulse. There was none. Mastaf was gone.

Among his people, death was part of life, and Abena accepted Mastaf's passing with equanimity. He closed the dead man's eyes, and with surprising ease, picked up the body and carried it a little way off the track. He laid it on the ground and began to thrust his sword into the soil, breaking it up and scooping out handfuls. Irzik helped him dig a hole just deep enough to bury the body. When it was ready, all four stood by the grave and Abena gave each an opportunity to say farewell to their departed friend. Then he and Irzik laid Mastaf in the shallow grave. They pushed the soil and chunks of clay over the body and Abena stomped all over it to pack it down. They went back to the animals. They traveled the rest of the day with a heavy spirit that manifested itself in their labored stride. Even the hard driving Abena became lethargic and preoccupied.

Around dusk, they started to exit the lake basin. Light vegetation began to appear and the air became cooler and less oppressive. They had lost time with Mastaf's death, forcing them to travel later than he would have liked. When night fell, Abena urged them to travel a little further until they got to an area with sturdier plant life. He called for a halt when he found a spot where they could camp for the night. They built a fire to keep away animals. After a snack of dried fruit and goat cheese, they attempted to go to sleep. Abena volunteered for the first watch.

Mastaf's demise robbed the convoy of its most sanguine member. Lying on his back looking at the stars, Rezan struggled with guilt for having brought a young man with great promise to die in a god-forsaken, unknown corner of the world. Mastaf's family will never know where his remains lie. For the first time, Rezan began to have serious doubts about what he was doing. He wondered whether journeying into unknown parts of the world was a poor substitute for venturing to the heavens - the true object of his curiosity. As the conflicting thoughts mounted, he grew depressed and discouraged. Finally, he told himself that there was no turning back. He had come too far. He forced the thoughts out of his mind, determined not to allow his feelings to get in the way of his purpose. Still, he grieved his young assistant.

Rasul also felt the weight of Mastaf's passing. From the moment they met, they connected. He found the young man intelligent and loyal. The lad did not volunteer for the journey because he had special skills, but because he admired Rezan and Rasul was also going on the trip. From a dark corner of his soul, a sudden rage exploded to the surface. He stood up, arms to his side, and fists clenched tight. He threw back his head and let out a long, anguished cry. He tore at his garment and beat his chest. The cry alarmed his companions and they rose to their feet. They could barely recognize the wild-eyed man cast in bizarre colors by the flames. Abena and Rezan ran up and held Rasul. He struggled and kicked at first but calmed down, though he still shook from sobbing. Irzik looked on, horrified.

"Why did he have to die?" Rasul asked in broken Shastani. "Why didn't I die instead? I abandoned my family. It is I who am not worthy to live!"

Abena and Rezan looked at one another, each hoping the other might offer the distraught man words of solace. Rezan was about to speak when he heard the fluttering of wings above them. A gray and white dove descended and landed a stride or two away. In its beak, it held a fresh twig with three leaves. Rasul looked at the dove and the twig. He recognized the leaves immediately. They were from the *chotti* plant common in Tandoon. On his walks around the village, he would pluck a handful and stuff them into his mouth, savoring the tangy flavor that sent his salivary glands into a squirting frenzy. He would chew on them, sucking out the essence until only the fiber remained. Then he would ball it and spit it out. On seeing the leaves, his glands involuntarily secreted their juices bringing him sharply to his senses. The dove dipped its head and opened its beak, dropping the twig on the ground. It cocked an eye toward him as if to indicate it had done its work. It fluttered its wings again and rose into the night.

As his companions watched awestruck, Rasul picked up the twig. He held it in both hands, raised it to his nose, and inhaled deeply with his eyes closed. He held his breath for a long time then released it in a rasping, "Aaah!" Still holding the leaves, he went to his spot, lay down in the fetal position, and fell asleep right away.

The other three looked at one another. Abena whistled in amazement and went back to sit by the fire. Rezan and Irzik likewise found their spots and lay down again. Rezan did not sleep. His mind was on the dove and its effect on Rasul. Then he realized that the heaviness he had been experiencing before Rasul exploded was gone. He was still sad about the death, but the sorrow was without the burden of guilt. He continued to think until it was time to relieve Abena. *What a day!*

They set out at first light and trekked without stopping. In the afternoon, Abena announced they were in Lefela's territory. His immediate older brother had chosen the land at the foot of the Gedi Mountain range. The ubiquitous sturdy bush was still in evidence, but there was a marked increase in the variety of plant and animal life. There were thick bushes with deep green leaves, a variety of twines and climbers, which grew on anything whose existence required no ambulation. The soil changed from the sand color to a reddish hue. Butterflies fluttered to protest the disturbance. Squirrels scurried down small trees and stood defiantly on the path, bushy tails held high. When the caravan closed in, they flitted off to watch from a safe distance. Increasing encounters with domestic animals signaled the presence of a greater herd up ahead. Rezan recalled the last time his group was in similar circumstances the bushes had erupted with armed men. He hoped the men in hiding would recognize Abena before they took any adverse action.

Sure enough, men emerged from the foliage, greeted Abena enthusiastically, then shook hands with Rezan, Rasul, and Irzik. One of them turned to Abena, apparently offering to take them to his master. With his stick across his shoulders, the man walked with Abena, talking fast and loud. They approached a clearing with five manyattas spread over the area. Upon seeing the visitors, a man came toward them with a big smile on his face. He had similar features to Abena though his hairline was receding and he had a thicker beard. They were about the same height and build.

"Lefela!"

The brothers kissed one another on the cheek and embraced. Abena turned and pointed at his visitors, introducing them by name. Lefela shook hands with each and smiled broadly. He led them to the shade of a large bush. Three women sat on the ground sifting through grain in wide reed containers. A woman in a *manyatta* stopped tending a pot on a smoky fire to look at the new arrivals. A group of children suspended their game, clearly torn between the desire to run to Abena and fear of the light-skinned strangers. The brave ones came to greet their uncle, but kept a wary eye on his companions. The brothers sat down and immediately got into a deep conversation.

As the brothers talked, two girls fed and watered the travelers' animals. The visitors, feeling left out, stood, and told Abena that they wanted to walk around a little. They unloaded their animals after the girls had watered them then strolled around the camp.

Later, a child came up to them, talking and pointing to where the brothers sat. Lefela, with a wide grin, waved them over. He offered each a cup of hot coffee. Before them was a platter of meat and bread, which they enjoyed immensely. When night came, the brothers continued where they had left off. Rezan took the opportunity to study the stars and find his bearings. They were still talking late in the night when he bid them goodnight and joined his friends who had already retired. They stayed two days at Lefela's camp in which time all the travelers related their journey to their incredulous host.

Over breakfast on the third day, with Abena acting as interpreter, Lefela told them that the best way to Xhaka's lands would be to cut across the Gedi Mountain range. From traders and travelers, he had heard of a man in the town of Tengit, deep in the mountains, who hailed from Xhaka's territory. He suggested they look him up as a possible source of information. Rezan thanked Lefela and presented him with gifts of jewelry and fabric. He accepted them with his customary grin.

One could tell the brothers did not agree on Abena making the trip. Lefela tapped his temple with his index finger, apparently questioning his brother's sanity. Nonetheless, they embraced and said farewell. The servants had already fed and watered the camels and the horse, so Lefela shook hands all round and they departed.

Chapter 14

Journey to Kwavantu

A day after they left Lefela's camp, the elevation of the land and vegetation changed perceptibly. The mountains, once an undulating strip on the horizon, now stood before them in stark relief from the flat monotony of the scrublands. There was increasingly abundant vegetation a greater variety of wildlife. This included dikdik, oryx, mongoose, zebra, and wild ass.

In the evening, the group sought shelter next to a large rock and built a fire to warm some food. What now bothered them was the vast number of tiny insects that buzzed around their heads and threatened to swarm into every orifice. The travelers wrapped scarves around their faces leaving only the eyes exposed. The insects let up only when darkness fell. Unfortunately, the mosquitoes took over. Though they did not come in large numbers, they were even more bothersome. Some buzzed around the ears at a high pitch that made the skin crawl. Others took advantage of this distraction to bite arms and legs, leaving angry red spots that itched for a long time. Initially, the travelers tried to slap them away or swat them whenever they attempted to land on the skin. Eventually, they gave up and went to sleep in spite of the nuisance.

On the third day, the path on which they traveled joined a more defined trail that marked it as a trade route. In due course, they encountered three large convoys traveling in the opposite direction. The first convoy consisted of people who looked like local highland dwellers. They had features similar to Abena's, with soft curly hair, sharp jaw lines, and tall, lean frames. They dressed in flaxen cloth consisting of two pieces - a robe that came up to the knees, and a shawl, which they draped over their shoulders.

The second convoy was largely of tall, dark-skinned, individuals with thick, black, kinky hair, which they kept short and well-groomed. Their teeth were remarkably white. They were bare above the waist, though one or two among them draped animal skins over their shoulders probably as a sign of authority. Their skirts were of fine linen in earth colors. They wore leather sandals whose laces reached just below the knees. Each had a short stabbing sword at the waist, a bow, and quiver of arrows over the shoulders.

The third and largest convoy had mix of individuals of various ethnicities. Some had features like Abena's while others were tall, dark, and lean. Still others were as light as Rezan and Rasul, with straight flowing hair. When Rezan communicated the intention to travel to Xhaka's kingdom, the traders confirmed they were heading the right way.

Over the next two days, they met only individuals or small groups traveling with a mule, probably on local errands. On the sixth day, however, a large caravan of mixed ethnicities overran them, forcing Rezan's group to step aside. At the head was a most intimidating man. He had a strong physique and though dark-skinned, he was of a lighter complexion than others like him. He kept his hair and beard short and well-groomed but the scars on his body bespoke a violent past. As he passed, he scrutinized Rezan's group and gave them a surprisingly warm smile. Rezan's convoy must have piqued his curiosity because he stood aside to let his own convoy pass while he waited for them.

The big man spoke to Abena in a different dialect of Shamaric with a thick accent, but they understood one another quite well. After introductions, the man told Abena he was head of the security detail many convoys hired for protection on the lucrative highway connecting the mountain towns with the big valley cities of Nubia. Abena told him that they were on a quest to Xhaka's kingdom, but did not elaborate. Through Abena, Rezan asked about security along the way. The man assured him it was safe in the mountains. The problem was on the plains, where traders had to contend with nomadic raiders making security escorts necessary. As the end of the man's convoy approached, he told Abena he had to go.

"Look me up when you get to Tengit. Ask for 'Leopard,'" he said. He shook hands with all of them and jogged after his charge.

On the evening of the seventh day after their encounter with "Leopard," they arrived in Tengit, a small town in the highlands. Thick fog shrouded the surrounding hilltops. The vegetation was thick and green with a wide variety of fruits growing wild by the roadside. From the large number of wool-packing stores lining the roads around the town, one could tell the locals raised sheep. They wore flax robes and draped woolen shawls around their shoulders.

Most houses on the outskirts were mud-walled with thatch roofs, but in the center of town, they were of red brick. Stores lined the road that ran through the middle of town. One or two small diners stayed open to serve travelers who would be spending the night in town. Behind some stores were corrals for caravan animals. Most were empty, but the smell of animals still rode the evening breeze. Only the caravan "Leopard" had escorted was in town.

The locals stopped to regard the unusual blend of travelers. The crowd following them grew in size. Abena good-naturedly talked to the children and answered questions from people walking alongside them, or those standing by the roadside.

"Are we going to find Leopard soon?" Rasul asked Rezan.

He was tired and cold and the children who walked by his side peering into his face irritated him. He felt Abena was enjoying the attention a little too much.

"Ah yes," Rezan replied. He called out to Abena to find out where Leopard lived. Abena posed the question to the children and promptly received a barrage of answers. Two boys, in particular, got into an argument, which Abena resolved to their mutual satisfaction. He looked back at Rezan.

"These boys will take us to 'Leopard.'"

The boys led them to the outskirts of town and up a steep hill, past vegetable patches and orchards. At the top of the hill, the ground leveled off and they came to a rudimentary structure that resembled a gazebo. Further up was a large mud and grass house with a wooden door. Behind it were other structures, which, by the sounds and smells, were probably animal sheds. However, the smell of cooking overpowered all other odors, reminding Rezan and his band they were hungry. The boys stood at the door and called out. Not hearing a response, they went around to the buildings behind the house. Rezan and his friends waited.

It would be some time before the boys came back with the man they immediately recognized as "'Leopard.'" He grinned widely when he saw them and shook hands all around. Leopard spoke to the boys who dashed into the house and came back with short stools, which they placed in the gazebo. He invited his visitors to sit down. He spoke to Abena who turned to the other travelers and made a gesture with palms pressed together against his tilted head with eyes closed. They interpreted it as an invitation to spend the night in his home. All nodded in the affirmative.

Leopard rattled off another set of instructions and the lads ran off again, returning with two athletic-looking young men. With Leopard, the young men unloaded the animals and took the goods into the house. When he stumbled over one of several children who stood watching, Leopard chased them off to their homes. Meanwhile, the lads built a fire in the gazebo after which Leopard sent them to one of the structures behind the house. They came back, each with a huge banana and a smile as they headed home. Watching his new host work, Rezan relaxed. He felt they knew what they were doing. The young men led the unburdened animals behind the house where they would spend the night with Leopard's livestock. It was dark by the time they finished. Leopard lit a lamp then sat down.

A young woman stepped into the gazebo with a pitcher of water. Leopard's face lit up and he took her right hand in his left and laid his right hand on his chest indicating she was his wife. To the visitors she could easily have passed for his daughter. Her name was Zawit and she was pregnant. The two young men were her brothers. Zawit smiled shyly and pulled her hand away. Leopard proffered his hands and she poured water over them, letting it run to the ground. They all washed their hands in turn and shook them dry. Zawit set the water aside and went to fetch dinner. It was a simple, but tasty meal of sour bread, lamb stew, and crunchy, green vegetables. Zawit served it all on a single platter and they ate in silence. At the end of the meal, Zawit reappeared, picked up the pitcher, and helped them to wash their hands. She went back to the kitchen with the platter and returned with cups of coffee sitting upon it.

Over coffee, Abena asked Leopard where he came from originally. Careful to include Rezan, Rasul, and Irzik as much as possible, Leopard told them he came from Kwavantu, one of the territories to the south, which had fallen to a mighty King called Xhaka. The name caught the travelers' attention.

"He came from Xhaka's land?" Rezan asked Abena.

"Yes." Rezan was about to speak again, but Abena beat him to it.

"How did you end up here?"

Leopard's face clouded over and he shook his head.

"I did some bad things in the past. I had a bad temper and was easily provoked. One day I got into a fight with a neighbor over our children. As we struggled, he tripped and fell back, hitting his head on a rock. He died on the spot and the village accused me of killing him. They banished me to the hill country where I met other people whose villages had expelled them like me. We were all bitter and mad at the world. When we became strong enough, we raided and destroyed villages."

He paused. Nobody interrupted him.

"We captured and raped girls and women, killed men and children…" He shook his head again. "I did this for many harvests. One night, we planned to enjoy a meal from one village's herd. We intended to kill the lead herdsboy then slaughter one or two cows and feast on them. The leader of our band, a young woman named Sujia, was ready to let an arrow fly when the hills erupted with spirit-warriors. The lead warrior, a most magnificent being, spoke of a child born that night who would become a mighty King."

By now, the visitors were listening with rapt attention.

"I tell you, it was a most spectacular sight. After he had made the pronouncement, all the spirit-beings broke into song and they ascended to the heavens. As they rose, they merged, becoming a bright light in the sky. The spirit-warrior told the boys if they followed the light it would lead them to the child. Though he did not speak to me, I joined the boys to follow the star. I was not about to miss the chance to see this wonderful thing."

Rasul jumped up in disbelief. "Are you saying the star we saw was a group of spirits?"

"Yes."

"How long did it stay up there?"

"I'd say half the night. I'm not sure. We were too busy running to notice."

Rezan said, "Half the night sounds right. That's how long the star I saw stayed up there."

"I agree. I watched it as long as it was in the sky," Abena added.

"This child… what is he or she like?" Rasul asked. "Is he a prince? Who are his parents?"

Leopard laughed. "No. Actually, his parents are very simple. Even the child is quite ordinary when you first look at him, but in his presence, you experience something not of this world. I… I can't describe it. It's a sense of peace, power, submission, and authority all rolled into one. I had lived the previous seven seasons doing all kinds of wicked things. Life meant nothing to me. I could snuff out a man's life as easily as I could tread on a cockroach. Yet, in the presence of the child, I understood the meaning of life and love. I felt I could love and be loved. As far as I could tell, he was human in every way. But there was something different about him and that's what had such a profound effect on me."

He stopped to reflect on what he had just said. They all did. Just then, they all looked at one another wondering if they had been hearing right. They had not communicated with gestures for some time, yet they had all understood each other perfectly, each speaking his mother's tongue. Rasul was sure he spoke and heard Nagrani. Up to now, Rezan, who had spoken Shastani all along, did not stop to wonder how the other three apart from Irzik, spoke it so fluently. Abena and Leopard neither picked out the different dialects they spoke nor questioned how the others spoke flawless Shamaric. Each now asked himself how this had happened. As soon as they asked the question, they realized the power to utter and understand different tongues had left them. No one wanted to be the first to speak for two reasons. First, the experience Leopard had shared moved them profoundly. Second, no one wanted to desecrate the Divine moment they had just experienced. Leopard stood up and motioned for them to follow him. He took the lamp and led them to the large mud house. He showed them where they would sleep and where the amenities were. He waved goodnight and retired.

Rezan and his friends stayed two days with Leopard. They learned that in the short time he had lived in Tengit, he had become a much loved and admired member of the community. He had learned to speak Shamaric and married a local girl, Zawit, whose name appropriately meant "gift." He felt that the Oracle had smiled on him and given him a chance to start anew. In turn, he spoke of his experience with the child of the star at every opportunity, saying the child had indeed saved his life.

The third day after their arrival in Tengit, the travelers were ready to continue. Leopard and his brothers-in-law loaded the animals for the march into Xhaka's territories. Leopard had spent part of the previous day curing meat, drying fruits and vegetables, and packing them for his guests. He arranged for each had man to have at least four sets of footwear to cross the plains. He especially pointed out an area called "The Forsaken Land," which was nothing but jagged rock. He also told them not to carry water just yet because there was plenty in the mountains.

In return for his kindness, Rezan attempted to offer Leopard a gift, but he declined, saying he received gifts from the caravans he escorted all the time. Unable to press him any further, Rezan thrust the roll of material in Zawit's hands. She looked at her husband in confusion, but he only smiled and shook his head in resignation.

"Zawit," Rezan said and they all laughed.

Since he did not expect a caravan to come into Tengit for at least two days, Leopard offered to lead them the first day. He asked his brothers-in-law to accompany him and they were happy to oblige. They took three horses, which they would ride back home.

The thick forest and the beautiful hills and valleys reminded Rasul of home. He always fought back thoughts of his wife and children. Now they came unbidden. Without Mastaf to distract him with lessons in Shastani, he had to face his feelings. He felt guilty because he had robbed Kulsam of the years they had been together, and also the rest of her life. Though he was the one who had left, the community would stigmatize her as "the woman whose husband left her." He was not sure she would take him back if he survived the journey. He was not sure he would go back to her in the first place. When he thought of his children, he felt even worse. No doubt, his mother, Bilqis, would look after them, but they still needed their father. He thought back on how much his own father had given him and realized there was no way he could excuse his absence from their lives. On thinking about the empty feeling he had experienced through the last year with his family, he realized he might still not have been happy had he stayed. Unfettered, his mind went back to his last encounter with his parents. His anger and self-loathing was complete. He did not know how the sword ended up in his hands, but in a rage, he cried out and loped off the top of a bush.

Rezan turned around at the sound..

"Rasul! Calm down." He coaxed the sword out of Rasul's hand and sheathed it.

The others also stopped. Rezan put an arm over Rasul's shoulder and turned him back to the trail. They walked in this manner for sometime with neither speaking.

"I miss my family too." Rezan said.

Rasul understood and felt comforted. He gradually emerged from his troubled mood.

Because he knew they were heading into arid land, Leopard wanted the travelers to save as much of the food they had carried as possible. As evening approached, he began to look out for a kill. Different kinds of animals made their home in the thick foliage of the mountains and he could pick any that crossed his path. The unfortunate victim was a beautiful brown stag with a white underside. He ambled onto the trail a few paces ahead and looked at the humans with no sign of fear. Leopard's arrow caught him just behind the neck. He crumpled and fell, twitching a few times before lying still. With the evening light that filtered through the trees, they made a clearing and set up camp. Leopard expertly skinned the deer and roasted it. He also roasted wild legumes that grew abundantly on the forest floor. They ate and went to sleep. Leopard shared guard duty with his brothers-in-law so the visitors could get the most rest.

All were sad to say goodbye the next morning. Though they did not say much about it, they all remembered the first evening when they had been able to understand one another's language through an entire conversation. It affirmed in their hearts that they shared a special bond and there was great significance to this mission. Leopard would gladly have joined them, but there was a price on his head in Kwavantu and he could not risk it.

"When you see the parents of the child, tell them Jambazi sends his regards and he will never forget them."

"Jambazi? What kind of name is that?" Abena asked.

"Just give them the message."

He embraced traveler before turning homeward with his brothers-in-law.

Rezan and his friends traveled three days in the mountains before the plains came into view, spread out below them in a sandy flatness that rushed into the blue at the horizon. Taking Leopard's advice, they filled their canisters at every opportunity. As they descended, the streams were fewer and further apart. The vegetation grew sparse, with less variety as the hardy bushes - masters of the scrublands, began to exert their dominance. The red soil ceded to the sandy soil at the foothills and the heat received them in a warm embrace. By the fifth day, the Gedi Mountains were mere shadows on the landscape behind them.

Nine days after leaving Tengit, they marched into the strangest land they had ever seen. It was flat and covered with chunks of porous, jagged, black rock. It had to be the Forsaken Land about which Leopard had warned. Even the self-confident bushes that boasted their ability to survive harsh conditions could only watch shamefaced from the fringes as a wicked-looking, pale-green cactus, with a thick waxen skin and hard dry thorns, took over. Walking in this part of the country was most challenging. Even the animals had trouble finding steady footing. Shoes wore out within two days though a misstep on the rough rocks instantly put a shoe out of commission. They were grateful for Leopard's advice to have extra pairs on hand.

The hardest thing about the Forsaken Land was finding a spot free of rocks or the angry cactus. It had to be a miracle, they believed, when each night, they found an area just clear enough they could sit down and rest. There was no need for a fire because there were no large animals in evidence. The land was so inhospitable even lizards and scorpions were scarce.

They were grateful when they got out of this stretch of land on the fourth day. With wounded pride, the bushes reasserted themselves. As if to make a statement, the bushes were larger and the vegetation thicker this side of the Forsaken Land. Herds of animals began to appear. Among them were deer, zebra, giraffe, and varieties of antelope. The animals left them alone - but not for long.

On the third days since leaving the Forsaken Land, a herd of elephants approached obliquely. If both parties were to keep moving, their paths would intersect. Abena told them to keep walking and not to show concern. The herd stopped and observed the humans. Suddenly, the large matriarch trumpeted, broke away from the herd, and made for the travelers. The horse spooked first. It bucked, scattering its load. Irzik grabbed and hung onto the reins. He tried to calm it, but the horse galloped away with Irzik flailing on his flanks. The elephant locked on Abena and chased him, ignoring everyone else. He ducked this way and that and behind bushes, but they were nothing to the mighty creature. She caught up with him and knocked him down with her trunk. He tried to get up, but she knocked him down with her right foreleg. Now his friends feared the animal would trample him underfoot. Also realizing this, Abena rolled, scrambled to his feet, and tried to get away, but she still outpaced him. She struck him a third time with her trunk, tossing him several paces like a useless doll.

Rasul had seen enough. Up to this point, he had tried to stay clear of the elephant, but seeing she was not going to leave Abena alone until she killed him, he ran and stood in her path as she prepared to charge the tiring man.

"*Oi! Oi!* Stop! Leave him alone!" he shouted in Nagrani, arms spread out.

The elephant was distracted for an instant, but it sought Abena again and charged. Rasul blocked her path again. She stopped and regarded him as if gauging what to do. He stood his ground. A feeling akin to what he experienced the night he faced Gulbit came over him.

"Get out of here! Go!" he shouted.

What happened next surprised them all. The animal reared on its hind legs and brought its forelegs down with an earthshaking thud and a cloud of dust. She turned and lumbered back to the other elephants, which had stood watching all the while. She stopped in front of her herd, turned round, and trumpeted what could only have been a pachyderm expletive before leading her charges in another direction.

Rezan, who had tried his best to control the camels, left them and ran toward Abena. With the immediate danger past, Rasul joined him at Abena's side. Shaken more than injured, Abena groaned. He breathed and sweated heavily. The smell of fear hung thick around him. He was cut, bruised, and covered in dust. A quick inventory revealed no broken bones. The greatest injuries he suffered were scraped hands and knees, and a bruised ego. Rezan cut a strip of cloth and poured a little water over it to clean the wounds. He dabbed a little myrrh over them to prevent infection. When he had recovered from the shock and was sure the elephants were not coming back, Abena looked gratefully at Rasul.

"Thank you. I owe you my life."

Rasul smiled and shrugged.

Rezan and Rasul helped Abena to his feet and went to help Irzik gather up the goods the animals had scattered as they sought to put distance between themselves and the elephant. They resumed their journey with a little more trepidation in the open country. Fortunately, they had no more such encounters though they still saw herds of wild animals.

After another twenty days of trekking through the scrubland, a mountain range began to appear on the horizon. Rezan told his companions he was sure their destination lay just beyond it. This information boosted their morale and a new gait sprang in their step. In subsequent days, the climate grew progressively cooler and the variety of plant life increased, just as it had happened when they ascended the Gedi Mountains. They also saw more settlements and encountered a few other travelers.

There was evidence of farming activity with people working on garden patches in front of their houses or on vast strips of land. The community kept cows, goats, and sheep, which grazed in the valleys and open fields. Chickens roamed freely around the small mud-walled huts with thatched roofs. Dogs barked warnings from the compounds.

Both men and women wore a dress made out of a single piece of soft leather tied over one shoulder and girdled at the waist with a strip of leather or twine. The women adorned their dress with beads and shells. Most wore a broad leather necklace with intricate patterns of beads and shells. The people were friendly and often saluted the travelers.

With evening approaching, Rezan thought they would need to find a place to spend the night. He managed to get the message across to some people working in a field. They led the travelers to the home of their headman. He welcomed them gladly and fed them a sumptuous meal. Afterwards, some elders joined them and they communicated using gestures. By this time, possibly the entire village gathered to look upon the travelers. At dusk, the headman's sons led Rezan and his friends to a large hut. The boys helped unload and secure the animals before leaving the visitors who promptly fell asleep. The same boys came to fetch them in the morning. The headman had prepared another heavy breakfast, which the travelers were at pains to eat because they were still full from the previous night. They gave the headman gifts of fine linen and a few trinkets to the elders with which they were delighted. They loaded their animals and set off.

The sixth day after leaving the friendly community, Rasul pointed out what looked like a city in the distance below them. It had to be Bora-ini. They were ecstatic. Finally, they were nearing the end of their quest. The thought added a kick to their stride. They noticed increased human activity and traffic the closer they got to the city. What they found disconcerting was that the people would step off the path completely and stare until they were out of sight. They did not return the travelers' greetings like the communities they had encountered earlier. They spent the night in the open, careful to observe their now refined safety measures.

Chapter 15

in kwavantu

One evening, a runner brought word to Bora-ini that a small convoy of strangers was making its way to the city from the north. They would be in the city by the evening of the next day. This was unusual because most caravans came from the east bringing goods that had come by ship from across the sea. Caravans from the north were rare and the few that came were usually Nubians in search of ivory and hides of exotic animals.

Mattu was at home playing with his children when he got the news. As a precaution, he dispatched a servant to Stimela to alert him of the arrival of this group. The servant reported that Stimela and other leaders were having a feast at the palace. This meant they should not be disturbed. One did so at his own peril. Mattu decided to take the initiative and meet the visitors. This would put him in a better position to answer Tamaa, whose wrath was like lightning. One could never predict when and where it would strike, so it was best to cover all possible angles. Mattu sent two guards to meet the convoy and invite them into his home. He sent another servant back to Tamaa with word that a small convoy of strangers had walked into town and he would keep them at his place and find out the purpose of their visit. Should Tamaa request it, he would release them to the governor. When he asked Fanta about accommodating them if he did not hear from Stimela or Tamaa, she said it would not be a problem. Mattu slept little as he pondered possible reasons for the unexpected visit.

Rezan and his companions were a little flustered when two men blocked their path. They stopped and one man spoke in his native tongue. Noticing they did not understand, he signaled what they perceived was a command to follow. They complied. After a short walk, they arrived at a large red brick house with a neatly thatched roof. Adjacent to it was a similar, but smaller building. The owner was obviously a man of stature. He now stood before them smiling broadly. He was about Abena's age, of medium build, and dressed in a colorful cotton outfit. He shook hands with each of them, uttering what one would presume were words of welcome.

"Mattu," he said, tapping his chest.

He invited them into the house, which they found surprisingly spacious and cool. They left the animals in front of the house for the time being. In the living room, they sat on intricately carved wooden chairs covered with animal hides and cushions. A servant came in with a basket full of fruits - bananas, passion fruit, pears, guavas, and avocados. She set it on the low table in their midst. Another followed with a metal jug of water and a basin. She knelt before each visitor and washed his hands catching the run-off with the basin. She handed each man a silver cup and filled it with water from a pitcher. After they had slaked their thirst, Mattu welcomed them to partake of the fruits.

As they ate, a slender, attractive woman entered the room. A girl of about ten and a boy of about seven followed her. From Mattu's introduction, they gathered this was his family. The woman went down on her knees before each visitor and took his hand in both of hers - something they all found a little disconcerting. When she finished, she rose and spoke to her husband. He nodded and she left the room, but her children sat with their father, never taking their eyes off the visitors.

Mattu's servant returned. He reported that the chief of the palace guards had said Tamaa was busy. Mattu decided he had done all he could for the time being. He would send word to Tamaa the next day. Meanwhile, he would get to know his guests and their mission. Fanta had informed him the guesthouse was ready. Mattu asked the guests to follow him. He pointed to the animals indicating their goods could go into the storage room. He called three of his servants to attend to this matter. Later, the servants showed the guests where they would sleep. They bathed and changed into fresh gowns Fanta had provided.

Afterwards, Mattu invited them in for dinner. From her quick assessment of the visitors, Fanta prepared rice and a fried flat bread called *chabadi* to go with spicy beef and chicken stew. This day was definitely special. She was glad when the guests appeared to enjoy the food.

While they ate and struggling to make conversation, Mattu was trying to find a solution to his dilemma. He was sure Tamaa would call for the travelers the following day and he did not want to leave room for mistakes. After racking his brain for some time, he remembered a widely traveled old-timer who spoke several languages. He excused himself and stepped outside.

"Femi!"

The servant came right away.

"Yes, Master."

"Do you remember Msafiri?

"The old traveler?"

"Yes. Do you know where he lives?"

"Not exactly, but as beetles to dung is Msafiri to cheap wine."

"Find Locho and Lindo and tell them to get here immediately."

"Yes, Master."

The two men appeared after a while. Mattu gave them instructions to look for Msafiri.

"I don't care who you have to disturb or wake up, but find Msafiri and bring him here. Don't fail!"

He went back to his conversation with the visitors. He knew the men were here on some quest for a star - the significance of which he did not grasp. He was further confounded when Rezan produced charts that made no sense. Finally, he allowed his tired guests to go to bed. His family also retired, but he sat waiting.

"Master." It was Femi. Mattu woke up with a start. He had fallen asleep on the chair. "Locho and Lindo have returned, Master."

Mattu sat up as his men walked into the room.

"We have good news and bad news," Locho began.

"The good news first."

"We found Msafiri." Locho paused. Mattu realized that was the extent of the good news.

"And the bad?"

"He's dead drunk. It took us half the night to find him, and when we did he didn't even wake up."

"*Eesh!*" Mattu swore. He heard the heavy alcohol-induced breathing coming from just outside the front door. "Help Femi, take him to one of the servants' chambers. I'll keep him overnight. We can't afford to lose track of him now. Good work, men. You may go home after that."

In the morning, Mattu was up before his guests. First, he checked on Msafiri and found him still asleep. The miasmic smell of stale beer on his breath filled the chamber. His mouth was red as though he had sipped on scalding hot soup. The half-open eyes had a deathly quality to them. His cheekbones were so pronounced they threatened to breach the pallid gray skin that covered them. If it weren't for the fact he was snoring, he might have passed for a cadaver. *What a waste of life!* Mattu knew that the man was once an intelligent businessman, knowledgeable in several languages and different cultures. His decline began with the death of his wife, Sumbi, several seasons back. Since then, he had taken to drink, seemingly determined never to set foot back in sobriety.

Mattu instructed Femi to clean him up and give him fermented porridge mixed with bitter herbs to ease the headache, clear his head, and quell the craving for more drink. He found his guests already in the main house. At the table was a breakfast of porridge, sweet potatoes, cassava, and fruits. As they ate, Mattu attempted to learn who the visitors were.

In the middle of breakfast, they heard the sound of hooves approaching. The visitors looked at Mattu for enlightenment. He looked down and frowned. He knew what it meant and he was not looking forward to it. The sound grew louder until it stopped outside his house save for the occasional "*clop, clop*" of a restless horse. Footsteps now approached and a tall, dignified man filled the entrance.

"His Highness Tamaa sends his compliments and begs the pleasure the visitors at the palace," the messenger told Mattu. "The horses are waiting to take all of you to him."

Though draped in protocol, it was an order to leave for the palace immediately.

"Right now?" Mattu sought to confirm.

"Right now," the messenger said impassively.

"Alright. Give us a little time."

He tried to convey the message to the visitors as best as he could. They read the situation better than he could explain, and nodded in understanding. They indicated that they had to fetch some gifts to present the ruler of the land. The messenger agreed and went to wait outside. Mattu called Femi.

"Get Msafiri ready now! I want him to come with us to the palace."

The guests were soon ready with their gifts for Tamaa.

"We're just waiting for one more," Mattu told Tamaa's messenger.

A while later, Femi appeared, doing his best to support the lugubrious Msafiri who swayed like a sapling in the wind.

"Is that thing coming with us?" the messenger asked incredulously.

"Yes. He's the only one who can interpret these men's languages.

"Fine. Your head, not mine."

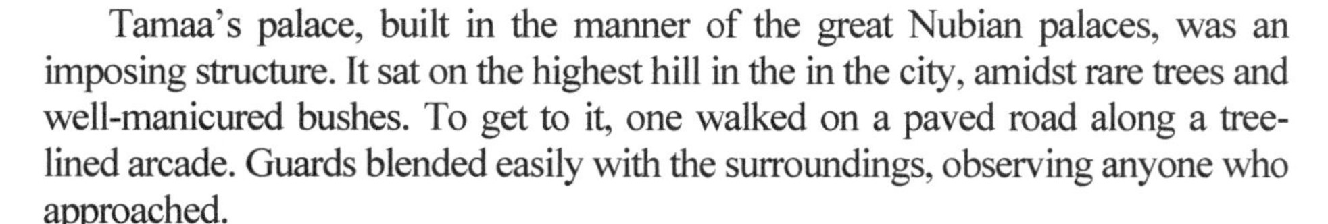

Tamaa's palace, built in the manner of the great Nubian palaces, was an imposing structure. It sat on the highest hill in the in the city, amidst rare trees and well-manicured bushes. To get to it, one walked on a paved road along a tree-lined arcade. Guards blended easily with the surroundings, observing anyone who approached.

The arcade led to a flight of steps and a brick false front, adorned with exotic plants and flowers. Beyond the front was a large tiled spa where guests and their families frolicked on hot days. It was made entirely of marble hauled in from distant lands. Around the spa were easy chairs made from polished hardwood and ivory. The spa stretched all the way up to the palace steps. The walls were of a specially baked red brick. Its heavy doors, made from mahogany and reinforced with decorative bronze plates and hinges, added to the imposing facade. Two warriors stood guard on either side. Under the escort of the royal messenger and palace guards, Rezan's company passed through with nothing more than a pat down.

The doors opened into a large chamber. Animal and human skulls lined the walls. Life size images of Tamaa in different attitudes greeted visitors as soon as they entered the anteroom. Palace guards confiscated all weapons before two large men opened the door to the meeting room. The circular meeting chamber had a raised dais opposite the door. Along the walls, guards stood with shields and spears. On the dais was a huge gold and ivory throne.

On the throne sat Tamaa, Governor of Kwavantu, in a white linen gown interwoven with fine gold thread that gave it a subtle sheen. He wore a narrow gold-rimmed leopard skin headband. On his delicately manicured feet were leather sandals with thongs tied midway up the shin. Above the throne was the stuffed head of a lion, intended to serve as an extension of his personality. In appearance, he was not what Rezan had imagined. Middle-aged and dark-skinned, he was obviously in good shape. His chiseled jaw, twinkling eyes, and easy smile endeared him to everyone on the first encounter.

Seated before him on either side of the throne were his twelve aides, advisors, and senior officials. They all seemed to mimic their leader. They smiled when he smiled and turned serious when he stopped.

Tamaa studied the visitors, his right hand that he tucked under his nose and his left arm resting on the throne. He maintained this posture when the Chief of Protocol announced the visitors. The travelers stood abreast, facing Tamaa. Mattu stood with them. Palace servants brought in the travelers' gifts and laid them before the governor.

"Your Excellency, Tamaa bin Tumbo," the Chief of Protocol, Bunduk, announced. "Great Governor of Kwavantu, today, an unusual group stands before you. These men all come from distant lands and last night, they arrived unexpectedly in your beloved city. Your servant, Mattu provided them accommodation until we were able to arrange this audience with you. Your Excellency, to help with the different languages these men speak, we brought in a man who has not been well, but he put his discomfort aside to serve you, O Great Tamaa. At your disposal, my Lord, is Msafiri, once one of the greatest travelers and traders in Kwavantu."

Msafiri, who up to this point still sagged from his perennial excesses, snapped out of his drunken stupor and stood erect. He bowed in affirmation of his readiness to serve.

Tamaa sat up, leaned forward, and interlocked his fingers. One by one, his officials adopted a similar posture.

"First I'd like to welcome you to our beautiful land. I'm sure you have seen more of it than have most of its citizens. Often when I have visitors from a foreign land, the ruler of the land will send a messenger to alert me of the upcoming visit. However, as Avantu, we welcome visitors anytime. I, Tamaa, welcome you to Bora-ini."

He spread his arms in a gesture of welcome. The officials nodded and smiled at the guests.

"Well then, my friends, tell me about yourselves."

Rezan spoke first.

"I greet you, O Great Tamaa. I am Rezan, son of Hammoun, from the city of Bhustan in Senna. I am a scholar and astronomer in the service of King Be'el-Sharrazz. We've journeyed a long time and are glad to be in your land and in this beautiful city. Your people have already treated us well and we feel welcome."

Tamaa looked at Mattu and smiled. Msafiri raised his voice and interpreted Rezan's words in Wahsil. Rezan then turned to Rasul who stood to his left.

"Your Excellency, I am Rasul Seth, son of Dev Seth, a businessman from Laksh, Chandustan." Msafiri interpreted his words.

Abena, on Rasul's right, spoke next. "I am Abena. I did not travel as far as my friends here did, but I am still a long way from home. I hail from the deserts of Nubia and am glad to be in your presence, O Great Ruler."

Rezan pointed to Irzik next to him. "This is Irzik also from Bhustan without whom this trip would be impossible."

"Very good," Tamaa said after the interpretation. "So, what brings you to our humble land from so far way?"

Rezan responded again.

"Your Excellency, several months ago, I was lying on the roof of my mother's house with my bride, enjoying the evening breeze. I looked up at the sky and saw a star form right before my eyes."

Tamaa assumed his favorite posture - right thumb under chin, fingers over mouth, left arm on armrest, as Msafiri began to interpret.

"The star gradually rose to a point in the sky and stopped. It stayed there a long time then faded. As a student of the heavens and an advisor to priests in the King's palace, I naturally wanted to understand the meaning of such a phenomenon."

Msafiri struggled to find appropriate interpretations for some of the terms, but he made it through. Rezan then explained how the sighting did not fit the pattern of stellar movements and not knowing what it meant bothered him. He related how Rasul had seen the same thing and started out on a journey to find its meaning. He talked about their journey across the Djanguan Desert, the Sea of Aldam, and the wilderness of Nubia, where they met Abena. Rezan mentioned that it could not be a coincidence that three men should see the same phenomenon, have an overwhelming desire to know its meaning, and end up coming together.

While Rezan spoke, Tamaa nodded in mild fascination at the fabulous account. He obviously wondered what would possess a man to leave everything to follow a star. The officials reflected this sentiment with subtle glances to one another and suppressed smiles. Rezan went on to talk about the trip in the Gedi Mountains where they met a man who claimed to have witnessed the formation of the star.

"The man was originally from Kwavantu." This got some reaction. Minds that had drifted off to savor a pleasant memory or anticipate a future event made a hasty return to the present. Rezan continued. "He lived in the hill country to which villages banish wrongdoers. He said one night they planned to rob some herdsboys when the hills exploded with spirit-beings. Their leader declared the birth of a child who would become King. A star led this man and the herdsboys to the child. We three, Your Excellency, all saw the same star. It is the reason we made this journey to pay homage to the child born that night. We believe our common experience means there's something special about him."

As Msafiri interpreted these words, the twinkle in Tamaa's eyes turned into a deadly glint that the visitors, in their innocence, did not notice. They however sensed the chill that befell the room. There were no more sneaky smiles or glances. Tamaa once again leaned forward and brought his hands together. This time the posture seemed more threatening. Even the smile he flashed took on the attitude of the lion above his head, which bared his fangs menacingly.

"Ah! That is good to hear my friends. It's a wonder you would come this far and risk your lives just to see a little infant from some obscure village. It must mean a lot to you. Well, you are welcome to find the child. In fact, I'll give you ten of my men to make sure you find him. When you do, come back and tell me about it that I too, may go worship him. Mattu, these men will remain with you tonight and leave to find the child tomorrow. Let Bunduk, the Chief of Protocol, know if you need anything for the journey. You must find this child. I am happy to have met you, friends. Again, come see me when you accomplish your mission."

Tamaa ignored the presents, making it clear that the meeting was over.

Msafiri interpreted what Tamaa said and they all bowed as Bunduk led them back into the anteroom.

After the visitors left, Tamaa sat back and looked around the room. All eyes looked down. One man, who seemed particularly discomfited, had turned into water as great drops of sweat fell at his feet. Tamaa rose and motioned to the guard on his right to follow him. He descended the steps slowly and went directly to the nervous man.

"Your Excellency, Great Tamaa. I was told the child and his parents were poor, insignificant peasants. Even Mattu can tell you that's what we learnt. I didn't know about these men. I couldn't have. I'm sorry."

Tamaa stretched out his arm and the warrior placed the spear in his hand. The man now fell to his knees and begged for mercy in earnest. Tamaa stood over him, cold and impassive.

"O Great Tamaa, Great Ruler, forgive me. Have mercy. I'll do anything you ask. Let me live and I'll..."

Thiukh!

Tamaa plunged the spear deep into the side of the man's neck, and then yanked it out. The protestations reduced to a strained gurgling. A red fountain spurted from the wound, splattering Tamaa and the man next to him. The victim fell sideways and lay still. Tamaa tossed the spear aside, regarded the body for a moment, then swept out of the room. After moments of indecision, the officials filed out into the anteroom. Servants came in to clean up. Stimela would not receive the burial due a man of his standing. The stray dogs that roamed the outskirts of the city would be fighting over his body shortly.

Tamaa left the chamber and went into the conference room where he held meetings with close associates. He walked up to a large wood carving of a warrior holding a sword and shield. He pulled on the sword and elicited the vexed groaning of a mechanical system roused from a state of inertia. The carving slid aside revealing a narrow door at the top of a flight of stairs. Tamaa descended the stairs into a cavernous room with furnishings similar to those in the anteroom. He pulled on another lever at the foot of the stairs and the cantankerous system shut the secret door. Flaming torches attached to the walls threw a ghostly orange light around the room. Presently another statue slid open and a shifty eyed individual, made more sinister in the light, stepped into the room. Tamaa addressed him without preamble.

"You heard what those men said?"

"Yes, my Lord. I heard everything."

"Tomorrow, they will travel to… what's that village?"

"Ronge, Your Excellency."

"Yes. Take ten men and pick the visitors up at Mattu's house tomorrow. Travel with them to find this child. Find out everything while you are there - what the people think about him, what they say about me, and if they plan to rally around another ruler. Come back the same way, but when you get to the land of the Vasua, kill them! All of them! Make it look like the Vasua ambushed you. Kill some of your men to make it look real. That way I can tell their respective kings bandits attacked them. But I want the visitors dead. This information is too dangerous to get out into the world. I'll take care of the child in the next few days. Do you understand what you have to do?

"Yes, Your Excellency."

"Good."

He waited for Kabala to leave before he slipped out through yet another secret door. He walked along a narrow tunnel that led to a trap door. He removed a brick from the wall. He took the key, replaced the brick, and opened the door. He took one of the torches and descended the steps, stopping to pull the door shut over his head.

The scantily clad young woman looked up in abject terror. He had come to do it again. She never got used to it. He did awful things to her. He beat her up and forced her to engage in horrible acts, sometimes with other men and women. He always cursed this person or that group of people when he did it. She could not fight back or escape. No one looked for her. No one would ever find her because he had killed her young husband - his own son, before throwing her in the dungeon. His blood-spattered robe told her it was going to be very rough.

"What just happened in there?" Rasul asked Rezan.

"I don't know. As soon as you mentioned the child, everything changed. Everyone in the room became tense."

"Did you hear someone crying and pleading as we left?" Abena asked.

They chorused in agreement.

"Something serious is going on," Rezan said. "We'll have to be careful in what we say and do."

They stopped talking when their escorts, courtesy of Tamaa, brought up the horses to take them back to Mattu's house.

Mattu stayed behind with the other officials. None of them would dare leave until Tamaa had spent his rage and they knew their fate. There was no point sealing it with an unnecessary act such as leaving without his consent.

The palace servant informed the travelers that Tamaa would send a band of warriors to escort them to their destination in the morning. Meanwhile, they were free to walk around the city. He did not tell them some inconspicuous individuals would shadow their every move and listen in on every conversation. When they later went into town, there was not much to see since no big caravans had come through lately and the next market day was three days away. Rasul, however, managed to converse with vendors. He learnt what they sold, where they got their merchandize, and how they transacted business. It tickled him that some spices on the market came from as far as Chandustan. He had to head back to Mattu's residence because began to draw a crowd of people gawking at his pale skin and straight matted hair.

In the middle of the afternoon, Mattu came home looking extremely distraught. He talked with his guests briefly then retired to the inner chambers. He reappeared just before dusk to inform the visitors what they already knew. They would leave early in the morning for Ronge. He dined with them, but said very little, prompting Rezan to ask if all was well. Mattu smiled, saying there was no problem, but his eyes were sad. Later, Msafiri told the travelers one of Tamaa's officials had died and the governor had appointed Mattu to take the dead man's place. The visitors now understood why their host was so despondent. They had already surmised Tamaa was no easy customer.

Chapter 16

behold the child!

As promised, eleven warriors showed up at Mattu's residence early the following morning. Their leader was a wiry, shifty-eyed man who did not look a person in the eye when he spoke. He told Rezan that because of the animals, they would take the indirect route to Ronge, avoiding the dangerous descent down the escarpment. The travelers, knowing no better, could only agree. Mattu bid them farewell and informed them they would be welcome to stay with him when they returned. He still looked troubled.

The leader of the warriors said very little and set a reasonable pace. Though the land was not as mountainous heading out on this side of the city, they still had a number of hills and valleys to cross. The vegetation was diverse while they were still in higher country. By the afternoon, they started the descent into the plains - the coolest in which they had traveled so far.

The warriors were a surly group, talking only amongst themselves. Their leader was the most lonesome among them and even his warriors largely ignored him. The travelers found the presence of the warriors a little unnerving after their experience at the palace.

"I have a bad feeling about this," Rezan told his companions.

"Me too," Rasul said.

Only Msafiri appeared clueless to what was going on, seemingly wrapped up in his own world in which he sometimes held quiet conversations with himself.

Toward evening, the warriors shot a zebra. They roasted it and shared with the foreigners. At night, the warriors took turns at keeping guard, but Rezan had his men observe guard duty as they would have done if they were by themselves.

The night went fast and very early the next morning the warriors were up and ready to go. About midmorning, Msafiri, the oldest among them, could hardly keep up. To the annoyance of the warriors, Rezan called for a halt so they could redistribute some packages to make room for Msafiri on the horse. Even on the horse he had trouble sitting up. When evening came, he lay down breathing heavily. His hands shook and he sweated profusely. A warrior came up and stared briefly at him, then turned aside and spat. His gestures indicated Msafiri missed drink and was suffering for it. Rezan looked through his supplies for an elixir he could give the interpreter. He found one his father used in emergent situations when he could not diagnose a condition with certainty. Rezan crushed a small amount of the grayish-green chunks in a small bowl, added a little water, and gave it to Msafiri. The drug knocked him out almost immediately. Rezan told his companions its effectiveness would show when Msafiri woke up.

When the warriors stirred the following day, Msafiri was already up complaining of a headache and a strange sensation all over his body. He, however, seemed more alert. Rezan prepared another potion for him. Afterwards, he gave the ailing man dates and sweet snacks as his father had done with his patients. Msafiri handled the start of this day better than the previous one and was somehow able to keep up. Later, however, he had to ride the horse.

By the afternoon, the mountain range appeared on the right, indicating they had gone round the southern end of the escarpment and were now heading toward the lower regions to the west. Tension began to build early in the evening as they approached what looked like a huge hump in the valley. The warriors now talked frequently among themselves, occasionally stealing glances at the foreigners. The shifty-eyed one appeared to differ with the rest over an issue, but they seemed to disregard his opinion. He seemed unhappy with the discussion.

To Rezan, the first indication of mischief came when they started to walk along the dry bed of a seasonal river with trees and thick bushes on each side. The warriors began to place themselves strategically behind his friends. First, two broke off to walk behind Irzik and Msafiri who were at the rear. A pair slid behind Rasul and another behind Rezan himself. He noticed two others take position in front of him behind Abena.

They now approached a point where the river dammed. Twigs, branches, driftwood, and other debris choked the area, leaving a narrow passage. Conversation ceased and tension mounted. The warriors handled their weapons in a barely perceptible offensive stance. Msafiri, who so far had given no indication of equestrian skills, suddenly spurred the horse forward and rode alongside Rezan with hitherto unseen expertise.

"Careful. They're up to something," he whispered in Shastani.

"*Weh!* Get back in your place," a warrior shouted.

"We have places?" Msafiri mocked.

Abena took the opportunity to stop and turn around. He looked straight at the warriors behind him, making it clear he was aware of their intentions.

"Keep moving. We're losing time," one of them barked.

"What's going on back there?" Abena asked, stalling while waiting for Rezan to draw closer. He saw the warning in Rezan's eyes and turned slowly to face the front.

"You drunk! Get back in your place!" the warrior warned Msafiri again.

Abena realized Msafiri was deliberately causing a disruption, so he slowed down and made as if he were going to reprimand him. This forced the warriors to stop. Abena laid his hand on his sword. Rasul noticed the movement and kept his hand ready for a quick draw.

Seeing their plan disrupted, a warrior shouted, "Kill them now!"

Abena did not need Msafiri's interpretation to understand the order. He drew his sword and faced the two warriors who had placed themselves behind him. He feigned an attack on the man to his left. The warrior raised his shield to ward off the blow. The other man struck out, not realizing it was precisely what Abena wanted him to do. He thrust at Abena who parried the blow and delivered one of his own, opening a deep gash along the man's arm. He used the momentum he had gained from avoiding the spear to run into the first warrior's shield, knocking him to the ground. But at that instant, he knew he was lost because Shifty Eyes and two other warriors who had been at the very front, now charged him. Besides, the injured warrior was still standing. Abena decided if he were to die, he would take the man on the ground with him. Kicking the fallen warrior's spear, he straddled him and raised his sword to bring it down on his throat, but the man twisted to evade the blow. At the same instant, Abena felt a sharp edge incise his belly. A moment later, the owner of the spear crashed into him and they tumbled to the ground. The heavy warrior pinned him down, staring at him strangely, then faded. Abena noticed the arrow sticking out of the right side of the warrior's neck. Warm blood was already soaking into Abena's robe and he fought himself free from under the man. As he stood, he saw the warrior whose arm he had opened also lying face down with an arrow in his back. A few steps away, Shifty Eyes sat on the ground, talking to himself and trying to dislodge an arrow in his torso. His chest rose and fell oddly. He too, fell back and was gone. Abena now knew someone else had attacked them and whoever it was had the power to hurt him as well. Ignoring his bleeding stomach, he raised bloody hands. The man on the ground, whom he had almost killed, also sat up and raised his.

Things also happened quickly around Rezan. When the warrior gave the order to kill, Rezan attempted to draw his sword, but he was not quick enough. The warriors, seeing his inexperience, decided to toy with him. One took hold of his hand in a tight grip while the other held him from behind in a chokehold. Rezan struggled, but it only added to the amusement of his tormentors. It did not last long. Both men suddenly registered expressions of surprise and relaxed their hold. When he saw the arrowhead sticking from the chest of the man who held his hand, he realized someone had hit both men from behind. They crumpled to the ground. Rezan looked around and saw Abena standing and a warrior seated on the ground with their hands in the air. He raised his too, though he did not know why.

For Rasul, the early years of training in swordsmanship and his recent proclivity for eruption served him well. As soon as he heard the order to kill, he identified the warriors who would present immediate danger. In two quick strikes, he decapitated their lances. In two similar blows, he sliced their shields in half, injuring one man's arm slightly in the process. The men realized they were dealing with a highly skilled swordsman and fell to their knees begging him to spare them. Rasul could have killed them both, but it was not in his nature to draw blood. He held his sword ready should they attempt to attack again. As the rage passed, he beheld the gory sight around him and felt sick. All but three warriors, counting the two before him, were dead. All his friends had survived though. He saw Abena and Rasul with their hands raised, but he did not dare take his eyes off his captives for too long.

Irzik, ever the camel driver, had no concern for himself when the bloodletting started. Bodies fell and arrows flew around him, but he worried about the animals and the goods more than anything else. When the horse reared and threw Msafiri to the ground, Irzik immediately reached for the reins. The animal quieted, and he stood looking around, bewildered at the sight of dead warriors and his companions who raised their arms. Irzik would never know that reaching to calm the horse had saved his life. He had not seen the warrior whose spear almost impaled him go down. He was equally oblivious of the spear that had struck the second warrior in the chest.

Msafiri sat on the ground where the horse had tossed him, watching open mouthed as the carnage unfolded. This time he knew for sure he was not having another wine-induced nightmare.

The camels could have cared less if the sky rained men with arrows driven through their temples.

Suddenly, it was all over. A long period of uncertainty followed in which those still alive knew a third party must have weapons trained on them. Then the bushes moved. A woman, barely a girl, emerged. She was rather tall, slim, exquisitely formed, with smooth dark skin. The high cheekbones and full lips gave her a regal bearing. She wore a two-piece outfit of soft brown leather. On her head, wrists, and ankles she wore bands made from leopard skin. Her necklace of multicolored beads fit snugly around a long elegant neck. Despite their distress, the travelers were spellbound. However, the bow and arrow in her hands and her unsmiling face grounded them in reality. From both sides of the river, men emerged, some with spears ready and others with arrows notched. They surrounded the travelers and warriors.

The girl approached the men kneeling before Rasul. She placed the arrow in her quiver, but still held her bow in her left hand. Ignoring Rasul, she got hold of the nearest warrior's cheeks in her right hand as an adult would when trying to see what a child hid in her mouth. The man slapped her hand away. She smiled.

"Where is your leader?" she asked calmly in Wahsil.

The warrior looked at her disdainfully and snickered. Without raising her voice or changing her tone, she asked the question again. Despite the calm delivery, its import was not lost on the warrior. He pointed grudgingly at the man who lay on his back with knees raised in an obscene posture and hands still clasping the arrow in his chest. Blood dribbled out of the right side of his mouth and his eyes looked skyward unseeing.

The young woman picked one of the broken spearheads and offered it to the warrior.

"Go cut off his head."

The man did not budge. A cocky smile cracked his face. His colleague muttered a comment at which they both laughed. With lightning speed, she smacked the second man across the forehead with the flat of the spearhead, breaking skin. Blood immediately flowed down his face into his eyes. The laughter ceased. She bent down and brought her face very close to the first warrior. Her eyes were more piercing than the tip of the spearhead. She handed it to him once more.

"Do it!"

The warrior made no further attempt at bravado. He rose, went up to his fallen leader, and began cutting through bone and sinew. It was a messy, gruesome sight. When he finished, he stood holding the head as it dripped blood on his foot.

"Take it to whoever sent you," the young woman said. "Make sure it gets to him or I will find you. Now go! All of you, go!"

Even Abena's would-be assailant scrambled to his feet and ran after his colleagues.

"Run, boys! Run!" a man hollered after them.

"Faster!" another shouted. To encourage them, they shot arrows at the heels of the fleeing trio. Their speed doubled instantly and they did not slow down until they disappeared from view.

The travelers had seen death up close, but had never seen it executed so coldly and efficiently. They had not understood what she said to the warriors, but it was easy to figure out. They wondered what power the ebony beauty held over her men. She asked them a question.

Msafiri stood up and interpreted. "She wants to know who you are."

Rasul, Rezan, and Abena responded and Msafiri interpreted each response in its turn.

"What brings you to these lands?"

"Several moons back we saw a bright light in the sky. We have come to find its meaning."

When Msafiri relayed Rasul's response, her reaction was completely at odds with what they had seen of her thus far. For a moment, her eyes widened and her bosom rose. She exhaled slowly.

"Sujia?" A bandit came and stood beside her, quizzically looking at her. She seemed to allow him a few more liberties than she did the others. She had a brief exchange with him.

"She wants to let us go," Msafiri whispered to Rezan.

Rezan noticed she looked weary all of a sudden. Once again, the travelers got a sense of her overpowering beauty when she was vulnerable. The bandit seemed to debate an issue with her. He pointed at the animals, but she was unmoved.

"He's complaining that they have not even seen what you are carrying. They planned to rob you," Msafiri added.

The bandit continued to appeal his case, but the renegade beauty did not answer. Instead, she rattled off some names whose bearers came to stand before her. At her signal, the rest of the men melted into the foliage.

"She has ordered these men to take you to Ronge. That's the village of the child."

The man tried to protest again, but she raised a hand to stop him. He walked back to the bushes in a huff.

Sujia turned back to Rasul and asked another question. She had forgotten he needed interpretation. Msafiri helped out, interpreting back and forth.

"How did you know you'd find the child in this land?"

Rasul told her briefly about his own journey from Chandustan all the way to the Gedi Mountains.

"Up to this point, we were just looking for the land of the star without knowing its meaning. Then we met a man who called himself 'Leopard.' He said he was originally from these lands."

Sujia shrugged. The name obviously meant nothing to her. Rasul continued.

"He told us how a few moons ago, they were about to attack a group of herdsboys when strange things happened around them."

She stiffened at this. Rasul did not notice. He was rather enamored of her.

"He said some strange beings told the herdsboys good news about a child who was born that night. In short, he left the people with whom he consorted and joined the boys to go see the child. He said he was never the same again. Seeing the child saved his life. And I believe him."

"You say his name is 'Leopard?'"

"That's what he told us."

"And he was happy?"

"Very happy. In fact he just married one of the local girls and they're expecting a child."

Sujia sighed deeply and shook her head.

"Leopard," she chuckled. "You're sure that was his name?"

Rasul wondered what was bothering her.

"Yes!" he said emphatically. "Wait! He mentioned another name… he told us to tell the parents of the child that J… Jab…"

"Jambazi?"

"Yes… that Jambazi sends his regards."

Sujia felt sick. A conversation she had overheard on the banks of another creek came to mind, each word clear as if it was yesterday. She recalled a woman talking with her husband about having a baby by the Spirit Father. The anger she had felt also cut through her guts briefly. It had to be the same couple these men had traveled so far to see. How it all now came together overwhelmed her.

"What is it with this child? Why does he keep coming up?" she thought aloud.

She hobbled over to a large rock and sat down with her head in her hands. Rasul and Msafiri followed. The rest of the party, realizing this was turning out to be quite intense, moved farther upriver to afford them privacy.

To Rasul, Sujia suddenly looked shattered. Defeated.

"Are you well?"

"I'm fine. You may go now."

"Are you sure? Why don't you come with us?" Rasul asked impulsively.

She did not answer for some time. Then she raised her eyes to him. They were dark beads that make him dizzy. In their depths there was pain. Rasul felt it because it triggered his own.

"Just go."

Her eyes became cold, hard stones again. Their eyes held for a long moment. He pushed hard, trying to force his way into her soul. She pushed back, fighting to keep him out. The memory of a similar encounter with another rogue female, "Gulbit," flashed in his mind briefly. He was not getting through with this one.

Locked in this battle of wills, tears welled in their eyes and ran down their cheeks at exactly the same time.

Msafiri, caught in the middle of this exchange, also stepped away to prevent his own emotions from welling to the surface. He knew what it was to have loved and lost and he did not want to see what these young people were doing to each other.

"Go!" Sujia ordered softly, firmly. She wiped away the tears.

Rasul knew what she meant, having heard that command earlier. He reached out and touched her shoulder then turned away sadly. Msafiri looked at the young woman who could easily have been his daughter. She gave him a withering look. He too, moved away to join Rasul and Rezan.

The warrior's spear had grazed Abena's stomach, tracing a short line across it. Rezan applied little myrrh and some dressing to take care of it.

"You are a lucky man, Abena. This is the second time you've wiggled free of death's grasp on this trip."

Abena clasped his hands in obeisance and looked heavenward, ascribing it to a higher power. With their new escorts, they hit the trail.

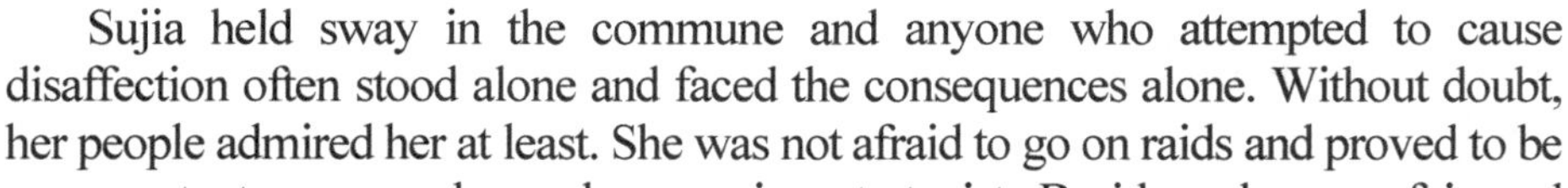

Sujia held sway in the commune and anyone who attempted to cause disaffection often stood alone and faced the consequences alone. Without doubt, her people admired her at least. She was not afraid to go on raids and proved to be a competent commander and a cunning strategist. Besides, she was fair and always divided the loot according to each person's effort. Unlike Asai, she did not take large choice portions for herself.

She had also transformed the bandits from a collection of rejects into a disciplined colony. Only a few moons earlier it was every man for himself, but she established a system that benefited the individual and the group as a whole. She began plan for their existence beyond the hills. For this reason, she made forays into the lands of regular communities in an effort to send them a message that they existed and had a right to do so. Therefore, when she gave a command, her men obeyed, even if they did not agree with it.

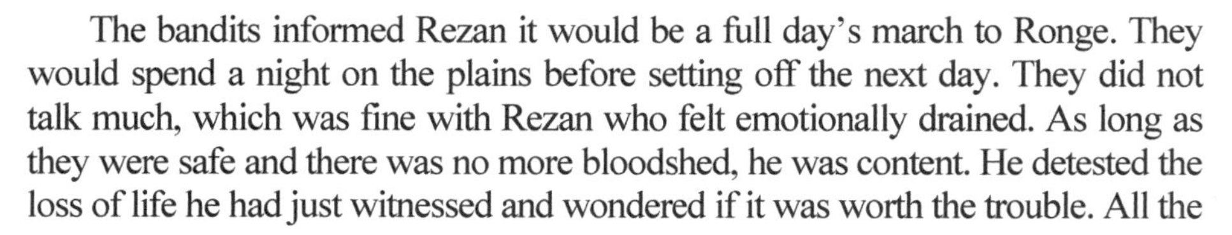

The bandits informed Rezan it would be a full day's march to Ronge. They would spend a night on the plains before setting off the next day. They did not talk much, which was fine with Rezan who felt emotionally drained. As long as they were safe and there was no more bloodshed, he was content. He detested the loss of life he had just witnessed and wondered if it was worth the trouble. All the men lying dead in the middle of the dry riverbed had given their lives for someone else's ambitions, aspirations, and whims. He wondered if they had families. He wondered how their families would feel when their loved ones did not return. *What a waste!*

Rasul tried to make sense of his feelings when he left Sujia sitting woebegone on the rock. He admitted to himself he found her beauty enthralling from the moment he saw her. He also realized she would not hesitate to take a life if she felt she had to. Besides, he was still married to Kulsam and developing affection for another woman was wrong. Oddly, he envied this woman's freedom to live in the wilderness doing whatever she pleased. He had seen right away she was a dark, lonely soul and he had wanted to take her in his arms to let her know he understood how she felt. She would not let him. He could not help wondering if he would ever see her again, but realized that was pure fantasy. He resolved to put her out of his mind and move on.

They spent the night on the plains before continuing the following day. As the terrain began to change, the bandits told Rezan that they would go no further. They gave Rezan instructions on how to get to Ronge before turning back toward the hill country. The travelers thanked them. With mixed feelings, they proceeded with what would be the last leg of their mission.

Seven moons had passed since Yssa's birth. Tradition required his parents to present him before the people for blessing, not only as their son, but also as a child of the entire village. They would also dedicate him to the Oracle, praying he would live a long, healthy life, have many wives, children, and livestock. It was a solemn occasion, which relatives traveled from distant villages to witness.

Yossou was glad his brothers could make it. As the youngest son, he automatically inherited the family land. He had sensed a little rancor when the time came for his brothers to leave home and find their own place. They had moved to the edges of Ronge territory and had to clear virgin land to build new homes for themselves. The advantage was they could claim as much land as they desired. At first, the distance with his brothers was both physical and relational. With time, and especially with Yanze's passing, they mellowed and often came to see him or welcomed him to their homes.

Ma'alia was glad to see Sabet and aunt Rodina. Death had robbed her of all her family before she was born or shortly thereafter. Being married to Yossou and the improved relationship with her mother-in-law had eased the sense of loneliness, but she was always happy to see blood relatives. However, nothing could match her feelings for the child they were preparing to dedicate. She could find no words to express how she felt about him. It was a deep sense of gratitude for him and this occasion was an acknowledgment of the Oracle's favor.

The Bagololi had heard about the child's conception and that Yossou was probably not the father in the physical sense. They also knew of the things that happened when he was born for which there was no logical explanation. However, like any other baby, he needed care and attention. It was, therefore, easy for people to forget he was special in any way and few thought of this occasion as anything more than a dedication and opportunity to meet relatives and friends.

While Yossou and Ma'alia waited in the ceremonial chamber, they heard commotion outside as a murmur rippled through the crowd. A lookout ran into the square panting heavily.

"Strange men… strange animals… heading this way," he said, barely able to get his words out.

"What do they look like? Do they come in peace?" Wiki-Zugu asked gravely.

"It's not… a war party. There're only… five men," the youth gasped. "Four look strange… pale… not from these lands."

"I'll go see who they are before they get here," Wind said.

"Yes, do that."

"Sande! Where's Sande?" Wind hollered.

Ma'alia and Yossou looked at one another, wondering who these visitors were. They listened as the buzz of conversation picked up, but they could not make out anything else.

When they parted company with the bandits, Rezan's party walked a long time before they encountered anyone else. Finally, they came upon a man leading two cows along the trail. On seeing them, he fled the path leaving his cows behind. His animals walked by themselves a while before they stopped. Rezan asked Msafiri to tell the man that they meant no harm and only wanted to find the way to Ronge. When they asked where Ronge was, the man pointed, but neither spoke nor approached. The travelers thanked him and continued, going round the cows, which did not budge.

After a few such encounters, they knew they were going the right way for the trail grew wider and more defined. The number of huts and fields also increased. Finally, the village came into view ahead of them. People looked at them with a mixture of curiosity and alarm, but most fields and compounds were empty.

As they drew closer, a tall man, with his hand in the air, stopped them. A younger man with a bow in his hand stood beside him. A few children and adults stood behind them. The travelers stopped several strides away.

"Who are you and what do you seek in our village?" Msafiri interpreted the tall man's question, but Rezan had already figured it out and nodded at him to go ahead and respond.

"These men have come from distant lands to find the child whose star they saw in the sky many moons back. They believe that the child hails from your village and have come to behold him."

The older man turned to the younger one and shook his head in wonder. He turned back to the travelers.

"What you say is amazing. The child of whom you speak indeed hails from this village. In fact, we are about to dedicate him to the Oracle this very moment."

Msafiri interpreted the statement.

"The fact that all four of us are here is a fascinating tale in itself," Rezan pointed out through Msafiri. "We saw are from different lands but we saw the same thing and had the same desire to know its meaning. That's why we all undertook this journey."

"I believe you. Come. Join us in the celebration." The tall man stepped forward and shook hands with Rezan. "My name is Wind. I was once the village hunter. This is Sande. He has taken over from me."

They all shook hands before Wind led them to the village square. A buzz rippled through the crowd at the sight of the strange men and animals. Wind asked them to leave the animals outside the bounds of the gathering and to follow him. He led them to an elderly man on a stool, next to three other men. Wind bowed and addressed the old man, turning slightly to the travelers. The old man looked at them long, shook his head, and hissed in amazement. He stood up, leaning slightly on his walking stick, and shook hands with each visitor. Not realizing Msafiri's role, he talked without pause. Msafiri interpreted in general.

"His name is Wiki-Zugu. He's the elder and he welcomes you to the village. He says they have seen many amazing things since the child was born. The fact that the Oracle and the spirits led you to the village on the very day and at the very time they were dedicating him is a wondrous thing."

"Tell him we are greatly honored to be here," Rezan said. "We also believe the God who did all these things sent us to be here this day."

Msafiri relayed the words to the villagers.

"Wonderful. Well, friends, these are our honored guests. This is Avoga, who also has an amazing story. This is Nkomo and Luginu. They are the child's uncles."

Wind, who had left briefly, returned with five lads carrying stools. He asked a few people seated next to the elders to move over and directed the boys to place the stools in the vacant spots. He asked the visitors to take their seats alongside the elders. After brief consultation, Wiki-Zugu sat down, as did the visitors. Wind remained standing to speak. Msafiri interpreted for Rezan and his friends.

"Our honored guests, Nkomo and Luginu, uncles of the child whom we dedicate this day, friends and relatives who have come from near and far, and fellow villagers, I salute you. I welcome you to this wonderful occasion. I… I don't know what to say… I really don't." He turned toward the visitors.

"There are no words for it," Wiki-Zugu agreed.

Wind continued. "These men have come farther than any of us. They come from lands unknown - lands most of us will never see. So what brought them here? It's the strong desire to see this child, Yssa."

The people responded with exclamations of wonder.

"I'll let them tell you about it themselves. For now, let's begin the ceremony for which we are gathered and that is to name and bless the child born to Yossou and Ma'alia. Yossou! Ma'alia! Present yourselves!"

The parents emerged from the ceremonial chamber, walking solemnly. Everyone noticed how radiant the child seemed. Wind sat down and the older Simi stood up, took the child from Ma'alia, and spoke next.

"This child came into our lives seven moons ago. We, of the household of Gondi, my late husband, are grateful for this gift. Having lost many grandchildren, I take no life for granted and I am constantly in prayer for the well-being of my children and grandchildren. This baby is special because he's the only male child in Yossou's household. We pray he will not be the last. As we dedicate him, we also pray The Mighty One will grant him many days upon this earth. And now, as his grandmother, I name this child Yssa, son of Yossou, of the house of Gondi, in the lineage of the Great King Adu, Son of the Oracle!" She lifted him before the crowd. They raised a chant.

"Yssa, son of Yossou! Yssa, son of the Oracle! Son of the Oracle!"

When the gathering eventually quieted down, Simi handed the child back to Ma'alia. The time to offer a sacrifice had come. His uncles brought forward a white lamb, which they paraded before the gathering. The people voiced their approval, after which M'mata laid the animal on the ground and Kofi slit its throat. M'mata collected the blood in a clay bowl and took it to the elders. Wiki-Zugu and the child's uncles dipped their flywhisks in the blood and with a single flick, each sprayed the child and his parents with the blood as a blessing. M'mata and Kofi then skinned the lamb and placed the carcass on the sacrificial fire in the middle of the square. As the smoke rose, the elders, uncles, and parents of the child said prayers of blessing upon him, his family, and the village.

When the time came for Wiki-Zugu to invoke the blessing, he tried to speak, but could not utter a word. Instead, he fell on his knees before Yssa whose presence grew stronger each moment and overwhelmed those closest to him. Wind, Avoga, and the child's uncles also fell to their knees chanting praises. A sensation akin to a sharp cold draft brushed over the travelers, and they too, could not remain seated. Words of praise to The Holy One came unbidden to their lips and they shouted out without self-consciousness. As Rezan raised his voice in Shastani, Rasul prayed in Nagrani. Abena, who never had a real concept of a deity, praised The Mighty One in Shamaric.

The people initially watched, wondering what was happening to the men before them, but they soon caught the spirit that swept across the square. Men and women knelt or lay prostrate with total disregard for the special garments they wore to the occasion. They chanted in Kigololi, praising The Mighty One, the Creator, the Holy One, or whatever aspect of the Deity spoke to an individual's heart at that moment. The entire square filled with the voices of men, women, and children shouting, uttering words in tongues they had never spoken before, and singing with complete abandon. No one cared what the next person said or did. Each gave expression in his own way, united in a common purpose - praising The Mighty One. The voices rose, blending into a beautiful fabric of sound.

A voice distinguished itself and picked up a strain. More voices attached themselves to Chizi's as she led them in a song of praise.

You are great
You are mighty
Though you come
In the form of a child

Your beauty
And majesty
Draws great men
From near and a far

Your wonders
We've seen
When, we peered
In the world of the Spirit

The aura that surrounded the child spread, covering everyone and everything in the square. The radiance spread even further, covering the entire village. It spread deep in their hearts, filling them with a sense of awe in the presence of The Mighty One who manifested himself to them this day. People spontaneously hugged and expressed their love for each other. Neighbors who had squabbled over land shook hands for the first time in many moons. A man who frequently abused his wife broke down and begged her forgiveness. A woman confessed she had approached a witchdoctor for potions to kill her co-wife. She said the bitterness was miraculously gone. People poured out their hearts and felt cleansed as a sense of healing took place.

Gradually, the mood progressed, becoming more animated. The people rose to their feet to sing and dance. They reached a climax when they sang and danced to the song in praise of the first-born, *Mwana wa Mberi.* They sang about the Oracle sending his son into the realm of men to live among them. As they sang, they brought gifts and laid them before the parents. Rezan and his friends brought the animals bearing gifts and unloaded them. As a personal offering, Rasul laid down the black pouch he had picked in the pass when bandits attacked his caravan. All the gold coins were still inside. Gradually, the singing and praising also died down. No one could yet speak before the people and they all quietly walked back to their homes without overt dismissal.

After the long travel and celebrations, the visitors were ready to retire. The ceremonial chamber also served as a guesthouse for special visitors. Wind led them to the large hut and made sure they were comfortable. They thanked him and all fell into deep, peaceful sleep as soon as they hit the bedrolls.

In the morning, excited whispering woke Rezan. A group of children peeked into the interior of the chamber until an adult shooed them off. Wind came in to check on the visitors. Seeing Rezan, he said good morning and uttered a follow-up question to which Rezan did not have a response. Understanding this, Wind motioned that a shower and breakfast were ready. He then left.

When Rezan emerged from the chamber, a little boy came up and led him round the back to a shower stall. He found a large clay basin of warm water, and a fibrous plant for scrubbing. It foamed when rubbed vigorously in the presence of water. Rezan always carried his own linen to dry himself for he did not know if his hosts would provide any. He washed and dried himself off then went back into the chamber. The others were up and bathed in turn.

The visitors had breakfast under the tree where they had sat the night before. Afterwards, they talked for some time with the elders and villagers. They learned the history of the Bagololi from the days of King Adu to the present under King Xhaka. The elders said they felt less of Xhaka's presence than that of his oppressive representative, Governor Tamaa bin Tumbo. The visitors could understand why they felt that way.

In the afternoon, Wind and Sande took the guests on a tour of the surrounding country during which the travelers shared their experiences on the quest they had now concluded. The two found the stories so fascinating they shared it with a few villagers when they returned. Word of the tale spread and more villagers asked to hear the story again.

In the evening, the villagers lit a bonfire and congregated for the storytelling. Typically, parents or grandparents shared stories with children in their homes sitting by the fire. Rarely did the entire village gather to hear accounts from other people. This was indeed a special treat. They listened with rapt attention as Rasul, Rezan, and Abena related everything they had been through in all the places they had travelled. Ma'alia listened in wonder, amazed that men who did not know one other, each from a different land, would undertake such a risky journey just to see her child.

For his part, Yossou felt blessed that the son of The Mighty One should call him "father." The visitors' accounts of their travels, especially the dangers they encountered, moved him and he felt humbled and undeserving of the privilege.

Later in the night, with light from fire and flaming torches, the village put on an impromptu show of song and dance involving groups of children, young people, and adults. They also held wrestling contests, which were crowd favorites because the wrestlers were actually competing and not merely trying to impress the visitors. The evening had more of a festive atmosphere than the somber mood of the previous evening, but it was no less meaningful.

With the evening well advanced, Sakul Wiki-Zugu rose to end the activities. He thanked the villagers for their hospitality and kindness toward the visitors. He thanked the visitors for heeding the voice of The Mighty One and making the long trip to an unknown land. He reminded his people they had a great gift in their midst and that they should heed what The Mighty One would tell them through the child.

The travelers expressed their gratitude to the villagers for their generosity and the warm welcome, adding they were now brothers and sisters, united through the son who had brought them together. They informed the village that they would be leaving early the following day, to which the people reacted with sounds of disappointment. Rezan and his friends went to bed early in anticipation of the long trek the following day.

They started the homeward journey intending to travel to Bora-ini as Tamaa had asked. Their hearts were inexplicably heavy at the thought of it, but they continued. They came to a fork on the trail where they could go south and around the escarpment to Bora-ini, or head north alongside the escarpment. A man stood on the trail leading to the south. Abena and his fellow travelers came up to him. He neither spoke nor moved.

"Kind Master, let us through," Abena begged. Still, the man did not respond. Abena tried to lead his camel around him. This time he moved off the trail to block Abena's path. Abena stopped and regarded him. His face did not reveal why he stopped them. Abena tried to go round the other side again, but the man moved to block the way. Abena stopped, completely at a loss as to what to do when...

He woke up feeling greatly distraught. His heart pounded and he had a lot pain in his chest. He had been dreaming. He felt relieved and his heartbeat slowed to normal. The pain in his chest also subsided. Day was breaking and he could hear sounds of the village coming alive. He rose and went outside. A woman saw him and called out to some men sitting by the large tree. Wind responded and came up to Abena. With gestures, he asked how he had slept. Abena signaled that he had slept well. Wind then indicated that there was warm water ready for him. Abena thanked him, fetched his linen, and headed for the booth. After they had all bathed, the visitors sat with Wiki-Zugu, Wind, Avoga, and Yossou for breakfast. With Msafiri interpreting, they talked about what the visit had meant to each of them.

Afterwards, the visitors loaded the camels with what they would take back. The villagers provided them with preserved meat, dried fruit and vegetables, sour milk, and water. Almost all Ronge came to see them off. Inexplicably, Rezan unloaded the horse and led it to Yossou. Surprised, he shook his head vigorously indicating he could not accept it. Through Msafiri, he tried to explain to Rezan he would not know what to do with a horse since it was not native to the land. Rezan's action also confounded his friends, but they held their peace when he firmly turned the reins over to a reluctant Yossou.

Each took a turn to bless the baby before they started their journey. The villagers escorted them to the outlying areas with singing and dancing. In their songs, they thanked the Oracle for the child and for bringing guests from distant lands. They invoked The Mighty One, asking them to protect the visitors on their journey home. On the outskirts of Ronge, they gradually fell away. Wiki-Zugu also said farewell and uttered a blessing on the visitors' journey. Wind, Sande, Kofi, Avoga, and Juma continued. Msafiri also went with them, still playing his role as interpreter.

In the afternoon, they got to a place where the trail forked. One part headed south and another would continue to the escarpment ahead of them. The visitors naturally took the southbound fork to go back to Bora-ini. The normally placid camels suddenly refused to move as though something on the path unnerved them. No matter how much they tried, they could not urge the animals any further. Irzik, who thought he could handle any camel, tried to bully the animal in his charge into compliance. Instead, he got a mouthful of spit in the face. The other camel sat down and refused to budge. While he was pulling on the reins, Abena felt a sharp pain in his chest and stumbled. Rezan and Sande ran to his aid. The men from Ronge watched in consternation. Then Abena remembered his dream. He pointed the direction they were heading and shook his head. He turned and pointed to the path leading toward the escarpment.

"But we go back by way of the city," Rezan said.

"No. We go that way," Abena explained in Houdini. "We do not go back to city. Last night I had a dream that warned us not to take that road. That's why the camels won't move."

Rezan could not counter the argument, so he told Irzik to turn the animals back to the other fork in the road. The stubborn camel turned round without a fuss. The other camel also got up and followed its companion. Rezan and Sande helped Abena along until he could walk on his own.

"That was strange," Rasul said.

"Very," Rezan agreed. "I guess we were not meant to go by the city after all."

When they got close to the escarpment, Wind stopped and held up his hand.

"Friends, this is where we turn and go back. These last two days have been the most memorable in the life of our village. I wish you could have stayed longer."

Msafiri interpreted and Rezan responded. "Our hearts are now much lighter than when we set off on this journey. We have seen amazing things about the child who brought us here. I can assure you of one thing - this is not the end. That child will change the world."

"I feel the same," Wind commented. "We could talk about it for a long time, but you have a long journey ahead of you and should be on your way. Travel well, friends. May The Mighty One lead and guide you."

"Thank you. May he watch over you and your people."

Msafiri stepped forward.

"Now I speak for myself. This is where I also leave you. You no longer need me. Thank you for everything. What I experienced with you and what I have seen has made me a new person. I am not going back to my old life."

Rezan was a little surprised. "That's good. What will you do now?"

"I'll go to the hill country."

"What? To become a bandit?" Rasul exclaimed.

"No. But they need me. The desire to do so came over me yesterday morning and it's been getting stronger each moment. I don't know what I'll do, but that is where I'll go. I wish you a safe journey. Perhaps we'll meet again."

Rezan embraced him. "Yes, indeed. Thank you, my friend."

Rasul also embraced Msafiri. As he did so, he whispered in his ear.

"If you're going to live among the bandits, look after that young woman. She's a hard person on the outside, but there's a beautiful person inside."

"I know. I saw how your hearts wrestled each with the other. She'll be like a daughter to me. I promise. Go well."

Wind and his fellow villagers waited until Msafiri had finished then wished the travelers a safe journey for the last time. They stood on the trail, watching the visitors for a long time before turning back toward Ronge.

Tamaa was not a happy man and all in the palace did their best to stay clear of him. He knew all his staff, advisors, and henchmen, were avoiding him so he called for people at random. The unfortunate individuals came like puppies trembling in a thunderstorm. He would torture them for a long time before putting them out of their misery. Their cries filled the halls as fear gripped the hearts of all within the palace and outside. Already two of his servants had taken their own lives to preempt such a horrible demise.

Things got worse when three of the warriors he had asked to accompany the travelers to Ronge returned the evening of the fourth day. They claimed bandits had attacked them and killed their comrades. They presented him with Kabala's head as proof. Tamaa did not fly into a rage, but they suspected he had not spared them. They were right. He fed them a hearty meal then ordered the guards to lop their heads off. He placed the heads on a platter, with Kabala's at the apex. Still, he was not satisfied and sank into a deep depression. He shut himself up for the next two days, neither eating nor seeing to anyone.

There was more bad news. When he emerged the third day, a runner reported that lookouts in a distant outpost had seen four strange looking men with two camels heading into Nubia. The description he gave matched the men who had been in his palace six days earlier. This time Tamaa fed the runner, gave him a bag of gold and sent him away a very rich man by most standards. He wondered who had compromised his plan to kill the foreigners and the child. But that was not a problem. He would find it out himself. He could not stand the thought of a child in a remote village whose parents harbored the notion he would someday rule over Kwavantu. *That will not be.*

"Get Asman here now!" he shouted down the hall from the private meeting room.

He did not address anyone in particular. With Tamaa, if someone was within earshot, he or she was the addressee. To assume the order was for someone else did not count. If there was no response in reasonable time, heads would roll - literally. A servant who heard the order ran into town immediately to find the leader of the city garrison.

Asman arrived at the palace promptly. Guards ushered him directly to the meeting room.

"Do you have any men near a place called Ronge in the land of the Bagololi?"

"The closest unit is in the highlands at an outpost called Matunda. It's halfway there from here."

"Can a band of men get to Ronge in less than half a day?"

"If their mission is brief and does not require much in terms of supplies, they can be there in about that time."

"Good. This is what I want you to do..."

Tamaa explained his wishes. Asman was horrified, but said nothing. His business was to obey. If he did not, Tamaa would kill him and find someone else to do it.

"I'll send the order by rider right away," Asman said when Tamaa finished.

"Don't fail."

"I'll get it done, Your Excellency," Asman assured him.

He did not relish the thought of his head sitting next to Kabala's on the platter in the middle of the room.

Chapter 17

Flight to Nubia

Yossou still could not comprehend why the young visitor gave him the horse. The only large animals he owned were two milk cows. He spent the afternoon trying to figure out what to feed the animal. The attention from the villagers made it nervous and complicated the task. He asked them to leave the animal alone to give it time to adjust. As darkness approached, the horse was finally able to have some peace.

Yossou found that it readily ate millet stalks, so he asked his daughters to gather some. He fed and watered it after he sent the girls to bed. He found it to be a gentle creature and made room for it next to the cows in the shed. Not sensing any aggression among the animals, he felt it would be safe for the night. He joined Ma'alia and the baby in his chamber. She was already asleep and barely stirred when he lay down next to her. The excitement of the last two days had probably worn her out, Yossou thought. He too, was tired and was soon snoring loudly.

Sometime later, sounds woke him. He knew all the usual night sounds. These were different. It was as if someone was trying to break into the barn or one of the animals was breaking loose. Yossou breathed lightly and listened intently. Someone was definitely out there. He picked up his club, which always lay by his side at night, and rose to investigate. Quietly, he removed the hide and stepped outside to trace the source of the sounds. The gleam of a sword caught his eye. A young man had taken the horse out of the barn. Yossou knew he had been awake long enough not to be dreaming.

"*Vaya!* What are you doing?" he challenged.

"Ssshh! Quick, Yossou! Rouse your wife and baby. You have to flee. Tamaa seeks to harm the child."

The young man continued to load the horse.

"Who are you?"

"There's no time. Go wake your wife and baby. You must leave right away."

Yossou had the feeling he had seen the young man before.

"Leave and go where?"

"Hurry! Your enemies draw nigh this very moment."

Too many strange things had happened in the last several months for Yossou to start arguing. He chose to flee rather than try to figure this one out. He went back to his hut and woke Ma'alia.

"Quick! Get up. We must leave now!"

"Where are we going?" she asked sleepily.

"I don't know. Let's go."

Even in the darkness, he sensed that she questioned his sanity. Nonetheless, she put on her garments, gathered up her baby, and joined him outside. The cold made her shudder. She exclaimed when she saw the young man with the horse.

"Both of you jump on," he ordered.

"I can't . . . I've never . . . "Ma'alia started.

"Put your left leg here and hike yourself onto his back," the young man told Yossou.

Yossou threw his leg over the horse and straddled it awkwardly before adjusting for comfort. The lad went to ensure he had found the other stirrup. He then took the baby from Ma'alia and handed him to Yossou. Grabbing Ma'alia by the waist, he hoisted her effortlessly to ride sidesaddle in front of her husband. He took the child again, handed him back to Ma'alia, and gave Yossou the reins.

"Don't worry about your mother and children. They'll be safe."

He smacked the horse on the rump and it set off at a gallop. Yossou looked back for one last glimpse of his home. The stranger was a shadow next to his mother's hut.

When Ma'alia was sure she would neither fall nor drop the baby, she asked Yossou what was going on.

"That young man said Tamaa wants to harm the child and we had to leave right away."

"Where are we going?"

"I don't know. I'm trusting in The Mighty One - and the horse."

"I guess that means I'll have to trust you."

"I don't have a choice. Neither do you."

Just then, he noticed lights up ahead. Instinct told Yossou an encounter with the bearers would be ill-advised so he did his best to turn the horse off the path. After a few attempts, he managed to guide it into the brush. Fearing they would hear the horse crunching leaves underfoot, Yossou struggled to bring it to a halt. The last thing he wanted was to attempt to flee through the thickets at night with no riding experience. He pulled back on the reins, and the horse stopped. He prayed it would hold still and the baby would not cry because the lights were, indeed, four flaming torches leading a band of warriors. Their grunting in unison and synchronized steps indicated they were on the warpath.

Right after they passed, the horse sneezed. Ma'alia turned to Yossou, eyes wide with panic. His heart sank. The last three warriors in the shadows of their colleagues turned to look. One of them stopped altogether, adopting an aggressive posture. He looked straight at the family for several moments. Yossou was not sure whether he actually saw them or just pinpointed their position from the sound. It got darker as the torchbearers continued toward the village. The warrior turned back to the path and took two steps, but he still peered into the bushes. Finally, he turned away and trotted after his comrades. Yossou exhaled with relief. The blood that had fled his body crept back in a tingling flow. He did not move just yet. Only when he was sure the warriors were out of earshot did he start the horse toward the path at a gallop.

Shortly after, they heard heart-rending screams from the village. Ma'alia looked at Yossou in horror, but he only shook his head. Flames from burning huts now lit the night, but Yossou did not stop. He afforded himself a little extra speed in order to put as much distance as possible between his family and the warriors. Ma'alia held the baby close to her bosom. Her heart broke for the mothers who would be rendered childless this night. She suspected she knew what Tamaa had intended.

Yossou and Ma'alia rode well into daylight before he slowed the horse to a trot. Still, he did not stop until mid-morning when he dismounted, leaving Ma'alia to ride with the baby. Initially, she was hesitant to ride by herself, but having no choice, she learned to balance quickly. Yossou avoided villages or homesteads along the way. They came upon a brook and Yossou thought the horse could use some rest. He noticed the young man had loaded gourds of water, dried food and fruit, and other essentials in pouches on the animal's flanks. There was a machete, extra pairs of tough leather sandals for both himself and Ma'alia, and bedrolls tied to the rear of the animal. He also found a small black bag of gold coins. He had only heard of the precious metal and its use as a form of currency. He suspected that everything on the horse was there for a reason and was glad the young man, whoever he was, had thought of all the important things.

He was about to lead the horse to the water when he recalled the night he went to rescue Ma'alia. He had felt the same "presence" this night as he had felt then. Even the voice was the same. *Could it be…*

"What's wrong?" Ma'alia interrupted his cogitation.

"Uh . . . nothing. I was just wondering…" he trailed off.

He allowed the horse to drink from the brook and then graze on the thick grass on its banks. Meanwhile, he and Ma'alia refreshed themselves in the crisp cold water. She dipped her hand in the water and ran it over the baby's body. She handed him to Yossou while she cleaned the mess he had made on her garments earlier. They finished and set off again. She rode while he led the horse at a brisk pace.

Yossou did not know where he was going but he had a definite sense of which path to take every time had to make a choice. The elevation of the land increased progressively and it got colder. Late in the afternoon, they came to the top of a wooded mountain from which they could see the valley below. There were signs of human habitation from the patchwork pattern of farms or gardens. Yossou felt it would be safe to pass through the community albeit with caution. They got to the edge of the village in the early part of the evening. They passed a few fields in which villagers were clearing weeds. They spoke a language whose inflections were similar to Kigololi. Work stopped as the family passed, the major distraction being the horse. Near the village, a short middle-aged woman addressed them in flawless Kigololi.

"Follow me."

Ma'alia and Yossou looked at one another wondering what she meant.

As if hearing their thoughts, she said, "Don't worry. The Mighty One led you here. You'll spend the night with me and my family."

She turned to a side path leading to two small huts. In her compound, they met her son and his young wife. Both were barely children, yet they had three of their own. They greeted Yossou and Ma'alia politely. She asked her son to unload the horse so it could graze. The women grafted Ma'alia into the kitchen where they had a pot of chicken stew simmering on a fire. On another fire, a pot of water boiled for *chima*. Ma'alia talked with them while they prepared dinner.

Yossou sat outside with the husband who was two or three age-groups his junior. Traditionally, they would not be sitting together, but the fact that the young man was married introduced a little parity between them. Still, he was not very conversational, preferring to play with the baby and the naked toddler. The eldest child clung to her mother's skirt as long as the strangers were in the home. Yossou tried to make small talk, first asking how long they had been married. The young man gave the briefest of answers and killed off any possibility of follow-up. Eventually, Yossou gave up and turned his attention to the sunset and the neighbors who stared at them as they headed home from the fields.

When supper was ready, the women joined the men outside. After the matriarch had given thanks, they ate. Ma'alia felt at home, talking and eating while nursing Yssa. When the meal was over, the woman instructed her son to tie the horse to a tree near the huts. Then she turned to Yossou and advised him to flee to Nubia. To get there, they would have to continue on the trail out of the village until they came to a river. They would cross it and travel along its banks. It would lead them into Nubia. She warned them that crossing further downstream was dangerous because of rapids in some sections, and crocodiles where it was calm. She then urged them to go to sleep early so they would be ready for the journey the following day. Ma'alia and Yossou suspected she had given up her chamber for them and would spend the night in the kitchen. She did not tell them her name and it was impolite to ask, so they addressed her simply as "M'ma."

Ma'alia woke to the sound of someone splitting firewood. It was not in her nature to lie around while others worked, so she rose and joined the woman in her chores. She helped prepare porridge and cassava for breakfast. The son's family woke up in stages. Yossou was last due to fatigue from the previous day's march. By the time the sun came up, they were ready to eat. After breakfast, the woman packed some food for the visitors while her son reloaded the horse. When it was time to leave, she uttered a moving prayer on behalf of her guests. Then all her family escorted them to the edge of the village. A few early risers hailed them, with some asking who the strangers were.

"Oh, they are wayfarers heading to another land," she responded vaguely.

The young man walked ahead with Yossou. They talked about everything, from the strange weather this harvest season to the bugs that caused havoc with the crop. When Yossou told him about his craft, he proved quite knowledgeable on the subject. They talked about roofing, furniture-making, and other subjects. The younger man was definitely more extroverted and Yossou enjoyed the conversation.

"The Mighty One be with you, my children," the woman said when they reached the edge of the village. "We now leave you to continue."

Her daughter-in-law hugged Ma'alia, saying she was glad to have found a new sister. Yossou and Ma'alia were a little sad to leave the family that they had known for only one evening. They did not have much, but what they had they shared freely.

About mid-afternoon, as the woman had said, they came to a river larger than any they had ever seen. It was at least twenty strides across and it awed them in spite of its calm, slow moving water. It was not hard to find the crossing point. Yossou asked Ma'alia to dismount and he took the food and other perishables from the horse. He used the soft leather mat to tie them in a bundle, which he placed on his head. He eased into the water, adjusting to the strength of the current as he went. It pushed him to the left and was strongest at the deepest point where it came up to his chest. That meant Ma'alia would be up to her neck at the same place. He decided to worry about it just yet.

"*Woi!* Be careful, Ba Yssa," Ma'alia called out from the bank.

"I'm doing fine," he assured her.

Silently, he besought The Mighty One that she would not panic when her turn came. If she lost her footing, they would perish. He made it safely to the other side and laid down the supplies. He went back across for his family. He patted the horse on the rump. It went unbidden into the water and waded to the other side. Yossou took Yssa from Ma'alia and carried him in his right arm.

"Take my hand and hold on tight," he told Ma'alia, offering his left hand. "Let's go."

When she was waist deep in the water, Ma'alia hesitated and pulled back. Yossou turned and was about to reprimand her, but checked himself.

"Ma'alia. We are both going to cross here and now, or we will not cross at all. If we don't, then what happens to us? What happens to our son? Let's do this and get over with it. Hold my hand tight and look straight ahead. Alright?"

Still with dread in her eyes, Ma'alia nodded.

Yossou pressed her hand reassuringly and turned to face the other bank.

"Let's go."

It was a challenge helping her stay on her feet, keeping his own footing, and holding on to his son. Where the water was deepest, Ma'alia hesitated again, but Yossou squeezed her hand gently and urged her forward. She moaned softly all the time they were in the water. They made it to the other side where the horse waited calmly with water dripping down its flanks. Out of the water, Ma'alia shivered. She sat on the ground to compose herself. Yossou gave her some time before handing her the baby. He put the supplies back on the horse and waited. When she was ready, he took Yssa from her and she mounted the horse. He handed her the child and they resumed the journey.

They traveled on a faint trail along the river's banks for the next three days. With the thick vegetation, Yossou's main concern was wild animals, especially because of the horse. Every evening, he built a fire and kept the horse close as a precaution. Ma'alia's calm disposition in the wilderness also surprised him. It was a complete antithesis to her reaction when crossing the river. She let him do all the worrying about what might happen to them.

The fifth day after their escape, they observed that the vegetation remained lush around the banks but further away from the river it was scrubland. It would be several more days before they came into the inhabited regions of Nubia. They encountered more people and the houses were of a more permanent design than the *manyattas*. Soon, a city began to take shape in the distance.

Kedem, the capital of Nubia, was the largest city south of the Kingdom of Zimri. With her resounding victory over the North in their last war, Nubia was enjoying relative peace on her own terms. Zimri had paid a huge tribute in gold, silver, and precious stones, and Nubia left her alone. With peace restored, King Ruok turned his attention to building cities and establishing the kingdom.

The city was even more impressive up close. The buildings were larger than any they had ever seen. Those in the main square were made of granite blocks laid with great precision. Yossou was humbled when he compared his work with the structures he beheld. Even the buildings that had awed him in Bora-ini paled in comparison to these majestic structures with tall pillars and magnificent statues. The architects had added elaborate carvings in bas-relief on the walls. Intricate statues of all shapes and sizes, and of different creatures, lined the edges of the walls. Even the path upon which he walked was paved with stone and was wide enough for a band of warriors to run on it with room to spare.

There were people from different lands who spoke different languages. The denizens were dark-skinned like Yossou and Ma'alia, with similar kinky hair. There was another group of people, who, though dark skinned, had soft, curly hair. Occasionally, they encountered a person of light skin, like one of the visitors who recently visited their village in Ronge. They traded in goods brought in from their respective lands to the center.

When the allure of the city began to wear off, Yossou started to ponder the next move. They did not know where to start. As he considered his limited options, a woman passed by at a brisk pace.

"Follow me," she said in Kigololi.

She neither looked at them nor slowed down. There was a familiar ring in her voice. By her attitude, she clearly expected them to comply. Yossou looked questioningly at Ma'alia who only shrugged, leaving the decision to him. He pulled at the reins and followed the strange woman. She turned into an alley without waiting. They hurried to catch up. She wound her way through a series of narrow alleys, past several shops and stalls. Behind the shops were one story and two story mud or brick houses. She stopped at a two-story house and knocked on the door. A stocky middle-aged woman opened it.

"Ah! They have come, eh!" She also spoke Kigololi, but with an accent.

"Yes. They'll stay with you until it is safe to go back home."

"I'm happy to have them," the second woman beamed. Yossou and Ma'alia liked her right away.

Then the mysterious woman turned to Yossou and Ma'alia.

"This is Melou. She came from Kwavantu a long time ago and settled here. You'll stay with her."

"I live by myself so you can stay as long as you wish," Melou explained.

"We don't know what to think," Yossou said. "We left in a hurry. There was no time to plan. We've never left our land, so this is all new to us."

The mystery woman smiled at the couple and said, "Don't worry. The Mighty One watches over you."

She and Melou unloaded the horse.

"I have to go now. You won't need the animal anymore," she told Yossou when they finished. She bowed before Yssa, then walked with the horse toward the alleys.

"Who is she?" Yossou asked.

"She serves the Great King."

The vague answer did not satisfy Yossou.

"That was a fine creature you had there," Melou said.

"Yes. We wouldn't have survived if it weren't for the horse," Ma'alia added. "And it's funny how we got it. We had guests in the village and they gave it to us the evening before we escaped. At first my husband refused to take it saying he didn't know what to do with it. Looking back, I see how everything worked out in a strange way."

"A wise observation, my child," Melou said with a knowing smile. "With The Mighty One, nothing happens by chance."

"Which king does she serve?" Yossou persisted. "Who is she?"

"I don't know. I've never met her before."

The admission left Yossou utterly dumbfounded. Ma'alia, who had observed and tucked away many things in her heart ever since Yssa came into her life, saw beyond the seemingly irrational and irreconcilable facts and events. Then it hit her! The woman who had just led them to Melou was the same one who had led the band of spirit-warriors on the escarpment the day after Yssa was born!

"What?" Yossou asked.

"Nothing. I was just wondering..."

Melou decorated her house in simple earth colors that gave it a warm, welcoming atmosphere. On the floor of the living room were soft, embroidered pillows around a low intricately decorated table. Beautiful vases standing in the corners contained spices whose scent filled the room. The walls were a pastel ochre and upon them hung traditional masks and flat woodcarvings. On a low table in the middle of the room sat a tray with a set of silverware - a jug and six cups. Melou poured fresh juice for her guests. After a hot day of travel, the drink was cool and refreshing. Ma'alia took a couple of large sips from her cup then put it to Yssa's lips. When he first drank, his face underwent contortions one would associate with extreme disgust. Ma'alia feared he might go into a spasm, but when she took away the cup, he protested loudly and pulled it back to his lips. He drank repeatedly, making faces each time, but he fussed whenever she attempted to move the cup away. Melou looked on with amusement. Unable to contain herself any longer, she reached out for him and Ma'alia gave him up. Melou poured out another cup of juice with which she fed him. After some time, she handed the child back to his mother.

"I could hold him forever, but I've got to go and see about supper."

She rose and headed for the enclosed yard.

"Do you need help?" Ma'alia asked.

"Not today, my dear. You've traveled far and need your rest. I had done most of the cooking already. I just need to warm it," she said stepping into the yard.

Yossou, with his back against the wall, was already snoring.

Melou gave Yossou and Ma'alia the upstairs room and free rein of the ground floor except her chamber. The kitchen was outside in the enclosed courtyard and they used communal bathrooms situated outside the compound. Melou took a year's rent in advance from some of the gold coins Yossou found on the horse. She deposited the rest with a local moneylender on their account.

To blend in, the family shed their leather garments from Ronge and adopted the textile garments of the city. Already Ma'alia and Melou had become fast friends and the family spent most of their time downstairs, only ascending to their quarters to sleep.

Melou was a successful fabric and jewelry merchant in her own right. She owned a store along one of the major streets in the city. Like most traders, her wares came by boat on vessels that plied the calm stretch of the River Koru. The fabrics came almost entirely from northern lands through Zimri, though she imported colorful materials, popular for special occasions, from territories to the west. Gold and silver ornaments also came from the north while precious stones made their way into the local market from far south in Azania. She also traded in hides, skins, and ivory, which nomads brought from the east. The number of competing stores was evidence of the commercial prosperity of Kedem and Nubia under King Ruok.

Every morning, Melou took Ma'alia to the store to train her in the business. By observing her new employer, Ma'alia began to understand how to place orders, bargain with vendors and customers, handle employees, and keep track of inventory, sales, and profits. She grasped the relative value of different currencies, from gold and silver coins to metal discs and cowry shells. In a short time, she mastered Deng, the language spoken in Kedem and much of Nubia. With traders from Zimri to the north, and lands to the east, it was an advantage to speak Falishi, and Ma'alia soon picked up key words and phrases in this language.

Most businesswomen took their babies to work, so Ma'alia naturally took

Yssa with her. She was amazed at how the baby captivated customers. Even strangers would stop and remark at how beautiful he was. Melou noticed an increase in business after Ma'alia came to work at the store. Ever the businesswoman, she found that with their guard down, women became highly susceptible to a sales pitch and she turned their fascination with Yssa into a pleasant shopping experience. Even men fell victim to his allure and divested themselves of silver coins, or a string of shells in exchange for a gift for their wives. Soon everyone knew "Ma Yssa," and customers missed Ma'alia when she was not at the store.

Yossou spent his first days in Kedem taking in the city. Starting from his new home, he was impressed with the strength of the walls and the manner of construction. They had more rooms than the huts in Ronge and were more spacious. What he did not like was the close proximity of the houses, allowing little privacy. In Ronge whenever he felt the need to relieve himself, he would find the nearest tree and water its base. For long calls, there was a bushy section in each homestead, specially designated for that purpose. At the end of such a call, one simply heaped soil on the mound and left it to nature's recycling agents - flies, beetles, sun, and rain. In Kedem, there were hardly any trees and one had to use communal facilities.

But it was the architecture and construction in the heart of the city, he found truly fascinating. On the fourth day since their arrival, he sat watching the work busy on another temple when the foreman noticed him and called him over. The man had a serious unsmiling face and sweat glistened on his forehead. Like most of the workers, he was naked, except for a loincloth held in place with a strip of leather. He was a local, probably a member of the Deng people. He asked a question that Yossou did not understand. The man got impatient and motioned him toward a group of workers behind him. Yossou then understood it was an offer to join the crew. Yossou smiled and nodded enthusiastically. He would be happy to be involved in building the magnificent structures he so admired. The man did not return the smile but turned round and barked an order. One of the men hauling granite blocks came over. After brief consultation with the foreman, he nodded at Yossou to follow him. He was now part of the crew.

It did not take long for Yossou to realize the work was not for weaklings. He started at the lowest level in the pecking order of the workforce - hauling sandstone blocks from the dressing crew to the masons. The heat made it even worse. He began to wonder if he had done the right thing accepting the offer. However, he was not one to quit easily, and he stayed on. At the end of the day, his trainer led him to a booth behind some construction material where they joined several other workers. When his turn came, he received his wage for the day - twenty cowry shells. He went home excited about his new employment. Ma'alia and Melou were glad he had found something to keep him occupied. He took a quick bath to wash off the grime and sweat. He sat down and fell asleep immediately.

He was back at work early the next morning, still excited he was putting up a magnificent building. In the days that followed, he drove himself harder than the rest of the crew. In a short time, he was offering suggestions to make the work easier and faster. He was always looking for improvements in personnel and process. The supervisors noted the increased productivity of the gang and its more positive attitude since Yossou joined. As he became proficient in Deng, his leadership developed and the foreman soon asked him to supervise his own crew. His pay rose to twenty-five cowry shells a day.

Because of his work, Yossou saw less of his family. He worked everyday from sunrise to sunset. When he got home, he was too tired to play with Yssa, let alone stay awake to listen to how his wife's day went. It soon led to a confrontation. One evening he was tickling Yssa and making him laugh when fatigue rolled over him. He fell asleep with the baby on his stomach, wondering why his father had stopped playing. Ma'alia, who was out in the yard with Melou, noticed the cessation in laughter and came to check. She heard the snoring even before she saw him. Yossou was lying on the floor, his head against the wall, arms by his side, and the baby looking at him in puzzlement. He woke up when Ma'alia picked Yssa up. He looked at her sheepishly.

"Oh! I think I fell asleep."

"You think?" After a short pause Ma'alia asked, "How long will this continue?"

"How long will what continue?"

"You leave early in the morning, you come back late in the evening. When you get home, you're too tired to do anything else."

"What am I supposed to do? I have to work, don't I?"

"That's true, but every single day from dawn to dusk? We don't see you anymore. Soon your son will hardly recognize you."

He sat up suddenly.

"Oh, come now! Do you want me to sit at home like a woman waiting for her husband to bring home the food?"

These words upset her.

"First of all, get rid of the idea that men do all the work while we sit at home. You don't know half the things a woman has to do to hold a family together."

"Ma'alia, we are guests in another land - in another home. You choose this time to shout at me? What's got into you? Just because half the town knows 'M'ma Yssa' doesn't mean you can now look down on me."

"That's not…"

"Well, what is it then?" Yossou shouted.

The baby let out a loud wail then cried as though someone had pinched his bottom. Ma'alia looked at him, then at Yossou, and stalked into the courtyard without another word. Yossou remained staring at the alley across the street in impotent rage. He left the house to walk it off, returning long after the sun had set. A bowl of food sat on the table. There was no one else in the room.

"That's your dinner," Melou said from her chamber. "Ma'alia's already gone to bed."

"Thank you," Yossou mumbled.

He did not feel hungry, but he knew it would cause more problems if he did not eat. He was still struggling with the food when Melou came out of her chamber and sat down across the table facing him. He glanced at her then averted his eyes.

"Look, I know you exchanged words with Ma'alia this evening. The truth is this matter has been bothering her for a while. She misses you."

"But I'm here everyday. I live here."

"That's true, but when you come from work, you are too tired to give either your wife or your baby any attention."

"Why are you are getting into this now? Just because…"

"*Ah ah!* I'm not trying to get into your business. I was just trying to say I understand how your wife feels. But you're right. I shouldn't get involved in your business. I'm sorry I overstepped my bounds."

"I didn't mean to jump on you like that. I'm sorry."

"Yes." She paused. "This is what I wanted to say. My late husband's brother owns a furniture store in town and I know he could use some help. I can tell you are a hardworking and loyal person. If you want, I can talk to him about hiring you. You won't have to work as hard as you're doing now, and I think the pay is a little better. Why don't you think about the offer and let me know. Take as much time as you need to do so."

"Yes, let me think about it."

"Good. Speaking for myself, I think you have a most wonderful wife and baby. Don't let this work, or anything come between you and them. Sleep well."

The next morning, Yossou got up early as usual and went to work at the temple. His colleagues noticed he was unusually withdrawn. During break, his friend, Achem, asked if all was well.

"Everything is fine," he said, but his tone and body language told a different story. He did not want to talk anymore. After the break, he threw himself into the work and still said little. At the end of the day he told the foreman he would not be coming back.

"I thought with your rapid rise on the crew you had aspirations for a career in temple building. Why leave now?"

"Personal reasons. I can't do it anymore."

"But you are doing very well. In fact, the priest in charge of this project was thinking of moving you to oversee the construction of another section. This is not the time to leave. You should reconsider, Yossou."

"I have made up my mind. I thank you for hiring me right off the street that first day, but I have to leave."

"*Akh!* By Zanzu! Suit yourself." He went back to studying the designs on the reed paper spread out in front of him.

Yossou left. After walking several paces from the site, he stopped to look back at the unfinished temple. He felt a measure of satisfaction in the thought that when it was complete, he would have been part of it. He was sure it would be one of the most beautiful buildings in the land. With a measure of regret, he went home to tell Ma'alia he would no longer work at the temple.

They sat down to a quiet dinner. Ma'alia still felt bad about the previous night's confrontation and she wanted to let Yossou know it. He too, seemed preoccupied and she was not sure what he was thinking. Noticing the awkward silence, Melou excused herself on a pretext.

"Yossou, I'm sorry about last night. I shouldn't have attacked you the way I did," Ma'alia opened when they were alone. "You have a right and responsibility to work wherever you can, and I should respect that."

"Actually it is I who should apologize for what I've been doing to you and Yssa. I was thinking only of myself and was never here for you. I was going to let you know that I stopped working on the temple today."

"Really?" Ma'alia was genuinely touched. "I regretted my words and attitude toward you and I wanted to let you know that I wasn't proud of what I did."

"All right, my dear. You're sorry, and I'm sorry. I thought I was doing the right thing all along and you had the right to confront me. Anyway, I told the foreman I won't be going back tomorrow. I'll have to find other work."

"I'm sorry. Did Melou tell you about her brother-in-law's furniture store?"

"She did. I think I'll take the offer."

"You're sure?"

"Uh… what do I have to lose?"

"Right."

"I'll tell her tonight. She'll be happy to know we haven't killed each other."

Ma'alia laughed and hugged her baby tighter.

The following morning, they all left for Melou's store. She opened up first and got the day going. She did not worry about leaving for a while because Ma'alia already had a handle on the business. Few customers came early in the day. Business usually picked up about mid-morning when seamstresses came to purchase material and accessories. Yossou played with Yssa while the women set up merchandize and organized the store.

When she was sure her brother-in law had opened and settled, Melou led Yossou down the street to Seydou's shop. The smell of wood welcomed them at the door. Seydou was sanding a large wooden chest on the display floor. Five men worked on different items at the back of the shop, hammering, chiseling, sawing, and generally making what might constitute a racket to most people, but it was music to Yossou's ears. Seydou smiled broadly when he saw Melou and came forward to greet her.

"*Ei, Savaji!*" he addressed her using the Kigololi term for sister-in-law. "How are you? It's been a while since I've seen you."

He shook Yossou's hand while still talking to and looking at Melou. Yossou found this rude. After the perfunctory questions on both sides about how things were, Melou came to the reason for their visit.

"This is Yossou from Kwavantu. He had to flee his homeland with his family because their lives were in danger."

"Oh, you are the family I heard about. I'm sorry about what you went through. At least you are safe here," he said, looking directly at Yossou this time and making up for the unfavorable first impression.

"Yossou was a builder in his homeland and has been on the crew building the new temple. He wants to do something else now. I was wondering if you could use him in your store. I'm sure he'll learn fast.

"Good! Actually, I need another worker. I've been unable to keep up with orders for doors and windows as the city grows and more people build. When can you start?"

Yossou was surprised at the quick offer. Melou smiled at his confusion as it caught him off-balance.

"Uh . . . I can start now . . . I mean . . . I'm not doing anything," he said.

"Very good! We'll put you to work."

"I think my work here is done," Melou said. "I'll leave you in Seydou's hands. He'll take care of you."

"Thank you, Melou. I'll see you at home."

To Seydou, Melou added, "Pass my greetings to Lakwena and the children. I'll come see them soon."

"I will. Go well, *Savaji*."

Melou left and Seydou turned to Yossou.

"What do you know about woodwork?"

"Not much. I was building huts back home until a few weeks ago when we had to leave. But I can learn fast."

Just then, an affluent looking man walked into the shop.

"That's good. Then you'll start by helping Mek with the windows he's making. Mek, show Yossou what you are doing. You are his trainer."

Seydou rushed to attend the visitor. Yossou went and sat next to Mek, who handed him a rough, flat faced rectangular stone with which he smoothed the side of a wooden window. This was the beginning of what would be his career for the rest of his days.

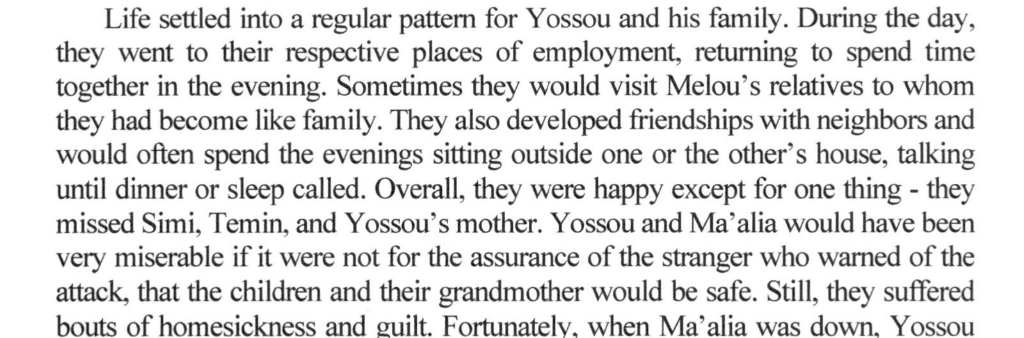

Life settled into a regular pattern for Yossou and his family. During the day, they went to their respective places of employment, returning to spend time together in the evening. Sometimes they would visit Melou's relatives to whom they had become like family. They also developed friendships with neighbors and would often spend the evenings sitting outside one or the other's house, talking until dinner or sleep called. Overall, they were happy except for one thing - they missed Simi, Temin, and Yossou's mother. Yossou and Ma'alia would have been very miserable if it were not for the assurance of the stranger who warned of the attack, that the children and their grandmother would be safe. Still, they suffered bouts of homesickness and guilt. Fortunately, when Ma'alia was down, Yossou would hold her up. When he was disheartened, she was strong.

Two moons after they arrived in Kedem, Ma'alia informed Yossou she was pregnant again. She broke the news to him one evening after they had gone to bed. It was the best news he had heard in a long time and all thought of sleep fled.

"How do you know?"

"*Eesh!* I'm a woman."

"Sorry, I'd forgotten. I'm happy to hear it."

He pulled her closer, drawing protest from Yssa, who slept between them. They talked a long time just as they did on their wedding night. They reminisced on their experiences of the last several months, their families, fellow villagers, and their friends. They thought of the women who had lost children and they experienced a twinge of guilt. The only way Yossou could deal with his conflicting emotions was to beseech The Mighty One. He launched into an impassioned prayer. Ma'alia cried out in agreement as he interceded for the victims of Tamaa's wrath. They fell asleep in the wee hours of the morning. The sun was already shining when they woke up. They found breakfast on the table and Melou gone. One look at the food and Ma'alia's stomach gave up its contents. Indeed something had changed.

Ma'alia gave birth to their second baby boy, eight moons later. Melou acted as midwife with help from Seydou's wife, Lakwena, and two neighbors. The women would not hear of Yossou being present at the birth, so he had to wait outside while Ma'alia was in labor. Only after Ma'alia had delivered and they had cleaned her and the baby, did they allow Yossou to see his new son. Yossou noticed the strong resemblance between the boys. *You'd think they had the same father.* He found the thought slightly irreverent and asked forgiveness of The Mighty One. In his heart, he loved both boys just the same and thought of each as his own son.

The new baby was a bright-eyed child who, within a couple of moons, had a ready smile for anyone who peered into his face. Later, in a simple ceremony they named him Jama. Even with another son, the family did not see the need to find another place to stay. In a sense, Melou stood in the gap for the elder Simi, and they could not imagine living away from her. She was warm, caring, and unselfish. Having never had children, she loved Yossou and Ma'alia as her own. Ma'alia continued to work with her at the store, which had moved to a more spacious location. The business had grown in the time they had been together and they had to employ extra help since items flew off the shelves faster than Melou could replace them.

Meanwhile, at Seydou's shop, Yossou had mastered the basics of woodworking and design. He was able to translate a customer's request into a specific design - something only Seydou could do previously. Yossou would then make components based on the given dimensions and put it together. This freed Seydou to pursue more business and keep clients happy. Yossou effectively became the manager of the shop as Seydou passed operations to him. As with Melou's store, Seydou's business increased after Yossou joined the staff.

Chapter 18

Return From Exile

One day, word came by traders from the east that the governor of the province of Kwavantu in Xhaka's kingdom had died. According to the reports, Tamaa was never the same after a group of visitors showed up in his city asking to see a child who would one day be king. They said he had sent his warriors to the villages of the child's people, killing every man-child who had not seen his second harvest. However, he was never sure the child was dead and the thought of it drove him insane. In his last days, the report said, he rarely ate and completely neglected himself. He became like a wild beast. For days at a time, he would lock himself in his chamber, which stank from his unwashed body, feces, and urine, ranting like a maniac. The servants and aides became concerned after they did not see him or hear his ranting for three straight days. A sharp odor also filled the hallway.

No one knew exactly how he died, but by the time the servants found him, slimy maggots were already wriggling on his body. Rats had deformed the once stately visage horribly. In a bizarre twist, Tamaa did not bequeath his son the governorship. Instead, he orchestrated an elaborate scheme that pitted his son, Ulafi, against the Chief of Protocol, Bunduk, upon his death. With support from some of his father's officials, Ulafi fended off the vicious onslaught to keep the throne. Like his father, the young ruler slaughtered Bunduk, his entire family, and anyone who even remotely supported him. This quashed any further designs on the throne.

King Ruok, ever mindful of the security of his kingdom, took nothing for granted. When he heard of Tamaa's death, he wondered what would come of it. He knew King Xhaka, whom Tamaa served, was a fierce warrior, master strategist, and formidable foe in battle. He decided to send a goodwill emissary to Kwavantu to assess the new governor and review their weak ties. He wanted Kwavantu to remain a buffer between Nubia and Xhaka's Kingdom proper, Azania, south of the province. Besides, the waters that fed his land flowed from Kwavantu. Therefore, it made sense he should sound out the new leader.

The emissary was a distant relative of the King. He would bear gifts for the new governor and the King Xhaka. In addition, he would look into possible avenues of trade between the territories. Though Ruok did not state it officially, his emissary would gauge the strengths and weaknesses of their southern neighbor, so the delegation included two strategists with a keen eye for political posturing. With everything in place, King Ruok set the travel date.

One morning, a regular customer came to pick up an order while Melou was away. She talked with Ma'alia about several issues for a while. Then she mentioned she had a relative who would be traveling to a land called Kwavantu.

"I'm from Kwavantu!" Ma'alia said.

"You are? So you heard about the death of your governor - someone called Tuma?"

"Tamaa. You say he's dead? I'm sorry, but that's good news. He was a wicked man."

"Yes, he's dead. That's why the King is sending a delegation to the province."

"I hate to say this, but that's one man the world could do without. It's good he's gone. He's the reason we're here."

"Oh, I didn't know that. Do you plan to return someday?"

"I would go back tomorrow if I could and if I knew my child would be safe."

"Your child? You have two. Which one are you talking about? What's so special about him?"

"Oh, don't worry. I was just talking."

"Hmm. I can talk to my kinsman about you. He might be able to arrange for you to travel with them, but I'm not promising anything. I have to go now. I'll see you soon." She picked up her materials and left.

"Go well, Safya."

When Melou returned, Ma'alia related to her the conversation with Safya along with her offer to talk to her kinsman.

"It would be perfect if you could travel back with them. It's certainly safer and more convenient."

"Yes, but I don't know if the emissary, let alone the King, would allow a lowly family to travel with his high-powered delegation."

"Didn't Safya offer to speak to her kinsman on your behalf?"

"Yes, but . . . "

"But what? Why are you here?"

"What do you mean?"

"Why are you here in Kedem?"

"We ran away. Tamaa was planning to hurt our child."

"Why?"

The questions puzzled Ma'alia for a moment.

"Oh! I see what you're implying," she laughed. "I'll talk to Yossou about it tonight."

When Ma'alia raised the matter at dinner, Yossou was thrilled at the prospect of going back home.

"If Tamaa's dead, surely we can go back. I'm dying to see my other children, my mother, Wiki-Zugu... By the Oracle! I've missed home!"

"Well, maybe it's time we made our way back."

"Yes, but how do we make our case to the King's emissary?"

"Didn't Safya say she'd mention you to her kinsman?" Melou chided. She fed Yssa while Ma'alia nursed the baby. "Don't you remember anything?"

"Oh yes, but she said she wasn't sure anything would come of it. I'll ask her the next time she comes to the shop."

While she was talking, a silhouette filled the doorway. There was no mistaking the royal messenger. Behind him were members of the King's guard. Usually, it was not a good thing when the king's men came to a person's door. All three adults fell to their knees, heads bowed and waiting to hear the worst.

"No! No! Get up. I come to you with a message from King Ruok."

They rose to their feet, still trembling in spite of the assurance.

"Relax, good people," he said. Reverting to his official voice and poise, he declared, "This is a message from the King Ruok, Conqueror of the Great River Kingdoms. The King wishes to know if you would be willing to accompany his delegation to the land of Kwavantu to pay respects to the new governor. Let this bearer carry your answer, whether it be yea or nay. If it be yea, you will travel the seventh day from today. The King will be glad if you would honor him with your presence the night before you leave. Let the King's servant know what is your pleasure."

Ma'alia and Yossou looked at one another in wordless consultation. Yossou turned to the messenger.

"My wife and I will be honored to accompany the King's delegation to Kwavantu. We will also be greatly honored to be his guests. This is our pleasure."

"Very good. I will take your answer to the King. You will present yourselves at his palace before sunset on the sixth day from today. You will not need to carry food or supplies. As part of the royal entourage, he will provide for all your needs. You will have a camel for your goods and horses to expedite travel."

"Yes, Master. Thank you."

After the messenger and his men left, concerned neighbors came to the door asking if there was a problem. The family assured them that there was no problem and that the men only came to deliver a message from the palace. This drew whistles of amazement and admiration.

"*Yayeh!* Who are you that the King sends his messengers to you?" someone asked.

"*Beh,* are you some sort of royalty we don't know about?" another remarked.

Ma'alia and Yossou did not answer the question. It was a paradox even to them, but they informed their neighbors they would be traveling back to their homeland in a few days. The neighbors were genuinely sad at the prospect of this pleasant family leaving. However, they extended to them their best wishes. In the days that followed, Melou and Ma'alia hardly did any cooking due to the dinner invitations that came every night. Neighbors wanted to spend as much time with the family as possible.

On the sixth day after the King's messenger paid them a visit, Melou did not go to the store, choosing instead to help her guests put together what they would take to Kwavantu. They would carry mostly souvenirs and keepsakes. Ma'alia took some material, a set of vases, bottles of perfume, and some jewelry. Yossou wangled some tools out of Seydou because he would not find similar items in Kwavantu. He also picked out two small ornamented wood chests he loved as soon as he saw them. They would be perfect gifts for Simi and Temin. For their grandmother, Ma'alia found a beautiful embroidered scarf of exotic fabric. She had thought of getting her a garment, but she remembered everybody else would be wearing leather, and it would be odd to wear textile. Over the last few days, they had picked out small items for every family in the village so no one would feel left out.

With the packing finished, they bathed, dressed in their best garments, and waited for the King's messengers. Sometime in the afternoon, they heard commotion outside and went to see what was going on. Coming round the corner was the messenger who had spoken to them a few days earlier. Children ran alongside the riders. Several adults also followed. The messenger held the reins of a camel while two assistants on horseback each led another horse. They stopped at Melou's door.

"Are you ready?" the messenger asked, dismounting skillfully.

"Yes. Everything is packed and ready to load."

"Very good! I like dealing with people who are organized." To his men he said, "Load up, boys."

With practiced hands, the assistants soon had everything secured on the camel. The neighbors, hearing that the King's men were at Melou's place, left their work and came to bid the family farewell. It was an emotional parting with much hugging and many words of encouragement. Melou was last to hug

Yossou and Ma'alia. She squatted to embrace both children. The outpouring of love toward this simple family impressed even the messenger and his assistants. In the end, he had to shout to the people to let them leave. He began to cut a path through the crowd with his horse. People lined up along the way right up to the palace.

"Farewell friends," they shouted. Soon the words changed to praise.

"Hail the King," some shouted.

"Great is the King," others responded.

Ma'alia sensed this had less to do with King Ruok than her first-born son who somehow always evoked such sentiment.

They were all at their assigned places at a long table in the royal dining room conversing quietly. Yossou and Ma'alia met Suping, who would lead the delegation to Kwavantu. They also met Koteng, Safya's kinsman. He told them he had mentioned their plight to Suping who relayed it to the King. Yossou and Ma'alia told him they were grateful his considerate action had led to the opportunity to go back home.

After some time, the Chief Steward raised his voice.

"All rise! Hail King Ruok, Conqueror of the Great River Kingdoms!"

The King swept into the room walking behind four bodyguards. A beautiful, stately woman in a flowing white robe and neatly plaited hair followed. No doubt, it was Queen Lekha. Behind her came four other guards. Everyone stood up while the King took his place at the head of the table with the Queen to his right. He asked them to take their seats and he did so himself. He threw a brief, knowing glance at Yossou who sat with Yssa in his lap. He smiled showing a set of perfectly shaped white teeth. He welcomed the guests and invited them to enjoy what the servers placed before them. To Yossou, the King looked rather young for such high office. His flowing robe further served to emasculate him somewhat, but for this misleading first impression, many a foe had suffered grief. Only the astute observer discerned the iron will beneath the gentle exterior.

The king did not spare any expense in what he spread before the guests. Neither Ma'alia nor Yossou had seen so much food and in such variety. Servants fussed over guests, refilling goblets even before they were empty. They carved slivers of different meats off skewers onto plates and passed around platters of salad, vegetables, and fruit. The King was a skilled entertainer, diffusing the tension of his presence right away with his easy manner and sharp wit. He allowed the conversation to take its course and occasionally turned to an individual to ask a question that would start a new discussion.

When he had eaten a little, the King excused himself, citing pressing duties. However, he encouraged his guests to dine as long as they desired. He left with six guards in tow. The Queen took over as host and the guests found her both knowledgeable and charming. Two guards remained with her. Presently, she also excused herself and the meal concluded shortly after. Servants approached the travelers to lead them to their sleeping quarters. The servant assigned to Yossou and Ma'alia approached them.

"Sir, the King would like to see you before you retire." They were surprised.

"The King wishes to see us? Why would the King want to see us?"

The servant's non-response was both a reprimand and a warning. Yossou relented.

"Uh… We will see the King right away."

They followed him down the hall.

Yossou and Ma'alia marveled at the immensity of the palace. It was much larger inside than it appeared outside. Wide corridors connected large rooms to waiting areas, all with opulent furnishings and decorations. The rooms had high ceilings and there were scores of torches whose light reinforced the cavernous ambience.

The servant stopped before a large door with two armed sentries on either side. He tapped the knocker on the door and it opened inward. Two more sentries frisked them before letting them all the way through. It was a large room with hundreds of scrolls tucked into shelves along two walls. On one wall was a display of exquisite weapons of all kinds from different lands. Along another were heads and hides of various animals. Strange instruments and devices sat on display in sections of the chamber. And there, before them, stood the King himself reading a scroll.

"Ah! I am greatly honored you could come to see me."

He rolled the scroll and dismissed the guards with a subtle wave of his hand. Yossou and Ma'alia were speechless. *Here was the Great King Ruok, Conqueror of the Great River Kingdoms, saying their visit honored him! Was it a trap?* Yossou stood holding Yssa's hand. Ma'alia cradled Jama in her left arm, rocking him gently. The King walked up to them and shook hands, banishing their fear.

"I must say I didn't know about you until a while ago. I'd been having this recurring dream about a beast attacking a family hiding in a cave. It tore away at the rock and soil around the cave, trying to get to them. Each time I had the dream, the beast appeared more frantic and vicious. The dream always ended without revealing whether or not the beast got to the family. In the dream, I had a strong feeling they were from the south. When I heard the governor of Kwavantu had died, it seemed to make sense. I also learned that a family had fled Kwavantu and was living among us. You are from Kwavantu, right?"

"Yes, Your Majesty."

"Well, I felt burdened in my heart that you wanted to, or needed to go back home - I don't know. I have political and commercial interests in sending the delegation to Kwavantu, but if this venture helps you return safely, then why not?"

"We are grateful for your thoughtfulness, Your Majesty."

"The gods dictate it. Usually, I do as I please, but this time I feel I'm only a vessel in the hands of your God."

Ma'alia and Yossou sensed this was probably the first time the King had bared his soul to anyone in such a manner.

"Now, is there anything you need of me? Anything at all? Don't be afraid to ask."

Yossou was not sure how to begin. He hesitated. "There could be something… We fled because the late governor wanted to harm our son." He looked down at Yssa. The King pursed his lips. "I understand you'll ensure safe passage for my family into Kwavantu, but what will happen when we get there? Will you expect us, as part of your entourage, to go all the way to Bora-ini? The son of the late governor now rules and from what we've heard, he takes after his father. Our son may not be safe there."

"That's a good question. You're under no obligations. You may leave the caravan whenever it is convenient and safe."

Yossou and Ma'alia breathed a sigh of relief.

"I have only one demand to make of you."

Yossou and Ma'alia looked at one another apprehensively.

"Not a word to anyone about any of this."

The King smiled and Yossou and Ma'alia relaxed visibly.

"Your Majesty, for what you're doing for us, the least we can do is to obey that command. Not a word."

"Good. I wish you a safe journey. If you ever find yourselves in Nubia again, remember my door is always open to you."

"Thank you, Your Majesty. We will always remember you, your kindness, and generosity. May The Mighty One grant you a long life as you lead this great empire."

The King smiled and pulled a lever along the wall. The guards reappeared, escorted the family to the big door, and let them out.

Their servant, who was waiting outside, led them to their quarters. The chamber was larger than Melou's entire house. Two torches behind silk screens lit the room, lending a soft touch to the ambience. The servant showed them how to put them out when they were ready to sleep. A small lamp would burn through the night so the room was not in total darkness. In the middle was a large bed enclosed in a beautiful white lace. The beddings and cushions were of a soft, shiny material. The floor was made of wood panels in perfect geometric patterns. All around were rugs with depictions of flowers, plants, and animals. A soft fragrance hung in the air and Ma'alia was spellbound. She could only stare open-mouthed at everything.

"Did you ever imagine you'd be a guest in a king's palace?" Yossou asked. He spotted Yssa pulling at the fibers of an intricately embroidered rug. "Stop that, son! That rug is probably worth more than all of us put together."

Ma'alia laughed. She pulled the lace aside and laid her baby on the bed.

"This is beyond anything I ever thought possible. Only the Great Father could have made this happen."

The workmanship of the furniture awed Yossou. In all his time with Seydou, he had not seen anything like it. Either these were master craftsmen or it came from another land. On close inspection, he determined it was both. The wood from which they were made was not readily available in Kedem, but the workmanship was also impeccable and not in the style of Nubia.

Ma'alia's interest was in the fabrics and ornaments that adorned the entire chamber. Just as Yossou had noted, much of what was in the chamber she had not seen in Melou's store. The lace was so fine it gave everything on the other side a fine luster. The material on the bed was soft and smooth and played easily on the fingers. Precious stones bedecked all the furnishings. Everything in the room was of the highest quality. Neither Yossou nor Ma'alia wanted to sit or lay down because they found everything perfect and intimidating. Only when fatigue set in did they finally crawl into bed.

"My lord, my lady, are you awake?" a voice at the door asked.

"Uh . . . yes," Yossou answered. "We'll be ready soon." He roused Ma'alia.

They bathed, dressed, and packed. When they stepped into the hallway, their attendant was waiting. He led them to a dining room smaller than the one in which they had dined the previous night. This time, only their fellow travelers were present and had already started on breakfast. When all had finished, attendants escorted them to the courtyard. It was just getting light. Koteng, the leader of the convoy was conferring for the last time with the chief emissary, Suping, while servants and other members of the entourage checked the luggage and supplies. When he was sure everything was in place, Koteng gave the order to start the journey. Yossou rode with Yssa while Ma'alia carried the baby.

It was an exciting moment for Yossou and Ma'alia knowing they were at last heading home after many moons of self-imposed exile. They were bursting with emotion as the horses took their first steps out of the courtyard, through the city and out onto the trade route along the banks of the Koru. By now, day had broken and it was completely light. Yossou stole a final glance at the city. The sun rewarded him with a breathtaking view of the temple on which he had first worked. The workers had made a lot of progress and the light hit it just right, accenting the structural highlights. In a moment of vanity, Yossou credited himself with part of that progress. He turned back to the route home, wondering how life had changed under the new governor. Then the sun bathed the caravan in orange-red light. With it, hope and anticipation poured into his heart.

To ensure the security of the caravan, two riders went a day or two ahead, announcing that representatives of King Ruok, Conqueror of the Great River Kingdoms, would be passing through en route to Xhaka's province of Kwavantu. This announcement was enough to put fear in every heart. Even bandits, who paid no heed to authority, with the view that they were law unto themselves, would think twice before attempting to spoil this caravan. In the past, those who had attacked a party in the service of the King had paid dearly. He flooded the area where the attacks had taken place with warriors who left nothing standing or alive. The people therefore treated the King's caravans graciously wherever they passed. The caravan leaders returned the favor, paying generously for the services they received in the towns and villages through which they fared. In his wisdom, King Ruok built a good name for himself through the generosity of those who represented him. Any report that one of his representatives had acted to the contrary bore serious consequences. This attitude had served him well in the campaigns against the northern cities, where grassroots support, nurtured in such simple ways, tipped the balance of many battles in his favor and reduced the cost of campaigns considerably.

The caravan took the valley route to Kwavantu, staying close to the banks of the Koru so as not to contend with mountains and valleys. They would enter the province from the north then cut across to the east. On the twenty-first day, they encountered people who spoke a language similar to Kigololi. It meant they were getting close to their destination. After two more days of travel, the vegetation and topography began to look familiar to Yossou. He sensed they were approaching Kilima, the Gololi village most toward the setting sun. When he saw the familiar hills, he knew they were home, but it would take half a day, even on horseback, to get there. Nightfall overtook them before they got to the foothills and the caravan spent the night at a trading post under protection the forerunners had negotiated.

The caravan made an early start the following day. The dark clouds that hung over the hills meant that it would rain soon. They got to the outskirts of Kilima about midmorning and before the rain. Ma'alia was excited and could not help calling out greetings to people she passed, though they stood at a distance from the caravan in fear. So far, she had not met anyone she recognized. Suping, sensing that the family might want to visit with residents, stopped his horse and waited for Yossou and Ma'alia.

"It looks as if you are home already. Do you wish to spend some time here before we move on?"

Yossou looked at Ma'alia. "You were raised here. You decide."

"I definitely want to see aunt Rodina and her family. At the same time, I can't wait to see my other children and I know you can't wait either."

"It's no more than half a day from Kilima to Ronge on horseback, so we can spend the rest of the morning visiting with your aunt and continue when the sun is overhead."

As if to contradict this proposition, a huge drop of rain hit his forehead splattering into several tiny droplets. Instinctively, they all looked at the sky.

"It's going to come down heavily. Let's try to get to the village square before it starts to pour in earnest. Ma'alia and I can lead the way."

"Go ahead," Suping agreed.

Ma'alia and Yossou made their way to the head of the caravan. Villagers ran toward the path to behold the uncommon sight, never having seen a horse or a camel before, let alone an entire caravan. When a horse sneezed, some ran away screaming.

"I don't remember the way so you may have to lead," Yossou told Ma'alia.

"No, it's easy. Once we find the wide path, it will lead us there."

They found the path and followed it to the village square. They stopped under the large evergreen tree. Yossou and Ma'alia looked at each other and burst into laughter simultaneously.

"What's so funny?" Koteng asked.

"The last time we stood under this tree, we were getting married. And that," he pointed to the large ceremonial hut, "is where we spent our first night as husband and wife."

"*Aah!* It must stir wonderful memories for both of you to be here!"

"It does. However, we need to find the headman to advise him of our presence. Ma'alia, who was the elder at the time we were married?"

"Emesi. He should still be alive."

Heavy drops now fell at regular intervals. Yossou dismounted and plucked Yssa from the saddle. He went up to one of the adults in the gathering crowd. Some stood under shelter of a hut, while others braved the increasing drizzle. All stared at the caravan wordlessly.

"Peace, my friend,"

"Peace," the man replied, but his face remained impassive. The reaction surprised Yossou. Traditionally, the Bagololi were always kind to strangers and more so to one of their own.

"I am Yossou from the village of Ronge." As soon as he said his name, the man's face clouded over - a reaction Yossou did not expect.

"What? What's wrong?"

The man looked away. Yossou was flabbergasted, never having suffered such treatment before. He turned for help from someone else, but the individual walked away.

"What's wrong, you people? I'm only asking to see Emesi, the headman."

In the end, a lad, who probably did not know better, offered to take him to Emesi. The drizzle turned into a fierce downpour as sheets of rain came down hard, drenching the earth. Yossou and the lad went back under the shelter of the tree.

"Let me hold your son," Koteng offered. "It looks like you need to take care of this situation first."

Yossou handed Yssa over and followed the lad, who picked his way from a network of narrow paths out of the square past a few huts. They came to a large hut and the lad called out a greeting. A voice answered from within and they stepped inside. Two elderly men seated on stools. Yossou entered and stood before them. Neither rose nor offered to shake his hand. The lad stood looking for a while then slunk back outside under the overhang.

"I greet you both, my fathers," Yossou began.

"You are back, eh?" Emesi asked with a hint of accusation in his voice.
A little boy who was leaning on his knee looked from one adult to the other as they spoke.

"What do you mean, father?"

"You brought a lot of trouble to your people, Yossou."

Yossou perceived he was referring to their flight from Ronge.

"I don't know… What happened?" he asked.

"Of course you don't! While you ran away to save yourself and your wife, Tamaa's warriors killed thirteen children in your village, eleven in Ngoma, twelve in Zigul, and eleven in Vogol. They probably spared us because it was almost daylight and they were tired. We feel no better, knowing our kinsmen lost their youngest for no reason at all. I've never attended so many funerals in my life. The land mourned from one harvest to the next after the attack. Mothers still mourn their children today. Our people have not been the same since." He paused, bowed his head, then he looked up at Yossou. "Why did you do it,

Yossou?"

"Why did I do what? I am confused." There was a tremor in his voice. "I have just come from a long journey - one which I did not want to undertake in the first place, and when I come back home you treat me like a leper. You accuse me of things I couldn't control."

"You knew trouble was coming and didn't warn the rest of the village," the second man, whom he did not recognize, said angrily. "You took your wife and child leaving those animals to slaughter other children."

Yossou could not believe what he heard and struggled to find the right words to respond. By this time, a group of people had gathered at the door, preferring a view of the inside of the hut to keeping dry. Just then, a figure broke through the crowd, and entered the hut, dripping wet. Emotions awhirl, Yossou did not recognize him until he spoke.

"Welcome back, Yossou!"

"Egadwa!"

They embraced. Egadwa clasped Yossou by the shoulders. He was about to speak again, but held his tongue and dropped his arms. He turned to the seated men.

"*Basakul*, each of you is old enough to be my father, but I have to challenge your handling of this situation. I heard what you said, and understand how you feel, but this is no way to treat one of your own. Yossou did not kill anyone so why should we banish him? He did not know what was going to happen that night and he barely managed to escape with his wife and son."

"How do you know this, Egadwa? Do you say this only because of your wife's kinship with Ma'alia?"

"Is it normal for a man, knowing band of warriors is on its way to slaughter his family, to leave even one of his children behind? If it were you, wouldn't you try to save all of them despite the risk?"

"What's your point?" the other man asked belligerently.

"The point is this," Egadwa stressed each syllable with thinly veiled irritation. "Yossou loves his girls as much as the baby with whom he fled. I know that, and I know Ma'alia loves them as well. Something else must have made them flee in such a manner. The spirits must have warned him to do so in order to save the boy, and there has to be a reason for it. Who then are we to question the will of the Oracle? If the Great Oracle ordained some children must die and this one should live, who are we to question it? Why did they spare our village, eh? We did not lose a single child. Are we any better than the other villages? Yet, here we are passing judgment on one man because his son lived. Think about it. Could it be that fate spared us so this family would find refuge here? After all, how is it they did not return by way of Ronge? The spirits must have ordered their steps to come to us first - we who missed the tip of the spear like they did. We cannot now sit here and play judge with things we don't understand. You all know the things that happened around the birth of this child. I certainly don't want to offend The Mighty One if there's more to it than the eye can see. Oh… and we have guests waiting to meet the village elder. What is your word, Father? Are we to treat them the way we are treating Yossou?"

The men thought for a while. Yossou could tell that they were struggling with what they had just heard. He knew Egadwa as a gentle and quiet man, but he spoke his mind and stood his ground when he believed in something.

"Egadwa is right, Asuu. I don't see how we can blame all those deaths on him, especially if we don't know what's going on in the realm of spirits."

Asuu grunted.

Emesi continued. "I know about the visitors. One of the lads had already alerted me. I cannot go out to greet them because if even a single drop of that rain falls on me, I'll catch a fever that will put me down for days. You take charge Egadwa. Make them feel welcome and see to it they have everything they need."

"I will. Thank you, Father.

"Yossou, welcome home," Emesi added.

The change of heart surprised Yossou. He was glad but speechless.

"Thank you, *Baba*," was all he could manage.

Egadwa smiled. "Let's go Yossou."

The people who had gathered and were blocking the doorway parted to let them through. They stepped into the rain and headed back to the village square. The water was ankle-deep water in certain sections of the path and the rain was still coming down hard.

"I presume Ma'alia's still at the square," Egadwa said.

"Yes. We couldn't go anywhere. No one wanted to talk to us."

"They'll get over it. Once you have Emesi on your side he'll change the attitude of the village."

At the square, the caravan still huddled under the tree. The rain did not hit them directly, but the drops worked their way down through the leaves, falling in a constant dribble. Koteng covered Yssa who played with the reins while carrying on an endless conversation in a language only he knew. Ma'alia tucked herself and Jama under a waterproof leather covering. When she saw Egadwa, she just about dropped the baby and almost jumped off the horse.

"*Koza* Egadwa!"

"Stay where you are, Ma'alia. There'll be time for greetings later," Egadwa told her.

However, he did come up to shake her hand. Ma'alia refused to let go.

"How's Senge Rodina? How are the children? Have you heard from

Yossou's mother and children? What about Wiki-Zugu?" In her excitement, the questions came fast.

"They are well. Everybody's well. Let me take care of our visitors first then we'll talk."

He patted her hand and pulled his away. He turned to Yossou.

"The animals can remain under the shelter of the tree. Your fellow travelers can gather in the ceremonial hut. There's room for most of them. Some families can host the rest for the short time they are here. Who is their leader?"

Yossou led Egadwa to Suping and introduced him.

Egadwa bowed. "Welcome to our humble village. We don't have much, but what we have we'll share with you."

Yossou interpreted.

"Thank you. We are used to traveling under all sorts of conditions in the King's service, so don't go out of your way to accommodate us."

Yossou interpreted back to Egadwa.

"Well, at least let's get you out of the rain and feed you some warm food." Speaking for himself, he continued. "Let me take that young man from you." He took Yssa from Koteng.

"Cover him with this."

Koteng shed his waterproof covering, handed it to Yossou, and dismounted. He yelled instructions and a number of his men followed Egadwa in a quick dash to the ceremonial hut. They sat on stools, or stood as water dripped from their garments. With gestures, indicating he would be back, Egadwa went to look for villagers willing to host the ten remaining travelers. Since all was eager to have one of the strange men in their homes, there was no shortage of volunteers. It would grant bragging rights for those chosen to host a visitor. Having settled all the travelers, Egadwa came back for Ma'alia and Yossou.

"Uh… I have a surprise for you," he said as he walked ahead of them.

"What surprise?" Ma'alia asked.

"What good is a surprise if I told you what it was?"

"Oh."

Egadwa directed the rest of the conversation to their experiences in the foreign land until they got to his compound. Very little had changed, Ma'alia noticed. Her kitchen was still the same. The hut in which she had lived after her mother's death was still standing. As they approached the main hut, she saw shadowy movements in her old hut. An elderly woman stepped outside under the overhang. Two girls followed her out and stood on either side of her. Yossou stopped Ma'alia's horse to observe them. The three also looked at them keenly. Recognition came to all at the same time.

"M'ma!" Yossou shouted.

"Yossou, my son!"

"Baba! M'ma!" the younger Simi screamed and tore from the shelter into the rain, running toward her parents. The older Simi followed.

"My children, you're back! My children!" she said.

Egadwa saw Ma'alia's dilemma and reached up to take the baby.

"This is the surprise, Ma'alia."

She barely heard him. Her eyes and attention were on Yossou's mother and children. She dismounted to join Yossou as he embraced his mother and daughter. Rodina and Kalhi came out of the main hut to see what was going on. They screeched with joy when they saw Ma'alia.

"Ma'alia! Ma'alia, my child."

Senge Rodina scrutinized her niece as if she could not believe what she was seeing. They laughed and cried at the same time.

Someone was missing from this reunion - Temin. She stood under the overhang, looking sullen. They all turned to her. She did not move. The younger Simi took Yssa's hand as her father went to talk to Temin. Ma'alia followed Yossou while the rest went into the main hut.

"Temin, I'm back. I'm back to see my little girl."

She fixed her eyes on the ground, pouting. Yossou reached out for her hand, but she snatched it away. Yossou paused then spoke gently.

"Temin, I know you're angry with me for leaving you. I can't tell you how bad I feel about it. Please forgive me."

"Forgive us both," Ma'alia added. "We are sorry we left you when those bad people came that night. Please understand we had to run away to save your little brother because a bad man wanted to kill him. We had to trust The Mighty One to take care of you."

"But why did you have to leave me and Simi behind?" she yelled. "Why couldn't you take us with you?"

"Temin, a spirit-being told us to leave immediately. We had no time to argue or to wake you up. We just had to go."

"You don't love me or my sister. You only love that boy and don't care about us. Only N'ne loves us."

Yossou held her by the arms. "Temin! Temin, listen to me…"

"No! I hate you. I hate both of you!"

Ma'alia put a hand to her own mouth. Yossou reached and hugged Temin, but she resisted and tried to break free. Unable to do so, she pummeled him with her tiny fists.

"I hate you! I hate you!" she screamed and struggled, but Yossou held her firmly. When she had spent herself, she sagged, still sobbing on Yossou's shoulder. Ma'alia closed in and put her arms around her daughter and husband.

Yossou assured Temin it was not their choice to leave her behind. He told her they were back and would never leave her again. They persuaded her to follow them to the main hut. As the family walked across the compound to the main hut, neighbors standing under overhangs or sheltered under trees ululated and shouted words of welcome.

This was a bittersweet homecoming for Yossou and Ma'alia. It was sweet because they were home. They were back together as a family again and genuinely happy to see each other. Unfortunately, it was also bitter because they returned under a cloud of suspicion. They were home, but not at home. Home was Ronge, but they could not go there due to resentment based on the assumption that they had betrayed fellow villagers. They all went into the main hut while Egadwa went to check on the visitors from Kedem.

The constant drizzle, occasional rumble of thunder, and "*plonk, plonk*" of drops falling into the puddles around the hut provided an eerie backdrop to the horrifying account Simi gave of the night Tamaa's warriors attacked.

My grandchildren and I were asleep after the visitors from distant lands left the village. In the middle of the night, I thought I heard talking outside, but I wasn't sure whether or not I was dreaming. Then I heard the sound of a large animal, which I now know was the horse, galloping away. I was still not fully awake, so I didn't investigate. Actually, I must have gone back to sleep. Next, I heard smashing and screaming. The night lit up with huts on fire. I sat up intending to run to the banana grove, but the warriors were already upon us. I sat holding my grandchildren, praying our deaths would be quick and painless. I knew they would kill me because I was too old to be a slave. What I dreaded most was they would ravish my granddaughters. I decided if it came to that, I would die defending them. But you know what? Twice, attackers came to our hut and stopped. They looked at us huddled on the floor and moved on! I know they saw us. Huts were burning all around us and the flames threw light on us. I tell you, they came up to the hut, looked at us, and left! I don't know what they saw or what stopped them.

The worst part was hearing the screams of mothers whose children were torn right out of their arms and killed. How do you console a person like that? What do you say? When it was over, there was wailing and confusion across the village. People stood purposelessly, lost in grief. Mothers held the bloody corpses of little boys whose necks those monsters had pierced with spears. Fathers cried over infants whose heads the warriors had dashed upon rocks. The question on everybody's mind was, "Where was The Mighty One in all of this? Where were the spirits that protect us from such mischief? And why? Why did it happen?"

Daylight broke only to highlight the havoc the warriors had left in their wake. We were still trying to make sense of it. Sakul Wiki-Zugu, the Oracle bless him, is a wise man indeed. He and a few men picked up the dead, cleaned them, and laid them at the square. He summoned the village and we mourned each mother's loss as if it was our own. That day we broke with tradition and did not take the dead to their homes. We allowed the grieving parents to be with their children among other parents so they would know they were not alone. I've never heard the people sing as beautifully as they did that day. We sang the praises of each child and lamented that he did not have the chance to grow and become all he could be. We praised the parents who had raised the children for the brief period they had lived. We praised the Oracle who ushered the children from the world of men into the realm of spirits, even if it was at the hands of madmen. It was a moving ceremony.

In the afternoon, Wiki-Zugu rose, prayed for the departed, and wished them well on their journey to join the ancestors. As usual, Goteng materialized out of nowhere, but this time, there were too many bodies for him to carry by himself. Several men offered to carry the children. I'll never forget the sight of them walking away, each with a child who had done no wrong - who never stood a chance against those beasts. We did not go back to our homes that night because the warriors had burned many huts. We ate together at the square and spent the night in the open.

Unfortunately, it did not take long for ugliness to rear its head. I began to hear people asking where you were. After all, they said, Yssa was the same age as the children Tamaa had slain. When eyes turned to me, I told them I did not know what happened to you, Ma'alia, and your son. Indeed, I too, was wondering where you were. I noticed a change in demeanor around me. I heard someone mutter that we had known about the danger, but did not warn the rest of the village. By morning, some of the bereaved women were outright hostile, accusing me of killing their children. It was painful to sit there and hear those accusations. Finally, Wiki-Zugu intervened and after a meeting of the elders, they concluded we could not stay in the village...

Simi choked back a sob.

...and they ordered us to leave right away. Some even called for our banishment to the hill country, but Wiki-Zugu restrained them. He said it was punishment enough to send us away. Right after he finished speaking, people rushed to our compound, tore everything down, and killed our animals. The irony is the raiders did not lay a finger on our home, but our own people destroyed it.

They even took the gifts the visitors from distant lands had brought. We have nothing Yossou. You have nothing there. Were it not for Wind, Sande, and Juma, we would not have made it here safely because other villages along the way had suffered the same fate and harbored the same feelings toward us. We are not welcome in those villages either. When the Baronge tore down our huts, they made it clear they have cut ties with us. This is the only village that will take us in, but only because Egadwa managed to convince many here that you could have done no such thing. This is now your home, Yossou.

To conclude the sad tale, the rain came down hard once more. Yossou stood up, went outside, and stood away from the door to watch it fall. His mother's narrative hurt him deeply. He was angry because he was not there to defend her and his daughters from the villagers' wrath. He was also angry that he was not there to defend himself against the accusation of selling out. He reminded himself most of the events of the last several months were beyond his control. He had to take the good with the bad and trust it was all working out for good somehow. After some time, the rain reduced to a light drizzle and the sun breached the clouds briefly. He shed his sandals and stepped onto the waterlogged compound. He untied Ma'alia's horse and began to leave. Little Yssa yelled and waddled after him.

"Where are you going, child?" Yssa only raised his hand.

His father propped him on the horse and headed to the square.

Egadwa and Rodina had mustered some village women to prepare a meal for the visitors. They ate in the ceremonial hut while conversing in gestures with villagers. Yossou joined Suping and they talked for a while. When the opportunity presented itself, he broached the matter that was on his mind.

"I'm sorry Ma'alia and I will not be traveling any further. We've just learned we cannot go beyond this village." He explained the situation briefly.

"Oh, it's no trouble. I'm glad that you are home, though you may not be exactly where you want to be. I'm sure everything will work out. I think we'll continue our journey now that the rain has let up."

"Why don't you spend the night and leave tomorrow?"

"That would be another day lost. With you here safe, part of our mission is accomplished."

Yossou wondered how he knew about this arrangement. Suping laughed as if he read his mind.

"I have not survived this long in the King's service without discernment. I understand my orders - spoken and unspoken. Now do me a favor; find all my men, and tell them we'll be leaving shortly."

"Sure."

Yossou commissioned some of the boys who now followed him everywhere to undertake the search. He asked them to find Egadwa to inform him the visitors were about to leave. The boys immediately scampered off to their respective assignments. While they waited, the women came in to clear the gourds and calabashes with which they had served the guests. Suping gestured to the women to wait a moment and gave instructions to one of his men who went out to the camels. The man came back with an etched brass bracelet for each woman. Suping smiled at their squeals of delight as they wore them and showed off to each other. They thanked him and went to boast to other women.

Presently other members of the delegation arrived and they prepared to resume their journey. Egadwa returned with a hobbling Emesi and the bitter Asuu. Ma'alia came along shortly after. With Yossou interpreting, Emesi thanked them for honoring Kilima with their visit and above all, for taking care of Yossou and his family. In turn, Suping thanked him and the village for their hospitality. As a gesture of appreciation, he gave him a bag of gold for the community. They shook hands and left the ceremonial hut. The men had already loaded everything and were ready to leave.

"Come and see us in Kedem sometime," Suping offered.

"You likewise," Yossou responded. "If you're ever traveling this way, be assured you have a place to spend the night."

Suping squatted and hugged Yssa. "Take care of your parents, son. You'll be a great man someday." Yssa smiled and handed him a clover he held in his hand.

"Thank you!" Suping rose and shook hands with Yossou and Ma'alia. "Goodbye, friends. I'll see you again soon, if the gods will it."

Koteng also came up to bid them farewell.

"Thank, you for everything," Yossou said earnestly. "This wouldn't have happened without you."

"And Safya," Ma'alia added.

"It was not our doing. Something tells me a higher power ordained it."

The following day, Egadwa gathered a group of men to start working on a hut for his niece and her family. They cleared a section of the compound uphill from Egadwa's hut and began to dig up soil for the wall. The previous day's rain made the digging easier and they did not have to fetch water for the mud. Other men came with long thin tree limbs and branches for the frame of the structure. They set about putting them in place, starting with the stout, vertical supporting limbs, then forming a grid with horizontal branches using strips of bark to tie the branches together. They then filled the grids with mud and smoothed it over. They had to wait for at least two rain-free days to harvest the grass for the roof since all spare material disappeared fast when the rains came and families made repairs.

By the fourth day, the hut had a roof. Yossou and Ma'alia moved in on the sixth day, after everything - the mud walls, the dung on the floor and the inside walls had dried. Ma'alia was especially glad. Finally, after several moons, she had a hut she could call her own. The elder Simi, the girls, and their cousin Kalhi, Rodina's daughter, used Ma'alia's old hut as their sleeping quarters, though occasionally, one or both girls would spend a night in their parents' hut. Chanzu, Egadwa and Rodina's son, divided his time between his parents' home and that of Egadwa's half-brother, Vakhum, who had three boys about Chanzu's age. Vakhum's family had all but adopted him. It was not unusual for a family to take over the child of a relative or even a friend. It happened gradually, as the child spent more time with a family other than his own.

Having been away for so many moons, Yossou had to reacquaint himself with his daughters. He was amazed at how much Simi had matured. She took the initiative doing chores at home and was always ready to help. She had a caring disposition and was very protective of her sister. As soon as she set eyes on her brothers, she took charge of them as well. Ma'alia appreciated the help both Simis gave in the care of Yssa and Jama. The family sometimes referred to her as *kam'ma* or "little mother."

Temin, on the other hand, lived on her own terms. She rarely helped with chores and her grandmother, Ma'alia, or Rodina often had to remind her of her responsibilities. Occasionally, they augmented their words with a thin stick administered to her derrière. She was closer to Kalhi than she was to her own sister. With regard to her father, the rest of the family could see what he could not. She knew how to get her way with him. Whereas he sometimes shouted at Simi when she erred, he did not use the same tone with Temin. When she got over begrudging him for leaving her, she reclaimed her role as the only one who took meals to him. Anyone who breached this arrangement risked a stern reprimand. In the interest of peace, all did their best to find her when her father's meals were ready.

With her penchant for the exotic, Temin wore the women down with requests to style her hair differently every day. She would then tuck a fresh flower in it and walk with a regal air. When she caught sight of the jewelry Ma'alia had brought from Kedem, Temin laid claim to a set of bracelets, a necklace, and some perfume. She especially loved the perfume. It was better than rubbing lime peels and flower petals together for fragrance as girls and women did.

Yssa's place in the home was most enigmatic. To Simi, he was the younger brother she always wanted. She defended and protected him, especially from Temin, who resented him as competition for her father's attention. Kalhi usually ignored him. For his part, Yssa did not ingratiate himself to anyone. Whenever he got into a disagreement, usually with Temin, he simply walked away instead of trying to prove himself. If it were over a toy, he would give it up rather than fight. Ma'alia observed this with the concern that her child was a pushover. She soon realized this was not the case. One morning as he played with his spinning top, a neighbor's child came along with his mother, crying that Yssa had taken his spinning top. Ma'alia was in her kitchen listening to the accusation, knowing it was false because Yossou had made that particular top for Yssa. She was about to intervene, but paused to see how it would pan out. Yssa did not protest or try to keep the toy.

"If you want play with my top, just say so, Bizi. Here, you can have it."

Ma'alia was impressed. She got up and watched from the shadows of the kitchen. Her son had knocked the wind out of the boy and his mother's claim in a masterstroke. His statement made it clear the toy was his, and he *had chosen* to give it up. He gave Bizi the top, and walked away with no sign of animosity. Mother and child looked at each other in confusion. To rub it in, and make a point, Ma'alia stepped into view.

"Oh... uh... peace, Ma'alia. Bizi only wanted to play with Yssa's spinning top so we came to borrow it."

Ma'alia smiled.

"Didn't I say you could have it?" Yssa reminded Bizi's mother. "How are you, M'ma," he said, blowing past her on his way to the grove.

She did not see him the rest of the morning. He reappeared in the afternoon to show her the most beautiful spinning top she had ever seen. He had designed it delicately and etched into the wood simple, but elegant patterns colored with extract from flowers and leaves. Later, he shared even this toy with Bizi and other boys. Through his willingness to share, he created a new culture among his peers. Like him, they relinquished absolute ownership of their toys and pets. They realized that when they shared, they had a lot more at their disposal. Those who kept what they had became a miserable minority. The lesson was not lost on adults who observed the change in the children's attitude and adopted it themselves.

Yssa soon outgrew the games and toys and took to spending more time with his father. He helped with all aspects of the work. He hewed logs in the woods with the men and dragged them back to the village. He learned to cut them into planks and to plane and file them.

Yossou tried to remember the design of tools he had used in Kedem and worked with Juma to make similar ones. He revolutionized the concept of doors and windows around Kilima, the neighboring villages, and beyond. The simple doors replaced the hides in many homes. They introduced new designs for stools, and the novel concept of a table borrowed from Kedem. To a people who served straight out of the pot onto a gourd, the table did not do well and they abandoned it. Still, the fame of father and son spread and people began to seek out their products.

Things also changed at the home. A few moons after their return, Yossou and Ma'alia welcomed a third son into the family. They named him Jani. From his early years, he was close to his brother Jama and it was rare to see one without the other. Moons later, Yossou received a delegation from his former village, Ronge. The elders said they were interested in a young woman in his compound as a possible bride for one of their sons. In the roundabout way tradition demanded, they informed his family that a young man named Dube was now of age and needed a wife. They said they had checked thoroughly and concluded Simi would be the perfect bride for him. She was hardworking, chaste, and came from a good home. Similarly, they indicated they wished to put the past behind them and renew their relationship with Yossou. They hoped the union would heal the wounds and reconcile him with his home village. Yossou said he would consult Egadwa, his wife, brothers, and mother and let Dube's people know. The Baronge agreed to come back another day. Yossou's family consented to the proposal. After many gifts, negotiations, and visits, Simi married Dube in a beautiful, well-attended ceremony. Shortly after, Temin also married a young man called Avedi from Zigul. Yossou and Ma'alia now focused on raising the boys.

Chapter 19

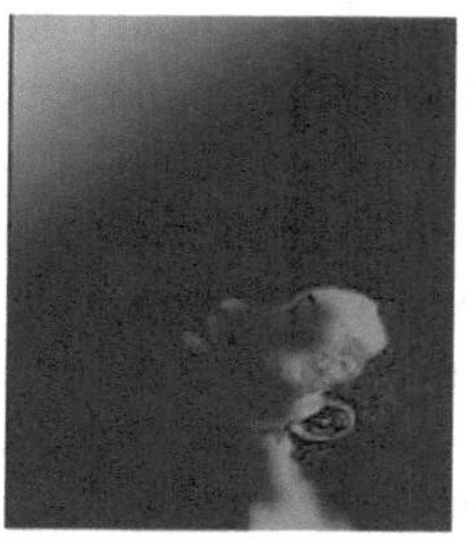

the calling

Circumcision was a community event to which all the clans brought their candidates. They celebrated those who stood firm and did not flinch when the knife incised the foreskin. Some who cried out or resisted became subjects of songs and folklore that told of what real men do not do.

After Yssa had seen eight harvests, it was time for his circumcision. It proved to be difficult time for the Bagololi because it evoked bitter memories of the innocent boys whose blood Tamaa had shed in his jealous rage. Both Ma'alia and Yossou felt a sense of guilt, but they reminded themselves that what happened in the past was beyond their control. Out of respect for the families whose children Tamaa had killed, Yossou and Ma'alia planned to have a quiet ceremony for their son and the boys from Kilima. Yossou mentioned this to Egadwa and together they went to ask M'losi to oversee the ritual.

"Why do you want to do it that way?" the medicine man asked.

Yossou explained. "All the villages hold the blood of the children who died over my head. I don't want to reopen the wounds of parents who feel I betrayed them."

"When they learn you've gone ahead and circumcised your son behind their backs what will they think?"

Yossou could not answer. Even Egadwa saw the point M'losi made.

"We can't go off on our own and do what the community does as one. We might as well spit in their faces." He turned to the medicine man and asked, "What then should we do?"

"Bring some elders together and visit all the clans on behalf of your kinsman. Remind them this age-group is ready to stand the knife. Tell them you understand some boys who should be there will not be there, but we cannot keep rehashing the past. See what they think. If feelings are still running high, then you have cause to go about it another way, but if they're willing to put the past behind, then we proceed as we've always done. We know the children who perished will be standing with the ancestors celebrating the initiation of their peers into manhood. At least give the villages a change to refuse."

The argument made sense and the men they agreed to try it. They requested a meeting of the elders in Kilima to consider M'losi's suggestion. The village appointed Egadwa, Emesi, and Bonaya to visit other villages to urge them to hold the circumcision for this age group in spite of the past. Over the next several days they visited each village, adding members of each clan they visited to their entourage thereby strengthening the case for the next visit. Eventually, only the Bavogol, who would not let go of their bitterness, opted out. The elders of the other clans agreed to hold the ceremony at the next full moon before the Festival of Sacrifice. They named this age group *Wadam* or "the age-group of blood," as a tribute to the boys who perished at the hand of Tamaa.

At the next full moon, M'losi and Vakhum came to pick up Yssa for circumcision. He was working with his father on a villager's house. Ma'alia sent a boy to fetch them. When Yssa arrived, M'losi asked him to shed his modesty patch. Yssa did so and stood naked. The medicine man produced pouches with white, red, and black paint. He painted Yssa's face and body while muttering incantations. The patterns would ward off evil spirits and help him to heal faster after circumcision.

When M'losi finished, he told Yssa to bid his family farewell. The men also went around the village, picked up Bizi and twelve other candidates, and marched to nearby woods. They built a makeshift shelter of twigs and leaves in which they would spend the night.

Early the following morning, the men and their wards began the trek to the Plains of Sacrifice. The boys carried long, thin sticks in their right hands and trotted to the chanting of the medicine man with heads bowed and eyes to the ground. Tradition demanded they should not respond to the crowd even if their own mothers called out to them. Villagers who came to see the boys off shouted encouragement, telling them to be strong when they face the knife.

On the banks of the River Dzodzo there was a special place reserved for the ceremony. It was part of the way to the Shrine of Sacrifice, but closer to the edge of the plains. The boys from Kilima found two boys from Vogol and one from Ngoma already there with their chaperons. The adults greeted one another somberly then went through an elaborate process of introducing the boys to one another. They emphasized that the boys will not only be friends, but blood brothers because the same knife will cut their foreskins and each boy's blood will stain its surface. In the evening, two boys from Ronge, nude and intricately painted, joined them. Their peers were already in the process of building a large shelter using sticks and leaves.

After breakfast the following day, they sat with their chaperons who affirmed their special identity among the people. Tamaa's slaughter of the children would etch itself on the timeline of their history. The adults filled the gaps in the boys' knowledge of the people's origin and journey through time.

In the afternoon, they divided them into three groups. The first had to find meat. The second had to find vegetables, roots, and fruit, while the third would cook what the others brought back. Under the guidance of the adults, the hunters learned they could expand their diet to include porcupine, hares, rodents, snails, bugs, and even snakes. The point was if they were in a situation where conventional food was scarce, they would have to be open to alternatives.

Similarly, the gatherers learned not stick with the usual herbs and legumes. They learned to identify edible roots, mushrooms, and other fruits, herbs, and plant forms that could be vital substitutes in a crisis. They identified those that were poisonous or led to sickness.

The chaperons taught the cooks how to start a fire using dry brush and sticks or stones and how to preserve embers for the next fire. Their duties included learning how to process and cook the strange meats and vegetables their peers brought back. Over the next two days, the groups rotated responsibilities to give each a chance to hunt, gather, and prepare food.

The adults continued to use the mornings to teach the morals and history of their people. They told the boys to view every member of the Bagololi as a brother, sister, mother, father, grandmother, or grandfather. Without going into details, they talked about the meaning of manhood, the purpose of the sex organs, sexual relations, proper relations with girls of their age, and marriage. The boys understood there were certain clans from which they could not marry because members of these clans were their blood relatives. Marriage or sexual liaisons between members of the clans would essentially be incestuous. The boys felt overwhelmed with all this information given the anxiety they already felt looking ahead to circumcision.

Very early on the fourth day, the candidates bathed in the river and washed off the paint before family members and well-wishers started arriving. Mothers and sisters came first, bringing breakfast for their sons. They placed it at a distance from the shelter lest they be seen and dishearten the boys. The men and other boys came later. The candidates finished their breakfast and waited for the ceremony to begin. M'losi was already pacing the riverbank, invoking the Oracle. Men walked around barking in guttural voices, "*Hoogh! Hoogh!*"

M'losi then raised his voice and declared it was time for the boys to prove they were men. Women ululated and men shouted. The chaperons emerged from the shelter and the boys followed. They lined up along the riverbanks, starting with the oldest, Manono from Ngoma. His uncle, who was also his chaperon, stood by his side and whispered to him.

"Don't even flinch otherwise they'll call you a girl and a coward. Look straight in front, grit your teeth, put your hands behind your buttocks, and plant your feet apart firmly. It will be over before you know it."

"Yes, *Koza*," the boy muttered.

M'losi was ready for him. Manono stepped forward and did as his uncle had instructed. He stared straight ahead and waited. The crowd quieted and murmured approvingly of his stance. With his left hand, the medicine man grabbed Manono's foreskin and yanked it twice. The knife flashed wickedly in his right. The boy neither moved nor flinched. M'losi pulled on the foreskin, cut it off expertly, and tossed it aside. Manono did not react. A rumble went through the spectators. M'losi then inserted the long nail of his left thumb between what was left of the foreskin and the head. Bright red blood ran down his thumb and forearm, dripping to the ground at the elbow. He cut all the way around, coming away with a ring of skin. A cheer went up from the crowd. The boy had passed the test. He was a man! His delighted uncle scooped him up carefully and took him back to the shelter. A special paste applied to the wound would stem the bleeding. *Tatula* leaves tied carefully around the member would protect it and accelerate healing.

With Manono having set the standard, the onus was on the next boy to show the same courage. Except for squeezing his eyes shut when M'losi cut the foreskin, he also did well. Three other boys followed with a similar display of bravery. The boy ahead of Yssa was having trouble staying calm. He moaned softly whenever the medicine man cut off the foreskin of those before him. His chaperon reprimanded him sharply for behaving like a little girl, but he did not stop. When his turn came, he would not budge. The chaperon nudged him forward, but he resisted and moaned louder. The crowd reacted with a mixture of derision, disappointment, and sympathy. The men were most derisive the while women were more sympathetic.

"Let the little boy go back to his mother," a man said in disgust. "He can come back when he's ready to be a man."

"And put us through all this again?" another man asked. "Just grab him, cut that thing off, and spare us the spectacle."

"That's cruel," a woman chided. "He can come back when he's older."

Meanwhile, M'losi was losing patience with the boy whose chaperon started to berate him. Yssa felt sorry for him and wished he could somehow help the nervous lad. Unsure of what to do, he just reached up and laid his hand on Shida's shoulder. Yssa could not explain what happened, but he felt a tingle when he touched the boy. Shida stopped crying and turned to Yssa with a nondescript expression. He faced M'losi again. The crowd, noting Yssa's gesture and the boy's reaction, observed closely to see what would follow.

"Cut it off," Shida told M'losi. The transformation puzzled the medicine man. He looked up at the boy doubtfully and reached for the tiny member. He yanked it harder than he had done with the other boys. Shida did not flinch.

"*Ee yeh?*" M'losi wondered. He yanked the skin one last time and swiftly cut off the foreskin. He watched for reaction and got none. The boy stared straight ahead. The crowd was silent, still unbelieving.

"Wait till the pain sinks in," someone whispered. "Then you'll hear him sing!"

M'losi used his long thumbnail to cut off the rest of the foreskin. The lad stood unmoved. He was a man! The crowd erupted into cheering louder than they had done for Manono and the other boys. His chaperon was overjoyed and swept Shida off his feet. He paraded him briefly before going into the shelter for treatment where the other boys bathed in glory despite the pain. They listened to the reaction of the crowd to gauge how each performed. They congratulated Shida when his uncle carried him in.

Yssa was next and his family moved to the front of the crowd. He could tell that his mother and sisters were nervous. His father made a gesture of encouragement.

"You'll do fine, my boy," Vakhum whispered. The rest of the crowd paid him scant attention. They were still talking about Shida when M'losi severed the foreskin from Yssa's member. Unlike other boys who looked away, Yssa kept his eyes on M'losi. The crowd barely noticed he did not even wince when the medicine man excised the rest of it. Vakhum carried him back to the shelter to a sputter of applause. His feelings would have been hurt if the reaction of the crowd had mattered to him. One of the boys asked him about it.

"Did you flinch? I didn't hear any cheering."

"Did you hear jeering?"

The rest of the boys did just as well. No one cried and few cringed. The witnesses said these were the bravest candidates they had seen in a long time. Even more amazing was how quickly they all healed. Usually it took at least seven days for the boys to be well enough to trudge home. These boys were all able to walk quite well by the third day. By the fourth, they were running around with abandon. That morning the chaperons had watched with amusement as they lined up to see whose arc would go the farthest. Ten small bodies leaned back, holding their members with both hands, their buttocks squeezed tight. Their contorted faces reflected the effort it took to send the lime-colored parabolas high in the air. When they had finished, they debated vigorously whose had gone the farthest judging by the splatter.

"Boys!" The adults shook their heads as they reminisced on their own childhood days.

"Today, relieving myself is like assembling a council of elders," Mlosi said.

"A long, slow process," Vakhum said, stressing every syllable.

Later when their families brought them food, they agreed that the boys could go home since all had healed completely. They tore down the shelter and headed back to their respective villages. To the Bagololi, it was nothing short of miraculous. They composed a song in praise of the courageous boys. The song cited Shida in particular. It made no mention of Yssa.

The Festival of Sacrifice followed about nine moons after the circumcision. It fell every fifth harvest, when the clans of Gololi gathered to thank The Mighty One and the ancestors for a good harvest. If it was not good, there was still much for which to offer sacrifice and be grateful. They gave thanks for life, health, strength, family, friends, and everything, which, at any other time they might have taken for granted. It lasted three days, starting with the march to the Plains.

By the afternoon of the first day, the people began to gather by clan - the Baronge, Bakilima, Bavogol, Bangoma, and Bazigul. They carried everything they would need, including food, firewood, and the sacrificial animals - usually a spotless lamb and a white rooster. The Dzodzo provided fresh water. Each clan gathered by family, and families gathered by household. Heads of household built makeshift shelters on lots the ancestors had allocated each clan and family going back generations.

In the throng, children were like leaves in an erratic breeze, drifting wherever cousins, friends, and play carried them. Parents were not concerned until the third day when they found themselves with a shelter full of children, none of whom was their own. This led to a long session of holding on to them and hollering for "the mother of so-and-so" while listening to other parents who might have their children. They would be lucky to find two of their children with the same family.

After breakfast the second day, they would spend the rest of the morning visiting with family and friends they had not seen in a long time. This was another reason for the festival - to maintain relationships among the clans so they would not drift apart to the point that they become hostile toward one another. Before Xhaka overran Kwavantu, the strength of a people was in direct proportion to the strength of the inter-clan relationships. The festival was a way of cementing those bonds.

After the visits, the clans would walk to designated areas along the river for cleansing. Each clan had an assigned priest to conduct the ritual. Young and old, they lined up before him. In turn, individuals would wade into the water and stand before the priest. He would scoop water in a bowl and pour it on their heads while praying over them. Then the individuals would submerge themselves briefly and rise again. So cleansed, they would step out of the river to wait on the bank for their kinsmen to complete the ritual.

In the afternoon, they sat in family groups singing somber songs and chanting prayers to the Oracle for protection, fertility, and peace with neighboring communities. During this session, priests in festive garb walked among the people, sounding incantations and occasionally shouting at an individual or group to chase away foul spirits. The ceremony of sacrifice followed at sundown. Heads of household slaughtered and cut up the animals they had brought for this purpose. Then they lined up to lay the richest portion of the meat on the flames of the altar before the priests.

The clans had last gathered just before Yossou and his family returned from Kedem. Yssa had attended his first Festival of Sacrifice after he had seen seven harvests. This was his second. He had shown a great interest in his people's traditions and practices, and their significance. He had a phenomenal memory for stories of historic events that formed the people's beliefs. He carefully observed what the heads of households, the clan leaders, and the priests did, finding it all fascinating. It created a hunger in him to know more about the spirit world, with which he felt a deep connection. It did not bequeath him a sense of privilege, but rather a responsibility.

When Yossou joined the line to lay his family's offering at the altar, Yssa asked if he could accompany him. His father thought about it for a moment, never having seen a child among the adults who went up to the altar. However, on seeing the sincerity in the child's eyes, he agreed, ignoring the disapproving looks of some men. Yssa followed his father and watched him place the offering over the embers. The fat awakened the fire, which sizzled in anticipation and stretched orange tongues to lick the meat. The smell of burning fat and meat filled the air and white smoke rose in a wobbly column, determined to make it to the ancestors in the heavens. The priest blessed the offering. Yossou prayed for each member of his family, for the land, livestock, and protection from wicked spirits.

When his father moved on, Yssa remained transfixed before the priest who stood behind the flames and smoke, blessing each offering. Yssa stepped over to one end of the altar. The priest did not appear to notice him and there was no break in the mutterings that poured out of his mouth. Yssa stepped back into the shadows to observe the gathering.

He felt the collective need of the people and saw the offerings as a mere token to mitigate that need. He watched people sway, supposedly in worship. He heard chants rising above the drone of the congregation. Some individuals were in self-induced trances. Men and women reached out to the spirit world, grasping for that elusive strand that would connect them with the sublime - the eternal. A woman walked backwards in circles, her back arched grotesquely in what would normally be a painful posture. With hands outstretched, she uttered strange things in an unnatural voice. She stomped on the ground so hard with each step that Yssa feared her bones would shatter. In another area, a man stooped like a fowl and ran headlong into people. They stopped his charge only for him change vectors and run down another group. When it got out of hand, onlookers wrestled him to the ground, ending his communion with the spirit world. With these two decommissioned, others replaced them with their own manifestation of transcendence.

When the offering of sacrifices wound down, the priests stepped away from the fire and disappeared behind the large rocks and boulders. Yssa descended the steps to join his family as they prepared to have the sacrificial meal. He reflected on his feelings when he looked at the crowd from his perch at the altar. He still felt the heaviness of their hearts and wondered about it. *Why should I bear the burden of so many?* He had no answer to this question. When the meal was ready, he ate reverently like everybody else, but his reasons had to do with weightier matters than mere reflection on the significance of the day. He listened as his father and other relatives seated around the fire talked in low tones about the day's events. They also talked about events of the past, and about benevolent and wicked spirits that influenced the life of the community. Yssa fell asleep, curled up next to his father, taking it all in.

In the morning, while families tore down camp and prepared for the journey home, the priests saw individuals with special needs. The demand for private divinations and healing was so heavy that to reduce the number of requests, the priests charged steep prices for the sessions. Still, people kept coming.

Yssa stole away from his family, went back to the shrine, and up the steps past the altar. He walked around it to see where the priests went after the sacrifice. It was a massive labyrinth of moss-covered boulders. A thick, musky scent hung in the air. After a few turns, he happened upon an open area where the rocks formed a relatively flat floor. Three warriors materialized from behind some boulders and stopped him. He must have interrupted them as they ate because each held a bone with juicy roast meat in greasy hands and their mouths glistened with fat. They did not reach for their weapons when they saw it was just a boy.

"Where do you think you're going, lad?" one asked.

Before Yssa could answer, a voice behind them spoke.

"Let the young man through. I'd like to hear what he has to say for himself."

It was the priest who had blessed the sacrifices the previous day.

"Come here. You had the audacity to come to the altar with your father, eh?"

Yssa wondered if he detected a smile in the voice. He followed the priest.

"I just wanted to see you perform the ceremony. I want to help people and deliver them from their troubles."

The priest raised an eyebrow. "You do?"

"Yes," Yssa replied unequivocally.

"I'm neither surprised at what you say nor to see you back. When you came to the altar with your father, right away I sensed there was something different about you. I'm Kefa, the Chief Priest. We are seeing the sick, the bewitched, and those troubled by wicked spirits. It's not easy work, son. Are you sure this is what you want to do?"

"That's why I came."

The response baffled Kefa. He was not sure the boy referred to his coming into the world, or his return to the altar. He led the boy deeper into the shrine and talked with him in earnest. He was amazed at the questions the boy asked and the answers he gave.

"Where's Yssa," Ma'alia asked Yossou.

"I thought he was with you."

"And I thought he was with you. He's been spending more time with the men lately, hasn't he?"

"Yes, but I haven't seen him. He's probably with some of our kinsmen."

"*Ai?* I don't know."

They were traveling with a number of people all heading for the foothills of their respective lands. One by one, clans and families broke away and Ma'alia became concerned when Yssa did not turn up. By the afternoon, only the Bakilima and their neighbors, the Bazigul, traveled the trail.

"I'm worried Yossou. Yssa should be with us by now. I've asked around and nobody has seen him or knows where he is."

"This is unlike Yssa. I wasn't worried because I know he has a habit of disappearing into the woods to pray. I thought that he wanted to be by himself again," Yossou said.

"Jama, where is your brother? *Thukhh!* Wipe that nose!"

"I haven't seen him since last night when he sat by the fire with Baba," the boy said. He ran his lower arm under his nose, leaving a glistening streak on it.

Yossou began to ask for Yssa urgently, going from family to family within the two clans. It began to emerge that he had probably not left the grounds of the shrine at all. There was only one course of action left.

"We'll have to go back. I will not sleep until I know where my son is," Ma'alia stated resolutely.

Yossou remembered his pregnant wife trekking across these same plains alone at night when he came to her rescue. The thought prodded him into action. He told his mother he and Ma'alia were going back to look for Yssa. Simi, who was also worried, said she would look after the younger boys. They began the journey back to the Shrine of Sacrifice. Several times, they had to explain to other travelers why they were traveling against the flow. No one recalled seeing the boy that morning. Traffic from the shrine gradually reduced to a trickle and this only served to heighten concern for the well-being of their son.

Yssa watched the priests conduct the healing session with a mixture of fascination and perturbation. He sensed the distress of the individuals whom family members brought before the priests and he desperately wanted to help. To him, the priests were akin to a mother hen squawking and flapping her wings as an eagle swooped down to snatch her chick. Their shouting and chanting could no more dispel the foul spirits than the cackling of the mother hen could stop the raptor or retrieve the chick from the talons of an eagle that had soared into the sky. Yssa wished he could explain to them the futility of it. *But what was the truth?* He had been searching for it daily in moaning and groaning to The Mighty One whom he felt he knew like a father. He had sought it in the long walks to the tops of the hills and in the woods. But how could he explain it? It bothered him that he could not explain what held the answer to the burdens of so many.

As he agonized, a man and a woman approached the priests. Another couple accompanied them, with the woman carrying a white chicken under her arm. Yssa felt so strongly drawn to this group. The first woman was clearly in pain and was barely able to walk. Sweat glistened on her forehead and her chest heaved with exertion at every breath. The effort served to accentuate her bony torso. With every movement, her breasts flapped against her ribs like empty wineskins.

One of the priests asked the couple to sit on the ground and explain what was going on. The husband told them her problems started about three moons back with frequent headaches and joint pain. She was always feverish and could not keep her food down. They tried all types of herbs, but nothing worked. Neither did the frequent visits to the village medicine man. The husband said he suspected a neighbor had thrown "the evil eye" at her out of jealousy because she had given him five boys whereas the neighbor in question had four girls and no boys. When he finished, the priests contemplated the woman as if trying to decipher her problems from an invisible aura around her.

"It is bad," one priest said.

"Very bad," the other priest agreed, affecting a dramatic shudder.

"We'll need the blood of an unblemished chicken to help her. I see bad spirits all around."

"*Aaagh!*" the second priest cried.

"We have the chicken. Here it is."

The second man took the chicken from his wife and held it before the priests. The priests looked at it long and hard.

"It's a good one," the first priest said. "Its blood will fight the spirits that trouble this woman."

There was a collective sigh of relief and the first priest got up and crouched like a leopard stalking prey. He approached the man with the chicken and stopped, looking at the chicken as if seeing it for the first time. Suddenly, he snatched it out of the man's hands, startling both. The chicken squawked briefly. The priest circled the woman in the same manner. Three times, he jabbed the befuddled bird at her. It cackled each time, but she stared ahead impassively. Each time he did so, the second priest would shout, "*Eeey!*" The first priest raised the chicken high above his head. This time it squawked loudly. He held it by the neck and brought it down, twisting at the same time. He tore off the head and tossed it aside. Blood spurted from the neck, spraying the woman and the seated priest.

"*Eeeeyiiih!*" the second priest shouted.

He rose and picked up a small clay bowl to collect the blood. The woman began to moan softly, swaying back and forth. Her three companions watched anxiously as the first priest laid down the headless chicken, took the bowl of blood, and resumed circling the woman in his hunched position. After a few revolutions, he stopped, dipped a finger in the chicken's blood, and dabbed it on her forehead. As soon as he did so, her swaying increased in amplitude and she almost knocked the bowl out of his hand with her head. Her eyes took on a manic expression. Without warning, she stood and took the first priest by the arm causing him to drop the bowl. He howled as her grip hastened him out of the trance into the reality of pain. She muttered incoherently in an unearthly voice, grabbed his other arm, and raised him right off the ground with arms pinned to his sides. She squeezed them in an attempt to crush him. He screamed. It was most uncanny to see the frail skeletal woman lift a grown, healthy man with such ease. The Chief Priest and the other men tried to break her grip on the unfortunate priest, but they could not move her. She was like the stump of a *mkuyu* tree firmly planted in the ground. The priest now howled shamelessly as she applied greater force. There was a sickening sound of ribs breaking and the priest let out a shrill cry that reverberated eerily in the enclosed area. Still, they were unable to free him. He started to pass out. In desperation, they all clung to her arms. She swung first her right arm then her left, discarding the men as an enraged bull would toss little children. Each landed in a heap several paces away. The warrior-guards come to see what was causing the commotion. They kept their distance when they saw how easily the woman flung the men aside. Now she picked the priest by the neck using only her left hand. His legs flailed uselessly. With her right, she prepared to strike. Given the strength she had just exhibited, it would be a deathblow.

When the troubled woman attacked the priest, Yssa saw that she was not the culprit. Evil forces had taken exception to the priests' meddling with their habitation. In that moment, a most brilliant light came upon Yssa and filled his person. He felt power flow into his being and his senses became sharp.

He saw the suffering of woman and the oppressive dark forces that played around her like flies on a mound of excrement. Their sheer weight smothered her spirit and did not allow her to express who she was. Like termites, they burrowed deep and destroyed from within.

Yssa knew their names - every one of them. He knew them from the time they had revolted against The Father at the dawn of time. The Father had flung them from their celestial home to wander the realm of men where they caused great mischief. In their eyes was deep hatred for humans. They sought to enslave, harm, and destroy them at every opportunity as they were doing with this woman. They now threatened to snuff out the priest's life. But the Father willed to save.

"*Riswa!* Come out!" Yssa ordered.

When she turned, it was not her face he saw, but the evil forms with jaded yellow eyes. They bared their teeth and shouted as one.

"No! This is our home. She's ours." The words came from the woman's mouth in a deep ugly voice.

Yssa spoke again. "Woman, you are free." He pointed to the dark vaporous things and said, "*Riswa!* Leave her now!"

"No!" she cried in the dreadful voice. "No! Noooo!"

Light flowed out of Yssa and enveloped the woman. With dreadful shrieks, the wicked forms fled into the ether with a loud "whoosh," leaving a wispy vapor and a most odious smell. The woman relaxed her grip on the priest and both collapsed on the ground like the dead. The four men got up from where they cowered and rushed to help.

"Let them be. They'll be fine," Yssa said.

The men stopped and looked at Yssa. He spoke with authority and his face shone with an otherworldly brilliance. His eyes sparkled, boring into those upon whom he gazed. His mere presence so overwhelmed them they began to tremble.

They fell prostrate at his feet. He bent down and touched the priest's shoulder.

"Get up, *M'sali,*" he said. "This is not the time."

He also tapped the woman's husband on the shoulder. He too, raised himself from his prone position, but remained on his knees. The other men also sat up, regarding him in awe. He went up to the woman and took her hand. She opened her eyes and her face came alive when she saw him.

"My Lord!" she said prostrating herself before him.

"Not now, woman," he said. "Not now." She sat up. He turned to the priest lying beside her and laid a hand on his chest. He too, opened his eyes.

"Thank you, My Lord," he said sitting up.

The woman's husband squatted beside her.

"How are you feeling?"

"I feel light. It's as if a crushing weight has fallen off my back."

"You're not in pain or anything?"

"No. I just feel light - and free."

"Oh! That's good!" He put an arm around her shoulder and rested his chin on her head.

Yssa sat down. He felt himself gradually returning to normal, though a little spent. This was the first time he had experienced something of this nature. The chief priest stared at him again with a mixture of awe and fascination.

"Who are you?" he asked.

Yssa turned to him, "I am Yssa, son of Yossou of Ronge."

"*Ee yeh?*" You are the one! Several harvests back we heard a tale from herdsboys about a star that led them to a place where a child was born. What happened here tonight reminds me of what they described."

The rest of the group gathered around to listen. The Chief Priest told the warrior-guards the priests would not be seeing anyone else and to send away anyone who asked to see them. Kefa turned back to Yssa.

"Tell us about yourself and where you learned to do such amazing acts."

"I did not set out to do what I did. The Spirit Father came upon me and showed me what to do."

"Who is The Father?"

"You are a priest of the Oracle and you don't know The Father?"

Yssa then told of childhood glimpses into the spirit world and the times he spent alone in the hills and woods. He talked about getting to know himself by knowing The Father. He explained that The Father was the one they worshipped as the Oracle, The Great Spirit, and The Mighty One. They were amazed at the ideas he related. Even the priests, who believed in good and bad spirits, could not fathom how a great spirit reigned over all. But they only had to think of what he had done for the woman to realize they could not dispute what he said.

Yssa was still talking when one of the warriors approached Kefa and whispered in his ear.

"I told you we're not seeing anyone else," Kefa said. The warrior whispered again.

"*Ah!* It must be him then." He stubbed his thumb toward Yssa. "Let them through."

As soon as Ma'alia saw Yssa, she ran and embraced him. His father stood behind her and both were visibly relieved to see him. Ma'alia released and chided him.

"Son, why did you treat us this way? You really had us worried. We've been looking all over for you."

"Why do you worry about me M'ma? You should know I would be about my Father's business."

Yossou turned his head sharply in his son's direction. Clearly, he was wondering what Yssa meant when he said, "my Father's business." Kefa did not quite grasp Yossou was in a quandary.

"You have an amazing son," he said. Those around agreed.

"We give thanks to the Mighty One for that," Yossou said absentmindedly. "Come. Let's go home. I don't want us walking home too late in the night."

They thanked the priest and rose to leave. Everybody else was still stunned.

Yossou and Ma'alia did not bring up the question of why Yssa had acted out of character. They were not sure how to broach the subject anyway. Yssa neither brought it up nor apologized.

Days passed and Yossou and Ma'alia pushed the incident at the Shrine out of their minds. He was a responsible, beloved child in Kilima. Though the community had a clearly defined pecking order based on age group and gender, certain individuals went beyond expectations by their exemplary leadership, respect, and unselfish service to others. No young man stood out like Yssa. He had a way of listening to others and offering solace and comfort. People came to him when they had disagreements they could not resolve. He listened patiently to both parties and asked a few pointed questions. He rarely dispensed advice, but his questions made antagonists wonder why they were in dispute in the first place.

Yssa developed a habit of not working every seventh day. He would disappear into the hills for the entire day. Some villagers who had secretly followed him reported hearing him invoke someone he called "Father." He always asked this "Father" to show him what to do. They said that though they listened until they were tired, they did not understand exactly what he asked. It was too deep and they left confused. Toward the evening, Yssa would return. His family had learned to respect his time alone and did not cumber him with tasks on such days. People started calling him "Son of the Oracle" because of his passion for meeting with this "Father." Gradually more villagers began to abstain from work every seventh day.

One morning, Yssa woke up early as he always did and went to the banana grove for his habitual prayer. His mother had just started preparing breakfast. When he finished, he came into the kitchen, saluted her, and sat down on a stool. He watched her stir the porridge and blow into the fire. She sensed a melancholy air around him. He asked how his sisters were faring. Ma'alia said as far as she knew, the girls and their families were all well.

"I miss them," he said.

"Me too. You have wonderful sisters and I think their husbands are very fortunate."

"Yes, indeed."

Ma'alia served him a gourd of porridge and he ate it with cold beans from the previous night. They reminisced on the good and bad times through which they had been. When he finished, he rinsed the gourd with a little water and set it down.

"I'm going to the woods for a while."

"Again?"

"Yes. I'll join Baba at the shop later," he said and left.

Ma'alia still could not get over the sense that her son was fretting over something. She wished she could help, but she had learned that if he did not tell her, it was best to leave him alone until he opened up. A sense of foreboding fleeted over her briefly. It was akin to the feeling one got when a loved one was leaving, never to return, or had died. She wished her mother-in-law were here. Simi was away, looking after an elderly relative who was gravely ill. Even when she took breakfast to Yossou, she did not say anything to him. She thought perhaps she was overreacting to Yssa's adolescent moodiness. She forgot about the episode - until that evening.

It had been over five moons since the last drop of rain fell and no one was sure if the rains would return anytime soon. The grass began to die. The villagers sent their animals to the marshes where thick green grass fended off the encroachment of the parched earth of surrounding areas. As part of their duties in the passage from boyhood to manhood, three to five young men would stay with the animals day and night for up to seven days at a time until the rains came. For this assignment, the elders of Kilima appointed Serem, Madira, Tonto, and Luseti. All were members of the *Wadam* age group. In a society that placed a premium on boys, the people of Kilima felt especially blessed to have them, considering what had happened to boys their age in other villages.

Over time, it became tradition that only the leader-apparent could relax along the slope of the embankment. One of his duties was to look out for danger. The other boys would remain at the bottom the whole time. Serem was not the oldest, but he was the leader.

Late in the afternoon of the second day of their assignment, Serem lay on the embankment cleaning his teeth with a chewing stick. In an otherwise clear sky, he observed a small cloud that resembled a fist. He wondered how a solitary cloud would materialize in the sky in this season. After a while, he paid it no further attention and his mind went to other things - Nambale to be precise. He had taken a fancy to Asuu's granddaughter, but she did not know it. He found every excuse to pass by her compound to see if she were outside, sweeping or grinding millet. In her presence, however, he always lost his faculty of speech. It did not help that they were from the same clan, and she was therefore his sister by tradition. Marriage was out of the question. He knew all this, but it did not stop him from dreaming about her.

The sun was setting by the time he realized he had to stop chasing thoughts of Nambale around in his head. His friends already had a fire going and were roasting edible roots. He looked at the sky and was surprised to see dark clouds gathering. Some had already overtaken the little cloud and moved toward the setting sun. It created an odd, ethereal effect with the low, ominous clouds that threatened overhead. Serem descended to rejoin his friends. For his amorous thoughts, he failed to notice the animals getting restless.

"Is it going to rain tonight?" Tonto asked as he turned the squirrel he was roasting.

"It would seem so," Serem responded, settling in the circle.

He picked up a yam from the edge of the fire and pressed it lightly. It was still hard and he put it back.

"Clouds never gather this fast in the dry season," Madira added. "This is strange."

"Indeed," Tonto agreed.

They rolled through several topics of conversation, ending with the upcoming wrestling match. Serem thought Hamma would remain champion of all the villages since he had won every match after defeating M'mata of Ronge and sending him into retirement three harvests back.

"*Heeeh!* Not this time!" Luseti shouted. Have you seen the way Palo of

Ngoma fights?

"Like a drunk?

Tonto and Madira burst into laughter. Luseti was not amused. Ngoma was notorious for its debauchery, but Palo was a focused individual. Serem only wanted to aggravate Luseti. An awkward pause followed during which the boys all became aware of a change in the atmosphere. Serem realized he should have seen the warning signs when the animals got restless as the clouds gathered. They had stopped grazing and moved around as though they smelled a predator. They ended up in a constantly shifting huddle. The boys also became apprehensive in the gathering darkness. Suddenly, a brilliant knife disemboweled the heavens and with a mighty ripping sound, they spilled their guts on the boys.

Yssa returned from helping his father well before the sun went down. He went into the kitchen where he drank a horn of water and took a handful of freshly cooked beans. He went to the chamber he shared with his brothers. Ma'alia got the same uneasy feeling when he walked into the kitchen just as she had in the morning. She did her best to brush it aside. She took a wicker basket and went to get grain from the granary. She saw Yssa sitting outside with his brothers telling them another story. They loved his stories because he told them in a way that made them seem real. Ma'alia would often listen in and find herself entranced. He spun tales and fables with beautiful, uplifting morals. She always marveled that a child his age could tell such creative stories.

Ma'alia noticed a tiny cloud in the sky. It was odd, but she did not dwell on it. She got a two wicker trays and began to winnow the grain. She glanced at the sky again and noticed dark clouds gathering rapidly. She picked up her grain and went back to the kitchen. She went down on her knees, scooped some grain, placed it on the stone, and began to grind it into flour.

She was not sure, but she felt as if she were having a flashback to that day when a stranger appeared to her some twelve harvests back. Even with the door open, the sense that the walls were closing in on her became palpable. She dropped the small grindstone on the big one. Its fall coincided with a lightning flash. Though she anticipated the thunder that would follow, it still made her jump. Then she saw Yssa standing at the entrance. She did not know how long he had been standing there. His eyes were sad but intense. There was a nervous tension around him and the disquieting feeling she had experienced earlier returned. He did not have to say it. She knew. He helped her up. His hand was strong and firm. He embraced her.

"Ma'alia, I go now," he said solemnly. "In due time, I will return."

Children did not call their parents by name, but she was not entirely surprised he did this time. She tried to process this along with the announcement he just made. He spoke with authority - not as a son. Then reality set in. The son she had born and raised was no longer hers. He belonged to The Father and he was now leaving to do his Father's bidding.

"The Mighty One is with you, Mother," he said.

He made for the door and almost collided with his brothers who came running to the kitchen. They clung to their mother fearing more thunder. Yssa looked on them with an equal measure of love and sadness. Then he was gone.

The rain came down in deafening torrents, soaking the thirsty ground within moments. White foam traced swirling patterns in the brown water flowing around the kitchen. Ma'alia went to stand outside under the overhang with the boys still clinging to her skirt. The reality of Yssa's departure cut through her heart like a red-hot lance. Her legs gave out beneath her and she slid to the ground against the rough mud wall. She felt neither the abrasion on her back nor the rain that pelted her legs as muddy water swirled around her heels. She did not hear the boys cry. For a long time, she gasped, unable to talk. Her mouth opened and closed like a dying fish out of water.

"My baby! Oh, my baby!" she choked when words finally came out.

epilogue

Kilum sat with three friends around a pot of wine. Each held a long *seke*. One end sat in the pot. They sucked in the bitter wine from the other end. They did not notice the steady progress of a little cloud across the sky until the heavens darkened.

"*Ee yeh!*" Okuda, Serem's father exclaimed. "Those clouds formed fast!"

Slightly tipsy, Gwele and Chole noticed them for the first time. They were not ordinary clouds. They were rain clouds - thick, and portent. Distant rumblings added to the menace they posed. Kilum, held his liquor well and his mind quickly went to his animals. He recalled the story of a herdsboy who died in the marshes many harvests back when it rained suddenly. According to the boys who survived, the victim had tried to urge a few dull creatures out of the ensuing bog. Villagers found his mud-crusted body several days after the rains had ceased. He had come to the surface in the thickets beyond the grazing grounds. The animals he tried to save had met the same fate and the villagers left their bloated remains in the mud.

"Okuda, your son and my cows are out there. If it rains, it could be dangerous for them."

"You are right. We need to get to them right away."

"It's almost night and with the clouds it will be dark altogether," Chole observed. "How will you get word to them in time?"

"We set off now!" Kilum fired off irritably. "I'll do it myself while you sit here talking like women!"

"*Esh!* That's not the point," Gwele started, but Kilum was already heading down the path that meandered through the village.

"I'll go with him," Okuda said rising. "Go tell Emesi we've gone to check on the boys and the animals. Ask him to send along a few strong, young men. We may need them. And don't finish that wine by yourselves!"

He ran after Kilum. The heavens delivered on their threat. With a flash of lightning and loud thunderclap, they let the earth have it.

The rains poured heavily as Gwele made his way to Emesi's compound. He explained what they planned to do.

"Good idea," Emesi agreed. "I remember how Firi died trying to save some animals. We all wondered if it was worth it. I hope none of the boys will try to be a hero in the same way."

"No. Hopefully, not."

Emesi turned to his grandson who always leaned on his knee. "Go call your father." The boy went to do so. He returned all wet and reclaimed his station on his grandfather's knee.

"*Eesh!* Couldn't you dry yourself off before you touch me?"

The boy only grinned. His father entered the hut, also dripping wet.

"Yes, Baba?"

Emesi cleared his throat. "Atsuli, we have an urgent matter on hand. These unexpected rains may put our herdsboys in danger. Get five or six young men to go with you to the marshes and see how they are faring. I understand Kilum and Okuda have gone ahead so you will want to hurry and catch up with them."

"Yes, Baba."

"Get Yssa to go with you. Those boys are in his age group and I have a feeling he, more than anyone else, will know exactly how to help them."

"It's strange you should say so. I thought of him as soon as you asked."

"Good. But hurry! There's no time to lose!"

"We should get the animals out of here," Serem said, barely audible above the sound of the rain. "Sakul Kilum will kill us if harm came to any of his animals. Let's move them to higher ground."

He made his way to where they stood. The other boys followed, sloshing through the rapidly softening earth. The water was already up to their ankles. They tried to direct the cows toward the slope, which was quite a distance away, but the animals would not cooperate. They avoided the sticks and arms the boys waved in the attempt to move them and turned back into the huddle. The water rose with every moment. It was up to their shins and it took a lot of effort just to lift their legs. The boys began to panic. Serem tried to move the animals again, but soon realized it was a lost cause. The sheep and goats were already half submerged. The cows were thrashing about in wide-eyed panic, some lowing in distress.

"I'm getting out of here," Luseti declared. He turned toward the slope using his stick for support and his left arm outstretched for stability as he struggled against the suction of clay at his feet. Tonto and Madira followed. Tonto was howling in despair. At one point, he sank in a low spot. He pulled on his leg a little too hard and leaned too far forward. When he freed it, he lost balance and fell in the water. He tried to roll over to keep his head above the surface, but went under again. Madira saw his friend's plight, and managed to take hold of him by the elbow. Somehow, he was able to help Tonto up and maintain his own balance. Unfortunately, Tonto had lost his stick without which, wading through the brackish water was impossible. He looked around but could not see it in the darkness and rain. Madira tried to hold his hand and make progress with the help of his stick, but now he could not move very far. Serem was in the same predicament. He could save neither the animals nor himself.

"We are lost!" he lamented. "I didn't even get the chance to see Nambale for the last time."

"Who will comfort my mother," Luseti moaned.

With surprising calmness, Serem raised his arm and voice.

"Brothers, we are *Wadam.* We should have died when Tamaa murdered our peers several seasons ago. We are fortunate to have lived to this day. The time has come for us to join our brothers in the spirit world. Let us face it as bravely as we faced the knife together."

Even Tonto calmed down just enough to listen to Serem. The water was now up to their bellies and the ground at their feet felt like a rapidly dissipating broth. Serem continued.

"We are not getting out of here alive. I now say farewell, my brothers. I will see you on the other side."

Serem leaned back and allowed the water to swallow him. Luseti and Madira watched in horror as bubbles rose where their friend had stood a moment earlier. They could not reach him to save him even if they wanted to. Tonto could not bear to look. He turned away. He was about to close his eyes when a movement caught his eye. He was not sure he saw right. He wiped his rain drenched face and looked again. A figure approached, cutting through the water as easily as a man walking through tall Kikuyu grass. Tonto realized Madira still held his hand and his grip had tightened as he watched Serem take his own life. Tonto yanked on the hand. Madira turned and Tonto pointed at the figure that waded toward them as they awaited certain death.

"*Wah!*" That was all Madira said. Luseti also noticed the strange sight.

"Who is that?" he asked.

"I don't know."

They had all forgotten about their drowning friend and their dire circumstances. They were more afraid of the stranger who was now upon them.

"Peace, brothers!" he said.

"Peace!" They responded hesitantly.

He passed the three boys and made straight for the spot where Serem had disappeared. He reached below the surface with both arms and pulled out the unconscious boy. He blew into Serem's face sharply. His eyes popped opened and he coughed, gulping in a lungful of air. He held onto the strange boy's arms. The newcomer broke the grip and led him by the arm to where his friends stood. Both moved through the water with ease.

The stranger pointed to the water.

"Follow the path. It will lead you to the slope of the embankment. When you are out of the water, do not stop. You'll find your way back to the village if you stay on the path."

Indeed when they looked in the water, there was a distinct path below the surface. The boys obeyed unquestioningly and made their way as the strange boy instructed. They did not realize how easily they glided through the water. The stranger turned his attention to the animals.

"*Sssuh!*" he hissed at them. Some tried to turn away, but he patted them on the rump and sent them after the boys. The animals found their footing and followed. The boys climbed out of the water and continued on a path they had never noticed before along the slope of the embankment. The rain still fell heavily, but they scarcely paid it any attention. Serem looked back and saw all the animals following single file. Some were still in the water, but all, even the goats and sheep, were making their way out. The strange boy, however, was not in sight. Serem realized the gravity of what they had survived when he noted the dry ground where they were roasting a squirrel a short while ago was now a huge black lake.

Kilum and Okuda stumbled through the rain with different concerns on their minds. Kilum thought of his animals and prayed none would be lost. Okuda thought of his son. Serem had escaped death when Tamaa's warriors did not attack Kilima. Okuda prayed the boy was not in danger this time as well. With these thoughts, both men descended the slope toward the grazing grounds.

Atsuli rounded up four of his peers for the possible rescue mission. He decided the four would have to suffice, since he did not have time to find a fifth volunteer. It was already dark due to the clouds and rain. Soon the real darkness would be upon them. He had to find Yssa quickly. With his friends, he went to Egadwa's compound. As soon as he turned into it, he knew something was wrong. Ma'alia sat by the door under the overhang that afforded her little cover from the rain. She did not seem to care. Her sons, Jama and Jani sat on either side of her, each claiming an arm. Her eyes were red from recent tears. The boys' faces were tear-streaked and their noses ran. Between sobs, Jani sucked the slime into his mouth with his tongue.

Atsuli hesitated and approached slowly.

"Ma'alia, is all well?"

"No."

Atsuli noted that Yssa was not in sight and he had a distinct feeling that had something to do with her despondency.

"Is Yssa home?"

"He's gone," she said without looking at him.

Atsuli hesitated again, wondering how far he could prod.

"Gone where?"

"He's gone," Ma'alia repeated.

By her tone, Atsuli knew she was through speaking. He made a mental note to ask some women to check on Ma'alia later. He turned.

"Let's go. We'll have to get to the boys without Yssa."

They made their way to the marshes, trying to get there quickly without slipping and falling.

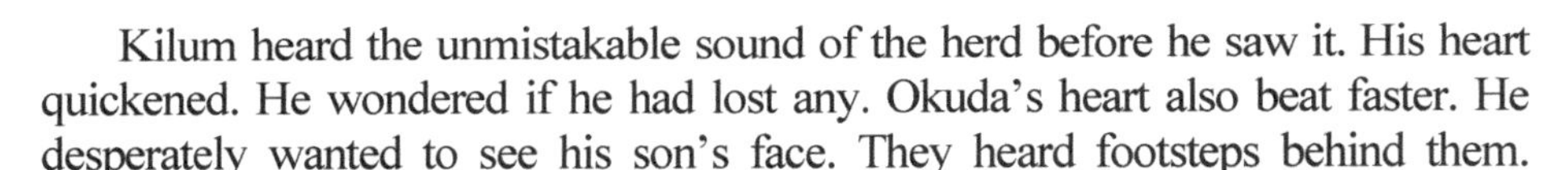

Kilum heard the unmistakable sound of the herd before he saw it. His heart quickened. He wondered if he had lost any. Okuda's heart also beat faster. He desperately wanted to see his son's face. They heard footsteps behind them. Atsuli and four of his peers broke through the bushes.

"We came as quickly as we could," Atsuli said. Then he addressed Okuda. "Yssa's gone. That is all Ma'alia could tell me. There was no time to learn more."

Before Okuda could respond, the boys came into view with Serem at the head.

"*Mwana wa!* I'm glad you are well." He ran to embrace his son.

"And you have all the animals, don't you," Kilum asked, his eyes scanning the herd behind the boys. "Yes, you do!" He was delighted.

"Yes, Sakul Kilum. Not one is lost," Serem responded flatly.

The men stood facing the boys.

"You are all amazing! How did you do it?"

"We didn't. We would all have drowned had it not been for that boy."

"What are you talking about, son?" Okuda asked.

"I'm saying the rain took us by surprise. It started suddenly and fell heavily. We tried to move the animals to higher ground, but we couldn't because the ground got soaked and the water rose fast."

"I know. The hillsides drain into the marshes. But what happened?"

"We were all stuck and waiting to die." Serem did not mention he had attempted to hasten his own demise. "That's when the boy came and pulled me out of the water. He showed us a path below the surface and told us to follow it out of the flooded grounds. That path led us here."

"What path?" They all looked at the ground. There was no path.

"And where did this boy go?"

"I don't know. We didn't see him again after that."

Atsuli turned to his friends and frowned.

Glossary of Terms

baba	Father
basakul	Elders
basiani	Young men
boma	Compound
bora	Rain; Also means "good" or "fine" in relation to quality
Bora-ini	Place in the rain. The capital city of Kwavantu
bundu	Bushy wilderness
chi	Expression of wonder
enza	Look
imbuya	Fabled inner turmoil
ingata	A hoop made from banana fiber that women use as padding to balance a pot on the head
Kam'ma	Little mother
koza	Uncle
m'losi	Medicineman, wizard
m'ma	Mother
m'sali	One who invokes the Oracle on behalf of others
manyatta	Dome-shaped hut made from sticks and hides
modi	Take heart
msiani	Young man
mwaza	Mercy
n'ne	Grandmother
pili pili	Hot pepper
riswa	An utterance to rebuke evil spirits
sakul	Elder
sasu	A plant with soft leaves
senge	Aunt
tatula	A short, broad-leafed plant with healing powers
vaya	Exclamation of surprise
wadam	Of the blood

Made in United States
Troutdale, OR
10/25/2023

14004313R00196